Also by Sherrhonda Denice

David's Passion Series

A Man's Heart (David's Passion Book 1)

A Man's Love (David's Passion Book 2)

Glue

Pathways

A MAN'S HEART

David's Passion Series
Book 1

Sherrhonda Denice

Lily Bird
PRESS

A Man's Heart (David's Passion Series Book One)

Copyright©2017 by Sherrhonda Denice www.sherrhondadenice.com

Published by Lily Bird Press, LLC

Cover Design: Colors in Cover

Edited by: Cheresse Graves (grammar.rulesatoz@gmail.com)

Library of Congress Control Number: 2016913480

ISBN 978-0-9801028-7-1 (Print)

ISBN 978-0-9801028-6-4 (ePUB);

Printed in the United States of America

 Formatted with Vellum

Daddy, this one is for you.
Thank you. Love you. Hugs and kisses.

My sheep hear My voice, and I know them, and they follow Me. And I give them eternal life, and they shall never perish; neither shall anyone snatch them out of My hand. My Father, who has given them to Me, is greater than all; and no one is able to snatch them out of My Father's hand. I and My Father are one."
John 10:27-30, NKJV

Prologue

The lifeless body of fourteen-year-old Michael "Squirt" Reeves lay near a garbage pile in an alley on Detroit's east side, with two gunshot wounds to the head. His blood seeped into the shallow grass surrounding his body and was beginning to summon rats. An old tire and a rusted-out, junked car were the only remaining witnesses to the execution-style murder.

Squirt's killer hadn't bothered to bind Squirt's hands or feet before the execution; he'd only made him kneel in front of him with his hands behind his back. He knew the kid wasn't going to run. The poor thing had been too scared. The killer had performed this ritual so many times; he felt nothing after he pulled the trigger to execute Squirt—or any of the others in the past who'd shared Squirt's fate. Although killing wasn't his main occupation, he was a professional when it came to murder. After every kill, he'd carry on with his day like everyone else: stop by the grocery store, pay his cable bill, and visit his mother. And hearing Squirt beg for his life hadn't fazed the killer either. The killer could not have cared less that the little guy had just turned fourteen the previous week. The way the killer saw it, Squirt should have known the rules of the game. *When you're in, you're in. If you want out, you die out . . .*

Chapter 1

Punch

Pastor David Kent Cole stood patiently in line at Smokey's Grill just around the corner from his church, waiting for his take-out order. The former hole-in-the-wall grill had recently been expanded to include a bar and an entertainment area with pool tables, pinball machines, and old-school video games. David observed all the patrons enjoying the loud music, food, and conversation. Several of the TV screens that encircled the bar were tuned to sports channels.

He leaned his six-foot frame against the padded bar rail. His broad shoulders and caramel skin were complemented by a prized athletic physique that was evident even underneath his coat and suit. Just a few days shy of his thirty-ninth birthday, he was an incredibly handsome specimen with a strong jawline and just a hint of softness that kept him from looking too harsh. His stature and commanding presence gave him a no-nonsense sort of appeal, which was a necessity in the neighborhood surrounding his church, Disciples of Christ Ministries, more affectionately known as DOC.

He was smack dab in the middle of Detroit's roughest neighborhood. The neighborhood's zip code was befittingly labeled as one of the most dangerous areas in the country. Nevertheless, it was the location that God had chosen for him to plant a church and labor in the harvest field. His radical ministry had earned him the nickname "The Turn-Around Preacher." With reckless abandon, he preached teens off the streets, out of gangs, and out of the drug life.

The neighborhood had seen a major shift for the better because of the work David had done with the young people in the area over the last several years. His dedication had been recognized both locally and nationally—even by the President of the United States, who'd invited him to the White House after news stories of his radical preaching and community activism had led to a significant decline in violence and crime in the neighborhood. David was proof that faith and hard work could make communities stronger.

Exhausted from serving at his church all day, he raked his hands over his head to wake up his brain and yawned. If he hadn't been so tired, he might have been a bit embarrassed by his cashmere dress coat and tailored suit. He was definitely dressed too professionally for a Friday night at Smokey's. His attire had been appropriate for his earlier think-tank meetings with city officials and other community activists as they strategized how to further lower the crime rates in the area with the help of its community members. Now, he looked overdressed and out of place. He prided himself on blending in with the people around him so that he'd seem approachable. His present dress code wasn't cutting it.

David rubbed his dark brown eyes and repositioned himself. He turned his head to the left, looking past the patrons at the bar. There was an extraordinary amount of clamor coming from the section near the pool tables. The noise was infused with the sounds of balls clashing together on the pool tables, glasses clinking, and loud talking. He found himself mesmerized by a woman who was sitting with a group that was dominated by men. The rambunctious bunch was celebrating something, talking over one another and laughing loudly.

"Stand up, Don!" one of the men called out. The gorgeous, petite woman stood accommodatingly, and the man continued with his beer mug extended in the air. "I just want to publicly say, you are the *baddest* chick I know!" The men gave her a feverish round of applause. David continued to intrude visually as the group toasted with heavy beer mugs and other alcoholic beverages, cheering for the young woman who had the most beautiful cocoa complexion. Humbled by all the attention, she covered her face with her hands momentarily, but she couldn't hide the perfect smile that had David fixated. Her dark, curly brown hair was pulled back into a ponytail that flowed down her back and swayed from side to side as she bowed for her audience. Her almond eyes beamed.

She was dressed casually in a fitted black T-shirt with Michael Jackson's face on the front. It was an *Off the Wall* era image of Michael when he still sported an afro. David had never seen Michael Jackson look *that* good before. He took note of the woman's small waist and curvaceous hips, which were put on display by a pair of body-hugging jeans. The woman's hourglass body made those jeans and T-shirt come alive in 3-D. It would have been nearly impossible for David or any other man in the room not to notice the woman's beauty, but he was skilled at checking his male drive. He knew how to appreciate and admire a woman without being lustful. *Lord, you ain't no joke. When you created woman, you weren't playing.*

Behind the bar, a statuesque Amazon goddess with fair skin and red freckles doubled as a bartender and take-out cashier. "What can I do for you, Pastor Cole? Did you call your usual order in?" she questioned David. Glancing at her watch, the goddess noticed it was nine-thirty p.m. "What happened to you at lunchtime? I had your meal ready for you," she continued her interrogation. The beauty with the MJ T-shirt on had cast a spell on David. "Pastor?"

"Oh, I'm sorry. How are you doing, Sharon? I had a couple of meetings earlier. Then I studied the message the Lord gave me for this Sunday's sermon. I didn't realize it had gotten so late." David motioned his head toward the group he'd been spying on. "Is this the typical Friday night thing going on over there?" he asked.

Sharon whispered. "Kinda. That's the crew—mostly cops, some SWAT. They come in here a lot, but tonight they're celebrating. They took down some fool who'd been holding his wife and kids hostage almost all day. He shot the wife and was threatening to kill the kids—six of 'em."

David's face twisted into a disturbed frown. "Wow. That's terrible . . ."

"You must have been studying pretty hard, Pastor. It's been all over the news. I think Lil Mama is the one who actually took the fool down, *and* it's her birthday. I guess that's the cover-up. It would be a little unprofessional and cruel to be celebrating killing somebody—even if the fool didn't deserve to live," Sharon offered before she disappeared into the kitchen. She returned with a hot cup of straight black coffee. It was David's go-to drink.

Being faithfully predictable, David ordered the same thing for lunch almost every day. Mondays through Thursdays, he ordered a grilled chicken salad. On Fridays, it was wing dings and French fries with a Vernors. And always a cup of straight black coffee. "Yeah, I've been studying pretty hard," he said, unable to take his eyes off the woman who had captivated him. *She is absolutely beautiful.*

Sharon followed the direction of David's gaze and raised her brow. She shook her head and kept her voice low. "That's *Dominique*. She may be pretty, but she is a *hot mess*," Sharon said. An incident that occurred more than a year ago was still etched in Sharon's mind. A familiar-looking gentleman had come into the grill begging Dominique not to end their "relationship." He was a handsome man who looked as if he hadn't shaved or washed in days. A disheveled-looking soul. Sharon had seen the man at the grill with Dominique on several occasions in their happier times, but the thing she remembered most about that evening was the coldness Dominique displayed toward the man.

Dominique had said only three words and walked away as if the man meant nothing to her. "*No strings attached.*" She had been as dismissive as a person accosted by a beggar on a dimly lit street in the clutches of midnight. The incident had struck Sharon as strange. It was a reversal of male and female roles if she'd ever seen it. She couldn't recall a time in her life when she'd seen a woman be that cold to a man before. In contrast, she had witnessed plenty of men break women into a million pieces—including her.

David chuckled. "Most beautiful women are a little challenging, Sharon. I'm sure there's a brother out there saying the same thing about you."

"I don't know about that, Pastor. I can't catch two men talkin' and I work at a place that is frequented by men!"

David laughed gregariously. Kindness and tenderness played on his face. "Well, trust me. You don't want to pick a man, you want the Lord to pick him. Whatever you do, get His assistance! Trust me, I know!"

"Pastor, you still got hope for me?" Sharon asked in a lower tone, looking at David with doe eyes that revealed her naïveté and need to be affirmed. David scrutinized her exotic beauty.

Although her stature was intimidating to some men, she was pretty in an irrefutably feminine way. Almost everyone in the neighborhood affectionately called her Red because of her light skin and red hair. Then there were those reddish brown freckles on her face that David deemed precious.

"Yes, I do, Sharon. If God doesn't give up, I sure won't. I'm still praying for you. The *right* guy will come along one day. He's probably right under your nose," David said. The two of them had talked many times about Sharon's desire to get married and have a family. She was a young, single mother, working her way through college, hoping to obtain a degree in education and become a teacher. At only twenty-two, she'd lived a rough life. Despite that, she was still doing what she needed to do to get her life together and take care of her three-year-old son, Marcus.

"Thanks, Pastor. I really appreciate it," Sharon said humbly. In her periphery, she spied a few women staring enviously in her and David's direction. Sharon knew what they were looking at—better yet, *who* they were looking at. David, with his fine self, had that kind of effect on women, but Sharon saw him as a mentor and father figure. Even so, his potent masculinity, street swag, and sexiness couldn't be denied.

"Excuse me, Red. Can I get an Amaretto sour? You can put it on Sarge's bill," Dominique said, interrupting Sharon and David's conversation. David hadn't even seen her approaching. Dominique had quietly invaded his space like a prowling lioness furtively nearing her prey.

"Coming right up," Sharon said. She turned away, took a bottle from the middle shelf, and began mixing a drink.

David gave Dominique an inconspicuous once-over glance. Then he averted his eyes. *Wow.*

Dominique spoke first. "Hi . . . how are you doing?"

"Hello. I'm great. How are you?" David returned politely,

feeling her presence like a Fourth of July sun, prickling his skin with heat and delight.

"Good."

A Santa Claus-bellied man emerged from the kitchen's double-swinging doors and handed Sharon David's bagged order as David's jazz ringtone played. He fished his cell from his coat pocket and answered the caller whose number was marked private. "This is Pastor David Kent Cole of Disciples of Christ Ministries. How may I bless you?" David said with a voice that was dipped in genuine care and sprinkled with professionalism.

"He got 'em! . . ." a young voice cried on the other end.

"Hello?"

"He got 'em!" the voice repeated.

"Got who? Who is this?"

"It's me, Pastor, Punch!"

"What's wrong, Punch?"

"He killed him, man . . ."

"Killed *who*? What's going on, Punch?" David's urgency caused Dominique to home in on his conversation.

"Squirt, man! He shot Squirt. He's . . . dead. Squirt is dead."

David banged his fist on the bar rail. "Jesus!" he shouted. "Where are you?"

"I'm at the church behind the—ow! Please don't kill me—please!" Punch cried.

"Punch! Punch!" David shouted into his cell.

Dominique eyed David empathetically. She was accustomed to the look of horrified eyes. In her profession, she had seen a lot of death and a lot of pain.

Fear consumed Sharon. "Pastor, what happened?"

"Squirt's been killed," David said, snatching bills out of his

11

wallet and tossing them on the counter. He grabbed the bag and hurried out of the grill to his truck.

"Oh, my God. No . . ." Sharon sobbed. David was already out the door.

* * *

Michael "Squirt" Reeves was Punch's younger brother. David brought the dynamic duo with him to the grill a couple of times a week for lunch. Squirt had a teenage crush on Sharon. Every time he saw her, he vowed to marry her when he grew up. Sharon had teasingly referred to Squirt as her little date.

Punch's real name was Brandon Reeves. David had nick-named him Punch—the same nickname David's father had given him—because Brandon reminded David of himself when he was his age. When David first met the two brothers, who were barely a year apart, he quickly took to Punch. It was his personal mission to keep the two from joining gangs and selling drugs. Just shy of fifteen, Punch was the older, angry one with a Mike Tyson punch. He was David's favorite kid.

Two years ago, David had broken up a fight as he was coming out of the supermarket near the church. The two contenders had been Punch and a young man named Mark Montgomery, the grandson of one of David's church mothers, of all people. Punch had whipped the snot out of Mark before David had had an opportunity to separate the two. Mark had a tendency to go for bad in the hood. David chuckled when he discovered the reason Punch whipped Mark so badly. It was all because Mark confronted Punch by walking up to him for no reason and saying, "I ain't scared of you—everybody else may be, but I ain't."

A defiant Punch countered by knocking the sense out of

Mark. "I showed that fool what er'body else scared of," Punch had explained to David. Since that day two years ago, Punch and his little brother Squirt had been David's sidekicks. He fought hard to keep them away from the gangs and the dealers. Now it seemed that his efforts had been in vain.

David jumped in his black Suburban and skidded around the corner on his way back to the church. The ringing of his cell was amplified through his car speakers. He touched a button on his steering wheel and patched in the call.

"Yeah," David said, eschewing his formal salutation. His heart thumped wildly against his chest.

A familiar voice with a deep, raspy coating responded, addressing David by what would forever be his 'hood nickname.

"DC, this is Bones. I got Lil Punch. He's safe for now. If you want to see him one last time before he disappears, meet me at our old spot in thirty minutes—no headlights. Don't be early, and don't be late. And do not—I repeat—do not call the police or tell anyone else about this. And don't even think about calling the mayor. This is way above Walt's head. Mayor or not, he can't do nothin' about what's goin' down in the city right now. If you make a wrong move, this little snot gon' take two to the head like his little brother—and you might not be far behind. " With that said, the call was disconnected.

David looked at the time. It would only take him fifteen minutes to reach the old spot. He had another fifteen minutes to spare. He thought of pulling over somewhere to kill the time, but then a thought popped into his head. He called his mother, Leah Cole-Montgomery.

His mother's voice was comforting. "Hey, honey," she answered.

"Ma, I need to stop by for a minute. I need you to come outside when I get there."

"Okay . . . but is something wrong?"

"Just come out, Ma. I'll call when I'm in the driveway. Let this stay between us."

"Okay . . ."

David headed towards his mother's North Rosedale Park home. It was a well-kept neighborhood on Detroit's west side. Some considered it a suburb within the city with its beautifully maintained Tudors, Colonials, and Victorian-style homes with lush landscapes. David thought of Bones' command not to call their childhood friend, Walt—more formally known as Walter Kincaid, who had become the city's mayor three years ago. Walter Kincaid was well respected and ran the city with a sense of integrity that Detroit hadn't seen in years. David knew whatever was going on had to be serious if Bones determined that the matter was over Walter's head. That's what frightened him like a victim in a horror movie. He had to keep repeating scriptures to himself to avoid focusing too much on the situation instead of the strength of his God.

The Lord had been with him in dangerous situations before, and surely tonight was no different. Being a pastor called by God to lead the city's teens away from street life into the arms of the Lord, David lived a dangerous life. His life had been threatened in the past, and his church had been vandalized. But through all of that, God had kept him. Pastor David Kent Cole had a lot of enemies who wouldn't think twice about eliminating him and his radical way of reaching the youth and interrupting the drug flow that had been established and was keeping some people financially solvent.

When David arrived at his mother's home, he shared all the details of what he knew so far, which wasn't much. If something happened to him, he wanted Leah to know what had been going on, or at least the part he played in all the drama. He had counseled so many mothers whose sons had been murdered, and the mothers were usually clueless as to what had been going on at the time of their child's death. Sometimes the mothers or fathers rarely knew why the victim had been at a certain place or with a certain person. David couldn't bear for that to be Leah's predicament.

"David, I don't know about this. Why can't you just call the police and let them handle it?"

"Bones said not to, Ma. Look, someone already killed Squirt. I just want to make sure Punch is okay. I have to."

"David, I know that you grew up with Bones, but you know and I know that underneath those supposed legitimate businesses, he is one of the biggest dealers in the city. How can you even trust him? How do you know he's not setting you up or something? How do you know Bones didn't kill Squirt *himself*? If somebody is cruel enough to kill a little fourteen-year-old boy, they'll kill you too!"

"Ma, everything in me is telling me that Bones didn't hurt Squirt. I'm not sure what's going on. But I know Punch is with Bones, and

I have to go meet Bones to find out what *is* going on. I don't have a choice. Remember, we fed Bones. He ate at our table when he didn't have anything. God put Punch in my life for a reason, and I'm going to see it all the way through. I have to do this."

David had long ended his friendship with Bones because of the paths their lives had taken. When he did see him, it was usually by happenstance somewhere around the city. David was fully aware that Bones lived on the other side of the law and the other side of salvation. He continued to pray for his childhood friend, but he kept his distance.

David looked at the time, then back at his mother. Her hazel eyes were misted with tears. The subtle streaks of gray that played throughout her curly brown and blond hair were a testament to her wisdom. But he had to listen to what he felt on the inside tonight. "I have to go, Ma. I love you." He kissed her forehead and smelled her hair—something he'd had a habit of doing since he was just a little boy. It was a sign of affection. Leah threw her arms around David's neck and squeezed him.

"I'm going to trust God tonight. And I'm going to pray," she said, wiping her tears.

"I'll call you soon. And if something goes wrong—if anything happens to me, all you know is that I got a call from Punch saying his little brother had been killed, and I went to meet him. That's it, Ma. Don't ever mention Bones or any of the conversation I just shared with you. And Ma, not a single word to anyone—not even Joe. It could get me killed. Promise me." David reiterated.

Leah nodded. "I promise, Punch. I would never do anything that would put your life in jeopardy, even if it means keeping this from my husband. I love you, son. God be with you."

"I'll call. I have to go."

Leah got out of David's truck and watched him pull out of the driveway. She stood there until she couldn't see his truck anymore.

She offered up her prayer right there. She knew God had called David to pastor and help the youth of the city, but tonight she had an uneasy feeling that something was going to go dreadfully wrong.

* * *

David eased the Suburban into the back of a building called The Ice Cream Shoppe. At one time during the early nineties, it had been an arcade that was mostly frequented by miscreants and others looking for some action other than arcade games.

16

One could find liquor, drugs, sex, gambling, and any other kind of vice. Back then, it was simply referred to as *The Spot*. He was glad those troubled times were behind him. But were they? The way things were unfolding tonight, he had to wonder. His heart grieved for Squirt, but he knew in the area of the city where he pastored, danger was always lurking around the corner. Sometimes it was so palpable he could feel it. Like right now. He felt the night closing in on him like the walls of a torture chamber—inching closer—squeezing the life right out of him.

David got out of his truck slowly and studied his surroundings. It was too dark to see anything. The ominous, black night seemed to be filled with something diabolically evil. His eyes adjusted and readjusted, trying to make out if anyone or anything was moving around him. By memory, he estimated the number of paces to the door. He reached it in ten paces and lifted his right hand to knock.

The bolted door creaked open. David's eyes zeroed in on a quick flash of light in the darkness that came from the silver and black .40 Glock 22 that Bones was holding. "Hurry. Go down the hallway to the basement. I'll be behind you in a few. Gotta make sure everything is straight out here," Bones instructed. His raspy tone was flat and short from smoking one too many cigarettes.

David hurried down the hallway and into the basement like he'd been told. Black-painted walls enclosed him. The room was furnished with a black leather sofa and loveseat, a small dining table with two chairs, a kitchenette, and a sixty-five-inch screen television. Four doors were also painted black and blended into the walls. It had been years since he had been in this place.

Punch nearly knocked David over when he ran into his arms. The boy was shaking so profusely that his teeth were rattling. David embraced the boy in a loving hold before pulling apart. "You okay, man?"

Scared to death, Punch was unable to use his voice. He shook his head from side to side as the tears streamed. Punch was eye to eye with David, six feet even with a medium build. He looked frail and pitiful, not like the kid that most others feared.

"Just sit back down, you little punk!" Bones commanded as soon as he entered. Punch scrambled back to the chair and sat like a scared puppy.

"Bo—" David started, but Bones threw his hands up in a stop motion. He set his weapon on a nearby table and lit up a cigarette. Bones was nervous. Or was it *fear*? Fear. *Bones?* Never. David had never seen Bones afraid of anything. Instead, Brian Bellamy looked like a man to *be* feared. His nickname was an oxymoron. He was anything but bones. He stood six feet four with a huge monster build. His skin was black as charcoal, and the scars on his face were symbolic of the street wars he'd been in since he was a teen. His rough, calloused hands had lived the lives of several men.

Bones took a long puff of the cigarette he held between his fingers. "DC, this is some serious stuff your little friend and his brother got themselves in," he said when he exhaled. He snuffed out the cigarette in an ashtray and stood. He walked over to Punch. "What I tell you, huh? When I saw you with him, I told you to stay away from him, didn't I?!" Shaking, Punch nodded. "These streets ain't nothin' to play with, boy! You had your butt in church; you should have stayed in church!" Bones yelled. He paced the floor before rummaging in his pocket for another cigarette. He took out a lighter and lit it. Again, he took a long puff. This time, however, he didn't snuff it out. He continued to smoke, pulling a chair right across from Punch. David sat nearby, not sure what he should do.

"Bones, what's going on, man? *Who* was he with?" David asked.

Bones chuckled in a semi-deranged way. "DC, you're like a brother to me. That's the only reason why I'm risking everything over this little snot," Bones responded. He pointed the cigarette at Punch. "I know how you feel about him, and I know what I'm about to say is gonna sound real cliché. But the less you know, the better."

"Bones, who killed Squirt?"

"A sick, demon of a man. And he is just a little cotton ball compared to the others."

"What others? *What* is going on?"

"What's going on is: if Lil Punch wants to live, he's got to go," Bones nodded, affirming his own words. "That's it. He can't ever come back here."

"Go where? Where is he going?"

"Someplace safe," Bones said to David. Then he turned to Punch. "You will *die* if you try to contact anyone or come back here for any reason. You understand me?"

Punch nodded.

Bones turned back to David. "DC, it's big, man. Bigger than I've seen in a long while. So what we gon' do is walk out of here, and everybody gon' go back to their lives—except for this little fool. But at least he'll be safe. But if he contacts his grandmomma, aunt, uncle, *you*, or anybody else, they will die, and he will too. What happened to Squirt ain't nothing compared to what could happen to him—or you—if the wrong people suspect you know anything." Bones turned to Punch. "If you break my trust, I will kill you myself. I mean it." He turned back to David. "Time for you to go, DC."

"Bones, I need some answers, man."

"Well, you ain't gon' get none. You a prayin' man. You better do what you do best. Brandon, say goodbye to Pastor

Cole. Thank him for trying to keep your little snot butt outta trouble." Brandon hesitated. "Get up, fool!" Bones demanded. Brandon jumped up from the chair and flung his arms around David.

"Squirt is with God right now, Punch," David said compassionately. "I know you're sad, but I want you to remember that, okay?" Punch nodded as David continued. "I love you, man. Read your Bible and do what's right." Punch only nodded.

"Come on, DC, I gotta let you out . . ."

David reluctantly followed Bones up the stairs and out into the pitch-black night. "Keep your lights off until you get a half a mile down, DC," was all that Bones said. David left with no more clarity than he'd come with.

Chapter 2

Kick

D avid sat in his church office with his chair reclined. He pressed his forefingers together, creating a steeple, and thought about the events that had transpired over the last two weeks. He'd preached Squirt's eulogy a week ago. He couldn't remember the last time he'd lost one of his kids to violence. His ministry had saved many of them from death on the streets. He had learned not to question God in situations like these. He knew his Father had a plan for everything that occurred in life—nothing was ever by happenstance. God was in control.

The corners of David's mouth turned upward when he thought of Squirt's spunk. He missed Squirt, no doubt. But he was certain Squirt was with the Lord. For that, he was grateful. Squirt had given his life to the Lord the Sunday before his birthday. David had had the honor of baptizing Squirt himself. That alone gave him a peaceful, satisfied soul. Out of all the other thoughts he had on his mind, the comfort of knowing that Squirt was with the Lord gave him a personal sense of pleasure and accomplishment. He'd gotten to Squirt before death got to him. With the power of the Holy Spirit, David had been able to lead Squirt to Christ.

David prayed aloud. "Thank you, Father. All that I am, all that I do is for You." He felt a familiar calmness envelop him, as if the Lord were wrapping His strong, mighty arms around him. Then his mind drifted to Punch. In his spirit, he knew that Punch was safe, but he felt uneasy about the entire situation. Sometimes he felt like a double agent. Like he was too close to the other side of the fence—the dark side. Dealing with gangsters and drug dealers sometimes took him to places emotionally and physically he didn't want to be. Through all of it, he'd learned to rely on God more. That was all he could do. It was all out of his control.

David's desk phone rang, pulling him away from his contemplations. He cleared his throat and pressed the speaker feature. "Good Morning, this is Pastor David Kent Cole of Disciples of Christ Ministries. How may I bless you today?" he said in a smooth, silky tenor. He still introduced himself the way he had in kindergarten—by stating his full name. His name was a source of pride because it connected him to his grandfather, Kent Cole, who had also been a pastor. The youth at his church often teased him for using his "government name," but some of them had started introducing themselves the same way.

"Good Morning, Pastor. I'm sorry to bother you, but you have a guest that is not on your schedule today," Greta, the church's secretary, said quite professionally. She had used the landline instead of the intercom so their conversation would be private. She lowered her voice to a whisper. "It's a lady police officer—says she has to talk to you about a *matter* . . ." Greta's tone was questioning.

David's brow furrowed. He wondered which one of his little darlings had gotten into trouble this time. He spent more money bailing people out of jail than anyone he knew. If it was

Rich Henry, he was surely going to kill him and deliver him directly to Jesus. He had warned Rich about shoplifting, and Rich had promised David he wouldn't do it anymore. It was understandable at first. Rich's mother was battling a crack addiction. The eleven-year-old did what he had to do to survive. But David, along with the help of the church counseling staff, had assisted Rich's mother with getting into treatment, and Rich was staying with a relative.

While he was considering, Greta butted in on his thoughts. "Officer Street," she said.

"Huh?" David said quizzically. "What time is my first appointment today?" He hadn't bothered to look at the calendar on his iPad mini or the Franklin planner Greta kept in his desk drawer—a hard copy—just in case. Greta was old school, but she was also more up-to-date with technology than most young people. At the ripe age of sixty, Greta could outdo the average teenager in terms of knowing about the latest technology. Her twenty-three-year-old son was a computer genius who had graduated from MIT. He kept her up on the latest technology, and she graciously shared it with her pastor.

"Ten thirty a.m. You've got an hour."

"Yes, ma'am. Send Officer Street on back. Hold my calls." David popped a mint in his mouth and straightened his tie.

"Will do, Pastor."

"Thank you, Ms. Greta," David said. He pushed back from the desk and stood. Then he walked over and opened his office door. He had a private wing in the church. There were no other ministry offices near his. His wing included two meeting rooms, along with his private office that was connected to an en suite, with a dressing area and walk-in closet. He spent more time at church than he did at his home.

David stepped into the hallway and almost swallowed the huge peppermint whole when he saw her. One of his idiosyncrasies was that his eyes popped extra-wide whenever he was surprised. As much as he tried to be cognizant that he tended to do it, he hadn't been that successful in controlling it. Right now, he needed a straight face, and his brain wasn't cooperating. *Come on, Pastor Cole, keep it together.* A moment passed before he was able to compose himself.

He'd found the professionalism he needed. "Good Morning," he greeted as Dominique neared. "I'm Pastor David Kent Cole. How can I help you, Officer Street?"

"Hi, I'm Dominique Antoinette Street," she smiled, mimicking David. She was wearing street clothes—the same as she wore the night he'd first seen her. A pair of jeans and that old familiar Michael Jackson T-shirt that was singing his name and moonwalking all over him. David made himself not eye her body. But looking at her beautiful face wasn't helping the matter. She did "it" for him. He felt that x-factor spark that happened when a person met the right one. "First, I want to apologize," Dominique continued. "I sort of flashed my badge to the receptionist—I don't feel like a lot of questions today. I'm not here on official police business."

David was taken aback. "Oh. How can I assist you?"

"I don't know if you remember, but we met a couple of weeks ago at Smokey's. You received a phone call about someone being shot. Red was pretty upset that night. She left soon after you did, but before she left, she shared with me that one of the kids you'd been working with had been killed. I saw her a few days ago and we talked about it. I was just checking on you to see how you were doing," Dominique said. She didn't bother to mention that after Sharon had given her Squirt's full name the night of the murder, she had immediately followed up with a contact at the police department to get more details. The murder was still under investigation. "You seemed pretty upset that night . . ." Dominique continued.

24

David didn't know if he was more blessed or confused. Had this beautiful woman come to see him personally about one of his kids? He hadn't been back to Smokey's since that night. "Officer Street, I greatly appreciate that. I thought one of the kids had gotten into trouble or something," he said, genuinely relieved.

"Nope. Nothing like that. And today I'm just Dominique Antoinette Street," she said, extending her hand.

David received her hand and gave it a firm Sunday morning shake. *I know your name. Dom-i-nique. Couldn't forget it.* Out of all that had happened that evening, David hadn't forgotten her name. "Right . . . right . . . Dominique. I remember," he said as if he'd all of a sudden gotten an epiphany. *Of course, I remember.*

"I didn't want to take up too much of your time . . . I know you're pretty busy. Red told me about all the work you do in the community with kids. I think it's great. She says you're famous," she chuckled.

"I don't know about all that, but Red is a sweet girl. I accept the compliment. It's God's work, not mine."

Dominique had run out of words. She hadn't come to be forward. Her coming to see him was a genuine expression of her concern. Nothing she'd said had been part of a come-on line. "Well, I have the day off today, and I've got a few appointments. Thanks for all that you do. And again, I'm sorry about Squirt."

"Thank you. We had his homegoing last Friday. It was a beautiful service."

"I'm sure," Dominique said. And there it was again, that precious parting of her lips that revealed brightness as luminous as the moon. She lit up David's day. "Well . . . take care, Pastor Cole. And if I can be of any assistance, please give me a call." Dominique handed David her business card.

He readily accepted it. "Thank you. Thank you very much. I appreciate the offer," David said, trying to zero in on what it was about Dominique that had him feeling some type of way. Like he'd been struck by Cupid. He was usually more reserved when it came to women. Honestly, he just hadn't had the time or the inclination to actively pursue a woman lately. His focus had solely been on his ministry. On the verge of forgetting his manners, David offered to walk Dominique out to her car. "Let me walk you out to your car, Officer Street."

"Sure, thank you."

Greta raised a discerning eyebrow when David passed by her desk, walking alongside Dominique. He ignored Greta with a mischievous smile that made Greta scowl at him playfully. David's armor bearer and assistant, Deacon John Lewis, was standing next to Greta's desk. For the sake of company, Deacon Lewis was formal. He normally referred to David as "*son*."

"Pastor Cole, do you need to be driven somewhere, sir?" Deacon Lewis asked.

"No, sir, I'm fine. I'm just going out to walk Officer Street to her car, Deacon Lewis." David's reply was formal as well, which made Deacon Lewis scowl at him just as Ms. Greta had. Then Greta and Deacon Lewis shared a whispered conversation.

Deacon Lewis was knocking on the age of eighty, but he was as mentally sharp as any middle-aged man, sometimes sharper. He was David's surrogate father and grandfather all rolled into one. The two shared a relationship that was only understood by them. Deacon Lewis felt God had appointed him to 'oversee' David's spiritual development since he'd been so young when he'd answered the call.

The two lovingly bickered about everything from sports to the dates of historical events. David never let Deacon Lewis win. Whenever he was right about something, he would tease

Deacon Lewis by saying, "Check your facts, Old Man," and Deacon Lewis would do the same. David had nicknamed him Old Man because his livelihood and inspiration were nothing like those of an old man. Deacon Lewis reminded David he was a young man in an old man's body.

On his way out the door, David winked at Juan Gomez, head of security. Juan gave him a knowing smile. September was kind, and the weather was agreeable. The sun sent a warm, soothing feeling over David. It was seventy-seven degrees and gorgeous. He gazed across the lawn and noticed the color change of the leaves—all the beautiful, brilliant colors that lay strewn about on the emerald green grass and waved from the trees. He was in awe of God's creativity. The landscaping was reminiscent of an English garden. He'd had the landscapers fill the campus with flowers and winding walking paths. He'd placed stone benches every few feet so that members could sit and have peaceful moments, enjoying God in creation.

The church campus was a place of respite. The latest addition to the campus included a small pond on the northwest side, which included fish. It was a favorite place of the church's nursery school students. The campus itself was an oasis in the middle of the surrounding eyesore of dilapidated, abandoned homes and empty lots. But there had been a lot of improvement since David had planted his church there. His church members had helped to clean and clear empty lots of debris and tall grass that could pose safety threats to residents.

"You have a beautiful church campus," Dominique said, admiring the peaceful scenery.

"Thank you. It's the result of a lot of hard-working people— mainly teens and young adults. That makes me extremely proud of it."

"You're doing a wonderful job in this neighborhood."

"Thank you. This is what God has called me to do, and I love it—it's everything to me."

"Great . . ." Dominique said as she stopped walking abruptly. There was only a corroded pick-up truck and a crotch rocket motorcycle in the nearest parking spaces. David was sure the pick-up truck belonged to one of the workers repairing some drywall in the teen lounge. An easy, satisfied smile worked its way across David's face when Dominique lifted a sleek, cheetah print helmet from the seat of the red-hot Kawasaki Ninja ZX-14. It was the thirtieth-anniversary limited edition. It looked brand new.

Thoroughly impressed, David nodded. "She rides . . ." he said, cheesing.

Dominique nodded, wondering what David was going to say next. "Yeah . . . I ride . . ."

"Can we have coffee together this week—maybe later this evening if you have time?" David couldn't help himself. She was intriguing. He wanted to know more about her, and he didn't see any reason to waste time.

Dominique stuck her tongue in her cheek. Then she pursed her lips. As good-looking and manly as David was, she wasn't interested. As politely as she could, she said, "I don't mean to be rude or anything, but I don't think I'd be interested in going on a date with a preacher . . ."

David broke into a hearty laugh. He quieted before saying, "Well, that's quite interesting, considering the fact that I haven't asked you on a *date*. I asked you to have coffee with me. And . . . um . . . in my book, having coffee with a woman and asking her on a date are two very *different* things. Sometimes one has coffee with another and discovers that's all there is to it. One may not even want to ask the other out on a date after having coffee—if one were even considering asking the other person on a date in the first place. Besides, I would only ask a woman out on a *date* if I had romantic intentions—i.e., I wanted to get to know her better for the purpose of establishing and maintaining a romantic relationship with her. Right now, I don't have any of those intentions. I'm just asking to have coffee."

David was so self-assured and direct, not to mention handsome as all get out with completely undeniable street swag. Dominique felt compelled to take him up on his offer. There was something about his presence that moved her in a way that was different than what she'd been used to. She knew by the mischievous smile on David's face that he had politely chastised her. She laughed at her presumptuousness.

"Okay . . . where and what time?" she conceded.

"How about seven o'clock this evening at the Barnes and Noble near Oakland mall? We can meet there. Because, as I said, it's not a *date*. If I don't like you, I can pick up some books I've been meaning to buy. And if you don't like me, you can go shopping until the mall closes."

Dominique read his playful sarcasm. "You've made your point. Sounds good. It was nice meeting you. I'll see you later." Dominique shook David's hand again and climbed atop her motorcycle. David decided that the view was too good and looked away. Dominique put on her helmet and revved up the engine. David watched as the red-hot vixen zoomed out of the church parking lot on a red-hot crotch rocket.

"That's nice right there! Real nice. Like a cup of straight black coffee. A woman with a little kick! Yes, indeed."

Watch and pray, David heard in his spirit.

"Watch and pray, son."

David jumped. "Whoa! Old Man, what are you doing sneaking up on people like that?"

"If you pay attention, you'll hear more and see more, son." David was still thinking about Dominique, and he chuckled.

"Oh, I'm paying attention alright."

"I meant to the right things. Your ten o'clock appointment canceled, so I'll be ready to drive you over to the Detroit Leadership Council meeting at two p.m. sharp."

David nudged Deacon Lewis and grinned, "Hey, I'm the pastor. I'm supposed to tell you when *I'm* ready."

"Yeah, maybe that would be true if God hadn't sent me to watch over *you*."

"I think He sent me to watch over *you*," David said, playfully boxing Deacon Lewis.

Deacon Lewis blocked David's jab. "You got it the other way around," he said, jabbing back.

David blocked his hit. "And you're quick, too. But not quick enough."

"Luckily for you, I ain't got all day to play with you. I'm 'bout to take me a walk." With that, Deacon Lewis turned in the direction of the walking path that trailed through the campus flower garden and circled the campus. David noticed that Deacon Lewis was still handsome at almost eighty years old. Although his caramel skin had seen younger days and his eyes now appeared grayish with time, his wrinkles reminded David of the ageless wisdom he possessed.

Deacon Lewis's naturally silky hair had grayed, but he had a luscious, full head of hair. He maintained it by brushing it over to the left and parting it on the right. He looked as if he stepped out of the 1940s. He exuded class and sophistication. The navy blue suit he wore was an updated style that David had purchased for him. Deacon Lewis took pride in his ministry assignment and his appearance. He had lived through many things, and God had blessed his health and strength. He was an integral part of David's life and ministry.

David's mind drifted back to Dominique, thinking how uncanny it was for Deacon Lewis to speak the same words the Lord had dropped into his spirit. *Watch and Pray.*

Chapter 3

Straight Black Coffee

Surprisingly, the Starbucks inside the bookstore wasn't overly crowded. That made it easy for David to secure a table. He decided to wait until Dominique arrived before ordering a coffee. He smirked when he thought about how she had said she wasn't interested in a *preacher*. He'd admonished her swiftly, yet delicately, and she'd handled the light rebuke with graciousness. David took out his phone and responded to emails while he waited. Seconds later, Dominique slid into the seat in front of him. She was on time. Gone was the MJ T-shirt. This time, she was wearing a ruffled, fuchsia-colored blouse, skinny jeans, and a pair of fuchsia-colored heels that gave her short, five-foot-three stature four extra inches of height.

"Hi, Pastor Cole."

"Good evening, Dominique. And please, call me David. It's nice to see you again. How was your day?"

Dominique nodded. "Very nice. The weather was perfect for riding, so I took advantage of the opportunity until I was pulled over for speeding," Dominique chuckled.

"Oh. Breaking the law, huh?"

"I wasn't trying to. I was just in my *zone*. Feeling myself, I guess. He let me go with a warning. I told him the truth. I was just blowing off some steam. As cops, we understand one another, you know?"

"I'm sure."

"Plus, he was trying to flirt. That helped, too."

David winked. "I bet. Women can always get away with the beauty card."

"If it saves me a hundred bucks, whatever works."

"What would you like?" David asked. Dominique held him in a sexually hungry stare. She hadn't heard a thing he'd said. "*Dominique?*" David said with his eyebrows raised, questioning.

Hearing her name snapped Dominique out of her deliciously wicked thoughts. "Huh?" she mumbled.

"*Coffee*. What kind of coffee would you like?"

"Oh. I take mine black—straight. No frills."

David could only show his teeth. That was just the way he liked his coffee. He stood up. Dominique allowed her eyes to roam over him. Earlier, he'd had on a suit. Now he was wearing jeans, and they were fitting his body well. It was evident from his nice build that he spent time in the gym regularly. He was mouth-watering, not what Dominique expected of a preacher at all.

"Is there anything else you want—a pastry or something?" David asked.

"No. Coffee is fine, thank you. I've eaten enough today."

"Okay. Coffee it is."

A few minutes later, David sat down with their coffees and handed Dominique hers gingerly. "Here you are. Straight black. No frills."

"Thank you," Dominique said, then took a sip. "Oh . . . that feels good going down."

"The best. So, what was the last movie you saw?" David asked.

"I'm a TV addict. I can't remember the last time I've been to a movie. I usually wait for stuff to come on DVD. What about you?"

"Uh . . . we took some of the teens at church to see Hunger Games. It was pretty good, actually. As far as TV, I hate it—except for sports. It's just so predictable. It doesn't stimulate my mind at all."

"So . . . what other things do you like to do?" Dominique asked, trying not to stare. She couldn't recover from his hotness. On top of that, David exuded a sense of raw maleness that she found irresistibly attractive.

"Well, my schedule is jam-packed nowadays, but I love to travel, and . . ." David looked around the bookstore.

Dominique laughed at herself. "Duh. My bad. Obviously, you like to read."

"Yes. I love reading. That's how I relax, honestly. It's like an escape after a long day. My grandfather used to do it every night. Sometimes he read the Bible, and sometimes he read history books. He was a history buff. I guess I inherited the reading bug from him."

"I'm just the opposite. I veg out on TV shows when I'm not working. Strangely enough, I love watching CSI, Law and Order, and shows like that. I have a DVR, so I record them and watch them on my days off. And I admit it; I do love American Idol."

David laughed. "I *hate* American Idol!"

"Opposites attract," Dominique said. She reached across the table and touched David's hand. It was a probing gesture that would have ignited a charge in any other man, but David was used to maintaining control when it came to women. He was ever mindful to separate lust from pure attraction. And he was even more mindful to walk cautiously into situations with the opposite sex. To sit back and observe. Evaluate. There was no reason for haste. Rarely were good decisions ever made in haste.

"So, what kind of books do you buy—Bible books and stuff?" Dominique asked after David failed to respond to her subtle temptation.

"No. Not all the time. I like books on politics and finance. And of course, history—like my granddad."

"Oh . . . that sounds kind of boring. Like a boring ol' preacher," Dominique teased. As soon as the words left her lips, she realized that they had the potential to be hurtful, like a poisonous bite that caused delayed symptoms. "I'm sorry. I didn't mean to offend you."

"I'm not offended because you don't know me, Dominique. I wouldn't characterize myself as a 'boring ol' preacher' anyway. I'm anything but that. My life and my work speak for themselves." David wondered if a minister had ever mistreated her, or if she just had some fixed idea about who he was because of stereotypes. "Is it me, or do you just have a thing against men of the cloth?" David asked.

"Honestly, I think a man is a man. I don't give any extra-credit points because someone calls himself a minister. Really, what is that supposed to mean?"

"It *should* mean that he has integrity. That he's in love with Jesus. That he lives a righteous life and can be trusted."

"Well, I haven't met too many men that fit that description—ministers or otherwise. I think being a pastor or minister is just a job like any other job. Don't get me wrong, I did take some time to Google you today. I admire what you've done for the community and the kids, but that wouldn't make me put you up on some kind of pedestal. You're still just a man."

"You're absolutely right, Dominique. I'm still just a man. The only man who should be elevated is Jesus Christ. That's what I try to do with my life."

"Should I expect you to be different from any other man because you do your *job*?"

David swallowed his coffee slowly, savoring the boldness of the taste. Then he responded to Dominique's obvious dig. "No. The Word says you will know a tree by the fruit it bears. In Matthew 7:20, it says: *Therefore by their fruit you will know them.* A man's actions and the way he lives his life are the things you should judge him by—nothing else. Not what he says, or who he is, but what he *does*."

Dominique looked as if she were considering David's words. She nodded, satisfied. "I like that."

"Now, that's not saying a person is going to be *perfect*—not even a minister. But the *totality* of one's life should represent who he or she is in Christ, not a few mistakes he or she may have made or will make for that matter," David continued.

"Are you speaking of yourself?" Dominique asked. She wondered if David was a *for real* minister or just one of those men who used the title to get what they wanted from weak-minded people. He was handsome enough to pull it off.

David laughed. "I'm speaking of *everyone*—you included." He leaned in closer. "Suppose seven years ago you had an affair with a married man, but since that time you've dedicated yourself to the Lord and His work and have been walking righteously before God. What fruit should I judge you by—the rotten fruit you produced seven years ago or the good fruit you've been producing all this time?"

"The good fruit," Dominique said quietly as if she'd been

chastised. She looked away for a moment and pondered. Then she turned back to David. "I get it."

"Did I say something wrong, Dominique?"

"No. I was just considering what you said, that's all." She changed the subject quickly. "What high school did you graduate from?"

"Union High School—you know it's closed now. Then I went on to Harvard, which was a shock to everyone, including me. I stayed there until I received my MBA. Then I worked on Wall Street as a broker for a few years—which I loved. I was doing *me*. Then one day I realized that doing 'me' is doing God, so I came back home and got my Master of Divinity from Hilltop Theological Seminary." David didn't want to talk too much about himself. He took a long pause. He wanted to know more about her.

"So, when did you know you wanted to be a minister?"

"I don't want to talk a lot about myself. I want to know more about you," he said.

"Let's finish talking about *you*," Dominique insisted. "When did you know you were *called*?"

David smiled, and Dominique found his jet-black eyes, dark bushy eyebrows, and smooth caramel-colored skin to be gorgeous. Not to mention that smile, and perfectly straight white teeth. His neatly trimmed goatee accentuated his full lips and made him a pleasing sight to behold.

"Honestly, as young as I remember, I had a love for church and God's Word. At seven, I saw myself standing over a congregation preaching. I just had this inner feeling. I knew that's what I was going to do. My grandfather was a minister, so he was a big influence in my life. But like most young men, I ignored the call for a long time so that I could 'do me' as they say."

Dominique hurled questions at him. "What did you do after seminary? Is that when you started your church?"

"No. When I first came home after working on Wall Street, I went to Christ the King Baptist Church and talked with Reverend Eugene Marshall and told him that God told me to preach and pastor His people. My grandfather had passed away while I was working on Wall Street, and he'd known Reverend Marshall for a while. Reverend Marshall took me under his wings. He made me go home and fast and pray for a week," David said. That period in his life had been as comical as it was life-changing. Thinking about it still made David feel joyful. "I came back to him after a week and let him know I hadn't heard anything different, so he told me to fast and pray for *another* week to be certain. I remember him saying: *'The call to preach and pastor is the most serious endeavor. You don't wanna be wrong and spend eternity in hell.'* So I prayed and fasted for another week."

"Wait a minute. You mean to tell me you weren't eating *anything?*"

"Nope. I only drank water."

"Man . . . that is crazy! So, tell me he was convinced the *second* time?"

"Nope. He told me to fast and pray one more week, and he said he was going to be fasting with me. So I gave it another week—no food—just water."

"Oh my goodness! Please tell me this man was convinced after three whole weeks."

David laughed. "Listen to this . . . he looked me over after the third week and asked if the Lord had given me a new revelation. I told him 'No!' Then I said, 'I hope He didn't tell you *nothin'* different because I. AM. HUNGRY!'" David said.

Dominique erupted in laughter, spitting out some of the coffee she was drinking. She quickly covered her mouth and laughed uncontrollably. When she finally calmed somewhat, she looked at David and said, "OMG! I would not have survived that! Three weeks? The most I've ever gotten through without eating was three days, and that was a long time ago. I'm not even sure I could do that now." She wiped her mouth and checked her blouse, glad that she hadn't sprayed any coffee on it. Again, she laughed a riotous laugh, shaking her head at David.

"I promise you, I lost about thirty pounds in three weeks! I was gonna be second-guessing my calling if I had to go without eating for another week! Whew! I know Jesus fasted for forty days, but twenty-one days was a little rough back then . . ."

"Pastor Cole, you are crazy!" Dominique said, taking David's hand. "Thanks. It's been a rough week. That was a good laugh." She squeezed his hand gently and then let it go. As sure as his name was David Kent Cole, David felt a definite spark between them.

"Anyway, I started seminary and worked as a minister-in-training under Reverend Marshall. I studied and prayed and became closer to God than I had ever been in my whole life. I fell more in love with Jesus, and I haven't been the same since. I started my church seven years ago, and God has blessed me all this time."

"Wow. I've never heard a man say that he was *in love* with Jesus. It kind of sounds like a couple's relationship when you say it that way."

"Well, I hope I conveyed the intensity of what I feel in my heart. Jesus does refer to the church as his bride. God called Himself Israel's husband. It demonstrates in our human mind the intimacy of a relationship with God. Most people can understand the intensity and sacredness of the husband-wife bond."

Dominique nodded. "That's deep. I never thought of it that way."

"Dominique, one thing I want to say about myself is that I *love* the Lord. My being a pastor has more to do with my loving God and wanting to make Him happy than it does anything else. I'm in love with Christ. That's my daily motivation. So, despite what you may believe, what I do for a living is *not* a job to me. It's my ministry. It's everything I am. It's my worship. It's my service. It's my thanks to God for all He has done for me. I *am* in love with Jesus. This is not some game to me. This is my heart," David said, patting his chest.

Dominique studied him. David saw her whole face soften. She looked at him with reverence. "I believe you are different, Pastor Cole. I really do. Maybe different enough to make me rethink some of my views. So tell me, what's it like being a pastor?"

"Well, I feel like I'm doing what I was put on earth to do. It has its stressors, but I truly believe I am fulfilling God's purpose for my life. And as I said, that's *everything* to me."

"Being a minister is just like being a celebrity these days," Dominique said. Despite her saying that, she truly believed David was different.

David wondered if Dominique had unconsciously passed judgment on him already. "Do you have a regular church home?" he queried.

"No. Not really," Dominique said. The look on David's face let her know that she'd have to expound. "Is that some sort of prerequisite for dating you?" she asked.

David sighed. "First of all, let me remind you that we aren't *dating*. I haven't asked you to *date* me. If I remember correctly, we're just having coffee. Why are you so defensive, Dominique? Did I say that was a prerequisite for dating me?"

Dominique looked David squarely in his eyes. "I just

thought that maybe being a pastor and all, you preferred a certain type of woman—some kind of holy roller."

David shook his head and smiled. Dominique Street was something else. As beautiful as she was, David sensed a lot of insecurity in her. "Let me be clear about something, Dominique. One of my strengths is being able to communicate with people in a way that they can understand. Right now, I'm having coffee with you. I don't have any preconceived notions about who you should be. Be who you are. If we find that we fit each other, that would be wonderful, sweetheart. And if we discover that we don't fit, that would certainly be okay too. It will be worth the journey either way. So please don't rack your brain trying to figure out what I want. I will let you know exactly what I want if we get to that point," David said with a penetrating stare that left no room for personal interpretation.

David's straightforwardness delighted Dominique. She had to admit that she was attracted to him. Working in a male-dominated profession, she was used to being surrounded by men who were brash and aggressive. She loved take-charge men who didn't take nonsense off anyone. That's the kind of man she wanted. "Okay," she said, aware that David had politely, yet directly, put her in her place for the second time that day.

"Tell me about when you accepted Christ," David said, continuing to ask the questions that he'd wanted answers to.

Dominique relaxed her shoulders, sat back in her chair, and reminded herself not to be defensive. "I was twelve. My dad and my mom had split up when I was nine. I did it at vacation Bible school. I was really hurting when my dad left, and for some reason, I felt like church could help me. When I told one of the church mothers how I felt about my dad, she told me God would help me and make that pain go away. So I accepted Christ, and I was baptized that Sunday."

"Do you talk to or see your dad now?"

Dominique shook her head. "No. I haven't talked to or seen him since I was about twenty—thirteen long years ago. We used to contact each other and start talking more frequently, and then all of a sudden, he'd disappear and not call. His phone number would be disconnected, and we'd just lose touch. I gave up on him."

"Well, that's one thing we have in common. I haven't seen my biological father since I was about five." David didn't want to talk about Jeff. "My mother's husband, Joe, raised me from the time I was about seven. What about your mom? How is your relationship with your mom?"

"Why do I feel like I'm in a therapy session?" Dominique asked.

"I don't know, sweetheart. If there is something you don't want to talk about, just say so. It's not my intention to pry. Like I said, I'm having coffee—and making conversation, trying to get to know a little bit about you."

"Okay. I'd rather not talk about my mom tonight. I don't want to dampen your mood or mine."

David put his hands up in a surrendering gesture. "Okay. That's fine, sweetheart. Tell me about some of your church experiences."

"Look, honestly, some things have happened that have kept me away from church. I'm not opposed to church. I know that I haven't and cannot lose my salvation. I realize that I need to be fed spiritually regularly. I just haven't found the perfect fit for me yet," Dominique explained.

"That's fair, Dominique. And that's honest. I like honesty. God can do wonderful things in our lives when we allow Him to."

"I think I could learn a lot from a man like you."

"My only hope is that you've seen or heard God in something I've said or done while we've been having coffee. For me, that's good enough."

They sat and talked until the bookstore closed. They talked about a wide range of topics from politics to religion. David enjoyed the easy way they communicated. Dominique was as feisty as she was beautiful, pulling no punches, holding back nothing that was on her mind. That pleased David. He sensed something had happened in her life that made her doubt God. He hoped that his life would be a witness to the goodness of God.

After the manager had politely given several hints that it was time for them to leave, David followed Dominique to the parking lot. She led him to a red convertible Corvette with a black top.

"Put the bike away?"

"Yeah. This is my other baby," Dominique said, patting the hood. "Gettin' my ride on before the snow hits. I don't drive her in the winter, obviously—this is Michigan."

"Beautiful woman with fast toys."

"Are you trying to flatter me?"

"No, I'm just telling the truth."

"I see . . . thanks for the compliment."

Dominique unlocked her car door, and David opened it for her. She eased inside, and he closed the door. She strapped on her seat belt and started the engine. She let the window down in case David had anything else to say. The seventy-seven-degree day had quickly turned to a fifty-degree night. The wind was nipping at her skin through her thin blouse.

"You're quite welcome. Drive safely. And thanks for having coffee with me, Dominique. It was nice meeting you and talking with you."

Dominique forced a smile. "You too," she responded as cheerily as she could. She was hoping David would ask her out for a real date. Now, she wanted to get to know *him* better. But maybe they hadn't clicked the way she thought they had. Maybe he *was* looking for a holy-roller type of woman.

"Goodnight, Dominique."

"Goodnight, David."

David watched her exit the lot before he strode to his truck and climbed in. He was grinning impishly from ear to ear. Dominique Street had to be handled a certain way. And he was just the man for the job. "I like her, Lord," he said aloud. He savored that thought all the way home. He made a quick stop by his mother's to get a plate of lasagna.

As soon as he was home, he showered and ate, smiling amusedly every time he thought about the look on Dominique's beautiful face when he didn't ask her out on a date. He pushed a button and elevated his bed so that his feet were propped up in the air. He reached over to the nightstand and picked up his cell phone. Chuckling, he dialed Dominique's number.

Dominique answered quickly. "Hello?"

"Hey, this is David. I'm just making sure you made it home safely."

"Oh yes, I'm good," Dominique said. She placed the call on speaker and rolled her eyes. *Did he not like her at all?*

"Okay, good night then. And again, thanks for having coffee with me," David said.

"You're welcome. Good night."

"Good night."

David pressed the end-call button, grinning like a Cheshire cat. "I got her good!" he said aloud. He let his bed down and went down to his kitchen and poured himself a cup of coffee. He came back a few minutes later and dialed Dominique's number again.

As soon as David heard Dominique's voice, he said, "Hey, it's me again. I hope it's not too late for you. I had a question."

"Sure. What is it?" Dominique asked hopefully.

"Your bike—is that the thirtieth-anniversary limited edition?"

"Huh?"

"Your bike—is that the limited edition?" David repeated, barely keeping his laughter in check.

"Yes, it is." Dominique sounded disappointed.

David could not keep himself from laughing any longer. He laughed gregariously. "I'm sorry, Dominique, that's not really what I called for."

Dominique wasn't sure where David was going with this conversation. "David, how can I help you?" she asked, trying not to sound as aggravated as she was becoming.

David responded seriously. "Dominique, I enjoyed your company this evening, and I'd like to see you again. I want to take you out on a real date and get to know more about you."

"Are you saying you want to go out with me because you have romantic intentions?"

David grinned. "Maybe. We'll see. How about this Friday evening?"

"I can't do Friday, but I can do Saturday."

"Okay. I'll plan to pick you up at about six o'clock for a nice dinner. What kind of food do you like best?"

"Big, juicy steaks."

David nodded. "Okay. Text me your address, and lock in my number in case there are any changes to your schedule."

"Where are you taking me?"

"You'll find out on Saturday, Ms. Street. Good night."

Dominique beamed. Her lips curled into a smile. "Okay. Good night."

Chapter 4

Boring Ol' Preacher

David felt a little rusty. He *was* rusty. He hadn't been on a date—a real date—in over a year. He showered and donned a pair of black slacks, a crisp white button-up, and a gray and black cardigan. It was a nice combination that complemented his chiseled frame. He reached for his three-quarter-length leather jacket and looked at himself again in his parlor mirror. He double-checked his shoes and decided his grandfather would have been proud. Satisfied that they were appropriately shined, he gave himself one last thorough check-over. First dates could reveal things about a person. He wanted Dominique to know that he had a little swag—some style. That he wasn't some 'boring ol' preacher.'

David arrived at Dominique's home twenty minutes early. Instead of calling from his cell to let her know that he'd arrived, he opted to ring the doorbell. He was nothing less than a gentleman. Dominique appeared at the door looking surprised. "Hi. I wasn't expecting you early. I'm not quite ready—but I will be. Just give me a few more minutes. I hope this is fine,"

Dominique said, turning, giving David a 360-degree view of the fitted red dress she wore.

Eye candy. "You look beautiful. And take your time. I just like to be punctual." David's eyes were fixed on her as she walked away. Immediately, he chided himself and meditated on a portion of Philippians 4:8. *Whatsoever things are just, whatsoever things are pure . . . think on these things.* "Lord, it's been a while, give me strength. Amen," he said in a whisper. He decided he needed to play some gospel music in the car.

Several minutes later, Dominique appeared before David again. "I'm ready, Pastor Cole," she said.

"Now what did I tell you about that? I'm *David*."

"Okay. It just seems weird. This is a first for me."

David was patient. "Let's get to know one another for who we are on the inside—not by titles."

"You are a pastor, though."

"I'm also a man, but that doesn't mean people go around addressing me as 'man' every time they say something to me."

"You have a point."

Maybe it was Dominique's nervousness that caused her to dwell on the fact that David was a pastor, or maybe it was her overall uncertainty. He didn't know which; he just hoped it wouldn't be a problem. He saw possibilities in Dominique's eyes.

David eased his sleek, silver, current-model Jaguar out of Dominique's driveway. He drove it only on occasion—never to church. It was one of his *hidden toys,* like his vintage 1964 Mustang, and crotch rocket motorcycle—the same model as Dominique's in midnight blue. He was careful about the impression he made in the community. Although he had been investment savvy over the years and could easily afford a plethora of extravagant luxuries, he purposely lived an unpretentious lifestyle. There were enough money-hungry, flashy, prosperity preachers in the world. He in no way wanted to be compared to any of those bozos. He paid himself a modest church salary that he hadn't increased over the years. He was blessed enough that he didn't have to rely on his church salary for income, but he made himself live off it.

Between the inheritance left to him by his grandfather, money made from investments while he worked on Wall Street, and his real estate portfolio, David was financially set for the rest of his life. It was his secret. He was a very low-key, multimillionaire. He had also strategically managed DOC's finances and had helped to build an awesome investment portfolio for the church, which allowed it to bless the surrounding community tremendously in tangible ways through various programs.

"So . . . where are we going, *David*?" Dominique asked.

David smiled at Dominique's sarcasm. "Well, you said you wanted steak. So, I'm taking you to Ruth's Chris Steak House. It's one of my favorites. Hopefully, you'll enjoy it as well."

"Never heard of it."

"I'm praying you like it," David joked. He did want to make a good first impression. He'd initially struggled with where to take her. He wanted to do something nice for their first date, but he didn't want to spend extravagantly straight out of the gate and have her focused on the monetary *trimmings* and not him. He was satisfied with his choice. It was a moderately priced steak house, with a nice atmosphere that would communicate that he put some thought into their date. Besides, he could always turn it up a few notches as their relationship progressed.

"What are we doing *afterward*?"

David raised a brow. "I really hadn't thought that far. Is there something you'd like to do after dinner?"

"I haven't been dancing in a while . . . but I don't know how you feel about that."

"Dominique, I'm not a caveman. It depends on what you have in mind. I'd prefer not to go to a nightclub. It sends a double message to anyone who might see me there."

Dominique wanted to keep the interaction civil, so she chose her words carefully. "I'm not sure where else we could go to dance, David, unless we are going to crash someone's wedding," she laughed.

"Dominique, I don't have a problem with dancing. Really. I just don't want to be seen at a nightclub. That doesn't reflect who I am."

"It's okay. Just forget about it."

"WHAT ELSE SHOULD I know about you?" Dominique asked with her head tilted. She pushed back a bit from the table and rested her body against the cushioned booth. David marveled at the fact that a woman of her size could put away so much food. He'd also concluded that she looked uber-sexy with her head tilted that way, but forced his mind not to go *there*.

"What do you want to know, Dominique?"

"Why'd you ask me out? I'm sure a man of your status has his pick when it comes to women."

"For one, you're beautiful and thoughtful. I thought it was compassionate of you to check on me after Squirt's death. And you intrigue me on a level I haven't experienced in a while. Why'd you *agree* to go out with me?"

"Because you're different and you seem so sweet and caring," Dominique admitted. "On top of those qualities, I find you very attractive."

"Ditto to that."

"Ditto as in you find yourself very attractive?" Dominique joked.

"Oh, you've got jokes, huh? Ditto, as in I find you remarkably and immeasurably attractive as well," David said, flashing his perfectly straight teeth. "Dominique Antoinette Street, the quintessential beauty."

"Oh . . . quintessential?" Dominique chuckled. "Is that one of your Harvard words?"

"No, that's a young man from the hood trying to impress a beautiful lady . . ."

"She's impressed."

David winked at her. "Good. And you know what? I have just the perfect plan for dessert tonight."

"Oh, really?"

"Yes. I think you'll love it."

David settled the bill with the waiter, and he and Dominique headed downtown. He loved driving. The forty-minute drive seemed to go by quickly as he and Dominique talked sports. When they pulled into the valet lane at Chase on the River, an upscale downtown restaurant, Dominique smirked. "David, I hate to break it to you, but there is *no* way we are getting in here on a Saturday night unless you have already made reservations."

Chase on the River was owned by Chef Chase Martin. His downtown location was the most popular, although he had just opened a new spot in Birmingham, Michigan. Patrons usually made reservations weeks in advance for the downtown eatery, which featured what Chase referred to as gourmet soul and seafood. The pricey, elegant restaurant was one of the most coveted spots in the city, along with Pat's Place, another upscale restaurant and contender, owned by a former NFL player.

A valet wearing a deep purple colored jacket with *Chase on the River* embroidered on the back opened David's door, while another opened Dominique's. The young valet on Dominique's side helped her out of the car, and a host greeted them at the door. "Good evening, I'm Jason. Welcome to Chase on the River. We regret that we are full tonight unless you have reservations," the young man said disappointedly.

Dominique shook her head. But she dared not tell David, "I told you so."

"No. I don't have reservations, sir. I'm on the owner's list," David explained. Dominique twisted her lips, and her brows inched up curiously.

"Oh, great! I'm so sorry for keeping you waiting, sir," the young man continued, as he tapped the screen of an electronic handheld tablet. "May I have your name, please?"

"David Kent Cole."

"Certainly," the young man said, nodding as he found David's name on the screen. Chase had put a tech-savvy system in place to protect the personal information of his special guests. The young man quickly glanced at David's picture, which was logged into the restaurant's owner's list, and looked back at David. It was a match. David winked at Dominique.

"Mr. Cole, how many will be in your party tonight?"

"Just two."

"Would you like to have your meals in the owner's suite or the owner's section?"

"We'll take the owner's section tonight, Jason."

The owner, Chase Martin, had renamed his VIP room and VIP section to the owner's suite and the owner's section after his wife pointed out that every person is a VIP and having a VIP room and section where only certain celebrities, sports players, or politicians could enter indicated that they were better than the general public. She said that having an owner's section communicated that the room was exclusive to the owner's special guests, but didn't communicate that the other guests weren't as important. Leave it to Chase to marry a social worker. He instituted the change the same week she'd pointed it out.

Chase kept an owner's list of his "former VIPs," which gave them access to a private, second-floor suite that was separated from the general dining area. It was glassed-in with one-way glass so that the guests in his personal suite had a view of the other guests in the restaurant, but could maintain their privacy. The owner's section was an area near the stage that consisted of a group of four booths and three tables. When those areas were full, privileged guests were escorted to the owner's suite upstairs. David favored the owner's section because it allowed him to be up close and personal with whomever was performing. An exceptionally gifted piano player, David loved music, and he basked in the experience of being so near that the instruments and singers' voices reverberated through him.

"Yes, sir. Right this way, Mr. Cole."

"Thank you, Jason," David said, squeezing Dominique's hand. He led her through the restaurant as he followed Jason to a seat that was in perfect view of the live band. David's attention gravitated to the female lead singer, who was crooning "The First Time Ever I Saw Your Face." He didn't hear his nickname called the first time. Dominique squeezed his hand to let him know that the *mayor* was trying to get his attention. David stopped in his tracks as Dominique pointed.

They'd passed the booth where Mayor Walter Kincaid sat with a tall, beautiful woman, whom David recognized as Arabelle, a world-famous French R&B artist. David had missed seeing Walter's security detail. Especially Duke. The big fella was hard to miss. David pivoted and walked toward Walter. Walter stood.

"DC, what's happening?" Walter Kincaid said, hugging David in a brotherly embrace.

"Hey . . . Walt. What's up, man?"

"Just hanging out a little bit tonight," Walter said. He paused. "Oh, excuse me. Let me introduce you to my lady friend," Walter said like a man who was hiding a golden goose behind his back. He was eager and excited, knowing good and well that David knew who Arabelle was. David could hear Walter thinking, '*I'm out with every man's dream.*' He smiled and nodded politely. Yes, Arabelle was a rare beauty. "Belle, meet my good friend, Pastor David *Kent* Cole," Walter said teasingly, emphasizing David's middle name.

"It's nice to meet you, Belle," David said casually.

Arabelle spoke with a heavy French accent. "Same here," she said, smiling flirtatiously at David.

David gently pulled Dominique to his side. "This is my friend, Dominique Street, Belle."

The two women exchanged salutations as David continued his introductions. "Dominique, this is my good friend and mayor, Walter Kincaid."

"Nice to meet you, sir," Dominique said formally.

"You too, beautiful," Walter said, winking at David. Mayor Walter Kincaid was certainly a charmer. David watched as Walter kissed Dominique's cheek. "Well, Belle and I are going to hang around here for a while, then do a little night-time sightseeing," Walter said.

"Okay, enjoy yourself. And again, it was nice to meet you, Belle," David said.

Arabelle's French accent was charming. "Thank you. You also," she said.

Dominique's eyes were wide. She hadn't expected to meet

the mayor *and* Arabelle. She didn't know why she'd become nervous all of a sudden.

Jason seated them two booths away from Walter and Arabelle. As soon as Dominique excused herself from the table to go to the ladies' room, David texted Walter. He couldn't resist.

> David: You better be in church tomorrow, man!

Walter responded minutes later with a long text.

> Walter: I can't even lie. You might as well tell the Lord to strike me down right now. Cuz you KNOW what I'm doin' 2nite! Bro, I ain't gon' have the energy to get up in the morning! LOLOL.

David put his cell phone away just as Dominique returned to the table. His phone vibrated in his belt clip.

"Excuse me. Let me turn off my cell, please."

"Sure, no problem. You can take your call if you need to."

David turned his phone off and placed it back in the clip. "No. No need, that's nobody but Walter. I texted him about showing up at church tomorrow, while he's over there romancing Arabelle."

Dominique hoped she didn't sound like some sort of groupie, but she wanted to know exactly what kind of relationship David had with her top boss. "You're on a texting basis with the *mayor*?" Dominique asked.

David shrugged his shoulders. "Yes. Walt and I grew up together, and we're still very good friends. There is a group of us—six to be exact. We're all pretty tight. My mother used to call us the brat pack. We've been buddies since elementary school. There's Mayor Kincaid, Reginald Williams—the mayor's chief of staff; Chase Martin, the guy that owns this restaurant; Pastor Corey Perry of Greater Christian Center Church; my best friend, Gus Merrick, and me. We all lived in the same neighborhood on the west side, went to the same church, and the same schools, and spent the night over each other's homes, driving our mothers crazy! We're like brothers. We don't see each other as often now, but the bonds are still there. Chase and Corey are best friends, and of course, Walter and Reginald are best friends, and then there's Gus and me."

"I see. All of you are so successful . . . what does Gus do?"

"Uh . . . Gus works in the area of internet security—hi-tech stuff. It's kind of private because he deals with the government a lot." What David didn't say was that Gus worked for the CIA on a special team that focused on cyber terrorism, and he'd had the ability to hack all manner of computers since eighth grade.

"Oh, I see. Sounds interesting."

David was quick to change the subject. He wasn't one for name-dropping, and he didn't want to seem pompous because of his relationship with Walter. "And to think, you thought we weren't going to get in this place!" David bubbled over with accomplishment. He'd nailed it.

"Well, I didn't know you were the *man* and all."

"Woman, you better ask somebody 'bout me!" David said playfully. Something about Dominique made him feel invincible. Maybe it was time to settle down with someone. He hadn't thought about that in over a year.

The woman who'd been singing so beautifully was now singing a duet with one of the male band members. They sang a sultry version of Marvin Gaye and Tammy Terrell's "If This World Were Mine." The song was a favorite of David's mother, Leah. Dominique swayed her head to the tune.

"Woman, whatchu know 'bout this song?"

"I know all the Motown songs—every artist. My mom loves everything Motown."

"Mine too. Come on, let's dance," David said. He reached across the table and took Dominique's hand in his.

"Huh?"

"Let's dance, Ms. Street. You said you wanted to dance, so I brought you somewhere we could dance. I *deliver*," David said. At that moment, he knew this would be the first of many dates he'd have with Dominique. Their chemistry couldn't be denied. He was certain that after this evening, she would be dying to see him again.

Dominique was pleased. "Yes, David. You *do* deliver."

David led her to the intimate dance floor. Shortly after, Walter and Arabelle followed. Dominique relaxed in David's arms, and he was mindful not to get too close. Dominique looked up at him with dreamy eyes and said, "Thank you, Dave." The shortened name seemed to fit him now.

"You're welcome. I hope you are having a good time with a 'boring ol' preacher.'"

"Yes. Certainly not what I expected at all. You're the best."

"Now that's what I like to hear . . ."

* * *

AFTER DANCING TO TWO SONGS, David and Dominique sat down for dessert. Chase Martin and his sister Mona, who served as Chase's business partner and public relations representative, made their usual Saturday night rounds, greeting the restaurant guests personally. David introduced Dominique to the brother and sister team. Then, at Mona's request, David and Dominique took pictures with Arabelle and Walter Kincaid. Mona seized the opportunity to add additional celebrity pictures to the restaurant's photo gallery wall. It was good for business.

David and Walter escaped to the lounge area connected to the men's restroom in the exclusive owner's section, where a few other high-profile men were assembled. Both were shocked when Mona walked in. She wore a skin-tight, purple leather dress that was cut low in the front and the back. Her ample hips and small waist made her look like a walking hourglass. Mona pranced around in a pair of silver, five-inch stilettos that gave her five-foot-two frame height. She looked like a baby doll.

Walter spoke first. "Woman, don't you know this is a men's lounge? What are you doing in here?"

"I'm sorry, babe. The staff told me it was clear. I was just coming to check to make sure it was up to par. There's a shift change in fifteen minutes," Mona said.

Walter stood, "It's very clean in there. Now come on over here and apologize right."

Mona smiled before sauntering into Walter's arms. She kissed him full on the lips and repeated the act twice. She whispered in Walter's ear, and he laughed a hearty player's laugh.

Mona took a Kleenex out of her bra and dabbed her lipstick off Walter, with her body pressed up against his.

"We don't want you to get into any trouble with Arabelle," she said seductively. "Bye, David," she said as she walked out.

"Bye, Mona . . ."

"Whew! She is somethin' else!" Walter said, nodding.

David had only one reply. "You're a big mess, man!"

"What?"

"You've got Arabelle—who is probably every man's dream —waiting for you at the table, and one of the finest women in this city kissing all over you in the men's lounge. You're a mess!"

"Man, Mona is worse than me! Ain't no holding her down. I tried that already!"

"I bet you did!"

"Oh, I did!" Walter laughed. "Mona ain't havin' that. She says she is single and loving it. Oh, but she's got skills, DC!"

"Unh-uh," David said. "I don't even want to hear it. I gotta keep my mind right." He covered his ears like a little boy.

Walter let out a roar. "Oh, I forgot you ain't gettin' none, preacher!"

"I don't want any. Bye, Walt."

Walter was still laughing as David walked out of the lounge. "Know he needs to get right with the Lord," David said aloud.

It was nine-thirty. David decided it was time to take Dominique home. He had to preach in the morning.

* * *

DAVID WALKED Dominique up the stairs of her Midtown townhouse. "Would you like to come in for a while?" she asked.

"No, thank you, sweetheart. I've got to be prepared for tomorrow. I need to rest," David said. He'd studied his sermon all week, but he still needed time in the morning to sit in the Spirit.

"Well, hopefully, we'll get together real soon," Dominique said. She didn't want to let on just how much she wanted to see him again.

Certain that they would, David said, "I look forward to that."

"Me, too," Dominique said before planting a kiss on David's lips. It was soft and teasing. The wind was whipping cold air around him, but David felt flushed from the heat inside of him.

He reciprocated the kiss with a closed mouth and pulled gently apart from Dominique. "Good night, Dominique."

"Call me Nik, please."

"Good night, Nik."

"Good night, Dave . . ."

"I'll call you tomorrow."

"Okay," Dominique said. She opened the door and stepped in.

On the drive home, David's mind was infiltrated by thoughts of Dominique.

Chapter 5

A Dime and A Dollar

It was Sweetest Day—a Midwest thing. A Hallmark holiday. Something someone made up to sell cards, candies, and flowers. But David felt like Dominique was his sweetie and worth the effort. He'd been dating her for almost a month, and things looked promising. He was feeling their vibe. He'd already made plans to see her later that evening. His morning, however, was solely devoted to his first love—God. This morning, he was scheduled to attend a special youth workshop held at Greater Christian Center, the church where Corey Perry, one of his childhood buddies, was the senior pastor.

David had seen a significant increase in the number of girls joining gangs in the area near his church, and he wanted to develop a special program just for them. Corey had spoken highly of a female dynamo at his church who was excellent at mentoring youth, and David had come to check the woman out and see if he could incorporate her into his plan for the girls at DOC.

He was impressed from the moment he pulled into the long

drive that led to the parking lot of Greater Christian Center. The newly built building was an architectural masterpiece. It was an enormous white brick chapel with stained-glass windows. David remembered a time when Corey's father, Pastor Charles Perry, had a little storefront church on the west side of Detroit. For the past three years, Corey had filled his father's position of senior pastor, having moved into that spot after his father's death. He smiled in awe when he noticed the parking lot was full. "Corey must be doing a great job over here to get the young people up at ten a.m. on a Saturday morning— on Sweetest Day at that," he said to himself.

David had made it a practice to hold youth events at DOC on Friday evenings because he usually received a better turnout that way. He exited his truck and walked up the winding walkway to the huge front doors of Greater Christian Center. He passed a gentleman he assumed to be a part of the mayor's security detail, dressed in plain clothes. He gave a discreet nod and walked toward Corey's private office. Two more plain-clothes officers were standing nearby.

A lanky young man who was about thirteen years old was serving as host. He was casually dressed in a white button-up shirt and khakis. "Good Morning. Are you Pastor Cole?" he asked politely.

"Yes, sir."

The young man shook David's hand. "My name is Stix. Pastor Corey is expecting you. Right this way, please."

David trailed behind Stix, impressed with the young man's professionalism. Stix knocked lightly on Corey's office door. It was a three-knock signal.

"Come in, Stix," Corey answered.

Stix opened the door and allowed David to go in ahead of him. "Hey . . ." David started. Walter Kincaid was closest and grabbed David in a bear hug.

"DC . . . I just saw the documentary about you on TV last night. It was awesome, man. You are big time now. And you have a New York Times Best Seller?"

"Just doing God's work. You know how they hype things up, bro." David was humbled by the attention he'd been receiving, especially about the book he'd written: *God Lives in the Hood.* The book's focus on city revitalization through faith outreach programs had caused it to be a staple at urban development and Christian conferences alike.

"You're looking good," Walter Kincaid said, checking out David's brown slacks and tan cashmere sweater. Walter Kincaid wasn't too arrogant or insecure to compliment another man when it was due to him.

"You're kind of crispy too, boss," David joked, sounding like one of his teens.

Walter Kincaid nodded. "Well, I'm the mayor. I have to stay crispy."

Walter Kincaid was one of the most powerful men in the city, after having won the bid for mayor just three years prior. His campaign platform had focused on ethics, integrity, and transparency. And he had not disappointed his constituents. He'd been leading the city and its residents without scandal. It was a known fact that Walter Kincaid was a single man on every high-society woman's most eligible bachelors list, but whatever escapades he may have had were kept private and never got in the way of him running the city with ethical politics. Walter was well-respected and admired, but to David and Corey, he was just Walt, the tall, ex-football star they'd grown up with since grade school.

Corey Perry walked up and embraced David in a brotherly hug. The two were the same height. Corey was sporting salt and pepper stubble on his chin. It was a nice contrast against his creamy vanilla skin color. He resembled his father. "So, I finally got you over here to GCC," he said to David.

"I had to come and check out this dynamo you keep bragging about. I want to start something special over at DOC with the girls who've been in gangs."

"Well, like I said, Dr. Cherelle Dupree is the *truth*. She is a licensed psychologist, Bible teacher, and a heck of a speaker. She's written seven books—both fiction and non-fiction. She can get up close and personal with the youth. They love her."

"And she looks good," Walter threw in, laughing.

Corey cut his eyes playfully at Walt.

"You already have too much going on. Arabelle *and* Mona Martin! That's too much for one man," David teased, taking some mints out of the glass jar on Corey's desk.

"God is still working on me, while I'm working on staying single," Walter admitted.

"Wait a minute! Walt, are you dating *Arabelle*?" Corey asked enviously.

"*And* Mona Martin!" David interjected again.

"Oh, you do have a lot going on!" Corey agreed.

David nodded. "Walt, we have to see to it that you get saved!"

"Man, Arabelle and I are just good friends . . ." Walter said, laughing.

Corey knew better. "Give it up, DC. He's not ready yet," he said.

"He better get ready."

"Come on, give me a break today, preach," Walter said as he patted David's back. "I remember when you were ice-cold with the women. I didn't know whether to call you Punch, like your mother called you, because you could knock a fool out in a second, or Ice because of the way you handled the women. You had the women going crazy, DC."

"Glad that's behind us," David said. He didn't even want to think about the old David anymore. It was shameful some of the things he'd done. He was glad God had delivered him from all that Grade A foolishness.

"Seriously, though," Walter started, "I'm proud of you both. You two are doing great things for this city. Corey, you are doing wonders with your job training and property ownership workshops. And David, what you've been able to do with the youth, as far as keeping them off the streets, has been helping me to do *my* job."

"Hey man, we are proud of *you*. You are the *mayor* of this city. Wow. No scandals. No negative reports every hour on the news. You have been doing a phenomenal job—with integrity, I might add," David complimented.

"I promised Mom and everyone who voted for me—no embarrassment to this fine city of ours. We have to restore it and leave all the debauchery and foolishness behind." Walter seemed to have slipped into politician mode, giving a speech.

"Walt, did you just say *debauchery*?" Corey joked.

"I did," Walter said, flashing his political smile.

"Hey, I might not be at church every Sunday, but I went to the same Sunday school as y'all two fools."

"Don't remind me about Mrs. Booth! Ooh wee, she didn't play! 'Walter Kincaid, Corey Perry, David Cole, Chase Martin, and Reginald Williams get up and recite some verses!'" Corey mocked in a scratchy voice, sounding like their childhood Sunday school teacher.

They all burst into laughter.

There were three knocks at the door, with a pause between each. "Come in, Stix," Corey called.

"Excuse me, Pastor Corey. Ms. Cherelle just arrived. We're ready for you to bless the food."

"Is your keynote speaker *late?*" David asked, looking at his watch. He was a stickler for punctuality.

"Nope. She had a TV interview this morning in New York. She just wrapped up a promotional tour for an independent Christian film she's starring in—it's her first acting role in a major film. I wasn't expecting her to be here at nine o'clock."

"You told us to get here by nine!" David said, feigning a whine.

"She's different . . ." Corey said. He stepped out of his office and into the hallway where Dr. Cherelle Dupree was walking toward him. Her coat was hung over her arm. Being alone in the hallway, the two embraced. Corey took her coat and purse, and they entered his office.

"Hey . . . how was your flight?" Corey asked in a sweet, low tone that caused David's antenna to go up.

"It was good. Thank you, Pastor Corey," Cherelle nodded in deference.

"Sister Cherelle, this is Pastor David *Kent* Cole of Disciples of Christ Ministries, better known as DOC. And you know Mayor Kincaid . . ."

"Good Morning, Pastor Cole, nice to meet you," Cherelle said, shaking David's hand firmly. She turned to Walter Kincaid. "Nice to see you again as well, Mayor Kincaid, sir."

"Same here," Walter said, hugging Cherelle. She looked a bit uneasy as Corey eyed her embrace with Walter. David took notice of that small detail. He made it his business to study people. He wondered what was going on. *Is Corey dating one of his members?* It was a no-no for David, but he wouldn't pass judgment if Corey felt that it was appropriate.

David wasn't quite sure what Walter Kincaid's angle was. He certainly sensed some familiarity in the way Walter looked at Cherelle and hugged her. If Walter intended to be inconspicuous, he was a poor actor if David had ever seen one. Corey had to be blind if he didn't pick up on it. David observed everyone quietly considering all these things in his mind. The Lord didn't shed any light on the situation, so he quickly turned his attention to what he'd come for—to observe Dr. Cherelle Dupree in action with the youth, get a feel for her personality, and see if she could be an addition to his youth ministry in some way.

Cherelle Dupree was girl-next-door beautiful. A good-looking woman who was well put together. She was what David referred to as *beautifully average*. It was his way of classifying an everyday-looking woman whose spirit, personality, style, or some other unique attribute captivated a man more than her physical beauty itself. She was dark chocolate with dark, slanted eyes and long, thick lashes that appeared to be natural. David hated the long fake lashes that some women wore, which made them look like some intergalactic creature on Star Trek.

Even with her modest outfit, David could tell that Cherelle Dupree had a nice figure. It was obvious that she had a beautiful smile as well. Although he didn't dwell on those things, they surely couldn't go unnoticed. There was something refreshingly alluring about Cherelle Dupree. It was her aura. Yes, her spirit. David noticed all of this in the short time Cherelle had been in the room, yet none of those details moved him in a profound way. That was partly attributed to the fact that he tended to be hyper-focused and sagacious when he was about the Lord's business. In addition, he had Dominique on his mind these days.

David observed every detail about Cherelle Dupree from the way she spoke, down to the way she dressed. She was wearing all black. She wore a fashionable knit skirt with lace-looking tights that drew attention to her knee-high black leather boots with two-inch heels. Not much of her legs were showing because her skirt ended just above the knee. There were a couple of inches of peek-a-boo space between her boots and the hem of her skirt, which to David was subtly sexy, but modest. Her top was a black satin, button-up blouse with short puff sleeves. She sported an afro puff atop her head. Her dark brown hair was perfectly kinky. David decided that she was feminine and chic, stylishly up-to-date, but still appropriate in attire. Her clothes fit her nicely but weren't too tight or too revealing. She was classy.

David had a good feeling about her from his first impression. Before he would even consider inviting anyone to work with his youth ministry, he checked the person out fully. Today's workshop was just the first phase of his informal interviewing process.

After Corey prayed that they would have a successful workshop, they exited his office, proudly escorted by Stix. David, Walter, Corey, and Cherelle made their way to the banquet room where the teens would have breakfast before the conference began. Upon entering the conference room, Corey blessed the food, and the youth ate and socialized with each other at the tables. There were one hundred of them this morning. The menu included made-to-order omelets, pancakes, waffles, grits, bacon, fresh fruit, iced coffee, regular coffee, and fruit smoothies. Instead of sitting with David, Corey, and Walter, Cherelle Dupree chose to sit at a table full of young women.

David studied her carefully as she interacted with them. Cherelle laughed unreservedly and took selfies with the young girls. She seemed to have a youthful spirit. Girls and young men from other tables came up to greet her. She had an excellent rapport with the youth. David could tell that the young people looked up to and trusted her by the way they interacted with her.

On Corey's prompting, Stix announced a seven-minute break when breakfast was over. Cherelle walked over to the table where David was sitting and asked to speak to Corey in private. David watched Corey get up and discreetly hand Cherelle a key. *A key to his office? There is definitely something going on between them*, David thought to himself.

"So, Pastor Corey," David started, "How do you know Dr. Dupree?"

Corey's response was cool and unrehearsed. "My dad introduced me to her before he passed. We found out that she was an excellent writer, speaker, and teacher, so we put her to work around here. She's been here for three years. She's a good woman. Good with the youth. She walks the walk. Lives a clean life for the Lord."

David nodded. "What's her latest book about?"

"Oh, it's great. It's called: *Teen Dating, Love, and Sex God's Way*."

"Hmm . . . that sounds pretty straightforward."

Corey nodded. "She's a straightforward kind of woman. The book is scripturally based, and she tackles some hard-hitting stuff. You'll see when she shares some wisdom with the youth today."

"I assume *Teen Dating, Love, and Sex God's Way* is about dating, love, and sex God's way. . ." David said, prodding. He knew how sometimes a catchy title was used purely to sell a book, whether it had substance or not.

"Absolutely. The book causes the teens to examine Scripture and take a look at what God says about how they live their lives. It's not condemning, it's truthful. It reads just as well for an adult, but it's focused on the teens. She's talking about self-worth, holiness, and honoring the Lord by not giving in to sex before marriage. She also delves into male-female respect in relationships. It's powerful, DC."

David nodded again. He'd wait to see what she had to say. *Then* he'd decide if it was powerful or not. If it was godly or not.

The break was over, and Cherelle returned looking even more alluring. She seemed to be glowing. Or was it just David's imagination?

With a small wireless microphone pack clipped on her waist and a clear earpiece that didn't detract from her beauty or outfit, Cherelle strode to the front of the room. "Let us pray. All heads bowed . . . all eyes closed . . ."

David felt moved by her prayer. It seemed to be right from her heart and not practiced or overly wordy.

"All black everything . . ." Cherelle joked with the room full of teens, as soon as they had said their amens. They stood, clapped, and cheered for her.

David could tell that Cherelle met them on their level.

"Thank you so much. I love you. I'm glad to be back with you. Today, we are going to honor God by learning His vision and purpose for dating, love, and *sex.*" Cherelle walked the room like a veteran keynote speaker. "We're going to start with sex because that's what everyone wants to talk about first anyway, right?" she asked, smiling at them.

They stood and clapped again. Some shouted their yeses. "Good. The first thing we need to do is crack open our Bibles. Get your Bibles out. If you are a Christian, the Bible is your authority. It's your ruler. Your law. Your instruction book. Not Mama. Not Daddy. Not Pooky. Not Ray Ray. Not Sha-nay-nay. Not Pastor Corey. Are we clear about that?"

The crowd responded in unison. "Yes!"

"Now, there may be some of you in the room who are not Christians. And that's okay. We're all here to learn today. And maybe, prayerfully, some of you will accept Christ after we share wisdom from God. For those of you who are *not* Christians, the Bible is still the authority. Whether you believe it or not, receive it or not, or do what it says or not, it is still the authority on life. It is God's Word and His will. Period. Put that on everything . . ."

David decided he liked her style already. He leaned over to Corey, "Is she a minister-in-training?"

"No. She's adamant about recognizing the call on her life. She says it's to exhort, which she does through counseling and writing, and to teach, which she's doing right now. She knows what her spiritual gifts are and what God has called her to do."

"Wow," was all David could say. He liked that. He knew that some people automatically claimed to be preachers because other people said they should become preachers. David admired Cherelle for being strong enough in her walk with Christ to know what He'd called her to do. That made her a powerhouse on so many levels.

Walter Kincaid seemed mesmerized. David wondered if Corey just ignored Walter's big eyes gawking at Cherelle, or if he was being ignorantly polite. After an hour of breaking down several scriptures and forty-five minutes of questions, David was satisfied. He would incorporate Cherelle into his youth ministry if his interview with her went well. He planned to order copies of her book and get started right away if she passed his scrutiny. He needed to make sure she was standing on sound doctrine on several issues.

"Pastor Cole, I want to meet with you and Dr. Dupree in Pastor Corey's office for a few minutes before I leave," Walter said after he had taken hundreds of photos with the teens.

"Sure . . ." David responded. *What does Walt have up his sleeves?*

Back in Corey's office, Walter took a seat behind Corey's desk while David and Cherelle naturally sat in the two leather chairs in front. From the way Walter put space between himself and them, David knew that whatever he wanted to talk about was business-related. He had so easily slid back into mayor mode. David had gotten used to the in-and-out transformation of his childhood friend.

"I've decided I want a youth task force. I'm going to totally overhaul the one in place now. I need a team to come up with programs that can be run by the city, and some that can be run by business partners or other foundations. I want you to serve as the chair," Walter said to David, "and you to serve as the unofficial co-chair because you live outside of the city. You'll be down as a consultant," he said to Cherelle. He handed a business card to David. "This is the budget we have to work with for now. Cherelle—Dr. Dupree, I need you to develop the curricula or programs and help Pastor Cole find some more partners. I want something ready to roll out in January."

Cherelle's eyes grew wide. "*January?*"

"January. I know you two can do this. Just sketch out some ideas. Brainstorm. Put something together that makes sense and that can have a positive impact on a long-term basis," Walter returned.

"Walt—Mayor Kincaid, it's October . . ." Cherelle protested.

"That gives you three months."

David had a bunch of questions on his mind. Didn't Walter have a staff at his disposal for this? "That doesn't leave us a lot of time, Mayor," David said.

"I need you. And I need it to be done this way. I can't go into a lot of detail at this time, but I want this kept under wraps for now. This is going to be part of the Kincaid legacy. I want it to touch as many youth as possible—not for me, for Him." Walter said, pointing upward. David was surprised by Walter's reference to God. Walter wasn't particularly religious.

"I'm in," Cherelle said quickly.

"Me too," David agreed.

Walter Kincaid looked at his watch. "You two get together and work out the details. If you want to add some more people to the team, I'll leave that up to you. I just want everything kept under wraps. I have to go." He stood and walked over and hugged David once again before hugging Cherelle. He whispered something in Cherelle's ear before pulling back. "Thank you both," he said before exiting.

David switched gears and went into administration mode. He loved to put his Harvard-earned MBA to good use. "Why don't we set a date for our first meeting within a week—does that work for your schedule, Dr. Dupree?"

Cherelle pulled out her iPad mini and checked her calendar. "No. I'm going to be out of town starting the day after tomorrow. I have a few conferences and a movie premiere in L.A. I won't be back for a week and a half. We can Skype or FaceTime if you like for the first meeting."

Corey walked in and went straight to his private restroom.

"No, let's wait until you get back. Since it's our first meeting, I'd like for us to bounce energy off each other and also touch and agree before we take on this endeavor," David said.

"Okay . . . Let's pray now," Cherelle suggested.

David prayed. When Cherelle sensed he was ending his prayer. She continued. "Continuing in prayer . . . let all of our actions, thoughts, and affiliations be guided by You, Dear Father. Give us wisdom and courage to do what You want done in our lives. Thank You for the opportunity to serve You in brand new ways every day. You are our sole provider. In Jesus' name. Amen."

David was stirred by her prayer. Her spirit was strong and fortified. He could feel it. He squeezed her hand and said, "Amen."

Corey had been praying silently with them. "What's going on?"

"Walter wants us to head a youth task force," Cherelle answered.

Walter? It was the second time Cherelle Dupree had referenced the mayor by his first name. *When did she get on a first-name basis with Walt?*

"You sure that's not putting too much on your plate? You're speaking at several conferences. And won't you have to be on the set for the new movie you're helping to produce?" Corey asked, concerned.

"I'll be fine, Pastor Corey," Cherelle said humbly. She hoped her tone was enough to jar Corey out of his overprotective state. She didn't want David to become suspicious about the two of them. She'd seen the way David's eyes widened when Corey commented on her schedule.

Corey caught on immediately. "Well, it's my job to make sure my *sheep* are not burned out from doing 'good'. You all have to take care of yourselves first."

Cherelle's cell phone rang. "Excuse me . . ." she said to Corey before answering her call. "Hey . . . yes. I'm excited. Already purchased the gown. It's an Armani . . . yes. Sure. I'd love that. Thank you so much . . . bye now!" Cherelle's smile was infectious.

"You're beaming, Sister Cherelle," Corey said.

"Pastor, movie director, Asa Miles, invited me to another industry party to informally meet with some more producers— money bags. They love the script I wrote!"

"Congratulations," Corey and David said in unison.

David chuckled to himself. He knew Asa Miles well enough. He'd attended high school with him. Although they'd fought over a young woman that they both had been crazy about in high school, David was proud of Asa's achievements in

Hollywood. He was another young man from Detroit who had gone on to do wonderful things.

"I've got to check on Mom. I will see you tomorrow for service," Cherelle said, exiting.

"Alright, take care," Corey said. Then suddenly he stepped into the hallway. "Hey, it's Sweetest Day, what are you doing later?"

"You're funny, Pastor Corey. Same thing I did last year. Nothing!" Cherelle laughed.

"I'll call you later," Corey said, lowering his voice. But it was too late. David had already processed their interaction. Something was going on between the two of them.

Corey reentered and closed the door behind him. A few seconds later, there was a knock on the door. The same code. Three raps with pauses in between each one. "Come in, Stix."

Stix entered, "Pastor Corey, my mom's here. See you tomorrow."

"Alright, man. You did a great job today. Thanks."

"Thank you, Pastor Corey." Stix turned to go out and then pivoted. "Pastor Corey, can I ask you a question? But I don't wanna get in no trouble. Me and Mark was havin' a discussion and . . ."

"Stix, you can talk to me about anything. You need privacy?" Corey said, looking at David.

Stix looked at David. "No . . . Pastor Cole is okay . . ."

"Spit it out, Stix . . ."

Stix smiled. "Is Ms. Cherelle your lady? She is a dime!"

Corey laughed. "No, sir. Ms. Cherelle is *not* my lady. She's a member of this church. And she ain't no dime. She's a dollar, boy! You better learn how to count!" Corey said, playfully punching Stix in the chest.

"Right . . . right . . . a dollar! I *like* her!"

"Get outta here. I'll tell her you said that."

"What's going on, Corey? I understand you'd want to keep things quiet because of your position and all, but *is* there something going on between you two? You guys do seem sort of *familiar* with each other."

"No, man. You know how kids are. I have *never* dated a woman at this church—Dad warned me against it. He didn't forbid it, but he warned against it. So, no. Cherelle and I are good friends. That's it. It's strictly platonic. Trust me."

"Okay," David said. But he wasn't sold. His phone vibrated. He looked down at it and grinned when he saw Dominique's number.

"Hi. Good afternoon. Wondering if we are still on for this evening?" she asked.

David loved the sweet sound of her voice. "Certainly."

"Okay, I was just checking. See you later."

"Yes, ma'am." David tried to play cool, but if he were honest with himself, he'd admit that he was smitten. "Bye . . ." he said.

"Why'd you ask me about Cherelle? Are you interested?" Corey asked when David put his phone back in his pocket.

"No . . . I mean, she seems like a great woman. She has a beautiful spirit. She's strong in the Word, and good-looking, but I'm working on something else right now."

"Oh, I see . . . Well, I hope that works out for you."

"Me too, and she's a dollar as well."

Corey laughed. "I'm sure."

Chapter 6

Sweet Like Honey

David was pleasantly surprised to find Dominique sitting in the lounge where he taught his noon-time, mid-week Bible study. His regular members were all accounted for. Dominique shifted in her seat. Her eyes revealed her fear that David would somehow draw attention to her. It was a contradiction for him to see her in this light. Her brash attitude hid other facets of her personality that were seeping out at this very moment. He smiled knowingly.

"Good afternoon. I'm blessed that you all could join me once again," David said, greeting the small group of thirteen, including Dominique.

"Good afternoon, Pastor," they said in unison.

"I see we have someone new joining us today. Would you please be so kind as to introduce yourself, sister?"

Dominique looked around as if David might be speaking to someone else, and then she smiled ashamedly. "Oh . . . hello everyone, I'm Dominique Street."

The regulars greeted Dominique with warm handshakes. And it seemed to David that some of her tension disappeared.

"Well, Sister Street, I'm Pastor Cole, and I'd like to welcome you to DOC. I hope that this study session blesses you tremendously," David said, not giving any hints to anyone in the room that he and Dominique knew each other. Dominique looked relieved.

"Thank you," she returned.

"Today, we are going to touch on the topic of forgiveness. How do you know when you have truly forgiven someone?" David asked the class.

"When you no longer want to kill them—like my ex-husband, Sam," Gayle Green interjected. The group laughed.

"That's certainly one way, Gayle," David said.

"When you don't hurt or aren't angry about it anymore," Someone else interjected.

Paul Porter, the church treasurer, disagreed. "I don't know about that. If you are hurting, forgiving someone doesn't take the hurt away. My little brother is dead because of a stupid gang war, and I have forgiven those who were responsible, but I still hurt over the loss, and sometimes I'm still very angry. Maybe it will get better with time, but right now it still hurts."

David nodded compassionately. "That's true. True forgiveness is giving up the right or feeling of needing to get even with someone or wishing them harm, like Gayle said. And forgiveness is for *you*, not for the person who wronged you. You all know the story of Joseph. His brothers sold him into slavery. Years later, when his brothers saw him again, they were afraid he was going to retaliate in some way, and they *needed* him during this time of famine. But what did he say, y'all? 'You meant it for evil, but God meant it for good.' You see, Joseph had let go of the need to get back at them, realizing that God was in charge. No matter what happens in your life—no matter what pain someone causes you—God is in charge. Sometimes the Lord takes our most devastating hurts and uses them to do something wonderful in our lives. So why should you forgive, class? Because God says so. Period. You may hurt, you may be angry, but the more you give it to God, the freer you'll become."

David taught the class with so much conviction that Dominique was convinced he believed every word he spoke. He was so sure about God—about God's Word. He taught as if he had spoken to God personally and had been given the lesson directly from God's own hands. His exuberance and passion for the Lord were threaded throughout the lesson. But Dominique didn't feel it. In her heart, she wanted to. The feeling wasn't there. It was ironic that David's Bible lesson was on forgiveness because Dominique had spent the evening before waiting for her father to return her call. She'd found a way to get in touch with him, had spoken to his current live-in woman, and was sure he would return her call, but instead, she got nothing.

Meeting David had renewed her desire to connect with her father, especially after David had lost his mentee, Squirt. Dominique was more aware that life wasn't promised, even when a person was young. She wanted to reach out to her father and resolve whatever differences they'd had over the years, just in case something ever happened to either of them. She didn't want their relationship or non-relationship to continue as it had been.

The sorrow in Dominique's eyes did not escape David. He willed himself not to stare at her. Katherine Morgan, whom he considered to be one of his nosiest members, didn't miss a thing. She would have all kinds of gossip started if she even *thought* David had a *female friend* at Bible study. Katherine was a church busybody. With all the young people in David's congregation, she had found plenty of insignificant things to do to keep herself busy under the pretense of keeping the young people out of trouble.

David taught for a half hour and then had the group assemble themselves in pairs to discuss a few talking points. Thankfully, Dominique was paired with Paul Porter. He was steady in his walk with the Lord. And Paul was married to a beautiful young woman who worked in the church's preschool, so David didn't have to worry about him flirting with Dominique. Why was he prone to jealousy these days?

David walked the room listening to the pairs' conversations, interjecting when needed. He could tell that Dominique and Paul were having a spiritually heavy discussion. He saw Dominique smile a few times as she listened intently to Paul. David trusted Paul's input. Paul was the church treasurer. He taught in the married couples' ministry and was a man of honor and integrity in David's eyes. David prayed that God was using Paul to help Dominique better cope with whatever had her looking so sorrowful. He'd been tempted to text her during class, but he would have been breaking his own rule about cell phone usage during God's time.

He couldn't very well go over and ask Dominique what was wrong. That would be too obvious. He'd have to wait until class was over and do it in such a way that wouldn't draw attention to them. He and Dominique were still new in their dating relationship, so there was no sense in giving others the wrong impression. David was ever so cautious about his image. He'd prefer to wait until they had solidified their relationship before they were seen as a couple at his church.

After a good class session, the group began to fan out. Most people checked their cell phones. David encouraged his members to turn their phones off during class and service, although he knew some kept their phones on vibrate. He felt that a cellphone being on was a sure distraction, even if it was on vibrate. The generation he was pastoring was filled with techies, so asking them to go without their phones for even an hour was like asking them to go without breathing. David answered questions posed by a few members, hoping Dominique would stick around. She didn't. From the corner of his eye, he disappointedly watched her exit. As soon as he had spoken with Paul about setting up a counseling session with him and his wife, he turned on his cell phone. His spirit lifted when he saw a text from Dominique.

> Dominique: Hey! The lesson was great! Come by for coffee now if you can. I'll have lunch waiting for you, too.

> David: Be right over! Thanks.

* * *

DOMINIQUE OPENED her door before David had an opportunity to ring her doorbell. She had changed from the dress slacks, and sweater she wore to Bible study and was sporting a pair of sweatpants and a sweatshirt that seemed too big for her petite frame.

"Come in. Let me get your coat," Dominique said. Gone was that sorrowful look David had noticed earlier. Dominique eased David's coat off and hung it in the closet.

"I hope you're hungry, Dave. I know you like—"

"Corned beef. Yeah, I smell it. That was so sweet of you," David said.

"You mentioned the other night you hadn't had any in a long time, so I thought I'd make you one of my famous sandwiches."

"Famous, huh?"

"Yes. To. Die. For."

"Well, I brought my appetite. Red had already sent my

chicken salad from Smokey's, but I put it in my fridge until tomorrow."

"Sit," Dominique said, motioning David toward her formal dining room. She'd prepared a nice place setting. His meal was already on the table. A triple-decker corned beef sandwich with all the trimmings.

David grinned widely. The sound of a kitchen timer traveled through the room.

"Be right back," Dominique said, hurrying back into the kitchen.

David stood. "I almost forgot my manners. I need to wash my hands."

"The second door to your left, Dave."

Dominique returned with hot French fries, right out of the deep fryer. It was a mixture of sweet potato and white potato fries. She loaded David's plate with fries and set the ketchup bottle next to him.

"Thank you, Nik. This was nice of you."

"No. Thank you. Ever since I met you, my life has been so different. You are like a breath of fresh air, Dave. Something I've never experienced before—even my relationship with God is on its way to being better because of you . . . "

It seemed to David that Dominique was a little sentimental, and he wanted her to know just how much her words meant to him. "Nik, you are so beautiful. I'm grateful that I have been a little light in your life. And I'm certainly glad that you are seeing God through new eyes. I pray that my life continues to be a good witness for Christ, for you, and for anyone else I may come in contact with. I thoroughly enjoy our friendship, and I pray that it grows even stronger."

Dominique took David's hands in hers. "Lord, thank you for lunch," she chuckled, feeling silly praying in front of David. He was so eloquent when he spoke or prayed or did anything.

"Thank you for bringing Dave into my life. He is truly a blessing, and I hope we get to know each other better and become stronger together, and in You. Amen." Dominique looked unsure of herself. She searched David's eyes to see if she had prayed correctly. David sensed her concern.

David brought her hands to his lips and kissed each one ever so gently. "Nik, that was beautiful. It was from the heart. That's all that matters . . ." His heart was warmed by Dominique's prayer. He was glad that their time together was bringing her closer to God. He was hopeful about a future with her. She was sweet like honey, and if it was God's will, David knew he would be the best man he could be for her.

Chapter 7

True. Love. Waits.

D avid tidied up his main conference room after his morning meeting with his church staff. He'd had Greta clear his calendar for the rest of the day so that he and Cherelle Dupree could begin working on the task force plans Mayor Kincaid wanted in place. David poured himself another cup of coffee and waited. He hoped Cherelle Dupree respected his time because tardiness was his main pet peeve. She was scheduled to meet him at ten o'clock. It was already a quarter til. He'd give her the benefit of the doubt this time. She seemed like a professional woman.

He sat in a rolling chair and twisted it from left to right, thinking of ideas for the task force. He wondered what ideas Cherelle Dupree had come up with, if any. He'd heard Corey say that she'd had a major acting role in a small independent film and that she had just written a script. She was as busy as he was. Greta knocked on the open conference room door.

"Pastor, Dr. Dupree is here."

Cherelle stood next to Greta, smiling.

David stood. "Good Morning, Dr. Dupree. Come on in. Is

there anything you would like to snack on? I have a feeling this is going to be a long, intense meeting," David said.

"No, I'm fine. I brought lunch with me."

"Okay, Pastor, I'll hold all your calls until four-thirty," Greta said.

She winked at David, which indicated that she liked Cherelle.

"Yes, ma'am. That's fine." David responded. He turned to Cherelle. "I created an agenda," he said, pointing to an agenda printed on pale blue paper that had been placed in front of the chair he expected Cherelle to sit in. "Our schedule will be from ten o'clock to twelve o'clock, mapping out the foundation of the program. We'll take an hour lunch break at twelve and resume promptly at one o'clock, and work until four-thirty. That way, we can give Walter an update and get some preliminary things in place."

"That sounds fine." Cherelle sat down at the conference table and took her laptop out of a designer tote. She looked over David's agenda. He'd been very detailed.

Cherelle was dressed in a navy blue pin-striped suit with a pencil skirt and a waist-length jacket. She wore a pink lace top underneath that showed no skin. She had on sheer gray stockings and navy blue heels. Pearl hoop earrings, a triple-strand pearl necklace, and a matching bracelet complemented her ensemble.

The adornment that caught David's attention was the ring on her left hand. He'd never seen one like it. It was a simple diamond-cut platinum band with a row of small diamonds in between each word of the familiar insignia David knew all too well. But he'd never seen a grown woman with one. He studied her soft-looking hands and manicured nails with hot pink polish. Cherelle was a true fashionista. She reminded him of his mother, Leah.

"Dr. Dupree, your ring is beautiful," David said as he took his seat.

She smiled. "Thanks. I had it made. So it's very special to me. And Pastor Cole, you can call me Cherelle."

"Okay, I will try to remember to call you Cherelle, and you can call me David. We're going to be working together a lot. I see no need to be so formal." Changing the subject, he said, "And I've never seen a woman with one of those rings."

"Really?"

"I'm serious. We have a lot of girls who wear them, of course, because we perform the ceremonies here at church. But this is the first time I've seen a *woman* wearing one."

Cherelle shrugged. "I think sometimes women need the reminder more than the girls," she said before shifting gears. "Have you come up with any ideas about the task force?" she asked.

"As a matter of fact, I have. I was thinking we should organize the programs by zones or areas, like by the police precincts, and find churches in those areas that could come alongside us. That way, all the responsibility wouldn't rest with the city. It would still be a city initiative, but sort of like a faith-based project. This will allow us to get some money from the Federal government that's allocated for the faith-based initiatives."

"That sounds good. I've only lived here for the last five years, and I don't know the areas too well."

"I can take care of that part. What we need is some sort of training for the kids. Like character building or something, for all the youth who will be involved. It will have to be age-appropriate for the different age groups. We can break those down later. Just so you know: there is a fine line when using faith-based initiative funds. But I always find a way to stick Jesus in without breaking any of the allocation rules," David said.

Cherelle nodded and typed rapidly on her laptop as David

spoke. "I could develop the curricula. Actually, I already have a couple. I just need to tweak them a little to support what we're trying to accomplish for the mayor."

"Sounds good."

David walked over to his interactive board. "Walt gave me a breakdown of the city according to the precincts. And I created zones that coordinate with the precinct numbers. Then I identified the churches in those areas that I know are sound, biblically-based institutions. Last week, I reached out to a few pastors in zones eleven, twelve, and thirteen. They have the worst crime rates outside of DOC, and they are all willing to participate. All we have to do is give them the plan. They have people who can carry it all out."

Cherelle was impressed. Corey had already given her the run-down on David Kent Cole. She knew he'd graduated with an MBA from Harvard and that he'd worked on Wall Street before becoming a minister. She could tell by the way he had processed the details that he was a very intelligent man. One thing Cherelle distinctly remembered Corey saying about David was that he ran his church like a business, but one that was owned by God. He merged his gift of pastoral leadership and his financial and business management skills so that God would be pleased by the way he handled the church's resources. Corey even wanted to institute some of the same processes at Greater Christian Center. David's church staff members were well paid, and the church was in the black. He achieved that without begging for money or having numerous fundraisers.

While they were in the middle of planning, David made a few more phone calls to various ministers he thought would be good assets to the program. Cherelle listened as he negotiated and explained how the programs would benefit the churches he'd contacted. Not one of them turned him down. David told them approximately how many staff members each church would need to run the programs, according to some figures he'd come up with. He did all of that without giving them full details of what the mayor had shared with him. He was a very shrewd businessman.

They worked two hours straight before David reminded Cherelle of their scheduled lunch break. He ordered his usual from Smokey's, and Red was gracious enough to walk it around to the church herself. For that, David gave her a twenty-dollar tip. Cherelle had brought a bag lunch. David watched as she removed her suit jacket and hung it on the back of the chair. He noticed her nicely toned arms.

"You like hitting the gym, Cherelle? Those are some nice guns!"

Cherelle laughed. "I have a home gym. And yes, I work out very hard. I have to."

"I try to hit the gym a few times a week myself. It helps relieve the stress."

"Tell me about it. It really does keep me sane."

David's cell buzzed. "Excuse me," he said to Cherelle, "I need to take this call."

Cherelle nodded. She marveled at the transition David made. His tone was perky and playful with whomever he was speaking. "Hey, you . . . how's your day going? You haven't had to take any bad guys to jail, have you?" he asked teasingly.

Cherelle watched as he morphed from a stern, serious leader and business manager to a tender and gentle-spirited man. "Sure. What did you have in mind?" David continued. "Oh," he said flatly. "I'd rather not. Hold on, sweetie. Cherelle, do you need anything? I need to continue this call in my office."

"No, thank you."

David stepped into the hall and walked down to his office,

and closed the door behind him. He put his cell on speaker and sat behind his desk.

"What do you mean, you'd rather not? I don't understand," Dominique queried.

"Sweetheart, I don't do Halloween. That's not something I participate in as an individual, nor does my church."

"Why not? It's just a party."

"It goes against Scripture, sweetheart. A Christian has no business celebrating Halloween."

"You don't have to celebrate it to go to a stupid party. You don't have to dress up or anything."

"It doesn't matter if I dress up or not. That's not something I want to do. Halloween is rooted in the occult. In Deuteronomy 18, it says that—"

"Dave, why does everything have to be a scripture with you?" Dominique interrupted. "It's just a party. I'm not in the occult. You're not in the occult. So it's no harm. Mack throws an awesome party every year. I'd like for you to come with me."

"No."

"What?"

"I said *no*, Nik," David reiterated.

"You've got to be kidding me, Dave. Are you serious?"

"No, I'm not kidding. And yes, I'm very serious. I can give you some literature on it if you like. And we can do something together on another day."

"Dave, haven't I been coming to your midweek Bible class ever since you invited me?"

"You have."

"Well, what is the big deal about you doing something *I* want to do?"

"Dominique, I'm *not* going to a Halloween party. Period. We can get together Sunday after church if you like."

"Bye, Dave," Dominique said without responding to his suggestion.

"Bye," David said, ending the call. Dominique was acting like a spoiled brat, and David didn't do "brat." He couldn't stand when people were overly emotional about insignificant things. As far as he was concerned, the Halloween party was insignificant. He wasn't about to compromise what he believed in because Dominique was having a brat attack. And if she thought sulking, pouting, and whining was going to win him over, she was wrong.

* * *

When David reentered the conference room, Cherelle was on a call herself. ". . . I know. I'm so sorry that happened. But you can't compromise your values and what's right by God to please someone else, Lynn. I know it hurts, but you just have to trust God. If he loves you like he says, he'll wait and marry you. Giving him your body is not going to make him love you or marry you, I promise you that. Been there, done that," Cherelle said before she realized that David had reentered the room. "Listen, I have to go. I'll come by your place as soon as the meeting is over, okay? I love you. Bye." Cherelle removed her earpiece and turned off her phone. She grunted.

"Is everything okay?"

"Yes and no. It's just that my best friend is not having a good day today. She's pretty torn up, actually."

David had heard enough of the conversation to understand just what had happened. "I'm sorry. I couldn't help but over-hear the end of your conversation. You told her correctly. Compromising on the things of God never brings forth good fruit. It can only end in disaster. If a man loves you, he's not going to pressure you for sex. If he wants you that badly, he'll be willing to spend the rest of his life with you. If a man is not willing to commit to you, then he doesn't really love you. No matter what he *says*."

"Amen. I guess that's why I'm still single," Cherelle chuckled.

"Well, it's better to be single than hooked up with someone you have no business being hooked up with."

"You're right."

"Where are you from, Cherelle?"

"I grew up in Louisville, Kentucky, and Florida. My mom is from Alabama, but she moved to Louisville before I was born. When I was about eight, we moved to Florida to stay with one of my aunts. I lived there until I went to college."

"Oh yeah? Where'd you go to college?"

"Juilliard."

"You went to *Juilliard*?"

"Yes, but I switched to NYU in my junior year, though. I didn't graduate from Juilliard."

"Still, that's impressive."

Cherelle smiled widely. "Not as impressive as an IQ of 155 and perfect scores on the ACT and SAT."

"Oh, man. Corey's been filling your head with rumors and gossip," David teased. He was grounded in humility when it came to his intellect and his achievements.

"Uh-huh. He told me you were one of the smartest people he knows, besides your best friend, Gus—better known as *Ghost*, who got near-perfect scores on both the ACT and SAT and has an IQ of 152. And whenever they get on your nerves, you remind them that they are academic and cognitive *peasants* compared to you."

David let out a bellow of a laugh. "Man, Corey gossips more than a woman!"

Cherelle winked. "You know he gave me the rundown on you."

"Ah, delusions of grandeur," David said with a posh, British accent, knowing that as a psychologist, Cherelle would catch the joke. "What else did Pastor Corey tell you about me, Cherelle?" he chuckled.

David's silliness earned him another wide smile from Cherelle. "Not much," she said, chuckling. "He just said that back in the day, you were one of the most feared people in the hood—that you used to fight at the drop of a dime. Your mother made you go to the gym and box from elementary to high school because she got tired of you getting into fights. Let's see . . . your family calls you Punch, but the folks from the old hood call you DC—short for David Cole, because you used to, and *still* introduce yourself by stating your whole name—David *Kent* Cole." David howled as Cherelle continued. "And he also said in your former life you were a ladies' man who had a plethora of women at your beck and call, and you ran the streets getting into all sorts of trouble." Cherelle laughed at David's widened eyes as he feigned innocence. "Let's see what else . . . oh . . . you are also a gifted pianist who was taught by your grandmother. I think that's about it."

"I need to have a talk with Pastor Corey, I see."

"He also said that you are one of the *realest* men he knows. And that you are wholeheartedly committed to Christ and the youth of this city. That you live for Christ. That you are a man of integrity, and that you love God with all your heart . . ."

David was honored to receive a compliment like that from such an upstanding man of God like Corey. "I guess I can't kill him now, can I?"

"No, not after all the accolades he gave you."

"So . . . Cherelle, you went to Juilliard, which tells me you are very creative and talented. What did you study?"

"Voice—opera"

"Oh. Let's hear something."

"No, thank you."

"Shy?"

"At times. But that's not my reason for turning you down."

"It's not?"

"Nope. Just not in a singing mood today," Cherelle chuckled.

David sensed Cherelle was keeping something from him. That she didn't want them to become too familiar with each other. He respected that. He'd be sure to maintain professional boundaries and not attempt to be too friendly, so she wouldn't feel that he was trying to be too personal. He could tell Cherelle had one of those A-type personalities. Everything in its proper place. Business was business. Personal was personal. She didn't mix the two.

"Who designed your purity ring?" David asked, surprising Cherelle.

"I did. But I had Donovan Stamps create it for me."

"*Donovan Stamps?* It seems that I've seen or heard that name before."

Cherelle slid one of David's Forbes magazines across the conference table. On the back cover was a model wearing a Donovan Stamps diamond bracelet.

David smiled. "Oh, you run with the upper echelon."

"I went to Juilliard with Donovan's sister, Meagan Stamps. He once had a crush on me, so I don't pay nearly as much as his celebrity clients."

"Can I see it?"

"Sure."

David moved from the seat across the conference table and sat next to Cherelle. She extended her hand to him so that he could get a closer look at her ring. David took her hand in his and studied the workmanship of the diamond-cut band with the engraved inscription: True. Love. Waits. He felt something strange the moment he touched her and quickly released her hand. For a moment, Cherelle thought she saw a look of disgust on his face. David went back to his seat on the opposite side of the conference table.

"That's very beautiful of you to make that commitment, Cherelle. God is pleased with you," he said resolutely.

"Thank you," Cherelle responded, confused by David's sudden mood swing. He seemed distant now and less jovial than he was just a few moments ago. He was back to being the serious leader.

"Cherelle, I don't know you at all, but God does. I'd be being disobedient if I didn't share what's pressed on my heart right now." He paused for a moment and then continued. "The Lord wants you to know that He hasn't forgotten about you. He sees you. He knows what's on your heart. Wait for Him to deliver. You will not be disappointed or ashamed. Your husband is going to be very pleased with you and will love you like God intended for a man to love his wife. Wait on the Lord. It's already done."

Cherelle gazed at David from across the table and swallowed the lump that had formed in her throat. She tried to compose herself in front of this stranger who had just spoken words of love into her life, but the tears trickled. There was no way David could have known that she had cried herself to sleep last night. That she had felt forgotten by God, even though she had been traveling the country proclaiming His Word at various ministry conferences.

Cherelle knew the words that David spoke were from God. She'd dressed so fashionably and paid extra attention to herself today because last night, she felt worthless. She'd had the foreboding feeling that no man would ever love her, and that pained her. Cherelle rose from the table. "Excuse me, David, where's your restroom?"

"It's right down the hall to your right."

David felt Cherelle's heavy spirit. He prayed while he waited for her to return.

Several minutes later, Cherelle strolled back into the conference room. "I'm sorry," she said, embarrassed by her earlier display of emotion. "I wasn't expecting you to say those things, and I was completely overwhelmed."

"I wasn't expecting to say those things, but I hope what I said blessed you in a way that only God can, Cherelle."

"It did. More than you know. I'm just overly emotional."

"It's okay to be 'overly emotional' in the Spirit, Cherelle. There is nothing to be embarrassed about when God speaks to us. Let me pray for you."

Cherelle stretched her hands out, and David held them in his. Railroaded again by a powerful emotion, he struggled with the thought of snatching his hands away. Instead, he prayed a strong prayer. "Father God, give us the strength to wait on You. Give us the measure of faith we need to stand on Your promises. Give us the will to live righteously and holy when things are not going our way. Give us the comfort we need when we feel lonely and out of place. Remind us that You are our God—a good God who will meet every need we have in Your time and in Your way. We will not lack nor be ashamed.

"Bless Cherelle now. Wrap your arms around her and give her the strength she needs to stand firm and still until You deliver. For God, true love does *wait*. And every word You speak is truth. Cover Cherelle's husband right now and bless him so that he will be just what she needs. That he will be a spiritual strong tower, Oh, God. A good provider and a good friend who is the priest of his home. Bless him to be nurturing and tender with Cherelle and their children."

Cherelle squeezed David's hand as the rivers of her heart flowed from her eyes. The word *children* had reopened an old wound. Cherelle suffered from Polycystic Ovary Syndrome, and she secretly worried that the diagnosis would rob her of the blessing of becoming a mother, despite her faith in God.

"Bless her womb right now, Oh God, so that the seeds that will be planted there will be healthy and strong, Lord. That her children will be obedient lovers of Christ, honoring both their mother and father. And now, bless every ministry You have placed in Cherelle's hands. Fortify them, expand them, and make them fruitful. We give You all the honor, in Jesus' name, Amen."

Cherelle wept profusely. She knew she'd made a mess of her makeup. She covered her face with her hands and praised God through her tears. "Yes, Lord . . . yes . . . thank you, Jesus," she repeated as if it were a chant.

David didn't want to touch Cherelle again. Just a moment ago, he couldn't wait to release her hands while they'd prayed. He didn't like the feeling that overpowered him when he touched her. However, instinct caused him to give her a brotherly hug. "God is a just God, Cherelle. You can count on every word He speaks to you." Cherelle sat down, affected by the weariness that came from crying so hard. David patted her back. "Trust . . ." he said. He reached over, grabbed a Kleenex box, and handed it to her.

"I'm so sorry. I am usually much more professional," Cherelle avowed.

"I don't know how anyone can remain *professional* when the Spirit is speaking to them, Cherelle. You go ahead and praise God. I'll be back in a bit."

David left Cherelle alone in his main conference room and hurried to his office. Confused, he plopped down in his chair. He held his hands out in front of him and surveyed them, contemplating the feeling that had come over him when he touched Cherelle. The thought frightened him. "Who is she, Lord? What is she doing here? What is going on? Speak to my heart, Jesus," David prayed aloud.

David's cell vibrated on his hip. He unclipped it and answered. "Hey, sweetheart."

Dominique was surprised that David wasn't angry with her. "Hi . . . I wanted to apologize for my behavior earlier. I was having one of my moments, Dave. I'm sorry. There is a lot I don't understand. I'm sorry for asking you to participate in something that goes against what you believe," Dominique confessed.

"It's fine, sweetheart. It's not that important. No worries."

"Can I see you later? I'll be home around five o'clock."

"Sure. I miss you. What would you like me to bring?"

"Just you. I put a roast in the slow cooker this morning. So I can at least feed you."

"Sounds wonderful. I'll bring some dessert."

"Okay. And I wanted to let you know that I read all of Romans. Thank you. You are changing my life in a positive way, Dave. It's different for me, but I like what we have."

"I'm glad, Nik. I like what we have, too. Listen, I have to get back to a meeting, but I'll see you soon."

"Okay. See you later."

"Later, sweetheart."

David's cell rang again. It was an unfamiliar number. "This is Pastor David Kent Cole of Disciples of Christ Ministries. How can I bless you today?"

"You better watch who you break bread with, preacher," the unidentified caller warned before disconnecting.

David rolled his eyes and put his cell back on his belt clip. He was not unused to getting threatening phone calls—sometimes even death threats. He thought nothing of the sweet little love notes.

* * *

CHERELLE HAD FRESHENED herself and reapplied her makeup. She was humming a tune when David walked back into the conference room. David felt an overwhelming sense of peace in the room, like the Lord was sitting in the midst. He looked around and pondered in his spirit. He and Cherelle worked diligently for the rest of the afternoon, and Cherelle stayed an extra forty-five minutes past their scheduled time to make up for any time lost during her little mini-breakdown.

David admired her diligence. She was easy to work with and remained focused on their agenda. They ended their first planning meeting with the major components mapped out. Cherelle would develop the character-building curriculum and assist David with contacting more supporters for donations, such as computers, tablets, backpacks, and money for trips for the kids. David knew he had added another thing to his already full plate, but young people were his passion, and he felt that the task force would be an extension of his ministry at DOC.

"I think we got a lot accomplished today, Cherelle. I like your work ethic. You work just as hard as I do," David said, winking as Cherelle gathered her things and stood.

"Thank you. Working hard without pay!" Cherelle joked.

"Right. How do I let Walt get me into these things?"

"I think he's going to do some creative financing to compensate us in some way for the time."

"I'm sure. This project is going to be very fruitful. I feel it. I've been praying about it since he first brought the idea to us," David said.

"Me too. I even fasted a few days," Cherelle admitted.

"Really?"

"Yeah. I wanted to be strengthened, and I wanted God to move through me. This is going to affect a lot of kids."

David nodded. There was an undercurrent with Cherelle. He didn't know what it was. On the other hand, there was a certain peace he felt in her presence. Mixed signals. That definitely couldn't be from God. "Next time, let me know when you are fasting about this task force so that both of us can be on one accord," he said.

"I will. And . . . speaking of money . . . " Cherelle said, as she slid her hand into her tote. She pulled a full-color brochure out and handed it to David. "These are the prices for the workshops you inquired about for DOC's girls. I included the prices of the books and three follow-up sessions. Pastor Corey will offset any lack if my prices are not in your church's budget. I also emailed this information to you. But I wanted to give you a hard copy just in case you're like me and you like to hold things in your hands—like books."

"Yes, thanks. Sit down for a minute if you don't mind. Let me look over this quickly and ask any questions I might have. Then, when we meet again, we can move forward with dates. Corey told me your schedule gets full pretty quickly."

Cherelle sat back down. "Okay. No problem. Take your time."

David looked over the brochure quietly, leaving Cherelle to wonder what he was thinking. She had priced everything moderately for the church. She hoped he was okay with her prices. She wasn't charging her normal rates because of the relationship David shared with Corey. And Corey had agreed to offset the prices if necessary. It seemed to be a win-win situation for David as far as Cherelle was concerned. But the blank look on his face made her wonder if he thought her prices were fair or not.

"Tell me something, Cherelle. Are these your *regular* prices?"

"No."

"Are your rates *lower* than this?"

"No. Actually, they're higher. Pastor Corey wanted me—"

David held his hand up. "I understand," he interrupted. "I tell you what, you have a skill and you should be paid for it. I'm not talking about your spiritual gifts, Cherelle, because it's obvious that you have the gift of exhortation and teaching. When you are training the body of Christ and it is your livelihood, you should be paid for it. Just because you are providing services to churches doesn't mean you should be paid any less, unless the Lord says so. This *is* your livelihood, correct?"

"Yes . . ."

"Well then, you should be paid for it. That doesn't mean that you don't offer gifts-in-kind to the body. From what Corey tells me, you go above and beyond in mentoring and ministry over there and are not paid. So send me your regular price list and tell Corey that I would like him to offset the costs of some workshops for a small church in Flint that's just starting. They don't have the resources that he and I have. I want to help out the ministry there. He and I can come together on that. I'll contact you tomorrow after I've gone over my personal schedule and the church schedule with Greta."

Cherelle didn't argue. "Okay . . ." Everything in her spirit was telling her to *listen.*

"Enjoy the rest of your day, Cherelle. It was nice working with you," David said, shaking her hand.

"You too. Thank you."

David couldn't wait for her to leave. He stuffed his hands in his pockets. Something about Cherelle disturbed him.

Chapter 8

Trigger

Dominique greeted David at the door, wearing a tank top, shorts, and a wide smile. David saluted her with a kiss on her cheek. "Hey . . . it smells good up in here!" he said, trying not to pay too much attention to the amount of Dominique's skin that was exposed.

She closed the door behind him. "Well, I'm not fully domesticated, but there are a few things I can cook very well, and a good pot roast is one. I made cornbread too."

"*Real* cornbread?"

Dominique laughed. "Don't get crazy! It's Jiffy."

"I'll take Jiffy, sweetheart. I'm grateful for the dinner. I brought ice cream for dessert—your favorite—Ben and Jerry's Chunky Monkey."

Dominique planted a kiss on David's lips. "Sweet!" she squealed. It was quick and innocent, but David's body couldn't tell the difference.

Within the hour, David was stuffed. Dominique sat on the opposite end of the sofa with her feet stretched across his lap. She'd complained that they were hurting, so David massaged

100

them through her fluffy socks. He didn't want to take her socks off. He was glad she didn't protest. He thought it better not to have too much skin-to-skin contact.

Dominique relaxed against a sofa pillow. "Umm . . . that's nice . . . . You are so tender . . . It's like night and day," she said.

"What?"

"The way you act."

"What do you mean, Nik?"

"It's like, I watch you preach and teach, and you are like this . . . stern, by-the-book sort of guy, but then here you are rubbing my feet and you feel so good . . ."

The lilt in Dominique's voice caused David's spiritual antenna to go up, or was he just imagining her voice sounding so seductive?

"Sweetheart, I wouldn't say I'm stern. I'm *serious* when it comes to the Word. But maybe, I guess, seriousness could be construed as stern by someone who doesn't understand exactly where I'm coming from. I hope God's love is coming through, though. I'm not a hellfire and brimstone preacher."

"No, you're not that bad," Dominique chuckled. "You're just sort of rigid. It's like you need to loosen up some. For instance, sometimes we can't even have a conversation without you saying a scripture. But I do like the way you break the Word down, Dave. I understand it when you're teaching."

"Well, the reason why my conversations are full of Scripture most of the time is because the Word is my filter. I filter everything that goes on around me—what I say and do, and what others say and do, through the Word. It's not something I'm conscious of when I'm speaking, sweetheart. It's just a part of who I am and what I do naturally. What makes you think I'm rigid?"

"My main example is the Halloween thing—I understand—but it's sort of rigid to me."

David wasn't going to go *there* and discuss that again. He was done with that topic.

"I see," was all he said.

"But you are tender. I can tell."

There it was again. That seductive pull David was either imagining or experiencing for real. It felt more real than imagined. He stopped massaging Dominique's feet. "You good?"

"Yeah. Were your hands getting tired?"

"Not really. I think I'm just tired overall. I had a long planning meeting today, and I did some studying."

"Oh. Too bad you're tired. There's something I want to do with you . . ."

In one swift motion, Dominique sat up and straddled David. He hadn't expected it and jumped. "Whoa!" He quickly locked his arms around Dominique's back to keep her from falling off the sofa. She steadied her hands on the sofa on either side of him and looked down at him seductively. Now, he wasn't imagining. She giggled mischievously. "Why'd you jump? You almost made me fall, silly!"

"I'm sorry. You caught me off guard, sweetheart." He was afraid to ask what Dominique wanted to do. *I hope she's not thinking what I think she's thinking. Oh, boy.* "What is it that you want to do, sweetheart?"

Dominique stared at David for a long while, subtly teasing him with her eyes. Neither of them moved. They breathed slowly and steadily in unison. Their eyes were locked together in a trance. Neither broke eye contact. Then Dominique burst into laughter as she crawled off David. She stood in front of him and reached out her hand. "Come on. Get up. You're coming with me . . ." She pulled him by his hands. She was too petite to move David. He assisted her by getting up on his own volition.

"Where are we going?"

"I want to do something that excites me. I'll be right back."

David was grateful that Dominique bounded up the stairs. He let go of the breath he'd been holding. She returned minutes later wearing jeans and a long-sleeved shirt. She had her gun in an underarm holster, and she was carrying a small duffle. She grabbed a down vest out of the closet. "Let's go. You drive. I'll tell you where."

David was relieved to get out of Dominique's place, but she resumed her sensual teasing in the car while he drove. Dominique placed her hands on David's thigh. "I want to teach you some things . . ." she giggled. That one gesture turned the twenty-minute drive into eternity. Finally, she instructed him to pull into an unfamiliar lot. David hid his smile.

They entered a brand-new, hi-tech, indoor gun range. The owner, Mack Dunn, had successfully copied the style of the high-end, nightclub-like gun ranges in Las Vegas. The lobby contained wall-to-wall naturally exposed brick. It was outfitted with sleek, red leather furniture with chrome legs. A variety of black and white gun photographs on the far left wall made the area look more like an art gallery than the lobby of an indoor gun range. A gigantic, black sand fish tank expanded the entire width of the opposite wall. It was littered with all manner of exotic, multi-colored species. Jazz played softly through the ceiling speakers.

As Dominique and David neared the counter, David took out his credit card and handed it to Mack, the retired narcotics officer who stood behind the counter with a Napoleon complex and a permanent scowl on his face. His rounded belly pushed against the counter because his once muscular body had also retired from the police force. His overall stature and weasel eyes reminded David of a shady character in a gangster movie.

Dominique gently took the credit card from David, slid it into his front pocket, and let her hand linger, causing David to feel a sudden jolt of electric current. "No, Dave, everything's on me tonight, but thank you," she said in a sultry tone.

Mack ignored David and Dominique's exchange. "Hey, Don. What's happenin' baby? Whatchu need?" he asked without looking at David.

"Nothin'. I have ammo with me today. I just wanted to see your handsome face," Dominique flattered him. The rest of her team and the other officers she knew secretly referred to him as Little Mack to distinguish him from the Mack on her team. One of the officers had slipped and called him that once, and found out just how big of an attitude he had.

"Look at you sweet-talkin' me," Mack responded. Then he eyed David and tossed a sly look at Dominique. Their eyes played a game. "I need paperwork on him, Don."

"Dave, this is Mack. Mack, this is Dave. Make it quick, Mack. He's with me, he's good."

"Business before pleasure, Don. Liability and irresponsibility don't stack dough," Mack said. He slid the safety paperwork and waiver forms to David.

David completed the forms and handed them back to Mack, feeling like he was being sized up by the guy. He watched as Mack and Dominique communicated silently with their eyes. Mack took a phone call at the desk, and Dominique flirted openly with David. She closed the space between them and looked up at him. "Did I tell you how handsome you look today?"

"No, but you can tell me now," David joked.

Dominique reached up on her tiptoes and kissed David. He met her halfway. He wasn't normally one to display public affection, especially when he technically wasn't in a relationship. He wasn't sure where he and Dominique were headed. He was still studying her, but he acquiesced and reciprocated the kiss.

"You're all set, Don. You're on lane eight."

Dominique chuckled. "You're funny, Mack."

"I sure am. Don't get in no trouble, Don. You know how *some people* are."

Dominique walked away from the counter toward the door of the main range. "I can handle myself," she said over her shoulder.

Mack chuckled. "Shoot, it ain't you I'm worried about. I'm talkin' bout your *guest*."

Dominique stopped in the second lobby before entering the firing range. She opened the small duffle and handed David a pair of ear muffs and safety glasses. She took the same items out of the bag for herself.

"What was all the code talking about?"

"Mack was just being nosy. Trying to feel you out. He's protective of me." That was only part of the truth.

"Why does he call you Don? I heard someone call you that at Smokey's the night we met. Is that short for Dominique?"

Dominique shook her head and laughed. "No, baby. It's short for *Don Corleone*—as in *The Godfather*. The guys say I'm cold like him."

"Oh, I see," David said.

David put on his earmuffs and safety glasses, and Dominique followed suit. She opened the door to the main firing range, and they stepped inside. Upon entering lane eight, Dominique programmed information on the digital screen to the left. "Twenty-five feet," she said. She took a Glock 43 out of her bag and kissed it. "Just got this baby." She laid it and the magazines on the bench. "Always point your firearm down the lane, even if it's unloaded," she instructed. David straight-faced her. "Now, this is how you load, " Dominique said, loading the magazines with rounds. "Next, you load the mag in the Glock. Just give it a push like this, and keep your finger *off* the trigger.

"Now, when disarming, always empty the mag first. Then, pull the slide back to release the round. Make sure you check the chamber thoroughly, Dave. A bullet could be left in the chamber—you don't want that. Check like this," she said, demonstrating. "It's all good. Back to a safe position." She laid her new Glock 43 on the bench. "Me first. Show you how it's done," she winked. She pushed a button on the wall, and a simulation screen came up with moving targets and wall blocks. A thirty-second countdown timer appeared on the screen. Dominique picked up her weapon and reloaded in real-time, not the slow-motion way she'd done while instructing David.

The game started, and Dominique fired in rapid succession. *Bang. Bang. Bang. Bang. Bang. Bang.* Perfect shots. David noticed her stance and the way she moved deftly, hitting all the moving targets on the screen. She hit every last one with expert precision. Her high skill level was accompanied by unparalleled confidence. The strength of her arms and her cockiness excited David. Dominique smiled victoriously after a few minutes. She unloaded her weapon and placed it on the bench facing down the range again.

"Okay, now you reload it like I showed you," she said. She watched David carefully to ensure that he loaded the weapon properly and safely. Satisfied she'd been a good teacher, she stepped back. She entered something on the keypad again. "Ready?"

David nodded and smiled. "I'm ready, sweetheart."

It was a zombie apocalypse. David grinned. *Bang. Bang.* He picked the digitized enemies off easily. More appeared. *Bang. Bang. Bang.* He aimed and met his targets, avoiding hitting the simulated innocent bystander depicted on the screen. *Bang.* The last one he clipped off with nonchalant ease. "Congratulations, David! You have saved the world!" a computer voice exclaimed. David ejected the empty magazine, pulled the slide back, and checked the chamber. He placed the weapon on the bench, aimed down the firing range like his grandfather had taught him at only eight years of age. He grinned mischievously.

Dominique's mouth was agape. "Dave, you didn't tell me you could shoot!"

"You didn't ask, sweetheart."

"Mmm . . ." Dominique purred. "You are just full of surprises . . ." she said, caressing David's arms.

David grinned. "I'm a country boy at heart. My granddad taught me how to shoot when I was a young man. We hunted together. I haven't been to the range in about a month, but I think I'm pretty good. And I didn't know anything about this range. It's nice.

"Mack is an ex-cop. This is his place. A lot of the guys come here to practice and get the monkey off their backs, you know. I didn't know you were so good . . ."

"You're learning," David smirked.

They shot a few more rounds, and Dominique was pleasantly surprised by David's skill. They rented rifles and shot on the simulated outdoor range, practicing long-range shooting before their gun range date came to an end.

* * *

"Dave, come in and have coffee with me."

"It's getting a little late, Nik. I don't want to keep you up. And I don't want to outstay my welcome."

"But I want you to . . . please . . ."

David gave in. "Okay. Half an hour, then I'm going to be a gentleman and say good night."

"Deal."

Dominique was competitive. She loved to play games. She

made David indulge in a hand of poker with her. She lost to him twice. David helped clear the table and wash their coffee mugs, setting them in the cabinet.

Dominique leaned against the counter, observing him closely. "So you know I wasn't expecting you to be so good. You outshot me on the zombie round, Dave. Unbelievable. If the guys knew that, they would never let me live it down."

"Don't worry. I'll keep our little secret until it's time to blackmail you," David said, taking her in. She was beautiful with a tough exterior, but he could sense the soft, pliable part of her that needed to be nurtured.

Dominique attempted to give him an open-mouth kiss. To that, he gently responded with a closed-mouth kiss instead.

"What's wrong, David? Is my breath good?" Dominique said, blowing into her hand and sniffing. She was being silly, and that made him smile.

David chuckled. "It's fine, sweetheart. I just want to make sure I stay within the boundaries."

"What boundaries? I haven't set any boundaries for you, Dave." That seductive pull was back again.

"I'm talking about the ones God has set, Nik. I want to make sure I don't do anything prematurely."

"You don't believe that passion and love sometimes just happen spontaneously?"

"Scripture says, *don't awaken love until it pleases*—meaning don't start anything that can't be completed the way God intended it. To put it more simply, don't become sexually involved outside of marriage. The 'pleasing' is the satisfaction of sharing erotic love in the commitment of marriage."

Dominique burst into laughter. "Are you trying to tell me that because you're not married, you're not having sex?"

"That would be premature, according to Scripture, wouldn't it?"

Dominique shook her head from side to side. "I don't believe you one bit. I don't believe it. Don't you date?"

"Yeah. I've been dating *you* for a little while now."

"You know what I meant."

"Actually, before you, I hadn't dated anyone in about a year. I met someone I liked a lot, and she moved away for her job. We decided that we would remain friends. We were never sexually involved. It was a romantic relationship, but not sexual. In the years before then, God let me know that it wasn't my time. If it were up to me, I would have been married and have children by now. I want to be a father one day. I want a spiritual and natural legacy."

"So you're saying you're not having *any* kind of sex?" Certainly, this deliciously sexy man couldn't be serious.

David felt like he was being ridiculed instead of being asked a question. He tried to remember that Dominique was a babe in Christ. He didn't want to lose his patience. "Dominique, I understand why you find that incredulous, but I've been celibate for quite a while. The Lord made it clear to me in several ways that my service to Him was above what I wanted at the time. I don't plan to *stay* celibate—I do plan to get married, Dominique. That's the purpose of dating, isn't it —to see if someone is a good candidate for a marriage partner?"

"Sometimes, I guess."

"Well, I don't date casually. I date with intent."

"Intent to do what?"

"Intent to be married. Dating is the process used to discover if you fit with someone or not," David said as patiently as possible.

"Don't you think that *grown* people sometimes date each other just because they like each other's company or enjoy one another physically? Two people may not even be interested in getting married; they might just like to spend time enjoying one another."

"*People* may like to do whatever they want, Nik. However, that's not God's way. The only person I can enjoy physically and still be in right standing with God is my wife. Scripture is clear on sex outside of marriage. It's a sin against one's own body, and it grieves the Holy Spirit."

"Yeah, they taught us that in youth camp at church."

"Were you *listening?*"

"I listened, Dave, but I was thirteen years old then. I'm a grown woman now. I'm thirty-three, not thirteen."

"Does your age make God's word ineffective—void? Do you feel that you can just ignore God's Word because you're a grown woman? Are you saying Scripture is for youth and young adults to follow and not adults who have the privilege of making up their minds?"

Dominique could tell by the way David triple-questioned her that he had stepped into his mode of what she considered religiously stern and by the book. "I didn't say it makes His Word void. But life *is* different when you're grown."

"But God's Word ain't different when you're grown. You can live until you're *four hundred* and thirteen. It ain't gonna change God's Word, Nik. Period. And just to be clear, I don't plan to be physically intimate with a woman again until I'm married. I have to follow God's Word, Nik. It's more important than what I want or what anyone else wants."

Dominique looked horrified. "You're not a virgin, are you, Dave?"

"No. But what difference would it make, Nik? I'm committed to following God's Word. I've been with women— *plenty*. But that was then, and this is now."

"So you're saying you haven't had sex since you've been a minister?"

David looked at Dominique seriously. It seemed that she was determined to make him a liar. "Dominique, I didn't say that. When I started as a young man in the ministry years ago, I made some mistakes. I hurt some people, and I'm not proud of that. But the more I've grown in my relationship with Christ and the more I've grown in my ministry, the more I've learned that God's Word is right and just. I've been walking righteously for some years now, and I know without a doubt that it's better to be on the right side of God, no matter what you or anyone else thinks."

Dominique could tell that she had exasperated David. She hadn't meant to. She'd just never met any man like him. He was an anomaly. And it was hard to believe all the things he'd shared about himself. "Please don't be angry, Dave. I'm just trying to understand you."

"I know, Nik. Look, it's time for me to go. We'll talk some more about it later."

David had retreated. Dominique couldn't read him now. She watched him leave and wondered what he was thinking about her. She wanted to make him happy. But she just wasn't sure how.

Chapter 9

King David

David sat at the head of his twenty-four-person conference table. Cherelle was scheduled to be at his staff meeting to discuss her involvement with his girls' ministry and upcoming youth symposium. She had already texted him to make him aware that she would *not* be on time. She had flown in from New York, and Corey wasn't on time to pick her up. One of his long-standing church mothers, Mother McDowell, had passed away, and visiting with the McDowell family had caused him to run behind schedule.

Cherelle knew David was a stickler when it came to punctuality, and he was even more serious when it came to meetings that involved planning God's work. He'd mentioned to her that it seemed to him that some people felt God's work was not as important as other things in their lives, because most people made it a point to be on time for their work or business meetings, and even fraternity and sorority meetings, but treated God's work casually.

David explained how he'd had to verbally correct two of his leadership team members for the infraction. And today,

Cherelle was on the agenda. The meeting started at five p.m., and it was already five fifteen. She was just pulling into the church lot. She hadn't eaten anything because she feared that stopping would have caused her to be even later. Everyone would surely be staring at her, and she could just imagine David giving her that disapproving glare she'd seen him give when one of the deacons hadn't been prepared for a meeting they were having.

One of the security guards walked Cherelle down to the main conference room. She hadn't bothered to change from the dress she'd worn on a daytime television show earlier that morning. She'd been promoting the new movie in which she had a lead role. Cherelle still had on the red-knit designer dress her former NYU roommate, Lourdes Artega, had designed for her. Lourdes had been a little-known designer, but she was quickly becoming a household name thanks to the First Lady of the United States being photographed wearing an Artega gown to a White House dinner. The whole buzz was taking the fashion industry by storm, as actresses scrambled to get Artega designs for red carpet events.

As Cherelle strutted down the hall, her feet screamed from the high-heeled boots she'd been sporting. She was donned in red and black. Stylist LaDonna Cartwright had handpicked Cherelle's black stone necklace, earrings, and bracelet. She looked glamorous. Her high-fashion glam mode would have to work for the meeting. If she'd been home, she would have chosen more business-like attire. Her hair was down in a twist out, and thankfully, nature had cooperated. No frizz. Her makeup was still stage-friendly. Because of stage lighting, the Hollywood make-up artist had 'beat' Cherelle's face. Her makeup was heavier and more glitzy than everyday wear. She looked gorgeous, albeit overdressed for a church leadership meeting.

Cherelle heard laughter and music before she even reached the door of the conference room. That was unusual. She also smelled food. Her stomach grumbled in response. She wondered what was going on. David was so rigid when it came to meetings and agendas. It didn't seem at all like him to have a *loose* meeting. Cherelle opened the conference room door and rolled in her overnight bag. David and his secretary, Ms. Greta, were tossing popcorn kernels across the table at one another. The rest of the leadership team was feasting on a smorgasbord of pasta, steak, chicken, pizza, and finger foods. It seemed that everyone stopped and stared at Cherelle. David halted mid-air while tossing another popcorn kernel at Ms. Greta.

"Hi . . . excuse me. I apologize for my tardiness . . ." Cherelle offered.

David stood and shook Cherelle's hand.

"Hey . . . Sister Cherelle! No worries. Today is our First Friday Leadership Meeting. It's a bit relaxed, as you can see. We fellowship first and start the meeting at six o'clock. We will be done promptly by seven thirty p.m. This gives people time to relax after work before jumping right in . . ."

Cherelle was surprised. "Oh, okay . . . that sounds good." David didn't seem like the *fun*-meeting kind of guy. This was different.

"Go ahead and get yourself something to eat, and we'll start in a while," David said as he nodded in the direction of the buffet table.

Ms. Greta eyed David before thoroughly eyeing Cherelle. David watched as Cherelle walked over to the food tables and prepared herself quite a plate. She hadn't eaten all day. Not wanting her stomach to appear bloated on national television, she'd only allowed herself a cup of green tea with lemon and honey that morning. David noticed that the women in the room and most of the men were secretly eyeing Cherelle, too.

Ms. Greta got up and scooped more potato salad and chips. "Dr. Dupree, that is a lovely outfit, you look absolutely beautiful—like a movie star. You wearin' that dress, girl. I mean you are workin' it!"

Cherelle blushed. "Thank you, Ms. Greta. And please call me Cherelle. I just left a talk show promoting a new independent film.

It's my first acting role in a movie. I love the arts. God has called me to exhort and teach his people in creative ways."

Greta nodded. "You are beautiful," she said, praising Cherelle in a motherly way.

Cherelle was humbled by the compliment. "Thank you so much," she said.

"What's the movie about?"

"It's about a young man who has planned to commit suicide because he feels his life isn't worth anything. And all day long, he documents parts of his last days by posting online. His teacher—well, I don't want to ruin the story, but she's instrumental in changing his plans. It shows how God can move in our lives when we least expect Him to. I think it's going to change a lot of people and help them to see God in their lives, no matter what pain they're going through. It's called *Status.*"

"I can't wait to see it! It sounds wonderful."

"Let me know what you think. It releases in theaters tonight."

"I will."

Ms. Greta sat back down and snapped her fingers at David. He knew what that meant. Ms. Greta thought Cherelle was *all that.* Cherelle sat down next to a young woman who seemed withdrawn and timid. The young woman pushed her glasses up on her nose. She was a beautiful woman behind her heavy black frames. No make-up. No fancy hairstyle. Just naturally beautiful.

"Hi, I'm Cherelle."

"Hi, I'm JoAnna," the young woman said, pronouncing her name, *Jo-Onna.*

"Nice to meet you."

"You too."

"If you don't mind me asking, do you have a stylist who picks your clothes out for you every day? I read a little about you on your website and looked through the photos. You always look so . . . polished. I want to dress more . . . together. I just need a little help."

"Aww... Thank you. I do work with a stylist, but not every day. I don't have *that* kind of money," Cherelle chuckled. "But definitely when I'm doing conferences or an appearance like today. Someone kind of puts things together for me based on my taste. I'm pretty good at choosing things for myself, but I use a stylist for special occasions. They are experts in the area of fashion, and it makes a difference."

JoAnna nodded. Cherelle observed the young woman's plain sweater and long skirt. She was still very pretty with a nice spirit. "Is there like a website I can get on?" JoAnna asked. "I definitely can't afford a *stylist*, I teach preschool."

"They have a lot of websites concerning fashion. "But I've had a stylist makeover my whole closet before, so I kind of know what to do. We could do some shopping together if you like. And I know how to stay on a budget. My mother was the budget queen."

"I'm serious, Dr. Dupree. I want to look *attractive*," JoAnna said quietly. She'd noticed how people in the conference had admired Cherelle when she'd first walked in.

"I'm serious, too, JoAnna. I'll be out of town next week, but I'll be back the following week and we can do some shopping then." Cherelle reached down into her bag and pulled out a business card. "My cell is on there. Just text or call when you're ready. Or we can just plan for that next Saturday at noon."

The two women shared an easy conversation, and David admired the way Cherelle befriended JoAnna. Cherelle had such a kind heart. It was like she automatically gravitated to people who were in need of healing. David liked that.

Promptly at six, David started his meeting. He introduced Cherelle to his leadership team, and they switched gears appropriately. "First, I need Sister Warren to report on the male panel for the girls' symposium, then you all can ask questions and work out the logistics of the workshops with Sister Cherelle."

"Well, Michael McAfee is confirmed for the panel," Felicia Warren beamed proudly. JoAnna, the co-chair of the committee for the girls' symposium, squirmed uncomfortably in her chair. The look on her face let David know that JoAnna was not in agreement with Michael McAfee, and neither was he.

"Excuse me, Felicia? I thought I told you I wasn't comfortable with Michael McAfee speaking here and that you needed to come up with another speaker instead. He has a documented history of violence against women. And I'm not going to send a wrong message to my girls about who I consider to be a role model for them."

Felicia challenged David's authority openly. "Pastor, you didn't *tell* me to get a replacement. You said, exactly, 'I'm uncomfortable with him; you need to consider someone else.' To me, that is a *suggestion*. I considered your suggestion and made a different decision based on my position as chair of the symposium."

"Felicia, when I said, 'You *need* to . . .' that was a directive—not a suggestion. And just by me telling you that I was uncomfortable with him should have been enough information for you to choose someone else."

Felicia became indignant about being questioned. "I did consider someone else, and it didn't work out. Mike agreed, and I confirmed him with a deposit."

"A deposit from where?"

"From the youth fund."

David gawked at Paul Porter, his church treasurer. "You cut a check without my approval?"

"Pastor, Felicia told me you had approved it, but you were running late, and she needed to get it completed by the end of the business day. That's happened before. I didn't think anything of it. I'm truly sorry," he said, looking at Felicia with disappointment. She had dragged him into her mess.

David turned his chair to the credenza behind him and picked up a stress ball from the basket. He put his hands in his lap and scooted his chair back to the conference table. Ms. Greta had a feeling David was squeezing the life out of the stress ball underneath the table. He nodded and spoke slowly. "You're right, Paul, that has happened before, but it won't happen again unless I call you myself." David directed his attention to the church secretary. "Ms. Greta, prepare a memo to go out that states no checks—no monies whatsoever will go out from this edifice without my signature or verbal approval to the treasurer—not anyone else."

"Yes, sir."

Ms. Greta knew for sure that the stress ball had taken its last breath. David returned his attention to Felicia. She'd been with him for three years. He appointed her as chair because he'd seen her dedication. More recently, however, he'd also seen that she was hungry for power. For that reason, he'd been extremely particular about what he allowed her to be involved in at the church. He thought the girls' symposium would be something she could handle without too much hassle. He was wrong.

"Help me to understand—wait—first, how much was the deposit for?"

"A thousand."

"A thousand *dollars*—for an hour-long panel?"

"That's part of his fee for any speaking engagement. A thousand up-front and a thousand at the conclusion of the presentation." Felicia spoke with defiance in her voice, and it didn't get past David. "Two thou—" David started before taking a deep breath. He paused, then said, "First of all, he has *no* business speaking at this church. He's been arrested *twice* for beating his wife. And several other women have come forth with allegations that he was physically and sexually abusive. I don't care how many praise albums he's sold," David said so calmly that Ms. Greta and everyone else in the room knew he was close to blowing a gasket.

Felicia banged her fist on the conference table. "She dropped the charges against him!"

David cut his eyes at Felicia and held a direct stare. "He's *not* speaking at this church until I have seen that he has been rehabilitated and committed to keeping his hands to himself. It will send the wrong message to the girls. You have three days to find another panelist—one who will volunteer his time, or we will go with three panelists instead of four. And you will call Mike McAfee and tell him he is *unconfirmed*. Prayerfully, he will do what's right and return the deposit to the church."

"The deposit is *non-refundable*. And a person has a right to change. God doesn't hold things over our heads. If he asked God for forgiveness, he's forgiven! That's what the girls need to see and know!"

Donald Clark, another leadership team member, interjected. "Pastor, Felicia is right. We should demonstrate *forgive-*

ness. And in all fairness, you didn't give Felicia a clear directive."

David had seen Felicia and Donald be friendlier than usual with one another. He thought it odd because Donald was going through a divorce. He'd attempted to provide counseling to Donald and his wife, Angela, but she'd flat-out refused to come to counseling. All David had was Donald's side of the story. Now, he knew for certain that things weren't as they seemed with Donald. He was having an affair with Felicia and had appointed himself her protector. "Felicia, Brother Clark, I'm done with that," David returned. There was a clear and distinct warning in his eyes.

"Well, you appointed me as the chair, and I made a decision based on the information I had. You should have been *clearer* about what *you* wanted. I'm not a mind reader. I didn't know when you said *'consider* someone else' you were giving me a directive," Felicia continued. Now she was being disrespectful.

David pushed back in his chair and crossed his arms over his chest. "Felicia, you are excused from this meeting. And that is a *directive,* not a suggestion. Thank you. You're welcome."

Donald Clark spoke up for the woman he'd been secretly dating. "Pastor, that's unnecessary . . ."

"Brother Clark, you are excused from this meeting. Thank you. And you're welcome as well," David said quietly. Felicia gathered her things and left. Donald followed her. David would deal with both of them later. He turned to JoAnna. "JoAnna, you will serve as chair of the girls' symposium until further notice. Do you have any suggestions for a fourth male panelist?" David said with a voice as pleasant and calm as a madman's. Cherelle could tell by the faces around the table that he was not one to challenge in a disrespectful manner.

Nervous, JoAnna's eyes grew wide, and she began to

perspire. Cherelle patted her hand. "Uh . . . yes . . . Pastor. I suggest Pastor Alejandro Miguel from New York. He's been here before, and he has a . . . uh . . . good personal history. His youth ministry is progressive but holy."

"Yes . . . Pastor Miguel. That sounds great. Good choice, JoAnna. Why don't you take a break now and get him on the phone if you can? His secretary is Melissa Alvarez. Ms. Greta has her number." JoAnna stood up. "And before you go, just so *everyone* is *clear*. When I say—if I ever say, 'You *need* to do something,' whether I use the word *consider* or the word *suggest*, I'm giving you a directive. I was raised by Leah and Joseph Montgomery. When my mother opened the door and said, 'You need to come in now, or when Joe said you *need* to be home by ten o'clock,' it wasn't a suggestion. It was a directive. When I give you carte blanche on an assignment, you can make your own choices.

"However, I am the pastor of this church, and I am ultimately responsible for the souls and ministries under my authority. So I may veto something if it doesn't line up with what God is telling *me*. Don't take it personally. I'm being obedient to the Spirit, and you all should be obedient as well. And if a leader doesn't know how to be obedient, they don't have the right to be a leader, here or anywhere else." The remaining leadership team members nodded in agreement. And Ms. Greta and JoAnna exited the room. "We will move to the next few items on the agenda until JoAnna has returned," David said.

He masterfully navigated through the remainder of the meeting, listening to the concerns of his staff, helping them to problem-solve issues they felt they couldn't handle without his input. He swayed between taskmaster and loving father. It was easy to see why he was so highly respected. The team had agreed that they would go a little over the scheduled meeting time so that they could wrap up some issues with the new nursery and preschool the church had built. David graciously gave them a fifteen-minute break. He needed it himself to go and pray about the rebellion that had crept into two of his leaders. On top of that, the wickedness of Felicia lying on him and having a check cut on the pretense that she had the authority to do so had gotten under David's skin.

Cherelle stretched her legs by heading to the ladies' room on the far end of the church instead of the one that was nearest the conference room. It looked empty. She went down to the end stall. A few minutes later, two of David's leadership team members, Katrina and Dorsey, entered, unaware that Cherelle was in their company.

"Girl, did you hear how he said, 'You are excused from this meeting'? He was so cool and unperturbed. His voice just sent chills through me." She lowered her voice to a whisper. "I was so turned on, is that *wrong*?" Katrina asked seriously.

Dorsey shrugged her shoulders. "I don't know. But if you were wrong, I was too, because I was feeling the same thing! Why does he have to be so *fine*? You see how he kept his cool even though you know he was super angry, especially when Donald jumped in trying to defend Felicia. I could barely concentrate on my notes."

"Right. And Felicia was so disrespectful. What's been going on with her lately? She acted a fool in front of company! We have a guest! Dr. Dupree must have thought Felicia was crazy!" Katrina returned.

Dorsey leaned against the counter. "Felicia *and* Donald. I thought something was going on with those two. They've been really close lately. I thought I had interrupted something that was about to turn into a kiss the other day, but—"

Both of the women's eyes bugged wide when Cherelle exited the stall and stood at the counter. She washed her hands methodically. Dorsey and Katrina looked at one another and then looked back at Cherelle.

"I didn't hear a thing," Cherelle said with a wink. She exited and headed back toward the conference room.

* * *

GRETA SPOKE in a low voice to Paul, the church treasurer, "I knew he was about to tear into her when he picked up that stress ball, honey."

"Ms. Greta, Felicia made me look like a fool, and I don't appreciate it. I'm gonna let her know, too. That was wrong on so many levels. I never would have done that to her or anyone. I don't want Pastor to think I'm rebellious and not taking my job seriously," Paul said.

"Paul, Pastor knows exactly what happened. He's not angry with you. Just let it go. Don't say anything to that woman. It's done with," Ms. Greta advised. "And you better believe Pastor ain't done with her tail or anybody else who thinks they are going to boss him around. Just disrespectful."

When David reentered, his jovial personality had returned. He joked with Ms. Greta about picking up the popcorn she'd been throwing at him earlier. Cherelle was able to answer all the questions about the workshops and break out sessions, and everything was in place for the symposium.

At the end of the meeting, Cherelle waited in the lobby for her best friend, photo journalist, Lynn Cooper, who was never on time. It was Friday, and just about everyone else had left. David walked up to the front door with Ms. Greta.

"Sister Cherelle, is everything okay? You're not having car trouble, are you?"

"No. I'm waiting for my best friend. She is never-ever-never on time."

"Okay. Well, let me walk Ms. Greta to her car, and I'll be right back. I'll wait with you until she gets here."

"Oh, it's no problem. You can go on with your evening, I'm fine."

"No. I wasn't raised that way, Cherelle. Be right back."

David walked Greta to her car and kissed her on the cheek. "I like her," Ms. Greta said.

"I know, Ms. Greta," David responded, turning back toward the church.

Cherelle had taken a seat on the sofa and was doing something on her cell phone. David came and sat beside her. "Did she call?"

"Yeah, she says she'll be here in twenty minutes, but that means thirty. I know her, so I've learned to calculate the time. We've been best friends for years. We met at NYU, and she's the reason my mom and I moved here to Michigan a little over five years ago. We're really close. So I know her like the back of my hand," Cherelle said.

David chuckled. "Well, that's good. It can keep you from blowing a gasket like I was about to do earlier."

"Yeah. I'm sure. You handled that very well. I need to start calling you *King* David."

David chuckled again. "Oh. *King* David? Am I that bad—you see me as a dictator?"

"No. That's a compliment. King David was a loving leader, even though he made some mistakes in his life. He cared about his people, and he loved the Lord with all his heart. He was *human*."

"Oh. I was surprised by Felicia's actions. If you have leaders like that, your church is on its way to chaos. I'm not going to have it at this church. If someone can't realize that God has called me to Pastor this edifice, they need to go somewhere else. I'm not going to have members *running me*. That's ridiculous. That's like going to the doctor and telling him what needs to be done. That's why I set up a non-denominational church in a way that leaves little room for the body to ever try to run me. I grew up in a Baptist church, and you have deacons and certain supposedly influential members telling the pastor what he *ought* to be doing. And most of them don't even pick up their Bibles and read during the week—no praying. Just interested in running something—being in charge of something. They vote on this or that. And sometimes those wicked and rebellious people vote on things that are not in the best interest of the body. And sometimes, the pastor's hands are almost locked— they can even vote him out. That's crazy."

"I agree. If you don't trust the leader, you need to be some-where else, not causing trouble for the church. Corey says that all the time."

David switched to something more pleasant. "So . . . Thanksgiving is coming up in a couple of weeks. What do you have planned?"

"I'll be over here at DOC with Corey helping your youth ministry serve the homeless."

David's eyes lit up. "Really?" *Corey and Cherelle have got to be dating.*

"Yeah. He told me you guys were teaming up this year to have a focus on the young people serving. So Greater Christian Center will be over here and so will I."

"That's nice. We're glad to have you. I'm proud of the work that we do. Last year, we fed two thousand people."

"I heard. That's wonderful. My mom is going to Florida to visit my aunt, so I'll probably hang out here and then do some Black Friday shopping the next morning until I can't walk anymore."

David laughed. "Oh, you're one of *those* women. You would get along well with my mother. Every year, she and all her little friends get together and shop all day long. My stepfather, Joe, and I sit back and work on leftovers. Then when she gets home, we 'ooh and ahh' over all the stuff she brings us back. It's a pretty sweet deal for us."

"Sounds like it."

David couldn't help but pry. "So what's Corey going to do after the homeless event? Is he going shopping with you?"

Cherelle looked at him strangely. "No. He'll probably be with his family." She didn't elaborate, and David took the hint to leave well enough alone. Cherelle was grateful. And just in the nick of time, she spied Lynn's two-seater BMW pull up in front of the church.

"I don't believe it; she got here early! I'm sorry to have kept you, David."

"It's no problem. I'm gonna go by my mom's, get some dinner, and head on home."

He walked Cherelle out to Lynn's car and introduced himself.

Cherelle had to nudge Lynn for staring so hard.

David stuffed his hands in his pockets, focused on something Cherelle had said earlier. There was something eerie he felt around her, like she wasn't who she said she was. Maybe it had something to do with her keeping her and Corey's dating relationship a secret and being deceitful about it. Maybe it was something else. But there was something strange about her.

Chapter 10

First Lady? Maybe...

Dominique was a fish out of water. Saying she felt uncomfortable was an understatement. She didn't belong at all. And why did they have a section for the pastor's special guests? It would have been better if she could have found an inconspicuous spot somewhere in the back. She'd warned David not to make her stand up and introduce herself or anything of that nature. It had been years since she'd been to a church service, barring her attendance at funerals.

The David Dominique saw in the pulpit, she didn't know. He was a different man. Not once did he look in her direction. To Dominique, David seemed to be in a trance-like state as a woman with a beautiful royal blue wrap dress made the announcements. David looked straight ahead as if his eyes were drawn to something. Dominique wanted to turn to see what or who it was, but she couldn't without being obvious. She hoped her dress was appropriate. She'd tried to find something that didn't cling to her so that she would look a tad more modest. David hadn't mentioned it, but she remembered a comment one of her fellow officers had made about dating a preacher. She had to look the part, and she wanted to impress David in a modest way, if possible.

During family fellowship, right before the Word was brought forth, David's eyes briefly connected with Dominique's. She smiled at him, and he smiled back and nodded, but someone immediately caused him to avert his attention. It was like he was a celebrity. The number of people who kept coming up to him nonstop had to have been exhausting. Dominique wondered if she could stand it all if she and David became a real couple. She wasn't sure she could. Her heart was beginning to feel something for him, and that made her uneasy.

She couldn't see herself as a first lady. It seemed that there were too many rules. You had to know when to stand up and when to sit down. Know all these hymns and gospel songs. Fit in with other church ladies. Attend conferences and serve on different auxiliaries. Dominique doubted she possessed the capacity to operate in such a religious role. But she couldn't deny that David was an anomaly and well worth the effort.

It was evident that he was serious about God. In addition to that, more than any other man she'd ever dated, he made her feel like she was the most important thing in the world when she was with him. And he had to be one of the most delectable-looking men she'd ever seen. If she were honest with herself, she would admit that she was looking forward to being with David in a more intimate way—a way she shouldn't be thinking about in church, of all places. She adjusted herself on the comfortable, cushy pew bench and tried to think of other things.

David preached about being true to your purpose—who you are. He used the prodigal son as an illustration. "You see, he took all his inheritance money and probably squandered it on women and partying, and all sorts of things that were beneath who he was. His father was a wealthy man. But because of poor choices, this young man was living in a manner that was beneath him. Beneath his upbringing. Beneath his heritage. And when the sense popped back into his head, he realized, 'Hey, this ain't me!'

"Have you ever been in the middle of doing something you know you had no business doing, or in a place you know you had no business being, and said to yourself, 'Hey, this ain't me?' People in the congregation responded with yeses and amens. "Well, you know you can always return home. That's what he did. He went back, ya'll. To the life he was meant to live. And his Father welcomed him. Just like Your Father will welcome you. He'll welcome you! Be true to who you are—to the purpose you were created for—the life you were called to live. You were called to live for Christ and Christ alone . . ."

David's words penetrated Dominique, but not in the way they should have. Instead of focusing on the message of Christ, Dominique wrestled with her identity. Who was she? Was she good enough for David? As she sat in her seat, tears rolled down her cheeks. *No, this ain't me. I'm just pretending to be someone I'm not. I can't do this* . . . .The thoughts bombarded Dominique until they crowded her head. She rose and began to move. The congregation clapped. David had extended the invitation to Christ, and the members assumed that Dominique's movement was an indication that she was making her way to the altar to accept the invitation. The clapping grew louder as Dominique exited the pew, but died down as she turned in the opposite direction of the altar. An usher met Dominique midway and whispered, "This is a sacred moment, sister. Except for extreme emergencies, we do not allow any movement during the invitation in order to honor God and not disturb those who may be wrestling with the Spirit."

Dominique's tears came more heavily. She looked back at the altar. It seemed that all eyes were focused on her, even David's. She felt a tug of war on the inside. A part of her knew she should just sit down until the whole thing was over. But what an embarrassment that would be to her and David. She had broken some holy code. The other part of her wanted to be free from this church—this whole idea of God and His perfection. She just didn't fit in.

"Sister . . ." the usher prompted Dominique.

Dominique turned her eyes away from David's and back to the usher. "I have an emergency, I have to leave *now!*" Dominique said through a strained cry.

"Okay . . . may the Lord be with you, my sister . . . ." The seasoned usher nodded to a young usher at the sanctuary door, and the young woman graciously opened the door for Dominique.

Dominique ran to her car and sobbed hard until her whole body shook. She banged her hands on the steering wheel, angry at herself for coming undone. Angry at herself for allowing David and all his holiness to get to her. She put the car in gear and decided to go to the one place she felt safe. The place where she could just be who she was.

As soon as the service ended, David sent Deacon Lewis to tell Minnie, the head usher, that he needed to talk with her. Obediently, Minnie stuck around until the receiving line dwindled and David had greeted the last of his members. It dwindled fast today because it was First Sunday, and DOC always served a meal on the first Sunday after communion.

"Hey, Minnie, how are you today?"

"I'm fine, Pastor. You preached a mighty message today. It blessed my soul."

"Thank you, Minnie. I have a question. The young woman

who left during the invitation—what was going on with her?" David asked.

"Pastor, I explained to her that it was a sacred moment and that we don't allow any movement except for extreme emergencies. She was upset about something because she was crying. She said she had an emergency and had to leave right away," Minnie explained.

"Oh, okay. Thanks, Minnie."

"Pastor, you know I don't let anyone dishonor God when I'm on duty. And none of my ushers either. They all know what to say and do to keep order in the Lord's house."

"I know, Minnie. You are doing a wonderful job. I'm glad to have you here."

DAVID ATTEMPTED to contact Dominique after service to no avail. He texted and called. The whole scene had caught his attention during service, and for a few moments, he had been distracted by it. He'd quickly forced himself to stay in the Spirit and repented for his lack of focus during such a holy moment. By seven p.m. that evening, David knew Dominique was avoiding him on purpose. It wasn't like him to jump to such conclusions, considering her profession. But he just felt it in his spirit. He'd listened to the news to see if anything was going on that would require her to be on SWAT duty. That would easily explain her behavior at church that morning. But there was nothing. He considered the fact that she could have had some emergency with her mother. But it was Dominique's normal pattern to text him during the day for a quick hello, just to see how his day was going. He expected her to do so now, especially since she'd left church so abruptly.

* * *

AN ENTIRE WEEK had gone by since Dominique's disappearing act. David didn't know what to make of it, and he had too many other things taking precedence in his life. God's church was his life. The work of the ministry required most of his attention. In addition to that, he and Cherelle had been working diligently to get the mayor's youth program up and running, and they were ahead of schedule. David lay in his bed, thumbing through the samples of the character development curriculum Cherelle had put together for the mayor's youth task force. He'd already read the curriculum she'd developed for the girls at his church. He realized that Cherelle had an awesome gift of the pen, and she was humble about her accomplishments.

David's cell phone buzzed. He reached over, hoping it was Dominique. He eyed the screen on his phone and smiled. *Dupree.* He had taken to calling her that because she was so prim and proper outside of teaching the gospel—prissy even.

"Hey . . . California girl, what are you up to?" It was ten p.m. Michigan time.

"We just wrapped up the filming for the day. I've been up since four a.m. this morning. We've been doing twelve-hour days. But I wanted to know what you thought of the curricula."

David chuckled. "You're worrying about the youth curricula and you've worked all day, Ms. Movie Star?"

"It's just another independent film, but it's great. I think this one is going to be a big hit. Really."

"What's this, your second acting role? And *Status* did very well at the box office. You are on your way to the top."

"I wish more Christian films were being made. I mean, this is a good movie and all—the script is great and it's a film about hope. But . . . " Cherelle's voice trailed off.

"Dupree, what's wrong?" They'd only known each other a couple of months, but they shared an uncomplicated camaraderie. They had spent so much time in meetings, on the phone, and on FaceTime, both felt like they'd known each other for years, so much so that David could already pick up on her moods.

"I don't fit in here, David."

"Explain Dupree," David said lovingly, "because if you are worried about whether you are good enough, I've seen *Status*, and your acting was superb. And you did it in a movie that was pleasing to God. That's *everything*."

"That's just it, David. On the set of *Status*, almost everyone was a Christian. It was just a joy to do that movie. Every day was beautiful. Don't get me wrong, Asa Miles is a great director, and this film is top-notch. Asa and I have even talked about working together to form a production company to bring more African American voices and projects to the big screen. But working with some of these people is the pits. They are so shallow. I'm trying to represent Christ to them with my behavior, but the attitudes, cattiness, *drugs*, and Hollywood crap are not me."

"Well, think of it this way, it's beautiful that you don't fit in, Dupree. Because you are God's. You're not supposed to fit in with those people. They are doing the movie because it's a paycheck. You're onboard because you believe in the storyline. Positive messages for African Americans. You'll be home soon. Continue to pray, and don't let it get you down. And I've been praying for you every day."

"One more month and I'm done."

"Are you still coming home for Thanksgiving?"

"Yes. Then I'll head back here. I'll be here for Christmas because of the filming schedule. Then I'll be home for New Year's Eve. Filming will be over, and I can rest a bit."

"I'm proud of you, Dupree. And to answer your question, both of the curricula are awesome. Really on point."

"Really? You think so?"

"I'm serious. And I can tell that you put so much work into them, Dupree. Even though the one for the mayor's project is not spiritually based because it's general character building, I see God all up in it. I feel it when I'm reading. And the girls' curriculum you designed for us is so well fortified in the Word that it blew me away. I feel the anointing on it. God has given you an awesome gift. I mean that. I can't wait until the youth symposium."

"That means a lot coming from you, Mr. Best Seller."

"You're next."

"I hope so. I need to keep the checks rolling in since I don't have a husband!"

David chuckled. "He's on his way. Remember our first meeting? God has that brother in the oven getting prepared just for you!"

"Well, amen to that. The brother had better hurry up. I'm getting weary. I go to everything alone. I need a date!"

"Be careful out there. And please, please, whatever you do, don't go get a man off Craigslist," David joked.

Cherelle was laughing hard. "Hey, it ain't that bad yet! Unh-uh!"

David spent over two hours talking with Cherelle until she was jumbling her words together and saying all kinds of things that didn't have anything to do with their conversation. *She is probably repeating her lines from the movie.* David smiled. The poor woman was delirious. She was normally in bed and sleeping by ten o'clock Michigan time. "Good night, Dupree," David said when he heard Cherelle's light snoring. "Bless her, Lord, and give her strength. Amen."

David put his phone in the nightstand drawer and turned off the lamp. He usually turned his cell phone off when he went to bed. The important people in his life had his home phone number. If there were ever an emergency, they'd call him on the landline. He didn't turn his cell off tonight because he had a feeling he'd be hearing from Cherelle once she realized she'd fallen asleep on him. Because of her A-type personality, she'd be so embarrassed, she would call him back and apologize. David smiled again. Dupree was alright. She had a good heart.

As soon as he had almost drifted off to sleep himself, his cell phone rang. "No worries, Dupree," he said groggily. He knew her so well.

"Dave, it's me . . ."

The voice jarred David out of his semi-sleeping state. He'd thought about her over the past week, disappointed that she had just disappeared without an explanation. He'd put God's work first, so he wouldn't be distracted by what was or wasn't happening between them. David scooted up against his head-board and turned on his lamp.

"Well, hello, Ms. Street. How have you been?"

"I'm sorry . . ." Dominique blurted out.

"I asked how you've been . . ." David said compassionately. That unraveled Dominique even more. She hadn't expected him to be pleasant after her little disappearing act. "And you'll have to clarify what you're sorry for. I don't want to jump to conclusions, sweetheart." David's light-hearted approach disarmed Dominique.

"I've been doing okay. I'm sorry for not calling you back. I had a lot on my mind, and I just wanted to be alone."

"You didn't feel that you could trust me with that informa-tion? Did you think I would stalk you or something?"

Dominique relaxed. "No, Dave, I didn't think you would

stalk me. And I *do* trust you. It's just that . . . I didn't know how to handle the situation."

"I didn't know that we had a *situation*, Dominique. I saw you leave church abruptly, and I didn't know why, so I called and texted and didn't receive a response. But I didn't know we'd had a situation."

"It was just me. I had a lot on my mind. I like you. I haven't dated like this in a while. I wasn't sure what I was feeling."

"That's fair. It's only been a couple of months. We can take our time and grow our friendship, Nik. I'm not rushing into anything."

"I know. Please accept my apologies, Dave. I miss you . . ."

"I miss you, too, Nik." David returned. And he wished he didn't miss her the way he did, because that meant his heart was on its way to being vulnerably exposed. He'd been praying about her, and there'd been no revelation from God. Just to watch and pray.

"Can we see each other for lunch or dinner—or breakfast? I just want to see you," Dominique asked humbly.

"Let's do breakfast around nine. I'll come and get you. No worries. Getting to know someone is a process. And loving God fully is a process, Nik."

Dominique didn't want to talk about God.

"Thank you, Dave."

"Good night, Nik."

Chapter 11

Thanksgiving

D isciples of Christ Ministries was filled to capacity and bustling with television camera crews, local celebrities, and volunteers. David didn't like all the attention. He knew why most of the celebrities were there. Mayor Walter Kincaid had added a spin to the Giving Thanks program David led every year to help feed the less fortunate and the homeless in the communities near his church. Walter had invited some local professional athletes and entertainers. There was plenty of food and plenty of volunteers. David wanted the work to get done and have DOC back to normal without all the extra people looking for PR opportunities. He wasn't into that. He served the Lord earnestly, and he wasn't comfortable with all the fanfare.

"Man, you might have to watch what you say around here. There are news people *everywhere*," Cherelle whispered to David.

David responded with his mouth covered. "And all these so-called celebrities. I wish I could get some of these folks to church on Sunday or to help mentor some of our youth. I'm not into the Hollywood thing."

"I understand. At least they're helping."

David looked around at all his youth. Many of them were wearing smocks and aprons with DOC embroidered on the front. They looked proud to be serving. "I guess. The kids are working hard, though."

"They are. They don't understand how much good they're doing by helping the less fortunate," Cherelle said.

"Yeah. Some of *them* are the less fortunate. But everybody can give God back something."

"True. I see your girls are enjoying themselves taking pictures with Trent Dobbs. He is nice looking in person, too." Cherelle teased, winking at David.

"Oh, so you like those basketball dudes, Dupree?" David asked. He shifted his glance to the area where a group of girls surrounded the city's star basketball player.

"Only if he's a man of God and not a *pretend* man of God. I've had my share of those."

"Some women like the private jets and the money—the celebrity perks. If a brother can give them all of that, I don't think most women care if he's a man of God or not."

"Well, as for me, of course, I desire to have someone financially solvent so that I can continue living the lifestyle I'm accustomed to—or better. But I would never trade a man who was really into Jesus for wealth and status. That's a no-brainer."

"Um . . . that's interesting, Dupree."

"Not really. When you grow spiritually, you see things from God's point of view."

David nodded. He liked what Cherelle said, and he agreed wholeheartedly. She had her priorities in order.

Seconds later, they were interrupted when David was grabbed suddenly. David grinned widely and said, "Hey, Bro, you made it." He hugged his friend tightly and gave him a shoulder bump.

"I told you I'd be here by three p.m. and here I am. I know how you get all bent out of shape when you *think* people are late," Gus said. He paused momentarily when he saw Cherelle. "I'm sorry, this beautiful lady must be *Dominique*," he said, taking Cherelle's hand and kissing it.

David's eyes bulged. *Leave it to Gus to mess up! I'm gonna kill him.*

Cherelle smiled humbly. "No . . . I'm *Cherelle Dupree*."

Gus quickly recovered, "Pardon me, *Dr.* Dupree. *'If I profane with my unworthiest hand/This holy shrine, the gentle sin is this:/ My lips, two blushing pilgrims, ready stand/To smooth that rough touch with a tender kiss,'"* Gus quoted Shakespeare's Romeo, still holding on to Cherelle's hand.

David pushed him playfully. "Man, get out of here with that," he said.

Cherelle's face lit up. She could never forget Juliet's response to Romeo. *"'Good pilgrim, you do wrong your hand too much/ Which mannerly devotion shows in this;/ For saints have hands that pilgrims' hands do touch/ And palm to palm is holy palmers' kiss',"* Cherelle responded. Then she said, "It's nice to meet you, Ghost."

She'd known by the way he and David interacted, as well as his quick recovery after mistaking her for someone else, that he must be David's soul brother. Gus was good-looking with an air of mystery. He stood toe to toe with David. If there was a height difference between the two, Cherelle would have bet that David had Gus by a half-inch. Gus's blonde hair was cut in a short fade, and he was clean-shaven. His snug-fitting T-shirt made a show of his muscular chest and biceps. To top it off, he had hypnotic blue-gray eyes that could charm a snake, but

Cherelle guessed he had charmed multitudes of women instead.

"Lovely, it's so nice to meet you as well. And please call me Gus. Only the Neanderthals call me Ghost," Gus said.

"*Peasant,*" David coughed out. Cherelle laughed as Gus rolled his eyes.

Gus Merrick was David's soul brother—Leah's "other" son. He'd grown up a few doors down from David, living with an elderly woman they called Grandma Jo. Ms. Josephine Tucker had taken care of plenty of children over the years as a foster mother. Gus had been one. In a neighborhood full of black kids, the pale, scrawny white boy stood out. His pale skin had affectionately earned him the hood nickname Ghost.

He and David met each other in seventh grade. Three boys had jumped David on his way home from school. David was known as the 'baddest' thing in the neighborhood, so challenges came with the territory. David lived up to his nickname, Punch. Gus had watched as David fought all three at once and decided he needed help to even the balance.

David's mother, Leah, often reminded him about the day he and Gus came through her door with bruises that looked like they had been in a fight with professional boxers. The whole left side of David's face was swollen, and Gus's pale white skin was purple on the corner of his right eye. Leah cried just looking at the two of them, until both of them proclaimed in unison, "We won!" They laughed heartily, boxing each other, reenacting how they had beaten three guys. One of their assailants was a high school student. The two had been inseparable since that day.

A young girl from Corey's church came and pulled on Cherelle's arm. "Ms. Cherelle, Derrick Dixon said he would give us signed jerseys if we came over here and got you to take a picture with him! Will you do it?"

"Uh . . . yeah . . . I guess . . ." she said as the young girl pulled her toward Derrick Dixon, who was newly retired from the city's football team.

David started in on Gus as soon as Cherelle was gone. "Man, *what* is wrong with you?! Why would you come over here and call her *Dominique*? Are you kidding me? You just broke every man code there is!"

Gus laughed. "Hey, bro, I'm sorry. I was watching you two when I came in. The way you were looking at her and interacting, I just figured she was *her*."

"You big dummy!" David said, popping Gus in the back of his head. "You're not in this city for five minutes, and you're already causing havoc!"

"Okay. My bad, bro. But I fixed it! She loved the way I quoted Romeo."

"Go help serve, bro. You need something to do."

"I am. But first, where *is* the mystery lady? I'm dying to meet her."

"She's in Vegas with friends. It was a pre-planned trip. So maybe on your next visit, you'll get to meet her."

"Does she know how special this Thanksgiving thing is for you?"

"Yes. But we've only been seeing each other for a couple of months. She had something else planned already, so I didn't sweat her about it. Now get to work," David said, changing the subject.

"Yes, mean old master," Gus said, strolling toward the kitchen.

* * *

DAVID HAD BEEN so preoccupied with helping to load trucks and serving dinners that he hadn't noticed that two hours had passed. He looked up and saw Gus sitting with Cherelle. He motioned Gus over to where he was standing.

"*What* are you doing?" David interrogated.

Gus knew full well what David was referring to, but he played innocent. "What are you talking about?"

David gave Gus his signature straight face.

"*What?*" Gus asked, feigning ignorance.

"What were you over there talking to Dupree about?"

Gus smirked. "Oh, *Cherelle?* She told me I could call her that, you know. We were talking about opera—Puccini's Tosca —*Vissi d'arte* to be specific," Gus said, rolling the Italian on his tongue. "She sang it in a production while she was a student at Juilliard. It's her favorite. I was telling her it's my favorite, too. She even sang a little for me. She has a *beautiful* voice, by the way."

"Vissi *what?*"

"*Vissi d'arte*, you uncultured heathen," Gus teased. "You need to get out and see the world more—experience more things." Gus knew that couldn't be further from the truth. David had been all over the world, and his studies at Harvard and subsequent travels had exposed him to a great deal of culturally relevant art.

David switched to his native tongue to make his point. "Don't be talkin' to her about no opera."

The two of them were little boys having a tug-of-war over the new girl in town. "Why not? We have a lot in common. I think she likes me."

"No, she doesn't. She's just being nice to you because you're my brother. She doesn't like you like that."

Gus intentionally sounded like a wounded seven-year-old. "That's not true. She likes me for *me*."

"Leave her alone, Gus. Dupree is really sweet. She's a for-real God-fearing woman—she's different."

"I know. That's exactly why I'm diggin' her. We've got a lot in common. She loves opera; I love opera. She writes books; I'm writing a book, and—"

"What?" David interrupted, unbelieving. "Since when have you been writing a *book?*"

"Oh, I've been working on one for quite some time now. In my travels and covert *activities,* I've experienced some things I think would make some great novels. In fact, *Cherelle* liked my ideas. She even said she would help me. And she's going to interview me for something she's working on. So see, she and I have a lot in common."

"Leave her alone, Gus. She's *absolutely off* limits."

Gus continued to purposefully rustle David's feathers. "Why? You've got *Dominique.*"

"Don't worry about who I'm dating. Leave Dupree alone."

"She thinks I'm good-looking. I can tell."

"I wonder how good-looking you'd be with a broken nose," David smiled ruefully.

"Such threats from a man of God? Shameful."

"Surely."

"I'm just messin' with you, bro," Gus chuckled. "But you've got me wondering why you don't want me talking to Cherelle."

"I don't want you harassing her because she's not interested in you."

"Why not? Because I'm *white?*" Gus joked.

"No. Because you're you, dummy."

"Truthfully, I'm not the one you need to be worried about," Gus said. He motioned with his head in the direction where Cherelle was sitting. Corey had come over, and Cherelle stood up to greet him. "I'd say Corey's in first place, trying to make something happen, and Walt is running a close second. See him over there on the other side of the room watching Cherelle and Corey? I bet you ten bucks that as soon as Corey steps away, Walt is gonna slide on over there and strike up a conversation. He's been watching her all evening."

David had to agree with Gus about Walter. But Corey had assured David that he and Cherelle were just friends. "Corey and Dupree are just good friends. That's it. He told me himself. They're not seeing each other."

Gus frowned, unconvinced. "Yep. That's probably what he told *you*. Check them out. See how there's very little space between them? That's a sign of deep familiarity," Gus elucidated. David indulged Gus and studied Cherelle and Corey. "And see the way she's looking up to him—almost with deference? That's surely a sign of some sort of intimate or close relationship. And you know what else? Notice how he's had his hand on her arm the whole time he's been talking to her, and she hasn't shifted positions or anything. That tells me that she is *comfortable* with him touching her. And more than likely, his touching her arm that way is probably a substitute for him holding her hand since they're in public. He doesn't want people to know they've got something going on. Didn't you say she works at his church?"

"Yeah. She's involved in a few ministries over there," David said, considering all of Gus's hypotheses.

"Okay, so Corey probably doesn't want anyone to know that he's dating one of his members until they get officially engaged or something."

"You think so?"

"Something's going on. Oh, wait! Now Corey's walking away . . ." Gus said. He and David watched as Corey walked away, and Walter Kincaid parlayed his way over to replace him, just as Gus predicted he would. "She didn't stand up for Walt," Gus said. They watched as Walter Kincaid took a seat and said something to Cherelle. "She glanced over her shoulder," Gus continued. "She's either checking to see if someone is around who may have overheard what Walt just said, or she's not that *interested* in what Walt just said. She's shaking her head, telling Walter '*no*' to whatever it is he's saying. Look at Walt. He's taking it like a man. He's got that political smile . . . he's accepted his defeat. She's getting up. Look at the way she hugs Walt—not getting too close . . . quickly sits back down. She's not interested," Gus said resolutely. Gus turned to David, "Stick with me, you might learn something. So . . . what's your angle, DC?"

"I don't have an angle. I'm interested in someone else," David said firmly.

"Uh-huh. Well, I'm gonna go over and finish talking to *Cherelle*."

"You're really pressing your luck, *Gustavo Adolfo Merrick*."

"Oh, why you wanna go and call a bro by his government name? That's cold."

"Don't get mad at me 'cause your momma named you after some eighteenth-century Spanish poet."

Gus grinned. "I bet Cherelle will appreciate the literary connection and think it's charming," Gus said, riling David's nerves. It was just like the old days.

They were brothers. He and David engaged in verbal sparring all the time. But Gus had given David something to think about.

THE DAY WAS COMING to an end, and the kitchen at Disciples of Christ Ministry was still overcrowded with celebrities and other guests, including Walter Kincaid himself. David hated the public relations efforts, but he realized that sometimes it came with the territory.

"Walt, you know most of these people are here just because

it makes them look good to their fans. I'd rather not have all the hoopla. I just like to put God first. They're just here taking advantage of an opportunity," David said as soon as he and Walter were alone.

"I know, DC, but these people are going to leave some money behind today—for your church and the city's youth project. And you're getting some necessary work done—who else is going to feed all these homeless people? Chase can't be out here by himself," Walter said, referring to their friend Chase, who usually closed his restaurant down on Thanksgiving to take meals to the homeless. "Who are you to question *how* God provides what you need? No one's doing anything illegal. It may not be in all of their hearts. But I know it's in yours, man."

David couldn't argue with that.

* * *

AFTER EVERYONE LEFT, David practically had to kick out his security team, assuring them he was safe with Gus. He promised to lock up and code out the church. David, Cherelle, and Gus sat in the serving area drinking tea and coffee, as Gus and David caught up. Cherelle sensed that the two had a deep bond. It reminded her of her relationship with her best friend, Lynn Cooper.

"You two are just alike!" Cherelle interjected as David and Gus argued, yet again, about some off-beat topic. Neither of them liked to be proven wrong.

"You better be glad you're my brother, man. I would have knocked you clean out by now!" David said to Gus, punching him lightly in the chest.

"Now, why would you want to hit someone who's had your back almost all of your life?"

"Oh, I remember when you didn't have my back, so don't go there."

Gus laughed. "Now that *one* time doesn't count. You asked for that!"

"It doesn't matter if I asked for it or not. Either you have a man's back or you don't."

"I did have it. I was just giving the situation some time to smooth over before I intervened . . ."

David rolled his eyes. "Yeah, okay. Whatever you say, Gus."

"Gus, did David get into a fight and you didn't back him up?"

Cherelle was more than curious.

"Cherelle, I wouldn't necessarily call it a *fight*. What your friend got himself into was a life-or-death situation. And I wasn't in the mood for dying that day!" Gus laughed.

Cherelle leaned forward and swallowed another sip of her tea.

"I've got to hear this," she said, setting her cup on the table.

"No, you don't, Dupree. It's not that interesting, is it, *Gustavo*?"

Gus mean-mugged David. "What did I tell you about that?"

Cherelle smiled. "I think Gustavo sounds very stately—like royalty."

"Now, see there, your little plan backfired. I already told her. Beat you to the punch," Gus said to David.

"A punch is what you're moments away from, man."

"Since you're threatening me, I'm gonna go ahead and tell this story . . ."

David tossed a sugar packet, hitting Gus.

"See the kind of violence I deal with from this dude, Cherelle? Anyway, so you know, DC went for bad when he was coming up. This one time we were about sixteen and DC and I had sneaked some liquor into Mama Leah's house and we were drinking . . ."

"No!" Cherelle said.

"Oh yeah. Mr. Pastor-So-Perfect wasn't so perfect back then," Gus teased before continuing his story. "So, to make a long story short, when Mama Leah came home, both of us were pretty lit. She got to yelling at DC. He mouthed off something to her, and she slapped him right across the face."

Cherelle's eyes were wide. "Aww, man!"

"Yes, ma'am. She slapped him silly! Now, DC was sitting down on the bed, but when Mama Leah slapped him, she hit him so hard it sort of made his body sway. It was the slap and not the liquor, trust me. This fool sprang up, towered over his mother, and said, 'Don't hit me again!' Of course, Mama Leah was outraged because it seemed as if DC were threatening her, so she motioned to slap him *again*! But DC grabbed her hand, held it tightly, and just glared at her, you know."

David interrupted. "You're really about to tell this?"

Gus laughed again. "Yes, I am! Stop interrupting *Pastor* Cole." He turned to Cherelle. "So DC has Mama Leah's hands —both of them now because, of course, she'd tried to hit him with her free hand. And he's just staring down at her. Mama Leah's telling him to let her go, but he doesn't. It's like DC was showing her, 'Hey, I'm stronger than you. You can't do anything about it.' And then all of a sudden, Papa Joe stormed into that room, and all I heard was, "Get. Your. Hands. Off. My. Wife!"

Cherelle sucked in a breath, hooked on every word of Gus's story. "Oh my goodness!"

Gus clapped his hands together in a prayer. "Cherelle, I promise you, when I looked up, I saw King Kong, The Incredible Hulk, and Godzilla all rolled into one superhero!" Cherelle howled. Gus continued his tale. "Papa Joe snatched DC up by his neck, and had him at least three feet off the ground—with *one* hand—I promise you! So Mama Leah is screaming for Papa Joe not to hurt DC. And that was the moment I knew I *wasn't* gettin' in it. Three little words, Cherelle. Papa Joe said, 'I've. Had. Enough!' And his eyes looked red as a bull's. DC couldn't have gotten loose if he wanted to. Mama Leah was looking at me to help do something. But I'm looking at Papa Joe. He's got DC by two inches, 'cause he's about six-two. But he was strong *and* mad! I was thinking to myself, *this ain't my fight!* And I stayed glued to the spot I was sitting in until Papa Joe let DC go. DC's body just fell on the bed—looked like he lost color. He was as white as me, I'm not kiddin'."

Cherelle looked at David, the cool and reserved, but tender-hearted man she'd come to know, and said, "I'm so shocked by you, David . . ."

"I was a silly young man with a chip on my shoulder, Dupree. But that day, Joe taught me three lessons: One, there's always someone tougher than you. Second, don't disrespect your mother. And third, don't *ever* disrespect another man's *wife*! I garnered a new appreciation for Joe that day. I respected him. Joe is a really quiet type of guy. Never says too much. My mother is the bossy, opinionated type. Joe has an easy spirit. He doesn't let my mother run him—he's not henpecked by any means. Just a gentle giant, you know. But that day, I had pushed every button. Joe had put up with me since I was seven years old and had never disciplined me—never put his hands on me. He'd always let my mom handle it. But that day, he let me know that if I stepped out of line with either of them, he was going to handle it from then on. When he said he'd had enough, he meant it!"

"Wow. Unbelievable," Cherelle said, shaking her head.

Gus eyed David and smiled. Then he turned to Cherelle. "Now, Cherelle, when you meet Joe, he's so quiet-spoken you would never think he'd do something like that, but he doesn't play when it comes to Mama Leah!"

"I heard that!" Cherelle winked at Gus and elbowed David. "Nothing wrong with a man protecting his wife—even from her own son!"

"Guilty as charged. Thank God for his transforming power!"

Chapter 12

Holiday Labels

David hadn't been able to spend Thanksgiving with Dominique, but he hoped she could spend time with him for Christmas. It just seemed reasonable since their friendship had escalated to terms of endearment. Although they hadn't quite defined what it was they shared, David did want Dominique to meet Leah. He and Dominique had grown closer since they hit that bump in the road a month ago when she disappeared for a week. Now, all of his free time was spent with her. She had completely infiltrated his life.

Tonight, they were scheduled to attend a community banquet at which David was the keynote speaker. David watched as Dominique twisted her long hair into a neat bun atop her head. When he first entered her townhome, she'd had it down. Somehow, after seeing what he was wearing, she decided to change her hairstyle. He couldn't understand the sense it made, but he knew better than to say that. He studied her as she strategically placed bobby pins in her mane to hold her style together. He imagined that moments like this could be a part of their future routine.

"So . . . I know we're just friends. And I don't want to put any pressure on you, but I'd like for you to join my family and me for dinner on Christmas Eve."

"Christmas *Eve*?"

"Yes. It's my mother's tradition to cook on Christmas Eve, and we have dinner. After dinner, around midnight, we open our gifts. That way, on Christmas, we can just chill or be free to visit other family members if we like. Most of the time, Ma and Joe end up spending Christmas Day in their pajamas, and I usually get around to visiting some of the sick and shut-in members of my church."

Dominique looked as if she were considering David's invitation. He picked up on her hesitation. "You don't have to stay until midnight, Nik. I just thought it would be nice to spend some time together. It will just be you, me, my mother, and Joe."

"Dave, I appreciate the invitation, but I don't know if I'm ready for the whole meet-the-parents thing."

David wondered why Dominique was so apprehensive about everything. He knew she'd been burned several times in relationships, but she was overboard when it came to being guarded. "Nik, you coming to dinner is in no way an attempt to make us more than friends. I respect that you want to take things slowly—so do I. Just think of it as being invited to a friend's for dinner. It's just dinner, Nik."

"What time?"

"We usually eat at six. I could pick you up and drop you off. That's no problem," David said, hoping to eliminate any excuses Dominique might conjure up.

Dominique finished pinning her hair and wrapped her arms around David's neck. She kissed him tenderly. He responded with a closed-mouth kiss. "Thank you for inviting me, Dave. I'd love to come."

"You're welcome. It'll be nice."

* * *

LEAH SENSED that Dominique was nervous, so she went out of her way to make her feel at home. David appreciated that. He hadn't brought anyone home for Leah to meet in over a year, since Desiree McKay, a woman who had aspirations as a political news writer. It was a promising relationship that God had said no to.

David watched Leah watch Dominique. Although she did it discreetly, David could see the wheels turning in his mother's mind. He'd already warned her not to bombard Dominique with too many questions. They were still just friends, not a couple. He didn't want Dominique to feel uncomfortable or pressured.

"So, Dominique, what kind of work do you do?" Leah inquired. Dominique smiled politely, fully aware that she wasn't going to make it through dinner without *any* questions asked of her.

"I'm a police officer."

David had already told Leah that, so he didn't know why she'd asked Dominique that question. But Leah was getting warmed up. Even Joseph knew that. He winked at David and shared an empathetic smile. David could hear Joseph's thoughts. *I hope she can handle your mother.* David exhaled and slyly scrunched his nose up at Joseph. Joseph knew exactly what David wished he could say aloud. *Can you please handle your wife?* But Joseph would do no such thing. Dominique would have to grin and bear Leah Cole-Montgomery. Joseph wasn't going to mess up his Christmas trying to tame a woman who couldn't be tamed.

"Dominique, have you met any of Punch's friends yet?" David knew what was coming next. Dominique had no idea.

"Umm . . . actually, I've only met Mayor Kincaid. He seems pretty nice," Dominique added.

"Did you get a chance to meet Gus on Thanksgiving?"

"I was out of town that weekend. I haven't met Gus yet."

"Oh . . ." Leah said, keeping David under surveillance as she spoke to Dominique. "Those two are best friends. They are like two peas in a pod. Gus is my other son. After dinner, I'll show you some photos of David and Gus when they were younger."

David chuckled. "I'm sure Nik doesn't want to see any old photos of me, Ma. It's boring, boring stuff," he teased.

Dominique evaluated Leah as well. "I'd love to see pictures of Dave when he was younger," she offered politely.

"Good. What do you think of DOC? We're very proud of the work Punch has been doing. He's grown the church, and the young people there just energize me to be and do more for Christ." Leah continued.

"It's a nice edifice."

"Is it weird watching him preach? He's like a different person, isn't he?"

"Yes, in a way . . ." Dominique wasn't sure if she was answering the questions the way she should.

"The first time I heard Punch preach, I kept thinking to myself: Is that my baby up there? It was such a surreal experience. God has gifted him mightily. He needs a strong woman in the Lord to support him and his ministries."

Dominique smiled and nodded. She didn't know how to take Leah's last statement. Was Leah saying that David needed a *different* kind of woman, or was she simply trying to match-make?

David intervened. "Ma, stop trying to get rid of me. God will send what I need when it's time."

"Hush. I couldn't get rid of you if I tried. You come over and get dinner every day. You need a wife to cook for you."

"Well, right now, I have you, my beautiful, loving, kind mother."

Leah shooed David with a wave of her hand. "That's right, pour it on thick, boy." She said before returning her attention to Dominique.

"So . . . Dominique, how long have you been putting up with him?"

"We've known each other for a few months—we're just friends," Dominique added so quickly that it caused Joseph to raise a brow.

David knew that wasn't going to satisfy Leah. Not one bit. He wanted her opinion of Dominique, and she was going to do what it took to give him her opinion.

"Well now, when you young people say *friends*, I'm not so sure just what that means. 'Friends' today means something totally different than what it meant in my day. Are you two friends as in buddies, or friends as in something more?"

Dominique swallowed her dressing and shifted uncomfortably in her seat. She glanced at David, then back at Leah. "We're friends. We don't have any labels other than that, Mrs. Leah. We're still getting to know one another."

"Okay. I was just asking because being a first lady is a big spiritual and familial responsibility. A woman has to take care of and support her man in his role as Pastor, *and* she has to take care of her man and support him in his role of being her husband as well. In addition to that, she's got to keep that family unit intact and train their children, sometimes not getting a lot of help from him, depending on what kinds of assignments God gives him."

Everything Leah said was true. But David could sense that what she'd said made Dominique uncomfortable.

"We haven't gotten that far yet, Mrs. Leah. No labels." Dominique repeated for the second time. Leah was prying, and Dominique had made herself clear on their title. There wasn't one.

"Ma, we'll cross that bridge when we get to it," David said, squeezing Dominique's hand gently. The gesture did not get past Leah.

"Dominique, I'm sorry if I said something to make you uncomfortable, honey. I'm just making small talk. I want you to feel welcome in our home—anytime. Punch hasn't brought anyone around in a long while," Leah said with a wink.

"It's no problem. I understand. But being a wife, mother, or a first lady are not things I've given a lot of thought to . . ." Dominique said. She noticed the shocked look on Leah and Joseph's faces, so she explained further. "Dave and I are still new . . . so . . . um . . . we haven't really discussed those things in detail."

Leah nodded. "I see." She knew it was time to change the subject.

* * *

DOMINIQUE WAS quiet on the way to her home. David wondered if Leah had truly upset her with all the questions and comments about being a first lady.

"My mother meant well, Nik. She was just trying to get to know you. And she wants grandbabies. So she was a little overzealous with the questioning and stuff."

Dominique shrugged. "It's okay, Dave. I expected to be grilled on some level, but we're not teenagers. Like I've said before, grown people date because they want to. There doesn't have to be a reason behind it . . ."

"Well, I'm hoping that we're cultivating a friendship that has the ability to blossom into something more if that's God's will."

"Let's just keep taking it slow, Dave."

Dominique's mind was someplace else. On something else. Maybe Leah had ruffled her feathers a bit. Maybe she just didn't like the prying. Leah was harmless. But maybe Dominique didn't see it that way.

"Again, Nik, if something my mother said was offensive or just got under your skin, I want to apologize. She means well. She's a loving and caring woman. Everyone loves my mom."

"I'm good, Dave. 'No worries,' as you say."

David put the car in park and reached down to the floor behind Dominique's seat. "I got you a little something for Christmas, Nik," he said, handing her a bag with two gift-wrapped boxes. "I want you to open them now since I'm not going to see you tomorrow."

"Oh . . . Dave . . . I didn't know you wanted to exchange presents . . . I didn't get you anything. I thought we were just going to have dinner."

"Nik, open your gifts."

"Okay." Dominique reached inside the bag and pulled out a smaller box first. David waited patiently as she opened it up. Her reaction pleased him. "These are so beautiful, Dave," she said, lifting the double-strand pearl necklace out of the box. She fingered the earrings and bracelet.

"I heard you commenting on Diana's jewelry after Bible study a couple of weeks ago."

"Yes, her pearls looked very feminine and pretty. And these are just as beautiful. Thank you, Dave." Dominique wasn't sure what else to say.

"Open your other box," David said.

Dominique replaced the jewelry and tore the paper from the larger box. She opened the box and picked up the blue, ruffled, chiffon gown. "Dave, you pay attention to everything! I don't know where I'd get to wear something so formal, but it is incredible."

"There may be some events coming up that call for a nice gown, you never know . . ." David said. He was thinking of the New Year's Eve service at his church. Some members had taken to dressing up for the occasion to thank God for getting them through another year. He'd seen her eye the dress in a boutique window next to a new restaurant they'd had lunch at a few weeks ago. He decided to get it for her. David knew she'd look beautiful in it.

"Dave, I didn't get you a gift because I thought we were just going to—"

David finished her sentence. "Take it slow. I know. Nik, whenever I do something, it's because I want to, not because I expect anything in return. I was raised that way. Merry Christmas."

Dominique threw her arms around David's neck and kissed him. He avoided a deep kiss. Dominique pulled back. "Merry Christmas, Dave."

* * *

LEAH COULDN'T WAIT for David to return from taking Dominique home. As soon as David stepped into the foyer, Leah met him.

"Punch, I'm so sorry. Joe has been fussing at me the whole time you've been gone. I was just trying to get a feel for who she was, that's all . . . I didn't mean to ruin your date."

David kissed Leah's forehead. "It's fine, Ma. No worries, okay? And it wasn't a date. We were just having dinner."

"What did she say? Was she angry, honey?"

"No, Ma. She wasn't angry. She's just a little different, that's all."

"You're not mad at me, are you, Punch?"

David hugged his mother. "Ma, no. I'm *not* mad. Dinner was beautiful. Everything was good. No worries." David took off his coat with his mother's assistance. She hung it in the foyer closet, and they walked hand in hand into the family room where Joseph was sitting in his favorite chair with his feet up, eating sweet potato pie.

"You started without me, Joe?"

"Son, you were taking too long. I tried to wait on you, but the pie was calling my name."

"Punch, I'll get you a slice. Go ahead and sit down," Leah said.

She headed toward the kitchen. David took a seat in the La-Z-Boy across from Joe.

"You know she's feeling guilty. I got on her about asking so many questions. That makes people feel like they're on the spot," Joseph offered.

"She's alright. It's not a big deal. That's what mothers do," David returned.

Leah returned a few minutes later with a huge slice of sweet potato pie and coffee for David.

"I should not be contributing to your coffee addiction, Punch, but Joe made me feel so bad."

"Ma, it's cool. Really. I'm serious."

"But honey," Leah asked, "does Dominique realize what dating you means?"

"What do you mean, Ma?"

"Does she understand that when a woman dates a pastor,

no matter how long she's known him, she's got to consider a life as a pastor's wife—because that may become her life?"

"It's like she said, Ma, she hasn't considered those things yet. We are still new—getting to know each other."

"Well, Punch, why is she dating you?"

"I don't know, Ma. I guess she's dating me because I'm interesting. And I like to think I'm good-looking," David joked. "But seriously, we have a good friendship. We're still learning each other and trying to see where we're going . . ."

Leah wasn't satisfied with David's answer. He wasn't satisfied with it either.

"Why are you dating her?"

"I'm trying to see if she could be my wife. I felt a connection when we first met. We had coffee one evening, and I felt like she was someone I could explore a relationship with. I'd like to get married and give you some grandbabies, Ma. Isn't that what you want?" David teased.

Leah sighed.

"Ma, just say whatever it is you want to say so I can eat this delicious pie you made just for me." Joseph cleared his throat, teasingly. "I mean just for Joe and me."

"Honey, it just seems to me that Dominique is just dating. I don't know how a woman could be dating a *pastor*—friends or not, and not consider what it would be like to be his wife. That's a huge life calling. How could she *not* think of that?"

"Ma, honestly, she's been through some bad relationships, and I think she's just a little gun-shy when it comes to intimacy. She's really a sweetheart. I think she's just being cautious."

"Have you prayed about her?"

"Almost every day."

"So you really like her then?"

"I do. She has her flaws, but she's growing. I care for her a lot. We'll see what happens."

David knew Leah wasn't too excited about Dominique. He couldn't divulge the things Dominique had told him about her father and the other men she'd loved who'd treated her poorly. That would stay between them. David understood Dominique's apprehension, even if Leah didn't.

* * *

A LITTLE AFTER MIDNIGHT, David checked his cell phone between opening gifts. He'd missed a call from Cherelle. He hurriedly called her back, knowing she was without family in California.

"Merry Christmas, David. Did you open your gift?"

"What gift? You got me a gift?"

"Yes, sir. I had Deacon Lewis give it to your stepfather. It's covered in red velvet-like paper with a black silk bow."

David called into the family room. "Hey, Joe! Did Old Man give you a box for me?"

"Oh, yeah. He sure did and left his usual envelope, too," Joe said, entering the dining room. He handed David the box and envelope. David had told Deacon Lewis at least a hundred times to stop giving him money for his birthdays and Christmas, but he never listened.

David opened the box and pulled out the baby blue and silver paisley bowtie and a pair of piano-shaped, sterling silver cuff links. "Nice, Dupree. Love the links. Very classy. I'm gonna sport these with my new tuxedo on New Year's Eve."

"I knew you would like your gifts, especially the cuff links. When I heard you play the piano at church, I was so flabber-gasted that you were so good. I had those made for you."

"You didn't go spending a lot of money, did you, Dupree?"

"Nah. I told you I get the Donovan Stamps family discount. I've gotten him so much business from people I've met on the movie set that I shouldn't have to pay regular price for a while," Cherelle said, chuckling.

"Well, thank you so much. Did you open the gift I sent you?"

"I'm opening it right now. Aww . . . thank you, David." The first thing she lifted out of the box was a scrapbook filled with photos of her and the girls in David's Girls for God ministry. The photos had been taken at the youth symposium Cherelle had presented at just a few weeks earlier. "This is special," Cherelle said, trying not to cry. The purple and red scrapbook also contained notes from the girls to Cherelle expressing how she'd blessed their lives. It truly was one of the most thoughtful gifts she'd received. The last page contained a photo of her, David, and the girls with a special letter of thanks from him.

"Dupree, you were such a blessing to our girls' conference. The girls loved you, and you brought the Word the way God intended. You deserved something special that would remind you how much we appreciate you at DOC. And Dupree, there's something else in that box. Should be another gift in there . . ."

"Aww, man! This is just what I needed." David had asked one of his church members who made specialty baskets to create a basket for Cherelle that was filled with natural products, soaps, teas, body scrubs, and oils. She was a natural enthusiast.

Content that he had made her smile, David ended the call after they'd chatted for a while. He sat up watching TV long after Leah and Joseph had gone to bed. He pondered over Leah's question. Why was Dominique dating him?

Chapter 13

What Are You Doing New Year's Eve?

David stood in front of his floor-length mirror, tying the baby blue and silver bow tie Cherelle had given him for Christmas. He was also sporting his piano cuff links. It was a classy complement to his charcoal-colored tuxedo. He couldn't wait to see Dominique tonight. He knew the elegant gown he'd given her for Christmas would look beautiful on her this evening.

He needed to get to the church early so that he could sit in the Spirit for a while. Dominique promised to be ready. She knew he was a stickler for punctuality. He texted her to let her know he was on his way. When he didn't get a response, he called.

"Hey, sweetheart, I was letting you know that I'm on my way."

"Dave, I'm not going to be able to make it. I've eaten something, and my stomach is killing me."

"Um . . . okay. Do you need anything? I could drop it off on my way to the church."

"No, I have everything I need. I'm going to lie down."

163

"Okay. I'll check on you after service," David said.

Disappointed, David wondered if Dominique was genuinely ill or had found a convenient way to back out of ringing in the New Year at church. He shunned all of those thoughts so that he could concentrate on the Word for the evening. Dominique had been hesitant about spending New Year's Eve at church. She'd commented that she'd never done it before. She usually celebrated with her friends. After all of David's convincing, she wouldn't make it after all.

David's dismay revealed just how much he'd developed feelings for Dominique. He'd wanted her to be on his arm tonight. He wanted her to share the things of God with him—the things that were most important to him. He had witnessed Dominique's spiritual growth in study and even in church attendance. He wanted to immerse her in his world so that she could see the beauty of what God was doing in his life—so she could see the beauty of what God was doing in her life. This Watch Night service was more than just another occasion; it was a time for him to share God with her in a different way. David's disappointment was full-blown.

David stood in the foyer of DOC talking with Deacon Lewis and his young, twenty-seven-year-old assistant pastor, Clint Hobbs, whom they all referred to as Pastor Clint. Clint was an average-sized young man with a big heart for God. Standing five feet ten inches tall and relatively slim, Clint had an unassuming disposition. His looks, however, drew attention. His dark chocolate skin and short, neat locks made him stand out, especially to women. His dark skin was so silky smooth that Clint looked like a teenager at times.

He had deep-set black eyes and twin dimples in his cheeks.

His lightning bolt smile and pearly white teeth that looked as if they had been chemically whitened added to his handsomeness. The oddity about Clint was the depth of his baritone voice. Looking so young, people were always taken aback when he spoke, because his voice sounded much older than he appeared. That was his woman magnet, whether he wanted it to be or not.

"Man, Pastor Corey sure is blessed," Clint said out of the blue.

David and Deacon Lewis looked in the direction of Clint's gaze and saw Cherelle and Corey walking toward them. They'd entered from the east wing doors. David watched as Corey removed Cherelle's coat. She did look beautiful.

"You better keep your eyes on the blessing God sent you," Deacon Lewis said.

"Sure better," David agreed.

"I'm just saying, she's pretty. She's going to make a beautiful first lady. There are benefits to being a man of God," Pastor Clint joked.

For some reason, David felt compelled to say, "They're just friends. I doubt if she'll be his first lady."

"*Friends?* Is that what he's calling *her?* I'm not the one who needs to get his mind right," Clint retorted.

Deacon Lewis popped Clint upside his head. "I raised this one already," Deacon Lewis said, tilting his head in David's direction. "I ain't got no time to be foolin' with you too."

David laughed. "I guarantee you, Pastor Clint is going to be much more trouble than I've been."

Deacon Lewis shook his head. "I don't know. He's just like you. Too much like you, if you ask me."

"Old Man, I've been keeping you on your toes for years."

"You've been worrying my nerves for years, is what you mean."

"You love every minute of it."

"No, I don't either."

"I love you, too," David said, hugging Deacon Lewis.

"Now here comes the most beautiful woman I've ever seen," Clint said, as his fiancée, Stormie Greer, came strutting up the opposite hallway.

"Don't ever forget that either. And make sure you stayin' *holy*, Pastor Clint," Deacon Lewis interjected.

"Yes, sir. Wouldn't think of doing anything less . . ."

"Keep it that way while you lookin' all starry-eyed."

"I'm good . . . "

Deacon Lewis wasn't that convinced. "Uh-huh . . ."

From a distance, David watched Cherelle and JoAnna Simms examine each other's dresses. Then he noticed something that caught his attention. Corey was discreetly eyeing JoAnna. He did it on more than one occasion as Cherelle and JoAnna conversed. There was a moment when Cherelle seemingly noticed and gave Corey a strange look before leaving Corey and JoAnna standing there alone. *Was she upset?* From David's vantage point, it seemed that Cherelle was discomposed. She walked toward him. He would get a few answers about Cherelle and Corey's relationship. Maybe.

"Hey, Dupree . . . you look nice. Everything good?" he pried.

"Thank you. So do you. And yes, everything is good." Cherelle glanced down the hall where Corey and JoAnna had stood just moments before. They were gone. David had watched as the two of them headed toward the preschool area. Corey had informed David that he planned to add a school to his church as well. Maybe Corey asked JoAnna to see the school wing. David had recently promoted JoAnna to the position of preschool director just a month ago after the original director moved out of state. JoAnna maintained her position as the lead preschool teacher as well as acted as the interim director. After praying, David was convinced that JoAnna Simms should take on the directorship.

David hugged Cherelle and was hit with a sickening feeling. He wanted to push her as far away from him as he could. *Lord, what is going on?* When Cherelle backed away from David, he eyed her again. She looked stunning in the black, sequined-looking jumpsuit that was modest enough and glamorous enough to make a statement. Diamond cross earrings dangled from her ears and matched her diamond-studded cross pendant necklace. She looked amazing, just like Pastor Clint had said earlier. It was hard not to notice.

David and Cherelle stood in a loose circle, talking to Deacon Lewis. Corey and JoAnna came walking toward the threesome a few minutes later. David searched Cherelle's eyes. It was apparent that she was purposely trying to maintain a straight face and show no emotion. But JoAnna's interaction with Cherelle caught all of David's attention.

"Uh . . . Cherelle . . . Pastor Corey asked me to show him the preschool wing. I hope you didn't mind." JoAnna was talking so fast and seemed so nervous that David had to rewind and replay her words in his mind. "He said he's planning to add a school next year . . ." JoAnna explained clumsily.

Cherelle was a bit too polite in David's opinion. "No problem. I was just catching up with Pastor Cole anyway," Cherelle said. Strangely, most of Cherelle's eye contact was with Corey.

"I—I didn't want you to think—" JoAnna began to explain again.

"JoAnna, it's fine. Really. I need to go to the ladies' room. Please excuse me," Cherelle said, silencing JoAnna for good.

David could have sworn that Cherelle's eyes misted. What in the world was going on with her and Corey? *Corey couldn't be that much of a lark to do something that would cause Dupree to cry, would he?* The way he just walked off with JoAnna had to be disturbing to Cherelle if she and Corey were more than what they claimed. *It would have been disturbing to me,* David thought to himself. Cherelle headed toward the restrooms near David's office.

Just a few moments later, that gave him a perfect opportunity to create an excuse and say he needed something out of his office before service. He instructed Deacon Lewis to seat Corey in the section for special guests and headed toward his office. Just as he'd planned, David ran right into Cherelle.

"Dupree, are you sure you're feeling alright tonight?"

"I'm fine, David. Why do you ask?"

"You just seem a little different."

"I have a terrible headache, and I have a lot on my mind as well."

"Well, I can give you an aspirin for the headache, and I can listen to what's on your mind."

"I'll take the aspirin, but I have no intention of sharing what's on my mind."

David chuckled. That's just what he expected. "Okay, let me get you some aspirin. Come on back to my office."

Entering David's office, Cherelle plopped down on his sofa and waited for him to bring her an aspirin. As soon as he handed her the aspirin, she took it and gulped it down with a cup of water. "Ugh! My head is banging . . ."

"If you need a moment, you can stay in here for a while. The door will auto-lock."

"No, I'm good. I'll be better when the aspirin kicks in."

David trailed behind Cherelle, and as soon as they stepped out of his wing, they heard JoAnna calling for Cherelle in the restrooms. Perplexed, they looked at one another.

"JoAnna, I'm right here," Cherelle said finally.

JoAnna raced over. "Cherelle, listen, please. I'm really

sorry. But I need to tell you this—and if you and Pastor Corey are more than friends—I was just being polite by showing him the wing . . ." JoAnna rattled on.

David wanted to hear everything, but he knew it was polite to mind his manners. "Let me leave you two alone," he offered.

"No. Pastor, please don't leave. I want you to hear this. I don't want you to think I'm the kind of woman who would—" she said without finishing her sentence. She was now hyper-verbal, and David wished she would slow down. The fast-talking was giving *him* a headache. JoAnna turned to Cherelle again. "Cherelle, I consider you a friend. You've been nice to me. I wouldn't do anything against you. Pastor Corey asked if he could call me, and I said it would be okay if there's nothing going on between you two. You said there wasn't, and he did too. But I don't have a good feeling. I'm attracted to him, but I don't want to do something that—I—I think Pastor Corey is a good man, I don't think he would lie to me about something like that. But I wanted to talk with you, Cherelle." JoAnna was almost tearful.

David knew why, but Cherelle was looking at JoAnna like she had just grown two heads. Cherelle rubbed her temples and said very quietly and slowly. "*JoAnna* . . . it is perfectly *okay* for Pastor Corey to call you if that's what you'd like for him to do. I am on his leadership team, and I assist him with ministry projects. Our relationship is strictly *platonic* and *holy*. That's all it is and all it ever will be. We are *friends,* okay? So please, calm down. I'm not sure what's going on, but I have a headache. So if I seem a little different, it's because I'm in pain."

JoAnna's vanilla cream complexion was now red, and her eyes were brimming with tears. She nodded and ran into the restroom.

Cherelle looked at David for some answers.

"Dupree, I will let her explain why she's probably so upset right now. It's not my place."

Exasperated, Cherelle said, "Let me take my seat."

* * *

DURING THE MEET-AND-GREET portion of the service, David couldn't help but look for Dominique. He hoped she would feel better and surprise him by showing up. He imagined her walking into the sanctuary wearing the beautiful blue gown he'd purchased. His hopes were lifted and quickly shattered when he saw a woman wearing a similar dress. It wasn't Dominique. David knew he was letting Dominique get to him. It was taking his focus off the Word, and he knew that wasn't okay with his Father. His mind wandered back to the conversation between JoAnna and Cherelle. Whatever Cherelle and Corey had going on—if they did have something going on was surely getting messy.

Service ended just past midnight, and David looked up and saw Cherelle smiling. At least she was feeling better. She was on her cell phone, probably talking with her mother, who'd opted to stay in for the evening. David hugged a few people as they headed to the serving area for breakfast. He detoured to his office and called Dominique. Her cell phone went straight to voicemail. It was unlike Dominique to be sleeping this early. She was a night owl. Maybe she didn't feel that well and had slept through the ringing in of the New Year.

David was forced to leave a message. "Hey, you. Happy New Year! I hope you're feeling better. Let me know if you need anything . . ." For the first time in a long while, David was missing something—the companionship only a woman could provide. And he was missing Dominique.

Chapter 14

Hiding All That

I t was already mid-March, and the youth program David and Cherelle developed for Mayor Walter Kincaid was in full swing. The mayor had met several times with the president, who was interested in the turnaround programs for youth, especially since he knew David was involved. Walter Kincaid had asked David and Cherelle to put together a presentation for the president.

In the mayor's conference room with papers strewn all over the mahogany conference table, Reginald reviewed Cherelle's agenda and PowerPoint for the president. They'd given the president the code name Number One. Reginald tweaked Cherelle's data and graphs. He was a numbers man. Cherelle was grateful because she wasn't a numbers person. Reginald studied a few spreadsheets and input some new numbers. After the first month, they'd seen significant drops in crime in most of the neighborhoods where the programs were running. Mayor Kincaid had a special meeting scheduled for the president himself to review the data, hoping that the programs could be duplicated in other cities.

"Okay, take a look," Reginald said to Walter. He turned to the projection screen. The city was broken down into geographical sections of different colors. Reginald took the laser pointer and centered it on the yellow section, which was one of the city's worst areas in terms of crime. "We have a fifty percent decrease here."

Multitasking, Walter paused mid-sentence from dictating a memo to his secretary, Alexis. "What? Are you sure? That seems too high," he said to Reginald.

Reginald smiled. "I'm absolutely, positively sure. I checked and double-checked. According to Cherelle's data and the data from the police precincts in that area, I'm right on the money."

Walter got up and walked over to the screen. "This is crazy. What programs are running over here?"

Reginald spun whimsically around in his chair toward Cherelle and spoke with an English accent. "Madame, would you kindly inform Mayor Kincaid of the resources you have put in place in this zone?"

Cherelle chuckled and threw a grape at Reginald. He intercepted it and popped it into his mouth. "Sure. Can you forward to slide number thirty? Lynn embedded a video in that slide. She stood up and walked over to the screen. Walter Kincaid couldn't help but notice how good Cherelle's hips and backside looked in her skinny jeans. The way her hips swayed as she walked to the screen caused Walter to divert his eyes from the PowerPoint to Cherelle's hourglass figure. She wore a yellow button-up sweater that screamed womanhood in Walter's opinion. Reginald caught him and smiled slyly.

Walter made a face at Reginald before Cherelle turned around. "Cherelle, if you don't mind, explain it to me like you're going to explain it to Number One," Walter said.

"Sure. For starters, what we have in this zone, which we deemed to be our most troublesome, are four churches that are now offering job skills classes, after-school programs, and Friday and Saturday night off-the-streets activities. These efforts are being co-funded by the Reach Foundation for Youth. We also have two high schools that have open gyms and pools on Friday and Saturday evenings. These programs are being supported by the Carter Family Foundation and the School and Community Partnership. The kids as young as five have specific programs per age group.

"They are using shuttles to transport the kids to the schools for safety. Everything is over by nine p.m. The kids have to sign a community pledge and attend a minimum of ten character education and life skills sessions presented at the churches. The sessions are all identical because I put them together that way. So no matter what church or base the kids are connected to, they're all being exposed to the same things. Pastor Cole worked with the gang leaders in that area to keep the peace. They are not recruiting any kids who are signed up for the programs. I'm not sure exactly what he did, or how he made it happen, but in a survey I gave the kids just two weeks ago, almost ninety-five percent said that they felt safe and that they would not be harmed or bullied into joining gangs. And ninety-nine percent said they hadn't been approached by any gang members since joining the programs."

"Wow. You guys did it! I am so proud right now," Walter said. "This is crazy. Number One was so impressed with the preliminary results that he was talking about me spearheading a national youth-in-cities initiative. But I couldn't have done this without you guys. This is what I'm talking about. This is part of the legacy I'm going to leave. Let's take a break for lunch and then run through the rest of the zones. By that time, DC should be here."

"Yes, he said his meeting would be over at one p.m.," Cherelle added.

"Lex, what time will lunch be here?" Walter asked his secretary. "In about ten minutes, Mr. Mayor."

"Thanks, love," Walter said. His secretary left the room and went on to some other task. He turned to Cherelle. "Okay, I was trying to wait, but it's time to cut that apple pie you baked, Cherelle. I'm gonna have my dessert before lunch today."

Both Walter and Reginald cut themselves huge slices of Cherelle's homemade apple pie. Reginald turned on the radio. One of Cherelle's favorite songs was playing. It was "Loving You" by Minnie Riperton. To Cherelle's amusement, both Reginald and Walter joined in, singing along to the song. It was hard to believe how Walter Kincaid could so easily slip in and out of normalcy. Walter switched gears like a true professional. Cherelle decided that this would be one crazy YouTube video. Both Walter and Reginald attempted to out-scream-sing each other in their untrained falsetto voices as they disastrously mimicked Minnie Riperton's five-octave range. Cherelle, however, hit the high note perfectly. Her voice was clear and crisp, pitch-perfect. Walter and Reginald stopped in their tracks.

A wide smile splayed across Walter Kincaid's face. "Aww, naw! No, you didn't hit that note, girl. You just made me fall in love with you! I ain't playin'!"

"Me too! Girl, you bad!" Reginald seconded. "I didn't know you were hiding all that!"

"Um. Um. Um," Reginald said before he winked at Walter. And Walter knew exactly what Reginald would say to him later in private. *"You better handle that, bro."*

Walter walked over and hugged Cherelle. "Girl, you got it going on. Forget the PowerPoint, I bet if we just cue up the music and let her sing for Number One, he'll probably give us a hundred million for these programs."

"For real," Reginald chimed in.

"Cherelle, you never cease to amaze me, baby! I'm so serious. God broke all kinds of molds when he made you! You are *it,* woman."

David strolled into the conference room looking like he stepped off a page in a men's fashion magazine. Cherelle moved away from Walter.

"Hey, David!" she said excitedly, walking toward him. They hugged briefly.

"Hey, Dupree. What's up?"

"We're getting ready for lunch. Let me run to the ladies' room."

Walter was still in awe. "Cherelle, girl. I. Am. Done. You have blown me away!"

Cherelle turned quickly and batted her eyes playfully. "Mr. Mayor! You've got to learn to keep some secrets!"

"Okay . . . okay. But, man . . . ooh wee!"

David smiled uncomfortably. He didn't like the camaraderie that was developing between Walter and Cherelle. He hid it easily. "What did I miss?" he asked in a tone laced with nonchalance.

Walter remembered what Cherelle said and chuckled. "Nothin', we were just messing around listening to some old-school tunes while we took a break from the project. Brought back some memories." It brought back memories all right—the ones Walter couldn't stop thinking about. He dreamed about Cherelle more frequently at night. "And she can cook?" Walter said to Reginald as he cut himself another slice of Cherelle's delicious apple pie. "You know her lovin' has got to be good!"

"Be respectful, Walt," David said.

"That's a compliment, DC."

"Some things a man needs to keep to himself."

"My bad, preacher."

When Cherelle returned from the restroom, David had

taken off his overcoat and suit jacket and draped them over the chair. His black tailored trousers and lilac dress shirt complemented his caramel skin color. Cherelle noticed everything about him, down to his initialed cuff links. She smiled. Walter's secretary, Alexis, had brought in their lunches, and David had already prepared Cherelle's plate. He'd taken the seat next to her laptop. He wanted to find out what the inside joke had been about.

Cherelle looked lovely. Even in a pair of jeans and a sweater, she was stylish. As soon as she sat down, David smelled her. Her aroma settled on him like magical fairy dust. Walter and Reginald were whispering about something. David didn't know what they were being so secretive about and didn't care. "Any changes to the presentation, Dupree?" he asked. "And by the way, the apple pie is delicious—almost better than my mom's."

"Thanks, David. And no, not many changes. Reginald just corrected the numbers. It looks really good. I'm nervous but excited."

"What are you nervous about? You speak in front of people all the time."

"I know, but this is different. It's not every day you get to speak to the President of the Free World."

"This will be our second meeting. You practically argued with the man at the last meeting," David teased.

"I was debating how much money it would take. Not arguing."

"I think he was smitten."

"Oh, please."

"And you know it was very rare for just the five of us to be there. Just you, me, Walt, Reginald, and the president. That was wild. I've only met with him alone once—right after the Time magazine thing."

"You're the one who's all chummy."

"No. It's just God. The Word says a man's gift will take him before great men."

Reginald snickered, and Cherelle wondered why until she heard the melody of Minnie Riperton's "Lovin' You" again. Walter had connected his playlist to the sound system.

Cherelle just smiled and tried not to make eye contact with Walter. He and Reginald were like two silly little kids. If she looked at him, she would burst into laughter, thinking about how the two of them banged up the high notes.

Walter sat back down at the table and winked at Cherelle. She winked back. That didn't get past David. He decided to ignore it and continued his conversation with her. "So what do you have planned this weekend?"

"Nothing much. I was thinking about—" The buzz of David's cell phone cut Cherelle's answer.

"Excuse me, Dupree," David said before answering his phone. "Hey, sweetheart. How are you feeling today? I didn't call earlier because I didn't want to wake you." Cherelle stared into her shrimp fried rice. Something about the way David said the word *sweetheart* shot chills through her. Her stomach ached with jealousy.

"Sure, sweetie. Is there anything else you need? No . . . it's no problem. No, babe. Don't worry about it. I'm going to bring my laptop so I can work there. I'll take care of you. I got you. Okay . . . got it. Halls cough drops. Cough medicine. Lentil soup—fresh from the Mediterranean grill in Hamtramck. Yeah, I know where it is."

Cherelle swallowed her feelings as another pang of jealousy pierced her. David's sweetness to the special *woman* on the other end of his cell was zapping her appetite. Extraordinarily attentive, his voice was gentle and caring. Cherelle was glad when he ended his call. She felt like she was bleeding internally. Especially when he ended with an *"I love you, see you soon."* Cherelle was sick to her stomach. David hadn't noticed, but the life had gone out of Cherelle. An hour and a half later, when the informal meeting was finally over, Walter worked his plan.

"I need to walk off all that good pie, Cherelle. You want to come take a short walk with me?" Walter Kincaid asked. "And Reg, you're welcome to join us," Walter said quickly. Reginald hid a sly smile. David smirked inwardly, not at all humored. Walt had just used *the code. "You're welcome to join us"* meant: You're *not* welcome. Cherelle was oblivious.

"Oh, no . . . You guys go ahead. I have to take care of some business and phone the wife," Reginald said. He knew exactly what Walt was up to, and he wanted to give him ample opportunity to make his move.

"Sure. No problem. That sounds good," Cherelle said. She stood and gathered her coat and purse. There was a pit in her stomach from David's conversation with *"her."*

As far as David was concerned, Cherelle was his friend. He cared about her. He knew Walter had no intentions toward Cherelle that weren't unquestionably self-gratifying in the end. David hoped Cherelle wasn't wooed by Walter's charm. By her admission, she hadn't had a relationship in over three years. That was a long time.

David hid his annoyance. "You guys enjoy," he said. He stood and removed his suit jacket and overcoat from the back of his chair and put them on. "Dupree, I'll check back with you later on the report for Number One."

"Okay. Talk to you later." Cherelle said as David exited.

Chapter 15

The Hair Thing

Dominique padded to the door with her Glock. She'd instinctively picked it up when she heard the loud knocking. She wasn't aware that the battery in her doorbell needed replacing. Her home had been broken into just two weeks ago, and she wasn't taking any chances. Spying through the peephole, she saw David's handsome face smiling back.

Dominique opened the door. The supposed-to-be-fitted stretch pants she was wearing were sagging. She looked frail. David had been out of town and hadn't seen her in a week and a half. Her petite frame was emaciated, and her normally bright eyes were dim. But in David's heart, she was still beautiful. "Hey you," he said when Dominique opened her screen door. David stepped in and locked the screen behind him. Then he closed and locked her entry door. Gently, he reached down to Dominique's side, covered her soft hand with his, and removed the gun from her hand. "You don't need this for me, beautiful," he said. He kissed her forehead. Being an undercover country boy, he was used to handling firearms. He'd proven that when

179

he outshot her at the gun range. Dominique couldn't help but crave him after that.

David hugged Dominique's body softly without pressing too firmly against her. He knew he'd brought Michigan's mid-March chill in with him. He set the bags on the counter and walked Dominique upstairs to her bedroom with his arm around her tiny waist. He placed the gun back in the night-stand safe where she kept it. Dominique loved that David was comfortable handling firearms. They made some of the men she'd dated feel intimidated, but handling firearms safely and using them—if necessary—was a part of her career, which made them a big part of her life.

David noticed a man's watch in the drawer. It may have been there for a while. It may have even been Dominique's. He'd seen her wearing men's watches before. On her, they looked feminine. It worked well with her sexy, tough-girl persona. Although he tended to be possessive and jealous in non-threatening ways, he didn't read too much into it. He closed the drawer.

"Get back in bed, sweetheart. I'll bring everything up to you," he said. Dominique complied with no "mouth" today. Moments later, David was in Dominique's kitchen re-heating her soup. He carried it up on a tray with her cough drops and cough medicine. Dominique sat up in bed when David reen-tered her bedroom.

Her voice was hoarse from constant coughing. "Thank you, Dave," she said.

"No problem, sweetheart." David took the cough medicine bottle, unscrewed the top, and filled the tiny cup. "Here, sweet-heart, take this," he said, extending the cup to her. Dominique took the cup from him and gulped the medicine down, making an ugly, disapproving face in the process. She looked like a contrary, but cute three-year-old.

David chuckled. "You whimpin' out on me?"

"Yes."

David kissed her lips lovingly. "Shameful," he said. Then he handed her the tray and sat down in the chair across from her bed—the one she usually tossed her clothes onto once she shed them. David watched her sip the soup.

"Come sit next to me, Dave." Dominique's voice sounded raspy, and David found it sexy.

"Are you sure?"

"Yes, I think I'm past the contamination phase," she joked.

"Baby, I ain't afraid of nothin'. I've been taking that cod liver oil my mom used to give me as a boy. It *scares* germs away."

David climbed atop Dominique's bed and scooted in close to her. Dominique turned up the television volume. She resumed watching the CSI shows she'd recorded with her DVR. David fell asleep within minutes. Dominique followed suit. David awoke two hours later, snuggled next to Dominique underneath the covers with his slacks on. He'd taken off his dress shirt and was wearing a white T-shirt. Dominique stirred in his lap. David played in the section of her hair that had freed itself from the hair band she'd tried to tame it with. It had frizzed and was swelling moment by moment.

With gentle, skilled hands, David massaged Dominique's scalp. He loved women's hair. He still remembered when he was a young boy, barely in preschool, how his mother Leah would bend down and talk to him. David held a memory of being captivated by her sweet-smelling hair. He often sniffed and patted it as a sign of affection. The smell of it was comforting. Now, he found comfort in the smell of Dominique's hair. It was a different kind of comfort than he'd experienced as a boy. It was a sensual sensation. Dominique stirred. Her lion's mane covered her face. She took a patch of loose strands and smelled them. "I stink," she said, almost embarrassed.

"Not to me," David said groggily.

"Yes, I do."

"Nope. You just smell *sick*. You've been sweating. That's natural when you're sick in bed with a bunch of covers, sweating out a cold."

"I need a shower," Dominique said. She moved and sat up in bed. She took another section of her hair and brought it to her nose.

"Yuck."

David couldn't help but smile. She looked so beautiful in her natural state. No make-up. No pretense. All woman. To him, she was flawless this way.

"Will you help me with it?"

"Your hair?"

"Yes."

"Sure. What do you want me to do?"

"Help me wash it. It's like a *wholenother* species."

"I can manage that. How do you usually wash it?"

Dominique laughed. She seemed to have gained some of her strength back. Maybe all it took was for her to see him again. Be in his presence. Feel his love. "Well, seeing as I haven't bathed in two days—" Dominique started.

"Ewe!" David teased, scrunching his nose.

Dominique took a pillow and swatted him. "Hush. I didn't have any energy. And I usually wash my hair in the shower, babe."

"Well, I don't think I can manage that, sweetheart."

"You can get in the shower with me, Dave."

It took a moment for David to process what Dominique had just said. He stared at her for a moment. "No. I can't. How about you take a shower and I wash your hair after you're done?"

"What's the matter—you don't trust yourself with me, Dave? I don't even have the energy to make lo—"

David was serious and firm in his response. He looked directly into Dominique's eyes and shook his head. "No," he said.

Dominique pressed anyway. "Dave," she countered, with her head tilted, "are you serious?" She knew he was.

David took her hands in his. "Nik, there is *no* way I can undress and get in the shower with you. There is no way I can *be* in the shower with you while you're naked—even if I had on twenty layers of clothing, sweetheart. I'm still a man . . . and I need to handle us a certain way—a godly way. Okay?"

"Okay. I understand, Dave," Dominique said. But her eyes told David that she didn't understand completely.

Dominique got out of bed and headed into her master bathroom. David heard the spray of water. He heard Dominique opening and closing drawers in the bathroom. He heard her electric toothbrush. It wasn't until he knew that she was in the shower that he relaxed. Just the mere thought of what she'd suggested had caused his body to respond in a way that he wished it hadn't. "Jesus," David said, rubbing his temples. A "need" headache had sneaked up on him. Talk about torture.

Dominique emerged from the bathroom twenty minutes later smelling lovely. By that time, David's body had finally complied with his will. But the scent of warm vanilla body lotion or perfume or whatever it was that was permeating throughout the room now that Dominique was standing a few feet away from him was driving him crazy with longing. She was wearing a short robe. David's imagination was starting to get the best of him. He needed to meditate on Philippians 4:8 in its entirety. His mind was treading in dangerous waters.

"Hey, I'll meet you down in the kitchen. I'll wash your hair in the kitchen sink—old school," David joked. He had to get out of her room. He didn't want Dominique to take off her robe in front of him. He had a feeling that she might, and he didn't want to see what he wanted to see. He picked up the serving tray before leaving the room. Downstairs, David washed the bowl and silverware and placed them back inside the cabinet. "Don't forget the shampoo and stuff, babe," he called upstairs to Dominique.

Dominique shuffled downstairs in a pair of yoga pants and a fitted T-shirt. David was grateful that she was mostly covered. It made no difference to his body, however. The thought had already taken root. Dominique sashayed over to the sink and handed David bottles of shampoo and conditioner. He placed them both on the counter.

Skepticism danced in Dominique's eyes. "I see you think you know what you're doing," she said.

"You'd be surprised."

What Dominique didn't know was that David was nothing like the 'boring old preacher' she'd wrongly assumed he was when they first met. He'd had his share of women in his days before Christ. And he had learned to do everything he needed to do to get what he wanted from them, including washing their hair.

Dominique had no clue as to how sensual it was for David to wash a woman's hair, and no clue that he was very skilled at the task. David turned on the water and put his hand under the stream to test the temperature. Satisfied, he said, "Okay, bend over a little farther, sweetheart." Dominique scooted closer to the sink with her head pointed face down. Why had he asked her to do that? *Stop.* David took the hose and gently sprayed the warm water over Dominique's hair. He saturated the mass with water before squeezing a glob of shampoo onto it and slathering it in like a professional. He massaged her scalp as he worked the shampoo through her long hair that had transformed into tight curls and waves.

Dominique moaned in pure satisfaction. David's strong, loving hands felt good. She was unaware of how enticing her moans were. Maybe this hair-washing thing wasn't such a good idea. How could something as innocent and simple as washing her hair do this to his body? David avoided getting too close to her. He was glad she couldn't witness the effect she was having on his body. "Jesus," David said quietly to himself. He washed her hair twice. The second time, he scratched her scalp well, which elicited more moans from Dominique.

"It never feels this good when I do it. You're almost as good as Anshelle," Dominique said, referring to the hair stylist she saw only a few times a year. Her swell of hair created a sound barrier that caused her voice to sound muffled. But David understood what she'd said.

"You're not me, and Anshelle doesn't make house visits with soup and cough medicine."

"I know, right?"

David blotted her hair with a towel and added conditioner. He worked it through and massaged her scalp. Her hair smelled soapy-clean and flowery. David lifted Dominique's head, and she stood in front of him.

"Okay, ma'am, that will be three hundred dollars," David teased.

"Dang, you're pretty expensive."

"That's because I give the best service."

Dominique smiled. "Yes, you do." She stood on her tiptoes and kissed David. He reciprocated and received her tongue. It was the first time David had kissed Dominique like *this*. Deeply. Passionately. He felt himself traveling to the edge of his boundary line. Dominique wrapped her arms around his neck and savored his kisses. She pulled back a bit and looked up at him so that she could see if she had affected him the way he affected her.

"I'm afraid I'm going to have to leave soon, so I can uh . . . stay focused . . ." David said quietly, willing his heart rate back down to a normal level.

Dominique seemed satisfied with his response, pleased to know he was *human*. Attracted to her. "Not until after you blow-dry me," she said.

"Okay . . . but no more kissing, sweetheart. I'm at the end of my rope today."

"Okay," Dominique said sincerely, "I respect you and what you're about, Dave."

"Thank you."

Dominique put a plastic cap on her head and set the kitchen timer for twenty minutes.

She motioned David over to the sofa, where she continued to catch up on her CSI shows until it was time for him to perform the arduous task of blow-drying her hair. She didn't have the strength to do it herself. David left shortly after he was done. He couldn't deny that touching Dominique's hair had been a sensually pleasurable act that had taken him to the edge of his self-control.

Chapter 16

Love Awakened

Dominique convinced David to accompany her to a birthday party for one of her SWAT members. David was immersed in her world now. Although they had no official label, they often went out as a couple. David had met Dominique's mother and most of her friends, so he knew she felt *something* for him. Her cautiousness didn't scare him. He, too, was taking his time. He thought about all of it as he danced close to Dominique in the basement of Elliot "Bag Man" Kirk's plush Sherwood Forest home. Elliot had been given the nickname Bag Man because he was a sharpshooter. Dominique bragged that if Elliot shot someone, the poor soul would leave the scene in a body bag.

Elliot's lower level looked like a nightclub. It was a party pad. Ordinarily, David would have said no to any such outing. Dominique had persuaded him by telling him it was a get-together. But there was way more going on at Elliot's than David expected. It was an all-out club scene. David might as well have been at a nightclub. The smell of cigars and marijuana permeated throughout the basement. Dominique promised him that they wouldn't stay long. She seemed happy just to have David with her in her world.

Dancing close to Dominique gave David an inebriated feeling likened to a sweet shot of Jamaican rum. He hadn't drunk socially since he was in his twenties, but being this close to Dominique reminded him of the feeling. In subtle ways, she teasingly unraveled his spiritual resolve. David inhaled the scent of Dominique's perfume, and he could distinguish it from the sultry smell of her warm skin. Her hair. Her scent. It permeated his nostrils, casting a drunken spell on him.

He had successfully kept *certain* thoughts at bay until lately. Dominique lifted her head off his chest and stared deeply into his eyes. David saw the wanting in those dark globes. The electric charge of Dominique's eyes meeting with his arrested David's body. She locked her arms around his neck and swayed to the music. With Dominique pressed so closely against him, David felt as if he were prey in a sensual web of desire. Again, she stared into his eyes, relishing erotic musings that David couldn't respond to despite the wanting he felt. The heaviness of his thoughts gave David a mild headache.

David knew that Dominique couldn't possibly comprehend what she was doing to him. He had to stay level-headed and concentrate on the sound of God's voice and not the sultry begging of Dominique's body. He was careful to hold her without caressing her. He needed to make sure that he was appropriate in public and in private. It was important to him because it was important to God.

The end of the song provided him some modicum of relief, and Dominique made good on her promise not to stay too long. She had volunteered to drive tonight, so she dropped David off at his home. "That wasn't so bad, was it?" she asked when she pulled into the driveway of David's North Rosedale Park

Tudor. It was a few blocks away from his mother and stepfather's home.

"Other than the weed and the cigar smoke, no."

"Everyone's not on your level, Dave. They're good people. I just wanted you with me."

"Nik, I was glad to be with you. It wasn't that bad."

"Partying is not something I do often. I just like to support my teammates. We're family. I don't smoke or do drugs. I might have an occasional social drink, but that's it, Dave . . ."

"Nik, I know who you are. You don't have to explain yourself to me. I get you."

"Do you?"

"Yes, I do."

"Let me get in the house. I've got a meeting with the mayor in the morning. It's formal, so I need to be on point."

"You mind if I come in and use the restroom?"

"No. That's no problem. Come on in."

David sat on his living room sofa waiting to walk Dominique out to her car, so he could get some much-needed sleep. When Dominique returned from the restroom, she had a peculiar look on her face.

"Nik, is something wrong?"

"I know you're tired, Dave. But can I please talk to you for a minute?"

". . . Uh . . . sure, sweetheart. What's going on?"

Dominique sat in the chair closest to David. He could tell from the look on her face that something was bothering her. She wrung her hands and stared at him, then sat without speaking.

"Nik, what is it?"

Dominique took in a deep breath and rationed it out. Fixing her eyes on David's, she finally spoke. "Are you gay?" she asked. The question imposed itself like a misfit in the silence. The absurdity of it caused David to sit still in disbelief. It had to be some sort of obnoxious joke. Dominique's eyes bore through David's with all the seriousness she intended. She waited for his answer, her eyes never diverting from his. She held him in a direct stare. She repeated herself. "Are. You. *Gay?*"

In a split second, David's mood metamorphosed from disbelief to anger. What was it about women these days? When a man respected them, showed them that he was different and not just out to conquer them, they assumed he was gay. Dominique's accusation incensed him. Didn't she know that in his days before Christ, he was known as David "Cold-as-Ice" Cole? He had never had a problem getting a woman or taking one to bed. As much as he'd tried to believe that Dominique was different, she was just as damaged as some of the other women he had encountered.

Since when did demonstrating self-control equate to being *gay?* David tried to squelch his anger. He'd been showering Dominique with nothing but love and respect. Her lack of reciprocity, compounded by David's ever-increasing sexual frustration, sent him flying over the edge. He rose to his feet. "No, Dominique, I am *not* gay! Are you kidding me?" His cool demeanor had been vanquished by her insult.

His voice rose to a chastising level. "First of all, can you please tell me *exactly* what I've done to make you even ask me something like that? We've been dating for over six months, and I would think by now you would know me better. I've been nothing but a gentleman with you. I have respected you and my God to the very best of my abilities. I'm not sure what is going on in your twisted little mind. Maybe you were right. Maybe we're just too different. Two different people. Two different worlds. You don't know me, and obviously, you are not trying to get to know me. I'm going to bed. Good night. Thank you. You're welcome."

Dominique evaluated David's disposition carefully. She had to be sure that he wasn't showing any signs of undue nervousness. She judged David's body language for any tell-tale signs that he might be lying about his sexual orientation. But she observed none. All her senses told her that David was being honest. And he was teed off. She'd never seen him this way.

David switched off the lamps in his living room as he always did before he went to bed. He had a meeting with the mayor in the morning, and he didn't have time for Dominique's garbage. Did she even understand the type of self-control it took to lie next to her and not touch her? Who was he kidding? It was apparent that he did need a woman who was more spiritually like-minded. Still, he didn't want to be rude to her.

"Look, I've got a meeting in the morning. I'll talk to you later. Let yourself out, please—and lock the door behind you." David said. He headed toward the beaming wood staircase that led to the second floor. Dominique heard the aged, creaking sound of the wood floor beneath him as he ascended each stair. She regretted that she'd upset him. She rose from the sofa and pursued him.

"Dave, wait! I'm sorry!" Dominique called to him from the bottom of the stairs. David was halfway up. He stopped and sighed heavily, but didn't turn around to face her. He wanted Dominique to go home; he had no more words for her tonight. He planned to deal with her tomorrow after he'd processed all of her nonsense and wasn't so exhausted. "Just listen for a minute, please . . ." Dominique begged. David turned and glared at her from his elevated position on the staircase. "Look, I didn't know what else to think," Dominique explained.

"We've been dating for a while now, and . . . you haven't even tried *anything*. The other night, you didn't even *touch* me."

David descended the stairs hurriedly. His anger had not at all waned. "Are you serious, woman?" He took in a deep breath. Let it go. Repeated the process. "Nik, I was respecting you! First of all, I didn't think it was a good idea for me to spend the night at your place, but I did because you practically begged me to. Honestly, that stretched me a bit, but I handled myself! You're the one who made a point of telling me about your past relationships and what you *don't* want in a man. I've been trying to meet you where you are, and be a man of God at the same time, Nik. If that causes you to think I'm gay, then you need to grow up, sweetheart," David said. "Surely if I had pawed all over you, you would have assumed that all men are alike, and lumped me as a *pastor*, right in the same boat as the rest of the scoundrels. I didn't want you to do that, because that's *not* who I am!"

David lowered his voice a few decibels and spoke as calmly as he could. "Dominique, you are a beautiful woman, and I physically desire you—trust me, I do. But I've been trying to ensure that I didn't put the cart before the horse. I thought I made myself *clear* when we first met."

He couldn't believe he was having this conversation with her. He truly regretted that she had asked him such a foolish question because up until that moment, he was quite sure he had fallen in love with her. Dominique ruined what had otherwise been a beautiful evening. Dancing with her, holding her the way he had at the party, confirmed what David had been fighting. It wasn't just the sexual feelings he'd been holding at bay. He'd been trying to avoid admitting to himself that he was in love with her because she'd been keeping him at an emotional distance. Love never worked under those circumstances.

Despite their differences, Dominique's free spirit was attractive to David. He loved the way she listened without bias. She didn't put him on some sort of pedestal like people tended to do, nor did she condemn him for being human. It seemed that knowing he was a pastor caused people to either treat him with disdain and cloudy suspicion, or like he was some holy anomaly. He was neither; he was just a man. Dominique understood that. She was a safe harbor from everything in his sometimes complicated world of demands and servitude.

Dominique humbled herself. "Dave, I'm really sorry. I wasn't trying to offend you. I've felt closer to you than any man I've known in my adult life. And yet, a part of me is still trying to figure you out. On the one hand, I'm so drawn to you. I find myself wondering what you're doing. What you're thinking about. And that is not me. I've had a string of short-term relationships because I just like to stay in my box, Dave. It minimizes the pain. Not opening up and trusting another person minimizes the *pain* . . .

"And it's crazy because I wonder about my hair, what I'm wearing—if you'll like it. Another part of me feels like I'm trying to be something I'm not—like I can't fit in your world. And I want to, Dave. Honestly, when you didn't touch me the other night, for the first time in a long while, I felt 'not good enough.' I know what you said about being on your walk with God, but I felt like you didn't *want* me. And that . . . hurt. I don't know what to think or how to feel anymore . . ." Dominique's body shook, and tears trailed their way down her soft cheeks.

Embarrassed, she wiped her tears with the backs of her hands, but each time more followed. Her strong emotional wall was crumbling. She had unwillingly lowered her shield. David could see the frightened little girl who'd been abandoned by her father. That was the betrayal that caused her to distrust all men and flee committed relationships, even one with God.

And as hard as she'd tried, she couldn't remain distant when it came to David. She wanted to bask in the love he had been showing her. More tears flowed, and Dominique turned away. She scurried to his front door, but David was right on her heels. She had unlocked and cracked open the huge wooden door David had recently re-varnished. He walked up behind her and gently pushed the door shut again.

"Nik, why are you crying?" he asked in a compassionate, soothing voice, softened by Dominique's vulnerable disposition. She refused to turn around and face him. She kept her face to the door. Her nose touched the deep crevices of the wood-carved designs in the center, and the fresh varnish drifted up her nostrils. Her eyes stung with tears—tears she didn't want David to see. He'd broken her down.

David reached out with tender hands and turned Dominique so that she faced him. Even with blood-red eyes, she was beautiful. Without a word, he kissed her face. He acknowledged every wet spot on her face with his lips. He cupped her face in his hands and smiled at her. "Talk to me, sweetheart," he said.

Trembling, Dominique shook her head. "It doesn't matter, Dave. Nothing matters anymore . . ."

"Nik, everything matters with us. *Talk* to me. *Please*, sweetheart. Tell me what's really going on."

Dominique drew in a breath and looked up at David. "This whole thing with us is driving me crazy. I'm not ready for this, Dave," Dominique said. She tried to keep herself from crying, but she couldn't. "I don't want to do this . . ." she repeated.

"Do what, Nik? What are you saying?"

"Dave, we're just getting too *close*! I just . . . I just want to go slowly."

David was sincerely confused. Wasn't she the woman who just a few minutes ago asked him if he was gay because he hadn't *touched* her in six months? "Sweetheart, I've been taking it slowly. I don't know what you mean."

"What is wrong with you? Don't you get it? This is too much for me!"

"*What* is too much, Nik? Please help me to understand. I want to understand you, sweetheart . . . " David pleaded.

"Feeling like this . . . like you can hurt me," Dominique said. She looked away, shamed by her confession.

David placed his fingers under Dominique's chin and turned her face back to his. He held her in a gaze that pleaded for understanding. "Nik, why would I ever hurt you? I don't want to hurt you, sweetheart. I'm *not* going to hurt you. Why would I do that to you? I've been giving you one hundred percent of me, showing you that I'm not like some of these other clowns out here. I want to give you something special—something real."

"Dave, I don't even know if I fit in your world. I love you, but I—"

Dominique's words caused David's entire train of thought to pause. "You *what?*" he asked after a few moments of hesitation. He'd first confessed those words to her a month ago, but she'd never said them back.

"I don't know if I fit in your world—" Dominique started. She purposely avoided repeating what David needed to hear again. She wished she hadn't let the words slip in the first place.

"And you *love* me?"

Dominique closed her eyes and inhaled again. "I don't want to love you, but I can't help but love you. And I need . . . you to love and want me too, Dave . . ." Tears flowed. Dominique tried to stop the flow by squeezing her eyes shut. She refused to open them. She refused to look at him.

"Nik, I *do* love you, sweetheart. That's what I've been trying to show you all this time."

Dominique's eyes snapped open. "But Dave, half the time I can't even read you. I'm not some sanctified church woman. I've been wondering, when you don't touch me or kiss me, is it really because of your faith, or is it just that you want something more? Something that I don't have. You're a pastor. I don't know anything about being with a pastor—I've never even read the Bible all the way through. I'm sure there are a million women at your church who could fit in and do all the right things. This is just too heavy for me, Dave . . ."

David calmed Dominique with an embrace, and she cried into his chest. She was afraid of loving. It surely made everything transparent for him. At least it explained why she'd been acting so strangely, even accusing him of being gay. *She's afraid of loving.* "Listen to me . . ." David said, cupping her face in his hands again. "I love you—just the way you are, Nik. You are *enough* for me. I'm crazy about you, woman. I just want to show you something different. That's all." He rested his forehead against hers.

Dominique inched back and searched David's eyes with her own. "I want to be yours . . ." she admitted in a soft, disarming voice. There was no denying what she meant. Just hearing her speak those words ignited a slow fire in David that abounded with every passing second. David's deep black eyes studied Dominique through lowered lids that were evidence of his arousal.

"No, Nik . . . I can't—we can't . . ." he said, breathing huskily into her ear. But David's body had its own desires. And at that moment, he had become more keenly aware of Dominique's sweet-smelling scent and the softness of her skin as he held her hands in his and brushed his nose against her neck.

Dominique responded to David's rebuttal by unzipping her jacket. She shrugged it off slowly and leaned back against the door. "Let me be yours, Dave. I want to be yours . . ." she repeated. And without thinking, David devoured Dominique in fiery, forbidden kisses that should have been harnessed until God's perfect timing. He allowed the urgent longing of his flesh to suppress his spirit. David took Dominique's hand and led her upstairs to his bedroom.

Chapter 17

After

David kneeled in front of his shower bench and prayed with a broken heart. The steady stream of water beat on his body from all directions, and he let his tears fall. His spirit was crushed by his wayward actions. A deep crater settled in the middle of his heart. David's voice quivered as he prayed. "My God . . . I humbly ask that you please forgive the sins of the flesh. Please do not move an angry hand against me, Lord, God."

Unlike other times in his life, David didn't have to rehash last night's events to know that he'd done all the wrong things. He had invited sin into his heart first and then into his bed. Yet, his heart loved Dominique. Nevertheless, as much love as he felt for her, he was undeniably heartbroken over the fact that he had defiled the very temple of God. Sincere tears streamed down his cheeks. A man's tears. "You have given me so many gifts and blessings—including Nik, Father. And I have failed You. I have failed every ministry under my leadership, and I've failed at being what I should have been for Nik. I'm so sorry . . . I love her. Please touch my heart and remove the things that

separate me from You. You, and You only, are my all and all—
my everything . . . In Jesus' name, I pray. Amen."

David dressed in his walk-in closet, robbed of his usual zest.
He walked out into his bedroom where Dominique slept,
tangled in a sea of white linen sheets. Parts of her bare body
were exposed. Those images curled around David's mind. He
looked away to quell the longing caused by the very thought of
her. Moving in slow motion, David walked over to the huge
dresser that he'd inherited from his grandfather and opened his
grandfather's small men's chest, which sat on top. He pulled
out a random pair of cuff links and looked back at Dominique.

Dominique stirred. Her long hair had swelled from their
interlude last night and had returned to its natural state of curls
and waves. David walked over to the bed and sat down.
Dominique's thigh peeked out from under the sheet. He shook
her gently. "Hey . . . I have to leave." Dominique awakened
slowly. David repeated himself. "I have to leave, Nik."

There was a distinctive sadness in Dominique's eyes. She
had been through this routine before with so many other men.
The morning after. When morning came, as politely as possible,
men always gave a cue that it was time for her to leave. Sometimes, they lied and said they had errands to run, and other
times they just said, *"So, I'll see you soon . . ."* No matter what
their method was, there was always *the cue.*

Dominique sat up slowly. "Give me five minutes, and I'll
get out of your way," she said.

David was surprised by the flatness of her tone. He
wondered if she had plans. "Um . . . do you have plans today?"

"No, but I guess you do."

David couldn't read her. "Sweetheart, remember last night,
I told you about the meeting with the mayor this morning?"

"Yeah . . . let me get dressed," Dominique said. She
wrapped herself loosely in the sheet and stood up. She didn't

want David to view her nakedness now. She felt utterly embarrassed as she reached down and retrieved her clothing from the tufted bench at the end of David's bed.

David stood. He could no longer avert his eyes. Dominique looked so beautiful. He made every mental effort to suppress last night's memories. "We need to talk when I get back," he said.

"Give me a call later," Dominique said dispassionately. She brushed past David as she entered his master bathroom.

David caught her gently by the arm. "Hey . . . you don't have to leave. I'll be back in a couple of hours. You can wait for me. I'd prefer that. I really want us to talk."

Dominique lied. "I have a lot of things to do, Dave."

Something in David's gut told him that Dominique felt like he was discarding her. She didn't know how much he loved her. And there was no way David could share the depths of his heart right now. There was not enough time and not enough words. "Nik, please stay. It's important to me that you do."

"Let's not make something out of nothing, David."

David moved closer to Dominique, fighting the urge to wrap his arms around her and show her what he was feeling right now. "Why would you say something like that, Nik? Last night was special to me. You are special to me, sweetheart. I love you." He placed a lingering kiss on her forehead before glancing at his watch. "Sweetheart, I've got to run. Please stay. Make yourself comfortable," he said, backing out of his bedroom.

* * *

DAVID WASN'T FULLY ENGAGED in the meeting. Instinctively, Cherelle took over. His mind was reeling with thoughts of his and Dominique's sin. He was painfully disappointed in himself. He knew better. How could he have let it happen? He'd given in to every unholy desire, and now he'd ruined his witness and possibly pushed Dominique away from Christ. Surely, she thought he was no different than any other man now. His being a pastor and a Christian probably no longer mattered to her.

The humiliated look on Dominique's face earlier that morning told a story of shame. David knew good and well that wasn't the way a person should feel after they'd made love to someone they loved and trusted. The moment had been cheapened by his lust. Why didn't he just tell Dominique, *"no"* last night? His mind was scattered.

David stared at Cherelle's purity ring. She'd been toying with it during the meeting. *True. Love. Waits.* But David hadn't waited, and the thought made him nauseous. He'd vomited this morning, just thinking about how he'd turned his back on what was right in God's eyesight. As soon as his and Dominique's physical coupling was over, David was filled with grief. He'd felt sick to his stomach. His relationship with God was real. He wasn't just a mouthpiece. He loved Christ. Yet, he had failed miserably and caused someone else to sin in the process.

"David, what's wrong?" Cherelle asked quietly as soon as their break started.

"Uh . . . just a lot on my mind, Dupree."

"Oh . . . is there something I can help you with?"

"No. Just a few things I need to pray about. And I'm not feeling too well either. No worries, Dupree."

"Okay. Well, if there is something I can do, just let me know."

"Okay, will do," David returned. *She has such a beautiful spirit.*

David couldn't help but reaffirm that Cherelle was truly a woman of God. Her conversation was always fitting. She spoke of Christ often and tried to model her life after His. Even though she had expressed that she dealt with loneliness from time to time, she had committed herself to celibacy and waiting to share herself with only her husband. She spoke of it proudly with excitement. "When the Lord sends me my man of God, I promise I am going to make up for lost time," she had joked with him once. He admired her for her convictions. David felt like an impostor sitting next to Cherelle.

He watched as Walter sidled up to her and flirted openly. Cherelle handled him politely and walked out of the conference room. David watched Walter lust after Cherelle's body, eyeing her from head to toe as she exited. Cherelle returned five minutes later, and Walter licked his lips teasingly. Cherelle hadn't noticed because she was texting. She bumped into Reginald.

"Oh, I'm so sorry . . ." Cherelle said.

"You're good. Don't walk and text," Reginald teased.

Cherelle laughed. "Right."

Cherelle took her seat next to David. Walter stepped out. He poked his head back into the conference room. "Reg, we have an update on the flight arrangements. I need your help."

Reginald hurried into Walter's inner office and closed the door behind him.

Cherelle was glued to her phone.

"You texting someone important, Dupree?" David kidded, trying to take his mind off the weightier matters in his life.

"Just Lynn."

"Oh, I thought you were scheduling a hot date."

"Nah. I don't think it's in the cards for me to date right now. The last one was a complete wash. But at least he was honest."

"Oh, are you talking about Johnathan—the guy you met at the writer's conference?"

"Yes. He said he wasn't 'into celibacy' and that he was 'looking for something *else.*'"

"Wow. What he meant is that he's looking for someone to have his way with, without a commitment," David offered.

"Basically. But it's okay because we got that out of the way on the first date—he brought it up."

"Well, you deserve to have a man who's going to be committed to Christ, and therefore committed to honoring *you* by keeping you pure until you are married." David felt like a hypocrite as soon as he'd said the words. But he meant it. He knew Cherelle was a quality woman. She deserved nothing less than God's best for her life.

"I'm just waiting, David. I know it will happen when it's time . . ."

"It will."

David texted Dominique.

> David: Hey, where are you?

> Dominique: Out and about.

> David: I want to talk. Can I see you after my meeting?

> Dominique: Not in the mood for a lot of talking, Dave.

David sighed. Dominique probably assumed he had brushed her off earlier that morning, and now she was returning the favor.

> David: Can I just come see you, spend some time with you? PLEASE.

Dominique: Sure.

David: Okay. I'll be by after the meeting in
about an hour.

Dominique: Ok.

* * *

"Hey . . . you look pretty," David said as soon as
Dominique opened her door. She stepped back a few paces to
allow him in. He had a bag full of snacks.

"You didn't have to bring anything," she said.

"I wanted to," he said, kissing her on the cheek. He put the
bag on the counter and hung up his coat.

"I was watching TV upstairs in the bedroom."

David looked Dominique over and noticed the way her
yoga pants clung to her body and the way her loose curls flowed
past her shoulders, and decided it would be best if he didn't
enter her bedroom.

"Is it okay if we sit down here?"

Dominique rolled her eyes subtly. "I guess. What's up,
Dave?"

"I want to talk about last night."

Dominique walked toward the sofa and plopped down. "I
thought I told you earlier that I *didn't* feel like talking."

David followed. "I'm sorry. It's just that I have some things
on my mind, and I need you to hear me out."

Dominique sighed heavily. "This is so unnecessary. It
happened, and it's over. One and done, you know? We had an
exchange. I made you feel good, you made me feel good. And
now it's done, okay?"

David stilled himself. He calculated his response thoughtfully. "Nik, I'm not sure what's all on your mind, but I want to let you know that last night wasn't a fling for me. I in no way intended for us to be intimate at this juncture in our relationship. I love you. I enjoy your company, but last night, I went against everything I stand for. And for that, I am truly sorry. I didn't represent Christ to you. You mean so much more to me than what we shared last night…"

Aggravated, Dominique said, "So what do you want, Dave? Just say whatever it is you want to say."

"Nik, I can't be sexually involved with you anymore. I have to obey God and protect the ministries He has placed under my leadership. I can't be duplicitous. It hurts my heart to hurt God. Last night, what we did hurt God—grieved Him. I don't want to live like that. I can't live like that."

"Dave, we don't ever have to see each other again if you don't want to."

"That's not what I'm saying, Nik. I want to continue seeing you. I hope you want to continue to see me. I just can't allow us to fornicate. It's not right."

"Fine. Is that all?"

"Nik, why are you being so mean and unfeeling? I'm trying to let you know what's on my heart. And I'm just trying to do right by God."

"You know what, Dave? If you don't want to see me again, just say that. Don't come in here with this *God* stuff! I don't see how you're any different from anyone else. I did everything last night to show you how I feel about you. If you don't want me, it's fine. You can go now."

"Nik, what are you talking about? Who said I *didn't want* you? I never said that, sweetheart. Come on, what's going on with you? All I'm saying is: I want to do things right between us. I'm not trying to leave you. I love you."

"Dave, you made me feel like a prostitute this morning. You basically put me out."

Damaged. She's damaged. David took in a deep breath. "Sweetheart, I'm so sorry. Please hear me out. That was not my intention. If I made you feel that way, I am truly sorry. I mean it. I love you, and I would never hurt you purposely. I thought I had shared with you that I had a meeting with the mayor early this morning. I wanted you to stay. Nik, I asked you to stay. You said you had some things to do. Remember?"

"What was I supposed to say, Dave? I felt like you were getting rid of me."

David held her hands in his. "Sweetheart, I apologize. Please forgive me. That's not what I was doing, Nik. I was just trying to make sure I made it to the meeting on time. I was just rushing. Please, please forgive me."

Dominique didn't want to cry in front of David again. This is exactly what she'd been afraid of—him controlling her emotions. But last night, something powerful had happened between them that went beyond the physical. She felt it. David had to have felt it too. "I don't know what to say . . ."

"Do you forgive me?"

Dominique searched David's eyes for sincerity. "Yes. I love you, Dave. I love you so much . . ." she said, locking her arms around David's neck and squeezing him close.

"I love you, too, Nik. Believe me, I do," David said into Dominique's ear. Feeling her tears against his face, he caressed her, and Dominique nestled snugly against his body. He needed her in every way right now. It took only moments for David to submit to the feelings he'd been fighting since he left her this morning. He succumbed to the fact that Dominique would be his toughest spiritual battle yet, as he gave in to his flesh again.

Chapter 18

Save Me

David was exhausted. His whole body ached from physical exertion and a lack of sleep for the past few days. He had preached more funerals, attended more meetings, and more youth events than was humanly possible without collapsing. He'd successfully made it home out of the April snowstorm that had shut down the city area by area. He sat in his garage and contemplated getting out and heading straight to bed, but his body rebelled. "Lord, thank you for the blessings," he said quietly. He'd learned a long time ago that it was better to have people call on you to do things than not. It spoke of his character and the calling on his life. He closed his eyes for a moment, but he fought the drowsiness. He remembered a story about a doctor who unintentionally killed himself when he fell asleep in his garage with his engine running.

He turned off his engine. Then he chided himself when he remembered that he'd run out of coffee. He couldn't start his Saturday morning without a cup of straight black coffee. He hit the remote, and the garage door lifted. He started the engine again. He would have to go to a nearby twenty-four-hour drugstore and get some coffee. As tired as he was, David knew that he'd be cranky in the morning if he didn't have a cup of straight black. It would ruin his entire Saturday. He backed out, noticing how much it had snowed in the few minutes he'd been sitting in the garage. The entire neighborhood was blanketed.

David's cell rang through his car speakers. It was Cherelle. "Dupree . . . I hope you're someplace nice and warm. The roads are terrible," David said.

All he heard was ragged breathing. It sounded like she was crying.

"Dupree?"

Cherelle's voice was strained. "David . . . I need help . . . can you come . . . get me . . . please?"

"Dupree, what's the matter?"

"I've been in an accident . . . . I hit a tree, and the car slid over into a ditch. I walked to a gas station. They said it would take about three hours to get towed. I'm cold and—"

David panicked. "You okay? You need to get to a hospital?"

"I'm okay. I just need you to come get me . . . please, David."

"Cherelle, where are you? What are you doing out in this weather?"

Cherelle sobbed. "A friend asked me to meet him at his place farther north . . . he said he needed to talk . . . and then things got crazy . . ."

David wanted to know who 'he' was. "What kind of man would have you outside in this weather? They've been asking people to stay off the streets for hours," David said, frustrated by the man whom he wished he could lay his hands on at the moment. He couldn't believe a man would ask a woman to come out in this weather. *He should have picked her up if anything. And why did she agree?*

208

"Please . . . come get me . . . I don't want to call Corey. I can't . . . I don't want him to know . . . I'm about twenty minutes away from my house, but I can't go there now. My mom will know something's wrong. I lied. I texted her that I was with Lynn, but Lynn is out of town." Cherelle was sobbing hard now.

That jerked David's heart. *She doesn't want Corey to know what? There's something else going on besides the accident.* "Dupree, what happened?" David pried. Cherelle only responded with more crying and sniffling. "*Cherelle,*" David said calmly, "Tell me where you are. I'll be right there, okay? It's alright. Just calm down. No worries."

Cherelle scrambled to pull her thoughts together. Still in shock, she stuttered " . . . Uh . . . I—I'm . . . at a gas station on Woodward near Quarton—across from an antique store."

David knew exactly where she was. He thought for a moment and then said, "Dupree, I'm going to have a friend of mine and his wife come and get you, and I'll meet you at their house. You need to get someplace warm, outta this mess. I'm on my way."

"Okay . . . thank you. Please . . . just . . . don't call Corey. Please . . . please . . . don't tell him anything."

"No worries, Dupree."

A myriad of thoughts bombarded David's mind. He had a feeling Cherelle had done something she regretted. He had an idea what that something was, and the thought disturbed him.

* * *

IN LESS THAN THIRTY MINUTES, Greg and Norma Kingston had picked up Cherelle and settled her into one of their guest suites. It was well past midnight when Cherelle lay down in the surroundings of their hunter-green painted guest room, furnished with an intricately detailed white, wrought iron queen bed. The focal point of the room was an antique, wooden Hayworth vanity and bench. There was a velvet hunter-green chaise in front of the window, which had bright white plantation shutters.

David had known Greg since his days as a Wall Street broker. Greg was twelve years older than David. While David had been in New York as a young broker, he'd worked on Greg's team, and Greg had mentored him in the financial industry and spiritually. They were both from Michigan. David worked with Greg for two years before Greg returned to Michigan to establish Kingston Financial Services and pursue degrees in ministry and pastoral counseling. Greg's wife, Norma, was a psychiatrist who also dabbled in her passion for interior decorating. David had formed a strong bond with the couple. Their three grown children, all in their early twenties, referred to David as Uncle David. Besides Deacon Lewis, Greg was one of the few men David trusted, and Greg hadn't let him down tonight.

"Hey Greg . . . thank you so much," David said. He patted Greg on the back firmly when the two embraced. Greg shut the door and helped David out of his coat, which was wet with fresh snowflakes. David stepped out of his boots and hurried toward the fireplace. When he turned around, Greg had a cup of coffee in his hands. He handed it to David.

"You're welcome. I thought you might need this."

"Greg, you read my mind," David said. He sat down on the sofa nearest the fireplace and nursed the cup of coffee.

Greg sat across from David. "So tell me, is Cherelle your *special* friend?" he asked.

"Uh . . . no. We work together on one of the mayor's committees. We're just really close, that's all."

Greg's brow rose with skepticism as he eyed David. He lowered his voice. "She was pretty shaken up," he said.

"Yeah, I could tell when she called me. I'm glad I could count on you guys."

"Always. And she must be quite a friend to have you braving the storm of all storms at this time of night, in these driving conditions."

David smiled. "It's nothing like that. We're just really cool. She's a good friend."

Greg nodded, unconvinced by David's explanation. The two chatted for a few minutes before David checked on Cherelle.

David knocked lightly on the door of the guest room where Cherelle was. She opened the door and leaned into David weakly. He stepped in and quietly shut the door behind him. Cherelle sobbed heavily on his chest. David held her and squeezed her before pulling back. "Let's talk, Dupree," he said, leading Cherelle to the edge of the bed. "Tell me what's going on . . ."

"I got a call from a friend about one p.m. this afternoon. He was really out of it. He said he was in some heavy stuff, and asked if I would come down to his spot—it's a place he uses as a retreat that no one else knows about except me. We had lunch and talked. Then he slept for a few hours. When he woke up, we talked some more. He's been working undercover, and he wouldn't tell me much. He just kept saying that he wasn't sure how it was going to end this time. He was scared and jittery. It's uncharacteristic of him to be that way. Emotions got high and um . . . we um . . . started kissing and touching," Cherelle started in between sniffs. "I let things get out of control, David. When I heard God speaking to me, I tried to stop before it was too late."

David's stomach turned again. *Had she given herself to another man?*

"But . . . h—he . . . was all wound up and he had me pinned down. He was literally pulling my clothes off. I started screaming . . ." Cherelle said. "I just remember kicking and fighting. He was too strong. I couldn't move him off me. I kept pleading with him. He just looked me in the eyes with a deranged look. It was like he was someone else . . ." Cherelle sucked in huge breaths as tears trickled down her face. "He wouldn't let me up. He held me forcefully against my will. I screamed until my throat felt raw . . . I begged him not to—" Cherelle cried.

David lifted Cherelle's chin with his fingers, feeling as if someone had hit him in the gut. "Dupree, did he *rape* you?"

Cherelle covered her face with her hands and was silent longer than David could stand. Finally, she spoke. "No. He finally let me up. It was like he came to himself all of a sudden and didn't know what was happening. I took that opportunity to run out of there. I don't know who he was at that moment. I never should have gotten myself in that predicament," Cherelle cried.

"It's not your fault, Dupree. You are a human being. I'm just glad you're okay." David said, relieved that Cherelle's *friend* hadn't taken from her that which rightfully belongs to God. He took her hands in his and prayed. Then he hugged her again, and it was as if he could feel all of her trauma. He felt a dark heaviness that he prayed away. "Listen, Dupree, get some sleep. I'll be in the room down the hall. Make yourself at home here. Greg and Norma are like family to me. You're home here. I'm gonna turn in. I'll drive you back home in the morning." He kissed her forehead. "See you in the morning. I don't want to give Greg and Norma the wrong impression about why I've been here in this bedroom with you so long," David chuckled.

"Okay," Cherelle nodded, understanding. David rose and walked to the door. "David, what about my truck?"

David pivoted. "Greg has a friend who owns a body shop. I had it towed there. He's going to look at it first thing in the morning. No worries. I got you, Dupree. Get some rest."

"Thank you so much. Good night, David."

"Good night, Dupree," David said, winking. He wanted to say something else, but he argued with God in his heart instead. As soon as he left Cherelle's room, he felt relieved. He was glad to be away from her.

In the morning, Norma provided Cherelle with brand-new sweats, brand-new underclothes, and a host of fragrant oils and soaps. While Cherelle showered, Norma prepared a grand breakfast. Initially, Cherelle was embarrassed, but Norma's sincere demeanor allowed Cherelle to relax and enjoy her hospitality. David came strolling into the kitchen, freshly show-ered and smelling like aftershave and cologne. He always kept extra clothes in a carry-on bag in his trunk. He looked like he had slept well.

"I know I smell chicken and waffles! Norma, you must have crept into my dreams," David teased, clapping his hands together. Norma's skin was the color of sand; her short curly fade was stylishly tapered, drawing attention to her oval face and light brown eyes. She was petite and slender, which made her look younger than her fifty-two years of maturity.

"I know it's one of your favorites. Have a seat," Norma said. "Greg is outside snow-blowing the driveway. He'll be in shortly."

Cherelle ate fresh fruit from a fancy gold bowl.

"Morning, Dupree," David said, kissing her on her forehead.

"Morning."

"You good?" David asked Cherelle quietly. Norma looked

over her shoulder and studied the timbre of David's voice as he spoke to Cherelle.

"Yes, thank you," Cherelle answered sweetly.

Norma turned back toward the waffle maker and smiled.

* * *

AFTER BREAKFAST, Norma and Greg gave Cherelle a tour of their home. David tagged along just so he could witness Cherelle's reaction to the palatial Bloomfield Hills estate.

"This is my dream home!" Cherelle screeched. "I would scrape up every dime I had to buy this home from you two."

"Sorry, Cherelle. We had this house built, and Norma and I are going to die in this bad boy!" Greg said, laughing. Cherelle found it adorable that Norma's height was just a notch past Greg's waist. At six feet four inches tall, he was a giant standing next to his wife.

"Speak for yourself," Norma said to Greg. She turned to Cherelle and said, "All of our kids and grandkids are in Arizona with Greg's family. I'd love to be closer to them."

"Only if I can pick up my house and take it with me! You remember? The one you made me go broke building," Greg teased Norma.

Norma twisted her lips, "Greg, you lie so much. You know you had more where that came from."

Greg winked at David.

"Ooh . . . look at this tub! It's big enough for three people," Cherelle said, gawking, as Norma and Greg showed off their master bathroom retreat. "And Norma, this rainfall shower is to die for!" Cherelle said.

"The lights change colors too—if you're feeling romantic," Norma said, elbowing her husband.

"I would absolutely love to have this house. I'm so serious,"

Cherelle said, trailing her fingers over the extra-wide marble shower bench.

"You better get to building, David," Greg said.

Both David and Cherelle cast their eyes downward as if they were hiding something. Norma assessed their physical responses. *Interesting.*

Cherelle was awestruck by the two-and-a-half-acre, seven-thousand-square-foot dwelling. She told David that as he drove her home later that afternoon. "That house has everything I want in a home. The pool. The movie room. The kids' rooms. The outdoor kitchen. It has it all. Norma has her own dance studio, and they have two workout rooms. I bet it was nice raising a family there—growing up there."

"Yeah, their kids had it pretty good," David said.

"I want my kids to grow up in a home like that." David didn't respond. He contemplated her words in his spirit. "And David, thanks again for last night. I'm sorry for dragging you out in the weather. I didn't have anyone else to call."

"Dupree, you don't have to apologize to me. There's nothing I wouldn't do for you," David admitted. The words echoed in his heart. And in Cherelle's.

Chapter 19

The Pull

On a sunny June morning, David sat on the sofa of his and Dominique's well-appointed Lake Shore Drive hotel suite, looking out at Lake Michigan. Even though David had planned this weekend getaway to Chicago just for Dominique because she'd said she needed it, he prayed that no one had seen him check in with her two days ago. He was even more concerned about the possibility of someone seeing them check out this morning. It didn't matter that he was in another state. David knew there was always a chance of being spotted. He'd been reduced to sneaking around. On top of that, he'd lied to Deacon Lewis, Ms. Greta, Pastor Clint, *and* Cherelle about his whereabouts.

Throughout his life, one of the main things David had taken pride in was being an honest man, even if he sometimes had to hurt someone's feelings in the process. Now, he could be counted as a liar *and* a fornicator. Spiritually, he was far from the man he'd been before Dominique came into his life. But was it her fault? He certainly couldn't blame her. He couldn't blame her for being beautiful. He couldn't blame her for the fact that he *wanted* her. Nor could he blame her for the fact that his heart now needed her.

David had slipped into an unscrupulous rhythm of living in a way that was unacceptable to God and himself. He'd given in to his flesh more times than he'd wanted. He considered his situation as he looked around the suite with its lavish, high-end furniture, fireplace, and modern designs. It was fit for a king and his queen, not some covert, unholy relationship.

His spirit was more troubled than it had ever been. In the past three months, he'd become comfortable sleeping with Dominique at his leisure, as if God had given him the right to do so. He knew he couldn't go on this way. He felt the spiritual distance from his Father, and he was walking in a hypocrite's shoes. God didn't deserve this in return for all the blessings He'd bestowed on him. David knew that. He knew with all conviction that he had to make things right with God. But the only way to do that was to—. He couldn't stand the thought of doing what he knew his Father wanted him to do.

He couldn't continue living in two worlds. He'd shared that with Dominique so many times. He'd even suggested marriage, but Dominique wanted David just the way she had him. Nothing more. Nothing less. David had put too much on the line. Too many ministries under his charge. Too many souls. His soul. Too much was at stake. He had to be a living example of Christ. He had to be about the business of his Father. He couldn't do that in this relationship.

Sneaking around wasn't God's way. A relationship that was good and pure didn't have to be hidden. David had become a double agent of the worst kind. How many times in the last few months had he preached on Sunday after he'd made love to Dominique? His duplicitousness was eating him alive. He'd heard God. He'd heard Him loud and clear. He could hear Him now.

End it.

I love her . . . I love her, Father.

End it, now.

What if I don't touch her— if we don't sin against You?

No. End it, now.

I want her, and I need her . . . please . . .

No. End it, now.

Pulverizing blows assaulted David. He lowered his head. Over his lifetime, God had rarely told him no. When he'd wanted to go to Harvard, God had said yes. When he wanted to work on Wall Street, God had said yes. When he'd wanted a church of his own with a powerful ministry, God had said yes. Rarely had he asked his Father for anything, and it wasn't given to him. But not this time. David couldn't dare disobey his Father *again.*

The words were strong and ringing in his spirit. He'd been rebellious for too long. David feared that God's patience would turn into a wrath he couldn't stand. The thought of his ministries becoming less effective, or him being spiritually disconnected from God in a state worse than he was right now, was unthinkable.

Dominique bounced out of the bedroom. Her face glowed with excitement. She was dressed and ready for their last adventure before heading back to Michigan. They were scheduled to visit Navy Pier and have lunch afterward.

"I'm ready, Dave!"

David lifted his head, and Dominique saw all the things she feared in David's eyes. She knew one day it would come to this. Every time they'd shared each other, David was distant afterward. This time, she saw something else in his eyes.

She walked to him, "Dave, I love you . . . just let us be. Please . . ."

David stood. "I can't anymore, Nik. I'm caving in on the

inside. I can't take the separation from Him. I can't live like this."

"We're good together, Dave. Let me show you . . . " Dominique said, roaming her hands over David's chest. She reached up to kiss him.

David took a step back and swallowed hard. He didn't want to let her go. He didn't want to do this. "I'm sorry, Nik. This has to end."

"Why do you have to be so perfect, Dave? Why can't you just be a regular man?!"

David backed away from Dominique. He belonged to God. He couldn't be what she wanted him to be. "I have to leave, Nik."

Dominique grabbed David by his arms. "Dave, just stay . . . let's just talk about it. Doesn't God want you to be happy, babe?"

"Yes, but not if—"

"Don't I make you happy, Dave?" Dominique interrupted, stroking David's face.

"Yes, but I'm moving farther away from Him, and I *can't* take it anymore. It feels unnatural. I feel like I'm *dying*, sweetheart. My obedience is more important than my happiness . . ."

"What about what I want, Dave? What about *my* happiness?" David knew if he stayed, he'd end up in bed with her again.

There was an impregnable pull between them. David had bonded with Dominique physically so many times that it seemed supremely natural for him to be with her that way. Yet it was unnatural. The thought of him being unable to connect with Dominique that way again gave David a vomitous feeling of withdrawal.

Leave now. Take the train back alone.

David took money out of his wallet and handed it to

Dominique. She snatched the crisp bills, balled them up, and threw them on the floor. "A driver will pick you up in front of the hotel at four p.m. and take you to the train station. Nik, I love you. I'm sorry. Please understand . . ."

Dominique screamed. "Dave, just go! I hate you! I never want to see you again! I hate that I ever *met* you!"

Chapter 20

Easy

David's front door was unlocked, just as he'd promised Cherelle it would be. He regretted that they had to get together today of all days. It had been a month since he ended his relationship with Dominique. But today, he was feeling the pain of their separation. He was reeling from a lover's withdrawal. He felt it both emotionally and physically. There was a raw, flesh-eating emptiness gnawing at his heart.

David's hands stroked the keys of his white baby grand piano masterfully. The vibrations reverberated through his soul, chased by thoughts of Dominique. As he thought back to their beginning, there'd been clear signs that she wasn't the right fit for him—wasn't God's choice for him. He had never experienced the feeling of inexplicable peace he usually did when God affirmed a decision he made. He had forged ahead anyway because of his pride and his desires.

It was all over now. He knew he'd done the right thing. It was right by God. He had to protect his relationship with his Father above all else—live a clean life for Christ. He couldn't be another hypocrite in the pulpit.

It had been a long time since he'd stepped out on a limb and put his heart on the line for a woman. The brokenness he experienced now confirmed for David that he had no intentions of ever doing that again. He'd been caught between his love for Dominique and his love for God. There was no greater torment.

* * *

As soon as Cherelle made it up the walkway to David's front door, she heard the sound of piano music. She turned the knob and pushed the huge wooden door open. The house was suffused with a soft, pleasant cloud of melodies. It was a familiar tune, "Easy" by the Commodores. With each chord, Cherelle felt something pressing in her spirit. She didn't bother to call out to David to make him aware of her presence. She doubted if he could hear her over the amplified sounds of his piano anyway. She knew her way around his home on the main level. Cherelle bent down and removed her sandals. The balmy July temperature had given her the opportunity to show off her newly painted pink toes.

David had viewed Cherelle's arrival from the small tablet he'd placed on top of his piano. He'd seen her pull into his driveway. He'd watched as she got out of her truck, smoothed her hands over her pink and white paisley sundress, and studied her surroundings. His fingers continued to stroke the keys with grace and precision. He communicated with the piano, playing out his emotions. He confessed all. His heart was a ragged, useless burden, and there was nothing he could do about it.

He'd heard God, but he hadn't liked what his Father said. When he was with Dominique, he'd been in constant turmoil because he felt separated from his God. Now that Dominique was out of his life, the separation from *her* was overwhelming. The tearing of soul ties had left a scar. David was irresolute, feeling rebellious, even though he'd done what God had instructed him to do. It just didn't feel right. *Guard thy heart . . .* He'd failed to do that.

Cherelle was careful not to disturb David, but his gift and emotion captivated her. She had a way of perceiving things others couldn't. She wished she could heal whatever it was that had David imprisoned in a dark space. He had never talked to her about Dominique. Not once had he mentioned that he was seeing someone. But Cherelle knew all along. There were those cryptic conversations on his cell phone, and times he would completely zone out while they were in meetings. It was uncharacteristic of David. He'd changed in a lot of ways.

Cherelle walked past David's music room and into the kitchen, where she washed her hands. She opened the refrigerator and retrieved the fresh-squeezed lemonade David had Leah make especially for her visit. On her last visit, they had fought over the last glass of it. Being a naturalist, Cherelle loved that Leah sweetened her lemonade with raw honey. David knew it was one of the treats Cherelle looked forward to when they met at his home. He had left a beautiful, hand-painted mason jar on the counter for her. The thought that Cherelle was smiling at that moment almost made David smile in return. He would have if he hadn't felt so empty.

Cherelle brought her lemonade-filled mason jar into David's music room. She set it down on the sofa table on top of a marble coaster and retrieved her computer from the tote bag she'd left outside the music room door. She curled up on the sofa across from David's piano and turned on her laptop. David acknowledged Cherelle with a nod but continued to play. He was in his world, separated from her and everything else that was transpiring at the moment, like the fact that Cherelle's sweet-smelling scent permeated throughout the small room, matching the way the piano's sound reverberated. Cherelle tucked her feet under her body and began to type her feelings on the computer in a story format, writing about herself as if she were a character in a book.

> *She watched him stroke the keys delicately. She listened to the sounds of his soul. She felt his fingers as if he were touching her skin. She longed to go to him and put her arms around him. She wanted to tell him that his playing was causing her heart to beat in sync with the notes. That she could feel his heaviness. Most of all, she wanted to tell him that she longed to soothe whatever pain he was feeling. If only he would let her in. But she knew that his heart was somewhere else—loving someone else. That made her ache inside. But in all situations, she'd learned to hide her emotions so well . . .*

David was appreciative that Cherelle hadn't said anything. She knew when to be *still*. She picked up on social cues effortlessly. David loved that about her. Well aware that they had important work to do, he needed his space at the moment. But he noticed everything about Cherelle. Like how her pink and white sundress complemented her dark chocolate skin and paid tribute to her small waist and plentiful hips. He understood full well why Walter Kincaid wanted to conquer her. David was enchanted by the redolence of the natural oils Cherelle used on her body and hair. They were uniquely hers. But nothing outweighed the affliction he felt.

Cherelle was extraordinarily quiet. After about ten minutes, without making a sound, she rose from the sofa and exited. She came back a few minutes later with another full jar of lemonade. Again, she tucked her feet underneath her and continued to work on her laptop. David didn't know if she was working on their project or if she was doing something else to pass the time until he was ready.

When at least forty-five minutes had passed, David stopped playing. It wasn't an abrupt stop. It was like a long ending to a concerto. His fingers softly crept back and forth over the keys, bringing his recital to a soft, lingering end. He rose from the piano bench. Only then did Cherelle make eye contact. She'd been fixated on her story.

David was dressed in a well-worn pair of Levis and one of his favorite Harvard T-shirts. He was barefoot. Cherelle tried to take all of him in without staring too deeply into his eyes. She was afraid of what she might see. David stood in front of her without speaking, as seconds ticked by. Cherelle stood finally, and David hugged her and placed a chaste kiss on her cheek.

"Dupree," he said quietly, "how are you doing?"

"I'm good. You?"

It was hard not to notice how the T-shirt stretched over his broad shoulders and muscular physique. Cherelle could only imagine the six-pack that was hidden underneath his T-shirt. David's jeans hung right at his narrow waist. His arms were ripped like he played professional basketball for a living. When he pulled Cherelle into his arms for a friendly hug, her breathing hitched.

"It's been one of those weeks, Dupree," David said resolutely.

"It's like that sometimes."

"Truly."

* * *

"Ok, so you know the mayor is going to kill both of us if we don't get phases two and three of these programs together. You know he's talking bigger and better!" Cherelle laughed. "I had a book deadline, and honestly, that was my number one priority. But I can't tell the mayor that so . . ." Cherelle said as soon as she and David were seated at a nearby sandwich shop. The weather was so nice she'd convinced him to get out of the house and enjoy a little sun. Then, they could go back to his home and work. More importantly, Cherelle needed the sunlight herself after soaking up all of David's emotions.

"My schedule has been packed too, but I've set aside today and tomorrow. We have a guest preacher from Los Angeles, so I'm off the hook for the sermon on Sunday," David said before taking a bite of his sandwich.

"Ok, well . . . I've got to admit something. I wanted to invite you out to my place to work this time. I have a lot of natural sunlight, and I thought it might get our creative juices flowing. But I thought my suggestion might seem forward or some-thing." Cherelle said, almost embarrassed by her thoughts.

"Come on, Dupree. You know we know each other too well for me to think anything negative of you. A change of venue might be good for us. We've worked at my place, the church, and the mayor's office. Change is good. Sounds good to me."

Nervous, Cherelle's body stiffened slightly. "My place is kind of far, but because you love to drive, I don't think the distance will be a problem for you. I have a large office with a decent-sized desk and table. I feel comfortable enough with you to invite you over."

"Hmmm . . . Oh really?" David teased.

"Stop it," Cherelle laughed.

David and Cherelle left the restaurant and drove back to David's home so he could pick up his car and computer. Then David followed Cherelle out to her Bloomfield Hills retreat. It was an affluent suburb about forty minutes outside the city. Cherelle lived in a serene, semi-wooded area. She owned a sprawling tri-level condo in a code-activated gated community. The door of her three-car, extra-deep garage inched its way up, and David was shocked by its cleanliness. Every gardening tool and other gadget had its perfect place secured on the walls with convenient hooks. Cherelle's garage looked like one in a hardware or auto parts commercial.

She motioned for David to pull to the left side of her "fun" car. It was a late-model Chrysler Challenger in jet black. The rims were beaming so that David wondered if the car belonged to a man—maybe a boyfriend. David got out of his truck and looked around.

"Wow. Your neighborhood is beautiful. And the wheels over here are pretty tight, too," David said when Cherelle stepped out of her Range Rover. He patted the roof of the sports car gently with his hand while he peeked in through the semi-tinted windows. He looked out of Cherelle's garage across the street at the lake. David counted only five homes in the cul-de-sac. Cherelle's house sat at the end on an extra-wide lot. "This is something else. It's like a vacation. This must be the perfect writer's retreat. You've got a lake view in the front and a wooded view in the back. That's nice . . ."

"Thank You. I love it," Cherelle beamed. "Come on in. Let me take you on a tour before we get to work. I think Mom is taking a nap because she's usually out here on the sofa watching TV," she said when they entered her foyer and living room area.

Cherelle had a modern-styled home, but it wasn't so ultramodern that it didn't have a homey feel to it. It had high, vaulted ceilings, skylights, and window walls. There was a waterfall feature near the front entrance. The cloud-white walls were splashed with colorful abstract paintings.

Cherelle's colorful, modular furniture made the house pop with life. Bright-colored sofas and chairs in pinks, purples, and reds filled her open-concept living room. It was busy-looking but stylish. David nodded. "Woman, you livin'!" he joked.

Cherelle's reading room was David's favorite, with its floor-to-ceiling, wall-to-wall bookcase and old-fashioned ladder. "Dupree, you gave city living up for this lil' *shack*?" David said teasingly.

That made Cherelle smile widely. "Pastor Corey found this place for me. He wanted to make sure I felt safe . . . and I feel safe here."

"Hey, I completely understand. I would want to make sure my lady was safe, too," David said. He was prying again on the sly.

Cherelle knew that, but the way he'd said, '*my* lady' stirred her on the inside. She loved it when a man was protective of his woman.

"So, do you throw crazy author parties?" David joked as he walked around Cherelle's basement. It had a separate kitchen, a state-of-the-art gym, and a living area with a movie projector screen and plush, theatre-style reclining chairs. "Your dates must love hanging out over here."

"The only other men who have stepped foot in here have been Wal—Mayor Kincaid and Pastor Corey. So not a lot of traffic. I'm pretty private, so I hardly ever invite people over."

"Oh, so there are levels to this?" David poked.

"I consider myself blessed."

David was tempted to ask Cherelle about her relationship with Walter. He wanted to know if she and Walter Kincaid had ever had some sort of *relationship*. Walter hadn't made a secret of the fact that he was sweet on Cherelle, and his choosing her to serve on the youth task force ensured that she'd spend a lot of time with him. David was no fool. He knew there was a good reason why Walter was keeping Cherelle close.

He wondered how Walter Kincaid had become aware of Cherelle Dupree in the first place. Maybe Corey had introduced the two of them. The way Corey and Walter went on about Cherelle sometimes made David wonder if there was some competition between the two men. Cherelle seemed oblivious to their admiration of her.

David was still in the dark about what was going on between Cherelle and Corey. There was undoubtedly something, even though both Cherelle and Corey denied it. However, several things had transpired to make David believe Corey and Cherelle weren't being quite honest. That had only left David curiously confused.

"So . . . how do you know Walter Kincaid?" David asked, hoping that since Cherelle was on home turf, she'd be a little more sociable.

Cherelle smiled. Then she said seriously, "You must remember I'm a licensed therapist, David. Is that the question you *really* want to ask me?"

"Well . . . I mean—I was just wondering if—"

Cherelle cut him off. "Why?" she countered.

"Man, you're making me feel all nervous and hot under the collar, Dupree." David laughed. "Like I'm being cross-examined."

"Ah . . . you said *cross*-examined, which means you recognize that you're prying into my personal business."

"Okay," David ceded. "I was prying."

"Why do you want to know, David? What is motivating you to ask about my *personal* relationship with a man—the mayor?"

"To be honest, I'm just curious. You may call it nosy."

Cherelle laughed. "Okay, so you're nosy."

"Certainly. And since I'm being nosy, fess up. What is the connection between you and Corey?"

"You are prying, David."

He chuckled. "I know. I'm just trying to get to know you better, Dupree. That's all."

"Corey and I have a special relationship. And it is most definitely, strictly platonic and will always be. Yuck!"

"That's odd, most women find the brother attractive. When he's been a guest preacher at DOC, some of the sisters go silly crazy over him."

"Yeah, well, Cherelle Dupree is not most women. He's extremely handsome, yes. But our relationship is platonic and personal—between him and me." She looked at David directly.

"Okay. But you didn't answer my question about Walt."

"The mayor and I have worked together before. We have a friend in common. We have a sort of bond because of that. Our relationship hasn't gone beyond that, and I won't ever allow it to. Now, let's get to work, so we can get phases two and three mapped out before our next meeting with Mayor Kincaid."

"Okay," David nodded. Cherelle was indomitable. David needed a key and a combination to get information out of her. Cherelle couldn't tell David that she and Walter Kincaid had connected because she had been his mother's therapist when she was dealing with suicidal ideations after her husband of forty years passed away.

* * *

AFTER THREE HOURS of plotting out the program components for phases two and three, Cherelle stared at David from across the table in her office. David had drifted off in thought. Cherelle didn't want to pry after she had jokingly chastised him earlier, but she felt in her spirit that she should.

230

"David, what's going on? What's on your heart? Whatever it is, I can *feel* it." Cherelle said.

David was startled out of his thoughts. "Uh . . . I'm good, Dupree.

Thanks for asking, though. I'm good." David returned, smiling.

"*David,* you're in emotional distress about something—someone. There's been this sort of cloud hovering over you since earlier—really for the past few weeks," Cherelle clarified. "I'm a licensed therapist. I know how to keep things private. I feel like you need to unload a burden. We've known each other for almost a year, and I know that doesn't give me the right to pry so deeply. I just feel like the Lord is leading me to talk with you about whatever is going on."

Without responding to her question, David looked at her with sincere eyes and considered her offer. "You mind if I get some more coffee?" he asked.

"Of course not. I'll get it for you."

David stood, "You don't have to do that, Dupree. I can get it."

Cherelle stopped him with a gentle touch on his shoulder. "Just sit. I got it." She returned a few minutes later with a fresh cup. She handed it to David and sat in front of him again.

"You are amazing, Dupree," David said after taking a few sips. "I don't know what to say. It's funny how the Lord sometimes interrupts our daily lives with someone or something to remind us that He is a real, caring God—not a distant God who is up in heaven unaware or unconcerned with our feelings . . . " David said. He let out a long breath and inhaled again. Cherelle nodded.

He didn't want to discuss it with her. He hadn't discussed it with anyone—not even Deacon Lewis or Greg Kingston, whom he could talk to about anything. David trusted the two men, and something in his spirit gave him the confidence that Cherelle could be trusted as well. He scratched the top of his head. "Dupree, I—I don't know where to start. A part of me wants to be relieved of the burden, but the other part of me is ashamed and embarrassed about the whole thing—that's the truth. I should have known better . . ."

"David, I promise I won't pass judgment on you. I would never do that," Cherelle said in a tone that was so compassionate and warm that David found it hard not to just blurt everything out all at once. But his relationship with Dominique was nothing to be proud of. The emotional fallout was still affecting him. He rose from the table and walked over to the window. He stared out in the direction of the lake and spoke.

"Last year, about a month before I met you, I met a woman, Dupree. Before she came into my life, I hadn't been looking for love. I hadn't been looking for anything. She was saved, but she'd been out of fellowship so long that . . . um . . . spiritually, we were on two different levels—in two different places. But I wanted her." David turned to face Cherelle. He had shoved his hands into the pockets of his slacks. He paced the floor for a moment before sitting in front of Cherelle.

"When I say, 'I wanted her,' I don't mean in the physical sense. Although yes, I can't lie, I desired her that way as well. What I'm saying is: I wanted her to be *mine*. Somehow, I felt my love could warm her heart. Make her want God more. Erase some of the emotional pain that was evident in her life." David stared at Cherelle with serious eyes. "I had every intention of keeping our dealings pure, Cherelle. I know some men of God —even pastors, don't control that one area of their lives, but I did—or I tried. I wanted to. It was important to me to show her God's way of doing things. But um . . . I let my guard down, and we became physically involved. From then on, I was stuck in a spiritually muddy place." Cherelle saw beads of perspiration bubbling on David's brow.

"That tore me in two," David continued. "I knew I had to break it off, even though we had never established a committed relationship in the first place. She never wanted to be in an *official* relationship, so to speak. She just assured me that I was the only man she was seeing. I knew she had a lot of pain from her past, so I accepted that. But there was always something deep down inside me telling me that she wasn't what God wanted for me—our relationship wasn't what He wanted for me. God made that clear to me, but I loved her. I truly loved her. When I finally broke it off, she told me that I was no better than any other man she'd been with in the past. That hurt me to my soul, Dupree. I haven't spoken to her since . . ."

Cherelle noted the changes in David's slumped body as he sank into the chair. She held her peace and waited for the Lord to guide her. She had tried to hold it in, but she couldn't keep herself from crying. She got up and pulled several tissues from the Kleenex box on her desk. She sat down in front of David again, eyeing him empathetically. Cherelle knew exactly what David was feeling, but David was puzzled by her reaction. He wondered why she was reacting so emotionally to what he'd just told her. It was strange.

Cherelle shifted in the chair. "David, what you just shared with me was not only for you to release a burden, but it also confirmed for me that I did the right thing by God, too," she said, wiping escaped tears. "You see, three years ago, I ended a relationship similar to yours. It's so similar, David, that it's uncanny. His name was Emory . . ."

David's puzzlement had turned to shock. He shook his head in disbelief.

"Yes . . ." Cherelle said, nodding. "He was a narcotics officer who spent most of his time undercover. He was tough. A go-getter. A man's man. But spiritually, we were and still are two *different* people. I loved him anyway, David. I wanted to be *his*. When I first met him, I was at a stage where I was frightened of never being married, never having babies. And that's what I wanted—what I still want." Cherelle swallowed. "I had been celibate for a long while when I met him. I was so engrossed in my ministry work that initially, I dismissed him as a possibility for me altogether. And certainly, when he realized that I was serious about my plan to stay celibate until marriage, he backed off.

"He checked on me now and then to see how I was doing, but he kept his distance. My heart was torn because we'd dated for over a year, and I had grown to love the man he was inside, even though he didn't understand God the way I did. Even though we didn't see eye to eye on celibacy. I had fallen in love, David, and it felt lonely without him. It had been several years since I had even *liked* a man, and he liked me back," Cherelle chuckled.

"Do you know what it feels like to go *years* without someone touching you, kissing you, and holding you?" Cherelle's voice cracked. "And I'm not talking about sexually, David. I'm talking about plain old affection from the opposite sex—someone holding you, and saying 'I love you,' or 'I miss you.' It was horrible. I felt like I was starving an emotional starvation. You know, church folk have a habit of dismissing every human problem with, 'You got Jesus.' And David, I know that. I *know* the Word. I teach the Word. But David, honestly, there were times when I wanted and needed *companionship,* especially after my mom had a stroke." Cherelle let her tears fall unashamedly. David reached across the table and held Cherelle's hand in his.

Cherelle swallowed again. "So, I did something that cost me more than I intended to pay. I turned my back on everything I knew to be right, David. I gave myself to Emory— mainly because of the way I felt for him, and partly because of the loneliness and fear. I didn't want to lose him—his attention —his affection. Deep in my heart, every time we were together intimately, I felt the tearing of my relationship with God. I kept thinking that soon, maybe Em and I would get married, and things would be right in God's eyes.

"And as guilty as I felt for allowing myself to be in that situation, I had never felt so loved and cared for by a man. The calls, the flowers, the time spent—it was all beautiful to me in a way. So I let it go on for a couple of years. And when I finally asked him what his intentions were toward me—if we were going to marry, his answer floored me. '*I don't know*' was what he said exactly. He went on to tell me about the stress on the job, this, that, and all the reasons why he couldn't promise me a future . . ."

David interrupted with a question. "Do you think he *really* loved you, Dupree?"

Cherelle shrugged. "Maybe in his mind—in his way. But deep down, I knew then and I know now, that I need a man of God, who is walking with God. One who can pray for me and be my strength, and I can be his. Most of all, I need a man who loves me enough to commit to me and only me, in a covenant that is ordained by God. And Emory simply isn't that man.

"That night I had the accident, I'd been with Emory earlier that evening. I went as a friend because he'd been so upset when he called. And when he snapped for those few moments, and I was positive in my heart that he was going to rape me, I promised God, if He let me get out of that situation, I would never look back again. And in the next moment, Em seemed to come to himself. He looked startled, like he didn't know what had transpired over the last few moments. He began to apologize. But I ran . . . " Cherelle said. "Sometimes we want what

God *doesn't* want for us, David. As His children, we've got to trust that He knows best."

David stood and pulled Cherelle up by her hands into the safe haven of his arms. She had no idea what she had just done for him. What God had done for him through her. It was time for him to release the pain and guilt he'd been holding onto.

Cherelle was comforted by David's touch in a pure sense. She felt his spiritual strength. She reveled in the comfort of being held by a strong man. She pulled back momentarily, looking up at him with a smile. "Thank you."

"No. Thank *you*," David said back. He wiped Cherelle's tears with the pads of his thumbs, and in an instant, they were drawn together by a force neither of them could counter. They leaned into one another slowly, and their lips touched in a feather-soft kiss. Then they surrendered to a free-fall kiss that comforted both of them, staying well within a spiritual boundary that protected them from going any further.

Cherelle's eyes fluttered open, followed by David's. "Dupree, I'm so sorry. I don't know what came over me," David said. "I can't even explain why I just did that . . . I'm so sorry," he repeated. "But I promise you, it came from a pure place in my heart. Not lust—not anything else. I promise. I just wanted you to know how beautiful you are in every way, Dupree. Spiritually, emotionally, physically—you are *beautiful*. I wanted you to feel the tenderness I have in my heart for—"

Cherelle interrupted David, covering his lips with hers. She allowed their lips to softly touch again before she laid her head against his chest and rested in his arms as he hugged her close to his body. For David, it seemed that time was suspended with Cherelle in his arms, and he felt at peace with her that way. He found his voice and whispered. "Dupree, you are an amazing woman. I knew that the moment I first saw you. You mean so much to me," David said. Not wanting to mislead her in any way, he spoke with complete honesty. "Right now, I'm in a place I've never been. I couldn't begin to give you what I know you deserve, but I don't want to lose our friendship—ever. Just having you listen to me tonight has done so much for my spirit. You've been a blessing to me since I met you, Dupree."

Cherelle understood more than David could say. Emotionally, he wasn't done with his past. She knew that. And it was something he had to be done with—when *he* got to that point. Nothing and no one, except God, could force him to emancipate himself. "Let us pray . . ." she offered.

Cherelle prayed so fervently that she caused David to drop to his knees. He bent over and lowered his face to the floor. He stretched his arms out and gave himself to God for healing. Instinctively, Cherelle bent down on her knees and covered David's head with her hands. "I rebuke every vile thing, every evil that threatens to attack him, Lord. Bless David's life with protection from danger. Give him strength and resolve. Bless him with a total release of his burdens, and grant forgiveness and cleansing in Christ. Mend his heart, Lord—every broken part. Restore what was lost. Restore his joy. Help him to let go and release the things that are not of You. Help him to walk in Your will for his life day by day . . . .The praise belongs to You, Lord." Unable to hold back his emotions, David wept openly. It was something he couldn't control. It was a release from emotional bondage. David's praise began as Cherelle's prayer came to a close. He felt God's presence and praised God in a voice that usurped all of his energy. He praised until his voice became a hoarse, whispery rumble.

* * *

DAVID AND CHERELLE lay on her office floor in their own spaces, David on his stomach, Cherelle on her back. They were stretched out like children on Cherelle's plush, bright purple rug, connected by intertwined fingers. They had prayed and praised until their strength was depleted. When David felt a small resurgence of energy an hour later, he rose to his feet and bid Cherelle good night. They agreed to meet in the morning to complete the components of phases two and three of the youth task force. The drive home allowed David more time to commune with God. It was the start of his healing.

Chapter 21

Act Like You Know Me

D avid arrived at ten a.m. sharp, just as he and Cherelle had agreed. Cherelle's mother, Eleanor, whom David referred to as Mother Dupree, was up watching her Saturday morning shows. David walked over to her and kissed her on her forehead. Cherelle and her mother both shared rich, dark skin, the color of milk chocolate. But Cherelle's features were distinctively different. She didn't bear that much resemblance to her mother aside from her skin color. David surmised that Cherelle must look more like her father.

"Mother Dupree, it's nice to see you again," David said. He'd met her a few months ago, when she and Cherelle had visited his church, along with Corey, for family and friends day.

"Nice to see you, too, Pastor Cole. How you been?"

"I've been good. Thank you."

"Well, y'all work hard and get that project done for the mayor. I'm so proud that the President of the United States has taken note of all the good work y'all been doin'. Ain't no tellin' where this could take the two of you."

"Mother, it's supposed to be confidential."

"Well, if I'm telling someone who already knows, that can't be breaking confidentiality, now can it?"

The stroke Eleanor had had four years ago had not destroyed her wit. She still had spunk, although the stroke had left her weakened on the left side. And David had no problem understanding what she'd said, even though her voice was slurred. He laughed at her wit.

As soon as David and Cherelle were in her office behind closed doors, David said, "Dupree, I need to talk to you about what happened between us last night. In no way do I want you to feel that I was using you or taking advantage of the moment. I really, honestly just acted—I don't know why I did it. I was just in the moment."

Cherelle twisted her lips. "Are you talking about our little *kisses*?"

"That's *exactly* what I'm talking about, Dupree."

"Well, first of all, I didn't feel that you were using me. We care for one another because we have a great friendship. I understand that doesn't negate the fact that you have stronger feelings—love for someone else. Secondly, if it were a matter of taking advantage of the moment, both of us could be considered guilty of that. Instead, I think it was a matter of two people acknowledging a pure tenderness for one another in a kiss that was precious and passionate—that we did not let lead to sin."

David wanted to tell Cherelle to speak for herself because he'd had to squash quite a few thoughts about Cherelle since last night. "Okay . . ." he said. "It's just important to me not to do anything that would cause you harm, Dupree. I sincerely care about you in a special way. I wouldn't want to do anything to hurt you. In the future, I promise to keep my lips to myself."

"It was our moment, David. We both were full of emotion

—so we sort of acted on it. It happened. It's fine. Is that going to make it difficult for you to work with me?"

"Uh . . . no. Not at all," David said. He hoped that remained true.

"We're fond of each other, David. But I know right now is not a good time for us to try to be anything more than friends, and we both know why. So let's just be friends—and keep our lips to ourselves so we don't stir up a passion that is not grounded spiritually and emotionally."

"You *are* amazing," David said.

"Thank you. So are you."

Cherelle's phone rang. She noticed it was Corey and placed him on speaker. His telephone conversations were usually quick and to the point. "Hey . . . Corey."

"Hey! Did I leave my tablet over there the other evening?"

"You sure did."

"I'm gonna swing by and pick it up within the hour."

"Okay. I'm working on the project for the mayor. I'll be in my office."

"See you soon."

"Okay. Bye."

"Bye."

David listened to their brief conversation and decided that maybe it was time for him to have a man-to-man with Corey about Cherelle.

Corey appeared less than an hour after his phone call. David remained in Cherelle's office, but he overheard Corey and Cherelle's conversation.

Corey greeted Cherelle warmly. "Good Morning. You look beautiful as usual."

"So do you—I mean handsome," Cherelle said, giggling.

"Thanks."

"Listen, there is someone I want you to meet. An old frat brother of mine from Tennessee. He's a man of God, and he's here in town for his job."

"What kind of work does he do?"

Corey chuckled. "Um . . . I really can't say—because he can't tell me. He's an army guy with one of those high-level security clearances, and whatever he does is confidential. His being here has something to do with that. But he couldn't elaborate. He's a good man. There's some kind of gala he has to go to next week. He said he'd look like a lame if he went alone. I figured you two might get along well. I've never done this before, Cherelle. But after our talk last week, I just thought it might be a good idea for you to get out. I totally and completely trust this guy. I stay with him at least twice a year and talk to him weekly. He is an upstanding man of God. I trust him."

Cherelle thought for a moment. She tilted her head and held her gaze on Corey.

"You're not mad, are you?" Corey asked.

"Not at all. I'll do it."

"Okay, great. I will have him call you. I didn't say anything to him about you *specifically* yet. I will. And while I do, I'm gonna be sure to let that brother know that I will *kill* his six-foot-three behind in a New York min—"

"Corey, is that you?" Eleanor called out. "Yes, ma'am."

"Get on in here and let me put my eyes on you."

"I'm comin', Ma Dupree."

Cherelle rolled her eyes playfully.

David stayed put in Cherelle's office, listening to every detail, hoping to get some clarity.

"You sure look handsome, sir," Eleanor said to Corey.

"Why, you're looking like a stunner, yourself, Ma."

She giggled. "I fix up on the weekends. I just got my hair done yesterday."

"It's beautiful," Corey said, admiring the long silvery locks.

"You so sweet. Just like your father. Give me some sugar, son."

Corey kissed her, and Eleanor eyed him. She couldn't believe how much he looked like his father.

"You stayin' for a while today?"

"No ma'am. I have to get ready for service tomorrow. But Cherelle and I are going out to dinner after service tomorrow, would you like to come with us?"

"I think I will, as long as you two let me eat what I want to."

"I think we can handle that," Corey laughed.

"Good. Then I will see you tomorrow after church."

"Okay, you got a date, Ma." Corey kissed her forehead and then gently took her frail hand and kissed it too. "See you tomorrow."

"Bye, now."

In the foyer, Corey looked at Cherelle and said, "I figured we could try this new sushi restaurant since Ma Dupree likes sushi so much."

"Yeah, my aunt introduced her to it, and now she can't get enough of it," Cherelle said.

He nodded. "Okay. It will be just the three of us—my mother won't be there."

"I understand."

Corey remembered something. "Oh yeah . . ." he said, opening his wallet. He pulled out three one-hundred-dollar bills. "This is for you," he said, putting the money in her hand.

"For what?"

"I don't know. I figured you might want to get your hair and nails done or something—a new dress."

"Corey, you don't have to do this. I'm good."

"I want to. I love you." He kissed her on the cheek and hugged her tightly.

David had stood on the side of the doorway in Cherelle's office out of view, spying. He'd seen Corey hand Cherelle money. But he'd also heard him say he wanted her to go out with a friend of his. What man in his right mind would offer someone as beautiful as Cherelle up to another man? David stepped out into the foyer. His presence startled Corey.

"Hey, Corey . . ."

"Hey . . . DC."

Cherelle quickly explained. "David is here working with me on the project for the mayor."

Corey rendered an odd expression with his brow raised. "Oh, I didn't know you were here," Corey said, looking directly at David.

David felt as if Corey was giving him a stare-down on the sly. "Yeah. Deacon Lewis insisted on driving me today. I think he just needed something to do. Cherelle and I are working on the next two phases of the mayor's youth project—expanding the program," David said. He evaluated the stare Corey poured on him.

"You could have worked at the church," Corey said. It was a quiet rebuke.

Cherelle's eyes widened.

"Cherelle said she'd be more comfortable *here*," David returned.

Corey nodded slowly. This time, he *was* sizing up David. He knew the old DC. "Let's step outside for a minute, huh?" Corey motioned to David.

David knew when some sort of man-challenge was happening. He didn't like it, and he surely would let it be known. "No problem," he said, following Corey out the front door.

Corey didn't hesitate to make *his* thoughts known as soon

244

as they'd stepped away from Cherelle's door and over to his car. "*Pastor Cole*, I'm not sure what's going on with *you*, but I do know what is going on with Cherelle Eleanor Dupree. Let your dealings with her be *business only*."

David's face contorted in disbelief. An anger that he'd learned to control years ago was bubbling. "What? Are you frontin' me, Corey?"

Corey stared at him again without flinching. "I meant every word I just said, DC."

"First of all, I don't like your tone. I don't know what you have goin' on with Cherelle, and I don't care. But I don't like the fact that you actin' like you don't know who you talkin' to," David said back.

Corey knew all too well who he was talking to. He'd grown up with David. He knew what David was capable of doing to him, and he didn't care. "DC, you *heard* what I said."

To some extent, David found Corey's bravado comical. He smirked before saying, "Whatever *dealings* I have with Cherelle are none of your business, so don't make it." He walked away from Corey and from his former self. The old David—the one that was known and respected by the name DC, would have laid Corey Perry out—right in the middle of Cherelle's driveway with one blow.

"Well, maybe it's the business of that little honey I saw you with at the W hotel in Chicago," Corey called out.

David pivoted and walked back toward Corey. "What did you say?"

"The honey I saw you with at the W hotel in Chicago—on the waterfront. I saw you take a honey into one of the '*Wow*' suites," Corey said, making air quotes with his fingers. "The way you were carrying on at the door, it looked pretty intimate to me. And I'm not judging. I'm sure we've all had our share of indiscretions—including me before I learned to walk a straight line with God. But leave Cherelle *out* of it."

David's heart sank. His indiscretion had not been private at all. His relationship with Dominique had cost him his witness and seemingly Corey's respect. He humbled himself and spoke in a quiet tone. "The woman you saw me with happened to be someone I loved. It wasn't a fling or a one-night stand—or anything like that. I'm not out here like that, Corey. Yes, I let our relationship cross the line that God set for me, but she was special to me."

Corey saw the telling signs in David's eyes. "And it sounds like she still is. I *repeat*, leave Cherelle *out* of it." Corey walked away and got into his car without another word.

Looking out her glass screen door, Cherelle wished she could hear what David and Corey were talking about. And what on earth had gotten into Corey? She'd never seen him be that cold toward anyone. What in the world was that about?

David looked flustered when he entered. A scowl hung on his face, and his brows were knitted into two slashes, partially forming the letter V. His whole mood had changed.

"David, are you okay?" Cherelle asked, but she could tell by the look on his face that he wasn't.

"Cherelle, can we pick this up another day? Monday or Tuesday? I need to go," David said. He would call Deacon Lewis and tell him they ended earlier than he expected.

"Sure . . . but are you going to tell me what's going on? What did Corey say to you?"

"Oh, so it's not *Pastor* Corey anymore?" David asked cynically.

"David, *what* is going on? Will you please talk to me?" Cherelle asked. She followed him into her office and closed the door behind her. She rested her body against the door. She watched him unplug his laptop and gather his things.

"David, please tell me why you're leaving."

"Dupree, why don't you just ask *Corey*?" he said, mocking the fact that Cherelle was so familiar with Corey that she referred to him by his first name.

"I'm asking *you*, David. I shared a part of myself with you last night. I opened up and let you into a private part of me. I'm talking about my emotions. My pain. My secrets. So . . . please, at this moment, after I've done that, don't treat me like this . . . please . . ." Cherelle couldn't explain her tears. Maybe she was crying because she had dredged up all those emotions last night. Maybe it was because she was just an emotional basket case, love-starved and crazy. Maybe it was because she had fallen in love with David Kent Cole.

David looked up from stuffing things into his backpack and saw her tears. He walked over to her and pulled her over to the chaise. "*Dupree,* please don't cry. You are making me feel like an absolute heel right now."

"I'm sorry. Last night brought up so many feelings. A lot of pain. Then there's you. I know how to keep this strictly on a friendship basis, David. I'm just asking you to tell me what's going on."

"Dupree, *what* is going on between you and Corey? It got pretty weird outside. Like he and I were back in the hood. It doesn't make sense to me."

"David, I want to share that with you. And I would right now. But honestly, it's Corey's business to tell—not mine. It would be deplorable if I broke his trust—I can't break his trust. Just as I would not break yours, David. I would rather it come from Corey. But it's *not* romantic."

"Well, you could have fooled me, the way that joker was carrying on. Back in the day, I would have laid him right on his behind for stepping to me so disrespectfully."

"That's not like Corey at all, David. He's kind and sweet."

"Dupree, I've known Corey Perry since elementary school —way longer than you. We don't interact the way he was talking to me outside. We go way back to the hood, Dupree. We *know* each other."

"David, what did he say?"

"He told me to keep my relationship with you 'strictly business.' It was like he was hot under the collar. Jealous."

Cherelle shook her head. "It definitely isn't jealousy; he may be a little overprotective."

"Why would he be overprotective of you, Dupree? How long have you known Corey?"

"A little over three years—since before Pastor Senior died. We've bonded a lot since then. Listen, David, I'm sorry if Corey is having a bad day. But I don't want there to be any strife between you and me."

"Dupree, there's no strife between you and me. Just like you shared a part of you last night, I shared a part of me. I told you my shortcomings. I *confessed my sins* to you. I haven't talked about the situation with Dominique with *anyone*. I need you to be honest with me, too."

Dominique. It was the first time Cherelle had ever heard David speak her name. In all that David had shared with Cherelle the night before, he hadn't said Dominique's name, although Cherelle assumed the woman David had been seeing was the same woman Gus had mentioned on Thanksgiving. Now she was positive.

"David, I *am* being honest. Give me some time. Let me talk to Corey," Cherelle said.

"He saw me at a hotel with Dominique."

"Oh . . . what was he doing there?"

"He didn't say. But apparently, Dominique and I must have been showing our affection for one another outside the door of our hotel suite, and Corey saw me. He feels that my indiscretion—my sin is grounds for me to stay away from you. Now, I'm not saying I wasn't wrong for being at a hotel with Dominique or for fornicating with her. I was dead wrong. There is no denying that. But it seems to me that Corey has deemed me and my ministry, and everything I stand for, unworthy because of my sin, and that's not true nor fair.

"Dupree, I've never been a womanizer while I've been in the pulpit. That was the old DC—before Christ. In the years since I've been pastor of DOC, the situation with Dominique was the first time I've been way out of line. I've always tried to live out God's Word. What happened with Dominique and me was the exception—not the norm."

Cherelle's doorbell rang. "That's odd. Excuse me for a second, David." Cherelle hurried to the door. "I hope Mama hasn't ordered something she shouldn't have," Cherelle said. She was shocked to see Corey standing at the door.

"Hey . . . I need to talk to DC," Corey said.

"He's in my office."

"Is there something going on between you two, Cherelle?"

"Not really, Corey. We do care for each other as friends. But David just got out of something, and he has a lot of residue. So we're just concentrating on being friends—platonic."

"Will you let us have a minute?"

"Sure. I'll go throw a load in the washing machine."

Corey walked into Cherelle's office and spoke before David had a chance to. "DC, we need to talk. First, I want to apologize for stepping to you like I did. I have a lot on my mind today. Today is my dad's birthday, man. And his death is as fresh to me today as it was three years ago. Secondly, I apologize if I demeaned you or your ministry in any way. I see what you've done with the communities in the city. I've talked to people whose lives you have helped to change with God's Word. I know you are a good man—a real man of God.

"I was at the hotel because my cousin Angel was getting married.

"Almost all of my family was staying there. When I saw you with the woman, I didn't immediately judge you. I saw the way you were looking at her. In my heart, I knew she wasn't some jump-off chick. I've been there before myself. I know sometimes it's a struggle for a single man of God to walk right-eously when it comes to that particular area. There are some jokers out here who have no regard for the Word, and they lay up with all kinds of women and even use their positions as ministers as a vehicle to get women. That's not me, and I know that's not you.

"We're *men*. But that's no excuse for not honoring the Word of God because Scripture says we are to have self-control, and that we have the power to control the flesh. I've come to the conclusion that I *need* to get married now. At first, it was just: *I would like to get married one day*. Now, it's a need. I don't want to fight with myself in the morning or the after-noon, or late at night or when it's raining, or when a Luther record comes on the radio," Corey chuckled. "I need a wife. I'm just trying to pick the right one so I don't end up in divorce court and tear my ministry all apart. So, I'm in no way judging you. I didn't mean to do that. It is apparent from the blessings God has bestowed upon you and the lives you have changed that the Lord is with you, DC. As I pulled around the corner leaving here, the Lord reminded me to remove the beam from my own eye . . ."

David nodded. "Thank you. I accept your apology. Cherelle and I had a deep conversation about Dominique—the woman you saw me with. She knows what happened. I told her *everything*. She is the only person, other than you, today, that I've talked to about it. I've come too far in Christ to throw my ministry out the window for anyone or anything. I ended the relationship with Dominique, but honestly, I'm still a bit raw.

"Corey, I won't lie to you. I care for Cherelle. I have *pure* admiration for her. And certainly, she is a physically attractive woman. I'm just not there. I've got to let God heal all the areas in my life that need healing. But I will *not* hurt Cherelle in any way. And for the record, if she were my sister, I probably would have reacted the same way you did."

Corey's brows shot up in surprise. "Did Cherelle tell you that she's my *sister?*"

"No. She was very adamant about *not* telling me the nature of you guys' relationship. But He did. As soon as you walked in that door again, I knew in my spirit, Corey."

Corey nodded. "Enough said. My father didn't find out about Cherelle until a few months before his death. He tried to tell my mother, but she didn't want to know. She said that if what he had to say wasn't going to cause him to stop loving her or her to stop loving him, she didn't want to hear it. She didn't want to hear any bad news or anything that might have stained her good memories of my father. She still hasn't said anything about it. I haven't told anyone, and I asked Cherelle not to tell anyone out of respect for my mother.

"My dad and Ma Dupree were in love. He came from a prominent, educated family, and Ma Dupree didn't. So, there was no way my grandmother and grandfather would allow him to marry Ma Dupree. Even though my dad was twenty years old—and by all accounts a grown man, he was under the influence of his parents. My granddad was a minister, and my dad wanted his blessing. So, my dad left the South. But before he left, he and Ma Dupree were together, and she became pregnant with Cherelle.

"Ma Dupree never told my dad she was pregnant because several months after he got to Detroit, he met and married my mother. She had the kind of pedigree that my grandmother and grandfather approved of, so my dad went on with his life. When Ma Dupree decided to tell my dad the secret she'd kept all those years, he only had six months to spend with Cherelle. The cancer had wreaked havoc on his body. At the time, Cherelle had just ended a relationship with some fool-behind dude, and she was taking it hard. My dad and I were there for her.

"My dad told me that he'd been wrong for letting his parents prevent him from marrying Ma Dupree because no one but God should choose who a man loves. He was sorry for what he had done. He told me that he had truly loved Ma Dupree and had wanted to marry her. He made me promise that, whether my mom ever knew about Cherelle or not, that I would take care of my sister and her mother, be a good uncle to Cherelle's kids when she had them, and be the brother that she should have had all those years. And that's what I'm doing, DC.

"I've seen Cherelle torn apart with her heart broken because she, like so many other women, had given her heart to a brother who was just plain undeserving of a gift like her. I don't ever want her to go through that again. She was losing my dad at the same time, so it was a lot for her to take. And these book publishers don't care. Cherelle makes money for them, and a deadline is a deadline. So through all of that, she had to keep it movin' when she was so broken. So yes, I'm very protective of her. I intend to do what my dad asked me to do . . ."

"I understand that completely," David said.

The two hugged and prayed together before Corey left.

Chapter 22

Sweet Thing

D avid sat enjoying the festivities of Pastor Corey Perry's seventies-themed fortieth birthday party at Chase on the River restaurant. He was seated at the same table with Mayor Walter Kincaid, Reginald Williams, the mayor's chief of staff, the restaurant's owner, Chase Martin, his wife Debra, and Deacon Lewis. Cherelle sat on the opposite side of the table, looking beautiful as ever. David hadn't seen her since their meeting with the mayor about the city's youth project two weeks ago. He'd just returned from a two-week mission trip to Nigeria the night before, and he missed her lovely face and smile, even though he was still emotionally raw and not ready for a relationship. But these days, he was never tired of seeing her.

Cherelle sat between Corey and Chase. As far as David was concerned, at least she was out of Walter's reach. Deacon Lewis sat on David's right. Walter was on his left, followed by Reginald. David was surprised that Reginald hadn't brought his wife, Juanita, with him. But then he remembered that Juanita was due to give birth any day, and maybe she hadn't been up to it. David watched as Cherelle threw her head back and laughed at something Corey said, then she lay her head on Corey's shoulder. Corey draped an arm around her, and the two clinked their glasses together in a toast. Cherelle continued to giggle uncontrollably. She was crying. She and Corey seemed to be enjoying some private joke because he was also laughing insanely. Corey put his head down on the table. David watched as Corey's shoulders hunched up and down. The music kept David from being in on the joke.

David tried not to stare, but Cherelle looked extraordinarily inviting to him in her metallic, royal blue paisley jumper with swirls of baby blue, pink, and yellow. She wore a matching head wrap. The halter-style jumper may not have looked particularly sexy on another woman, but on Cherelle, it seemed as if she had stepped off a page of Essence magazine circa 1972. It certainly accentuated her nice figure. She was a real-life Foxy Brown. Cherelle triggered a myriad of emotions in David. When she looked his way, David averted his eyes. He didn't want to step out of the perimeter of the friendship they'd built.

"Are you enjoying yourself, Old Man?" David poked at Deacon Lewis.

"Oh, yeah. This is a mighty fine place and a mighty fine party."

David stole a furtive glance at Cherelle again. "Yes, it is," he said to Deacon Lewis, unable to keep his eyes off Cherelle.

David loved John Lewis as much as he had loved his biological grandfather. He loved that he could bring joy into Deacon Lewis's life in small ways, like allowing him to tag along with him. Deacon Lewis had no living relatives. His wife, Essie, had passed away years ago.

Deacon Lewis leaned into David's ear. "This here is a nice band," he said.

David agreed. "I was just thinking that."

"Ms. Cherelle is lookin' really pretty." Deacon Lewis whispered in David's ear.

David smiled. "That's always . . ."

"Watchu gon' do 'bout it? That's what I want to know."

David whispered back. "We had that conversation. You know I'm not ready for that right now." David had finally gotten around to telling Deacon Lewis about his affair with Dominique and his feelings for Cherelle.

Deacon whispered into David's ear again. "You better *get* ready, son. Walter Kincaid barkin' up yo tree."

David watched as Walter Kincaid winked at Cherelle. Cherelle smiled back. Those two gestures unnerved David like a rash he couldn't rid himself of. Corey's mother, Cynthia Perry, came over to the table and spoke to everyone. She stood behind Corey and placed her hands on his back. Cherelle stiffened for a moment, then fidgeted with her head scarf. Then Cynthia Perry was gone.

Cherelle had confided to David that Cynthia Perry was polite to her but not necessarily warm. Corey still hadn't shared with his mother Cherelle's identity. His father had cautioned him to wait until Cynthia was ready. For that reason, Corey hadn't broached the subject with her. He remembered how upset she'd been when his father had attempted to tell her. Cynthia Perry had made it clear she didn't want to know one way or the other. That was three years ago, and nothing had changed. Corey was careful not to bring Cherelle to family gatherings, but he was getting tired of the façade.

Cherelle excused herself from the table. She had to pass David and Walter. Walter Kincaid stood and caught Cherelle's arm. "You're not leaving, are you, *Dupree?*" he asked.

"No. Just going to take care of something for the birthday man."

Walter held Cherelle's hand a moment too long. "Okay . . . I didn't want you to leave without me walking you out properly."

Reginald hid his smirk. Walter was grating on David's nerves, especially the way he'd said 'Dupree'. *Why is Walt all of a sudden referring to Cherelle as Dupree? I'm the only one who calls her that. Walt knows that.* Surely Walter Kincaid was getting under David's skin. Cherelle stopped and bent down between David and Deacon Lewis after Walter had released her. "Are you two handsome gentlemen enjoying yourselves?" she asked.

Deacon Lewis was quick to respond first. "I know I am."

The scent of the oils that were Cherelle's signature scents wafted up David's nostrils. He inhaled the scent of her hair even though it was covered by a fashionable head wrap. Either her perfume, natural body scent, or both was mesmerizing. "Me too," David said.

"Good." Cherelle stood up straight, and David couldn't help but watch her walk away. The jumper poured over her curves and fanned out to wide-leg bell-bottoms.

Walter sucked his teeth and let out an expletive. "Ooh wee!"

"You better hurry up and handle that, bro," Reginald chuckled.

"Man, I've been tryin'. She ain't cuttin' the *mayor* no slack."

"You need to step up your game. That's the first lady of this great city right there, bro. You better kick your knees up like you're marching in a band," Reginald teased.

Walter Kincaid stood up straight and began marching in place, kicking his knees up high. Reginald howled. "There you go, player! That's what I'm talking about. Get on your job!"

Chase and his wife laughed at Walter's antics. Corey took a knife off the table and pointed it at Walter, scrunching his face like Popeye, which caused Walter and Reginald to laugh even harder. David didn't find any of it amusing. He took his phone out and pretended to be checking messages, ignoring them all.

The lights on the stage dimmed low, and a white cloud of smoke crept across it. The lead guitarist of the band spoke with a deep, husky baritone voice. "Can everyone take their seats, please? We have a special presentation for the birthday guy." The few people who were up complied almost immediately. The lights dimmed all the way down, making the room pitch black momentarily. Then, the spotlight shone on a woman in an all-white halter jumpsuit. It had a metallic sheen like the one Cherelle had been wearing. The chords of Rufus and Chaka Khan's "Sweet Thing" began to play. The lights inched up two more settings, creating a full-body halo around the woman, and David's jaw dropped. *Dupree.* What a chameleon Cherelle Dupree was. Her hair, which had been previously covered with a head wrap, was set free and untamed in a full twist-out. It was wild and flirty.

From the moment Cherelle took command of the first note, David groaned inside. Her soft, sultry voice transported David to another space. She gazed out into the audience with her slanted, bedroom eyes and sang as if she were living the words. David didn't know the words "sweet thing" could grip him so tightly. Cherelle made eye contact with every person at Corey's table, but it seemed to David that when he gazed at Cherelle, she was singing only to him. She swayed smoothly to the music.

Over the last year, David had observed Cherelle in multiple capacities. He'd seen her command meetings in the presence of the President of the United States, teach the Bible on a level that some preachers couldn't, and create a storyline or script based on a brief interaction or observation of someone while she was people-watching. He knew what made her smile and what she cared about most. He was acquainted with all of her moods. It had gotten to the point that he could predict her responses to different situations.

But the woman on stage was an intensely different Cherelle. A sensuous Cherelle. The sway of her hips and the power of her voice as it floated through the atmosphere and through David revealed elements of a mystery. "Lord, Jesus," David mumbled.

Reginald shook his head at Walter. "Bro, if you don't handle *that*, I'm gonna have to take your player card!"

Awestruck, Walter shook his head. "Is this the same woman whom I've seen lead people to get saved with her teaching and speak her mind to the President of the United States? Man! I don't know what to say . . ."

"You better start going to church, bro!" Reginald instigated. "You've got to come up to her level. She's smart, funny, a woman of God, *and* sexy? You can't get no better than that. I wouldn't tell you nothin' wrong, chief!"

Walter laughed. He taunted Corey from across the table. "Corey, I'm coming to church next Sunday. Yes, sir! I'll be at church on the front pew," Walter said.

Again, Reginald roared. David was aggravated by the two of them. In his mind, Cherelle was precious and sacred. David knew that no matter how much effort Walter Kincaid put into pursuing Cherelle, she'd only end up being another one of his conquests in the end. The only thought that kept David sane was that he was confident Cherelle didn't want Walter in that way. She had said it herself. Walter was hardly trying to live a godly lifestyle. And no matter how many times he'd tried to convince Cherelle that he would, Walter wasn't ready to throw bachelorhood out the window. He had power, prestige, and almost any woman he wanted. He was living most men's dreams. Walter wasn't ready to give all of that up for one woman.

Cherelle continued belting out that beautifully sweet melody, strolling to the other side of the stage, where she elicited shouts of approval from the party attendees. Slowly, she swayed back to the center spot where David could eye her unabashedly. He swore his heart stopped beating when Cherelle clinched the climactic note of the song perfectly. Almost every person in the room stood and applauded. David was locked in his seat, his mind and heart fixed on the chocolate wonder. *She's not the only one who is about to go crazy. She is about to drive me crazy.*

Walter was out of his seat, clapping like a deranged man. "Sing, baby! Sing, girl! Whew!" he slapped Reginald on the back. Deacon Lewis was on his feet and stayed on his feet. He shook his head in awe as well. He turned to David. He didn't have to say a word; he'd already said what he needed to say. David heard the warning again. *'You better hurry up. Walter Kincaid barkin' up yo tree. . .'*

David was in a conundrum. And he was selfish. He didn't want Cherelle to *get away*. But he'd be a liar before his God if he said he didn't still have residue from Dominique. He didn't feel that there was any room left in his warped heart to let anyone else in—not even Cherelle. That truth alone pained him because he knew there was no guarantee that Cherelle would still be available when his wounds finally healed.

The band slowed the song down and infused it with jazzy tunes. The saxophonist slid right next to Cherelle and played softly, providing the perfect instrumental accompaniment for Cherelle to scat. She turned, twisted, dipped, and curved her voice skillfully over notes that caused tiny aftershock waves to pulse through David. The audience clapped wildly again before Cherelle finally brought the song to a close.

Corey beamed with pride. One of the professional photographers followed closely behind Corey with his camera as he took to the stage and hugged Cherelle, lifting her off her feet. She'd sung his favorite song with the perfection of a professional singer. He hadn't known she had been hiding *that* voice.

David was still taking it all in when Deacon Lewis made his way to the stage. David wondered what the old man was up to, but he decided to let Deacon Lewis enjoy himself in whatever way made him happy. He watched as Deacon Lewis nudged Corey playfully out of the way and hugged Cherelle. He watched the two talk. Then Deacon Lewis turned to Corey and spoke briefly with him. They shook hands, and Deacon Lewis patted Corey on his back. The trio was asked to take pictures. They smiled for numerous photos, changing poses a few times before Deacon Lewis returned to his seat.

"What are you up to, Old Man?" David asked.

Deacon Lewis smiled like a man who held a secret. "Mindin' my own business," he said.

"Uh-huh," David said, unconvinced.

A scowl marred Cynthia Perry's pretty face. She walked over to Corey's best friend, Chase, and pulled him aside. Then the two walked down the hallway where Chase and Mona's offices were located. Chase returned a few minutes later without Cynthia. Corey tried to make his way back to his table but was being held hostage every few steps by birthday well-wishers who requested to take pictures with him.

Walter seized the opportunity to take several photographs with Cherelle. David wanted to wring Walter's neck. Then Cherelle finally returned to the table.

"Hey . . . let's get some pictures for my scrapbook," Cherelle said to David.

David felt a little flushed. His heart played a song of its own. "Oh . . . okay . . . sure," he said, but his brain was mush. Cherelle had him under her spell. He stood, and they walked over to a spot where several photographers were clicking away.

"Lynn, can we get a couple of different poses?" Cherelle asked her best friend.

David tried not to encroach on Cherelle's personal body space. Her scent was intoxicating.

"Pastor Cole, can you move in a little closer to Cherelle and look the other way? Just forget I'm right here," Lynn said.

"Sure."

Cherelle slid her arm around David's waist. The scent of her hair was sweet.

"Okay, Pastor Cole, stand behind Cherelle, and both of you look at me." Lynn directed.

David switched positions and stood behind Cherelle. He prayed hard that his body didn't betray him. Cherelle was ever so cognizant of not resting her backside on him. David let out a gentle sigh of relief. He had to sit down. They smiled for the camera.

"Okay, that looked good. We're done," Lynn said. "Cherelle, I'll get them to you sometime tomorrow, after I go through and make sure they're polished. I know how you are."

"Thank you, precious," Cherelle said. She kissed Lynn on her cheek. They shared something in quiet voices, then they giggled. "Bye, Lynn," Cherelle said.

"Enjoy your night," Lynn said. "And girlfriend, you sang the mess outta that song!"

"Thanks, Lynn. And thank you, David. I'm gonna head to the ladies' room."

"You're welcome," David said. He hadn't even told her how wonderful she sounded or how marvelous she *looked*. He reconfirmed in his spirit what he'd known all along. Cherelle

Eleanor Dupree was a modern-day Proverbs 31 woman. She loved the Lord with all her heart, *and* she knew how to have fun. She was the kind of woman who could be whatever a man needed.

Chase's sister, Mona, crept up alongside David with basketball player Trent Dobbs attached to her like a Siamese twin. "Hey, Pastor Cole," Mona said formally. David wondered what she was up to. "I want to introduce you to my special friend, Trent, and also give you that package I told you about the other day . . ."

David caught on right away, and this time, he was able to prevent his eyes from popping wide with surprise. "Sure . . ." he said to Mona before directing his attention to Trent.

"Hello, how are you, Trent?"

"Oh, I'm good, Pastor Cole. It's nice to see you again. I saw the documentary about you. I think what you're doing with the kids in the city is awesome. And I enjoyed helping out during Thanksgiving."

"Thank you so much," David returned.

"Baby, Pastor Cole and I are like brother and sister. We grew up together."

"I keep hearing a lot of good things about you, Pastor Cole," Trent offered.

"I appreciate it. Come join us for worship one Sunday, Trent. We'd love to have you."

"I promise to do that when my schedule is good."

"Oh, baby . . . let me talk to Pastor Cole for a minute so I can give him a package," Mona said to Trent. He loosened his grip on her.

Trent kissed Mona on her forehead. "Okay, baby . . ."

Mona took David by the hand and dragged him down the hall to her office. There was a tall man at the entrance way. "Hey, Carter," Mona said to the private security guard. Then she turned and looked at David. "Man, I thought I'd never get away from Trent. He is so *clingy!*" Mona complained.

"Mona Martin, you just put me in a lie?"

"No, I didn't, *David Kent Cole*. I *do* have a package to give you."

"Oh, really?"

"Really." Mona took an electronic swipe card that was wrapped in a Kleenex out of her bra. She unwrapped it quickly and slid it into the electronic reader on her office door. It clicked, and she re-wrapped and returned the electronic key to its place.

David was curious as to what was going on. He stood on the outside of her door. Mona turned to see that David hadn't followed her in. "Come in, DC. What are you just standing there for?" David reluctantly came inside. Mona walked over to her desk and scribbled something on a piece of paper. She folded it and handed it to David. "This is your package. Give that to Walter immediately. His cell phone battery is dead."

"Don't be putting me in the middle of you guys' mess."

"DC, would you please not give me a lecture? I won't ask you to do anything else."

David didn't feel like arguing with Mona. It was of no consequence anyway. "Make this your last time, Mona."

"I said, *okay*. Pray for me," Mona said flippantly.

"I've been doing that."

"Well, don't stop. Let's go before Trent comes around looking for me. He doesn't know Carter is half crazy. He won't let anybody in this hall without permission. Even if he has to take a head or two off," Mona said.

"I believe it. He looks like it."

The two of them stepped into the quiet hallway. They heard shouting coming from Chase's office. The door was slightly ajar.

"Corey Charles Perry, you tell me the truth right now! Was Cherelle Dupree your father's *lover*?!"

Corey's voice remained low and calm. "No. Why would you think something like that about my dad?"

"Is she *your* lover?"

Exercising a great deal of patience with his mother, Corey answered. "No. Of course not," he said.

Cynthia's voice cracked. "Is she your father's *daughter*?"

"Yes. She's my *sister*, Ma."

"Oh, Jesus!" Cynthia Perry cried. It had been a little over three years since her husband of thirty-eight years had passed away, and she was still grieving. "I feel so betrayed by both of you—you and your father, Corey Charles!"

"Ma, calm down. It's not what you think. Cherelle happened before Dad even met you. It was before he moved to Michigan. She's older than me. She's forty-two and I'm forty—do the math. Ma, Dad was always faithful to you. He never cheated on you. He told me that himself before he died." There was a sprinkle of aggravation in Corey's voice. He had been so close to his father. He took it personally that his mother would ever think ill of his father. "He tried to tell you, but you didn't want to know. Dad didn't find out about Cherelle until six months before he passed away. Ma Dupree never told him she was pregnant because she discovered that he had come to Detroit and gotten married. She loved Dad so much that she didn't want to interfere with his happiness, so she never told him he had a daughter. And she never told Cherelle who her father was until she found out that Dad was dying. She couldn't live with the secret anymore. She didn't want him to die without knowing the truth. That's love, Ma. And Dad didn't tell you because you wouldn't let him . . ."

Cynthia Perry ran her fingers through her curly bob. "I'm sorry . . . I just—I couldn't take any more at the time, Corey. I knew your father was slipping away. And when he said he wanted to tell me about something in his past, I didn't want to hear anything that was going to put a blemish on our thirty-eight years together. I just couldn't take it." Cynthia cried. "I walked into his hospital room one day, and Cherelle had scooted next to your father in his bed and had laid her head on his chest. Your father had his hands in her hair. He was weak, but I watched him stroke her hair gently while she cried. I saw tears in your father's eyes. I perceived the matter as something altogether different. It looked like a man sharing an emotional moment with his lover . . ."

"It was a man comforting his daughter—a daughter that had been kept from him for thirty-nine years, Ma. It was bittersweet for him. He had the joy of knowing he had a daughter and the pain of knowing he hadn't been able to be a father to her, and would never be able to because he was dying . . ."

"Corey Charles, please forgive me. Your father was my *whole* life. He's the only man I've ever fully known. He was my *one and only* love. I just wanted to hold on to what we had . . . I'm so, so sorry. Please, forgive me, son," Cynthia cried.

Corey wrapped his arms around his mother. His eyes were full of tears for both his mother and father. "It's alright, Ma. I love you. I understand . . . and Cherelle understands."

"She must think I'm a horrible woman. I haven't been that warm towards her . . ."

"No, she doesn't think you're horrible, Ma. Cherelle understands the power of love. She's a beautiful person on the inside and out."

Cynthia looked up at her son and chuckled through her tears. "And she's surely got a voice on her."

"That too."

"Bring her here. I want to talk to her, Corey."

"Right *now?*"

Cynthia nodded. "Yes. Life is not promised, and time doesn't wait," Cynthia said, quoting her late husband.

"Okay."

David and Mona tiptoed out of the hallway and back to the party. David was relieved that Cherelle and Corey didn't have to hide their relationship anymore. He had heard that all sorts of rumors about Corey and Cherelle were in full swing at his church, so much so that Corey had thought to discuss it with his congregation. He just hadn't figured out how or when.

Corey found Cherelle and took her back to his best friend's office, where Cynthia was waiting. He left them alone to talk, while he made his last rounds to thank all of his guests as the party wound down.

Cherelle walked in apprehensively, not knowing what to expect from Cynthia. At times, the polished, full-figured woman seemed standoffish. Cynthia walked up to Cherelle and took a good look at her. That's when she noticed Cherelle's eyes. Those slanted eyes that were Charles'. And Cherelle's semi-straight nose belonged to Charles as well. Cherelle looked like Charles Perry painted in a different hue. Charles had been covered in smooth French vanilla, and Cherelle was a mirror image of him in smooth dark chocolate. Cynthia didn't know how she could have missed such a striking resemblance before. She cupped Cherelle's face in her hands, and then she hugged her. She was holding a part of Charles Perry, a man she'd loved all her life. And her tears poured out. "I'm so sorry, sweetheart, please forgive me . . ."

"It's okay, Mrs. Perry. I understand."

Cynthia pulled back and took Cherelle in. "Thank you. I want you to call me Ma from now on. You are a part of my husband and a part of my son. So that makes me your mother, too. Please do me the honor of calling me, Ma."

"Yes, ma'am."

* * *

COREY WALKED onto the stage and commanded everyone's attention without saying a word. His presence alone caused a hush to fall over the room. "I want to thank everyone for coming out tonight, especially those from Greater Christian Center. It shows that you can love the Lord and still have a good time without being sinful." The members clapped. "And I also want to clear up a matter and thank someone very special to me. Cherelle, come on up here," Corey said. Cherelle rose from her seat and crept up the stairs to the elevated stage. She joined Corey, looping her arm around his waist. "I've been asked a lot of questions about Sister Cherelle. 'Is that your honey? Is that your fiancée?' And I've given the same answer for the last three years, which is: Cherelle and I are good friends. That's the truth. We are good friends, but she's also my older sister." A few gasps could be heard across the room. "So, if you've noticed that we spend a lot of time together, and I'm protective of her, I am," Corey chuckled. "My dad was blessed with Cherelle before he came to Michigan from the South, and unfortunately, he didn't find out about her until he was in his last stages of cancer. So, we have been learning each other and growing as a family. I thank all of you who have respected and supported my mom and me through the process of grief. And again, thank you for a wonderful birthday celebration . . ."

The guests clapped. "Please enjoy the last dance. And I will see you all next Sunday."

This time, David had enough sense not to let Walter Kincaid get in his way. David handed Walter the note from Mona. Walter read it, smiled, and slipped it to Reginald. Walter and Reginald disappeared. David wondered how Mona managed to slip away from Trent. It was apparent that she and

Walter had something planned for the evening. Walter certainly didn't deserve Cherelle.

David met Cherelle as she and Corey stepped off the stage. "Can I have the last dance, Dupree?" David asked coyly.

A beaming smile spread across Cherelle's face. "Yes, you may," she said.

"Keep your hands where I can see them, or I'll throw a steak knife across the room and hit you right between your eyes," Corey said. He was halfway serious.

David couldn't help but chuckle, "My, my . . . so violent, Pastor Corey."

"Whatever."

"Now, *this* is my all-time favorite song," Cherelle said. She made sure not to dance too closely to David. They were in public view, and Cherelle didn't want to do anything to tarnish his reputation. David sensed that Cherelle knew just what to do and what not to do.

It took a split second for David to ascertain the tune. "'*With You I'm Born Again*' by Billy Preston and Syreeta," David said. "I know this. I can play it on the piano."

"Well, you'll have to play it for me one day," Cherelle said, before she began to serenade David.

"Dupree, I realize that you've been told this more than a hundred times tonight, but I've got to tell you again. Your voice is so . . . beautiful."

Cherelle searched David's eyes and nodded her thanks, continuing to sing to him. David wanted to pull Cherelle closer. He wanted her to rest her head on his chest like she'd done a few weeks ago in her office when they'd shared private conversations about their past failures and heartbreaks. But he knew this was not the place or time. And there it was again, the feeling that overpowered him when he was around her. It was frightening. He didn't want there to be a time when Cherelle

268

wasn't in his life. And yet, his heart was torn in another direction. He struggled on the inside with the plethora of emotions that begged for first place.

David had conflicting feelings about the song ending. As much as he wanted to keep holding Cherelle and continue listening to her serenade him, there was another part of him that wanted to escape the feelings she caused in him. His wounds were too new.

Bright lights popped on, and the restaurant staff began to reorganize Chase's restaurant for business the next day. "I guess this is goodnight. Did you drive yourself?" David asked Cherelle.

"You know Corey did not let me drive here. He didn't want me to have to drive back to my place so late by myself."

"Is he taking you home?"

Confused, Cherelle asked, "Are you joking?"

"No. Why?"

"Deacon Lewis said you two were taking me home. Corey has an early dentist appointment in the morning. He's got to have a root canal."

That sly, old, brilliant rascal. "Oh . . . yes, we're taking you home. I didn't know you had confirmed it," David said. It wasn't a lie.

"Are you sure?" Cherelle asked, somewhat skeptical.

"Positive."

"Okay. Let me go get my things. I'll be ready in a few minutes."

David couldn't have been happier on the inside. "Take your time, Dupree."

David found Deacon Lewis in a loose crowd. "I guess you are good for something, Old Man," he teased.

"One of us has to be."

"You told Dupree we were escorting her home?"

"Who else was gonna do it? You're the one who needs to kick his knees up and march."

David nodded. "Maybe so."

"I know the Lord done spoke to you. Open your eyes and behold your gift, son."

* * *

DEACON LEWIS INSISTED that David drop him off first. David assumed that was part of Deacon Lewis's master plan to allow him and Cherelle the opportunity to spend time alone. Cherelle settled in the passenger seat of David's Suburban. She let her head fall back against the headrest and reclined her seat. She'd taken her shoes off and was humming along to the gospel CD that was playing. "I enjoyed myself tonight, David."

"Me, too. Chase put out a luxurious and scrumptious spread for Corey," David said.

"Yes, he did! That must have cost a pretty penny. There was shrimp, lobster, crab, *and* steak. I ate some of everything!"

"I think I added some pounds myself, Dupree."

Cherelle let her window down a little more and let the late-night August breeze blow through her natural hair freely. David stole a glance at the way the wind gently moved it. "I can't believe I'm still awake," Cherelle said.

David looked at the clock on his dashboard. It was a quarter past nine. "Me either, Cinderella. It's past your bedtime."

"Once my head hits that pillow, it's on!"

"I know."

"So, David, your birthday is coming up soon—next month."

"Yes, ma'am."

"How do you feel about turning *forty*? I think Corey has been going through something for the last few weeks. Spending all kinds of time at the gym working out, and going shopping. I thought for a moment that he was afraid to get old," Cherelle said, chuckling.

"Honestly, I'm feeling good, Dupree. God has brought me a long way. I'm still in good shape. I've got my health and my strength. I'm trying to be like Deacon Lewis."

"I'm sure. He's still so active for a man who's eighty years old—and handsome."

"Don't make me jealous, Dupree."

"Hush."

"So are *you* worried about aging, Dupree?"

"Not at all. I try to stay in shape and enjoy life. I have more wisdom now than I did when I was younger. I wouldn't want to go back. I think all of a person's experiences make him or her who they are."

"Are you saying you're looking forward to aging?" David asked.

"I don't know about all that. But I'm okay with it. Two years ago, when I turned forty, I felt accomplished."

"Oh, that's right. Corey did say you're two years older than him, which makes you two years older than me. Dupree, you're a *cougar*!"

Cherelle laughed. "You are crazy!"

"Really, you're more like a kitten. That's what I think I'm going to call you from now on—Kit," David said, nodding. "Yeah, *Kit*. I like that. It will stay between you and me," he added, thinking about how Walter had called her 'Dupree' earlier.

Cherelle shook her head. "Ok, crazy."

"Kit," David said again, trying out Cherelle's new nickname. With a loving tenderness, he took Cherelle's hand, brought it to his lips, and kissed it. He threaded his fingers through hers and placed their hands on his thigh. Cherelle relaxed. She closed her eyes and let the summer breeze cool her. David enjoyed her this way. What he admired most about Cherelle had more to do with her spirit and her personality than her sensuality or physical attractiveness, but he was fully aware that she was a total package. Even Walter Kincaid knew that.

David became lost in his thoughts on the drive to Cherelle's place. The hypnotic rhythm of the tire treads meeting the road created a secure thinking bubble. Cherelle was so quiet that David thought she'd fallen asleep. When he pulled into her driveway, he turned to find her staring at him. Her dreamy eyes concealed a secret. David put the car in park and turned off the engine. "Let me walk you to the door and make sure you get in safely," he said.

"No. It's okay. You don't have to," Cherelle said. She didn't break her stare.

"What's wrong, Dupree—I mean Kit?" David smiled.

Cherelle's composed response settled in the confines of the truck. "Nothing. I'm fine."

David reached out and tipped Cherelle's chin toward him. He searched those slanted eyes. "What are you thinking about?"

Cherelle moved David's hand from her chin, brought it to her chest, and pressed it against her heart. She held it there, wanting him to feel her heart beating. The act sent pulses through David. Cherelle tilted her head and spoke in a quiet voice. "I'm wondering, *David Kent Cole*, if you know that *this* heart," she said, with her hand covering his, "can satisfy you in every way—spiritually, emotionally, and physically—in Christ."

David leaned closer, his lips a breath away from hers. "Oh, Kit . . . I know. Trust me, beautiful. I *know* it . . ." he whispered.

Cherelle backed away and pushed herself against the door. "Please don't kiss me, because I want you to kiss me. And please don't touch me, because I want you to touch me, David."

Cherelle sighed. "I need to go." She took a finger and placed it over David's lips. It was an inadequate substitution for the feeling of her lips against his. "Good night, David," Cherelle said. She unlocked the door and opened it. Stepping down, she grabbed her bag off the floor and closed his car door without making eye contact with him again.

* * *

THOUGHTS OF CHERELLE left David uncertain how to proceed and mentally depleted. And his body still hadn't adjusted to the time change from being in Africa for the last two weeks. He decided that whoever said there was no such thing as catching up on sleep had no idea what they were talking about. Tired as he was, there was no way he could have missed Corey's fortieth-birthday celebration. He hadn't realized how much he'd missed Cherelle either. He couldn't get her words out of his head. *"This heart can satisfy you in every way —spiritually, emotionally, and physically—in Christ . . ."*

David's cell phone ring amplified through his car speakers. He looked at the screen on the dashboard. It was an unfamiliar number. What in the world was anyone doing calling him this late? It was approaching ten p.m. on a Sunday evening at that.

"Pastor David Kent Cole. How may I bless you?"

"Hi Dave, I need to talk to you. Can you come by, or can we meet someplace?"

David heard God's voice immediately.

No.

"Uh . . . I'm on my way home from a birthday party for a friend, and I just got back from Nigeria last night. I'm truly exhausted. Another time would be better."

Dominique's voice was unsteady. "Dave, please, it can't wait . . ."

The warning came again.

No.

Despite his Father's voice, David pressed the accelerator, eased over to the far right lane, and took the exit that would place him closer to Dominique's townhome. "I'll meet you at your place," he said.

Chapter 23

The Wages of Sin

David observed that Dominique had barely touched her coffee as they sat in a booth at a twenty-four-hour Coney Island. They were the only two patrons in the establishment. Seeing Dominique again brought back a tidal wave of memories and emotions that David wished he could get rid of. That was the reason he'd picked her up from her place and suggested that they talk in a public place. He didn't trust himself enough to be alone with her in private. He remembered what Dominique's kisses tasted like and the way her body felt connected with his. Residue.

His love for her hadn't completely vanished. Those feelings had to dissipate on their own. He couldn't just make them go away, despite what he knew he felt for Cherelle. Across from him, Dominique squirmed on the cushioned seat of the booth. He hadn't wanted to rush her into a conversation, but his body was begging for rest. "Nik, what's going on?" he asked.

"Dave, I'm pregnant . . ." Dominique confessed. No hesitation. No beating around the bush. Just a straightforward fact. Her eyes quickly filled with tears. David rose from the seat across from her and scooted in next to her. He squeezed Dominique to his body, and she buried her head in his chest and cried. David felt her warm tears seep through his shirt.

Devastated, He spoke into Dominique's hair with a low, soft voice. "I'm right here with you, Nik. I know this is scary, sweetheart, but together we can do this . . . ." This was his fault entirely. He knew it. He'd been so comfortable with her, so careless. He remembered that while in Chicago on their weekend getaway, he'd loved Dominique freely as if she were his wife, not being mindful of the consequences.

Dominique looked up at David. "Dave, I'm scared. I can't think right now. I just want to go home."

David left enough money to cover their bill and something extra for the waitress. He guided Dominique out of the restaurant and to his truck. The ride to Dominique's had David's stomach churning, while Dominique's solemn disposition foreshadowed their future.

"Nik, I know this is a lot to handle. It's a lot for me, too. But there are two of us. And together we can work this out. I'm right here. We could get married . . ." What was he saying? He knew God didn't want that.

"This is not about you, Dave. This is bigger than you!"

David tried to stay calm. "What do you mean, it's not about me? You are carrying my child, Nik."

"Dave, like I said, this is not about you. I feel like you're suggesting marriage so that you can protect your image as a pastor, and that's not fair to me."

David refrained from saying what was on his mind. He didn't want to lash out at her at a time like this. She was partially right. But he didn't know any other way to correct the situation. All he knew was that she was carrying his child.

"Nik, as far as my image is concerned, I will stand before my congregation and confess my sin. I'm not above that at all.

But what I'm *not* going to do is let my child grow up without me being in his or her life. Image has nothing to do with this, and you know it. The sin was committed when we lay down together. My child is not a sin."

"It's not that easy, Dave. I've got my career to think about."

"Dominique, you can always take time off and go back when the baby is a few months old. I don't see why that has to be an issue."

"Dave, I'm not sure I'm ready for a *baby* right now."

David tried not to let her comment crush him. "I can understand that. But we have to deal with our situation."

"Dave, you know I love you. I know you'd make a great father and husband. But I don't think that's the life for me. And I don't want to put myself in that position. What if I don't want my baby to grow up in a church, but be able to make his or her own choices about religion when he or she is old enough?"

David eased into the driveway. He let the engine idle. He wondered where all of this was coming from. Dominique never expressed this level of aversion to church before. And she knew full well that he desired for his children to be raised with the fear of God.

"My child is going to be raised under the Word of God, Nik. Period. There is no other way. My family and I will serve the Lord. I want my child in my life. I don't want to be some weekend, part-time dad. No. That's unacceptable."

"Dave, have you considered the fact that I may not *want* a baby?"

David's resolve was stone. "Dominique, you're pregnant now, what other option do we have? This is where we deal with our mistakes and move forward."

"I have another choice, Dave. I don't have to have a baby. I can get an abor—"

"No! Absolutely not! Dominique Antoinette Street, you

listen to me, and you listen to me good; you are not going to *murder* my child! That's off the table! It's not a discussion we are going to entertain. I can't believe you would consider murdering our child because we sinned. What are we going to do, commit a sin on top of a sin—murdering our own child—the one we created together? No. No way!"

"Dave, I need to do what's best for me!"

"What about what's best for *us*? What about what's best for *our* child?!"

"I can't do this!" Dominique screamed. Her voice echoed in David's ears. She breathed in deeply, trying to catch her breath. The Suburban filled with silence.

David backed down. "Nik, let's not scream at each other. I just need to think—we both need to think and figure out what's the best thing for *all* of us."

Dominique spoke from a faraway place. She had mentally retreated. "I'm tired. I need to lie down."

"Let's talk tomorrow. I'll come by in the morning. I don't want us arguing. I love you . . ."

"Good night, Dave," Dominique said, opening the car door suddenly. She got out and hurried up the winding path to her front door. Tonight, David didn't bother to get out and walk her to the door. He was vexed. Mostly, he was pained. Why on earth had he allowed this to happen?

Dominique fumbled with her keys. David shook his head. He'd told her to replace the bulb at the front door months ago. Then he remembered that she had tossed her sweater onto the back seat. He got out and opened the back door on the driver's side. "Nik, you left your sweater!" he called out. He grabbed it off the seat and shut the door.

Dominique had turned to face David when the zooming sound of a speeding car caught her attention. Seconds afterward, gunshots pierced through the quiet night like a sudden hailstorm. David watched Dominique's body plummet. She writhed on the porch, attempting to reach for her weapon. David ran toward her, and in an instant, bullets careened through his body as he dived onto Dominique, covering her. He felt the first explosive shot burn through his back, but he didn't feel the others.

David's limp, heavy frame pinned Dominique underneath him.

"Arghhh!" Dominique grunted. She wiggled to free herself from his solid wall of muscles. She'd taken a bullet to the left shoulder. "Dave!" Dominique screamed. Blood filled David's mouth and flowed from the corners. Dominique struggled to reverse her position and cradle his head in her arms. David's smooth, honey-brown skin was marred with his own blood. As Dominique cradled David's head in the bend of her right arm, she felt his warm blood. *So much blood.* Dominique let out a loud, animalistic shriek as David's body jerked.

The numbing pain she'd felt moments ago in her left shoulder was vanquished by the pain that now choked her heart. "God, no!" Dominique screamed so loudly that the vibration of her voice scorched her vocal cords with the severity of hot coals. All of her professional training was useless as she watched the life force spill from David's body. Still in shock, she rocked involuntarily, dazed by the sight before her.

Bernard Jackson, Dominique's next-door neighbor, was out of his door and on Dominique's small porch in seconds. His nineteen-year-old twin grandsons, who were visiting from college, followed swiftly behind him. "Get the truck, Antonio!" Bernard shouted to one of the identical-looking young men. Both of them were six feet tall and handsome with dark skin and dark features. "He's gon' die if we wait on an ambulance!" Bernard continued. "Antoine, help me lift him," he said to the other twin.

None of them noticed that Dominique had also been shot until Bernard and Antoine lifted David's body. Dominique's shirt was soaked in her and David's blood. She gritted her teeth and panted out heavy breaths that didn't reduce the burning heat in her shoulder. Antonio jumped out of the four-door pick-up truck that he'd pulled onto Dominique's lawn and assisted her inside. Bernard and Antoine laid David on the back seat.

As soon as Antonio helped Dominique inside the truck, he hopped into the back seat, where Antoine had taken on the job of cradling David's upper body. Antonio stretched David's legs across his own. Bernard jumped into the driver's seat and threw the truck into gear. He skidded across the lawn and into the street. The pick-up raced down the block and screeched onto the main road. As a retired cop, Bernard Jackson's driving skills were impeccable, but the tires of the four-by-four protested as the truck perfected a street racing drift around the corner.

Dominique sat on the passenger side, slumped against the door. Every bump and dip in the road sent waves of pain through her entire body. "Is he breathing?" Dominique heard one of the twins ask the other. When she heard no response to the question, she let out a loud cry. She forced herself to look back at David's bloody body. Both of the twins' white Michigan State University T-shirts with green lettering were ghoulishly painted with blood. Dominique cried, "Please, God . . . don't do this!"

"Almost there," Bernard said calmly. "Hold on." But Dominique could only think of David. He'd been hit at least three times. She'd felt the growing wet spot on David's back when she'd put her hand underneath him. There was another stain on the right leg of his pants. He'd been hit there, too. *But his head.* Antoine had a towel underneath David's head. Blood gushed out.

It seemed to Dominique that Bernard was driving like a

little old lady. But in reality, he was zipping past other drivers, weaving in and out of lanes like a professional racecar driver. Bernard barreled down the busy street and headed toward City Memorial Hospital. Finally arriving, he skidded into the emergency lane. Antonio hopped out and ran inside. Within seconds, a team of medical professionals swarmed the vehicle and removed David.

Loading David on a gurney, the team raced him through the ER area. Bernard provided the desk staff with all the information he knew, while the emergency team whisked David away. Bernard made a call to his wife, and two minutes later, Leah Cole-Montgomery was calling his cell. Leah had known the Jacksons since she'd met her husband, Joseph.

"Bernard! What happened?" Leah cried into the phone.

"Leah, just come on down to City Memorial," he said. He didn't want to tell her all the details over the phone.

"I'm on my way! You tell me what happened to my baby!" Leah screamed into his ear. Bernard heard Joseph in the background telling Leah to calm down. "What happened?!" she demanded.

"Pastor Cole's been shot, Leah."

"Jesus, No! Jesus, please . . . . Is he alright, Bernard?"

Bernard choked up. "I—I don't know, Leah . . . there was a lot of blood," he said. Bernard swallowed hard. His mind had just caught up with the images he'd seen moments ago. They weakened his normally tough demeanor. "He's got more than one wound . . ." Bernard said hesitantly.

"Good Lord, no!" Leah cried before the call disconnected. Bernard signaled for his grandsons, and they prayed in the emergency waiting room.

Chapter 24

Wake Up the Mayor

Mayor Walter Kincaid slept soundly. He'd sent all his household staff home. It was well after midnight, and he was snoring louder than two old men. Every muscle in his body was relaxed and rested. He did not hear the buzzing of his cell phone on the nightstand. However, Reginald, his best friend and chief of staff, was persistent. He called back several times.

A full thirty minutes passed before Walter rolled over. The discordant sounds of his doorbell ringing and cell phone buzzing woke him from a delightful dream. Walter grunted. He reached clumsily over on his nightstand and snatched up his phone. He knocked something over in the process. It made a bouncy, tapping sound on the floor. It was a giant blue cup with a Superman emblem on the front. Walter heard the water pour onto his hardwood floor. He squinted at the phone screen; he'd missed several calls from Reginald. He got up against his body's wishes and went to the intercom and screen near his bedroom door.

"You must not like your job . . ." Walter said to Officer

Diane Ramsey, one of the two officers serving as detail for the weekend.

Officer Ramsey wanted to smirk, but she knew his royal highness could see her face, so she straight-faced the camera instead. "Sorry, Mr. Mayor, sir. Mr. Williams said it was urgent that you call him. He's on his way here." Walter was just a big pushover. One had to know him to know that. His tall, athletic build made him look more intimidating than he was. He rarely joked in public outside his circle of friends, but Diane concluded that Mayor Kincaid had a great heart. Her partner, Jeffery Smith, had coaxed her into delivering the bad news. He figured since she was the prettier of the two, the mayor wouldn't be as angry. Walter clicked off the camera without saying anything and dialed Reginald.

"This better be important," Walter said as soon as Reginald answered his phone.

"You got honey-company?" Reginald asked.

Walter looked over at Mona, who hadn't budged. She'd had too much champagne and too much Walter Kincaid. "Mona. But she's knocked out."

"Well, we have an emergency. We've got *big* problems."

"Nothing you couldn't handle alone?" Walter yawned.

Reginald hesitated. "Walt, DC's been shot. And one of our officers, too." Reginald said. He refrained from saying Dominique's name on the cell phone. He'd learned to monitor everything he did. "And the officer is loosely tied to the *Flight Arrangements,*" Reginald spoke in code. That's what they'd nicknamed an investigation the city's police department was conducting with the FBI, or rather, subordinately conducting, because the lead DEA agent, Jay Delgado, seemed to think that the city's police department worked for him personally. He was a rogue of a man, and more arrogant than Reginald.

"What?!"

"It's true, Walt. I've got confirmation from the hospital. They took DC up for emergency surgery two hours ago. It was an apparent drive-by. He's sustained three gunshot wounds. One in the left shoulder, one in the right leg, and . . . um . . . he's got a head wound. He's pretty bad off. My contact at the hospital says they don't think his chances of survival are good. He sustained a 'non-survivable injury,' is what she said exactly. It's . . . uh . . . not good, Walt." Reginald said somberly. David was their brother.

Walter let out an expletive. Then there was nothing but silence. The normally charismatic orator was at a loss for words. He wasn't the mayor right now. He was Walter Kincaid, a lifelong friend of David Kent Cole. They'd all gone to college to escape the violence they'd witnessed as young men growing up in the city. Now, the very violence they'd attempted to escape had ensnared them anyway. Walter let out a long breath. It was Reginald who hid his emotions by switching gears. He had to remain the voice of reason for the mayor of the city. That was his job.

"Mr. Mayor," Reginald acknowledged, alerting Walter to his civic duties, "We've got a department leak bigger than the Mississippi River. A news report is going to tie our officer to the Flight Arrangements, and I wouldn't be surprised if DC gets thrown in the mix somehow. It's all bad, Walt. You're going to have to give a statement tonight. Nothing is in our favor right now. I think we should go see about DC and handle the rest later."

Walter let out a string of expletives this time. He'd kept his administration scandal-free since he'd been elected. "What about the *clown?*" Walter asked, referring to Brent King, a narcotics officer with the police department who was as dirty as they came. He was the centerpiece of the Flight Arrangements investigation.

"Chief says Internal Affairs questioned him about an unrelated incident last week, but they didn't go hard. Natasha Savage in IAD is the only one over there who knows he's the FBI's link to the drug cartel. She didn't want to spook him. The feds don't want to blow the case. I'm downstairs," Reginald said, entering the Mayor's mansion with his key.

Walter pressed the end-call button on his cell and hopped in the shower. Afterward, he dressed as fast as he could. He did not wake Mona. Instead, he left a note for her to call him as soon as she awakened. He figured he'd be back before then. She was sleeping hard, and she'd turned her cell phone off.

When Walter entered his study, Reginald gave him the rundown. "Okay, here's what we know so far . . . Brent King—the clown, has apparently been seeing Officer Dominique Street on and off for two years—along with some other women. He gets around."

"Where does DC come in?"

"DC dated Officer Street for a short time. The two started seeing each other last year around mid-September. They stopped dating around June of this year. Officer Street placed a call to DC sometime around ten p.m. last night—right after Corey's party, probably. There had been no other calls between the two since June. But she's been talking to the clown at least twice a week, and he's made frequent visits to her in the last few months—and they weren't playing Monopoly."

"How do you know all this?" Walter asked.

Reginald rolled his eyes. "The Boss," Reginald said, referring to FBI agent Delgado.

Reginald's sarcasm didn't get past Walter. "He sure knows a lot."

"Or at least thinks he knows. Anyway, the IAD interview with Officer King was based on an anonymous tip they received about a murder that went down near Grady's Liquor store. King swore that Officer Street could back him up on his whereabouts. But when she was contacted by IAD, she didn't corroborate King's story. That's all I got from Delgado. Let's get movin', Walt. We've got a long day ahead of us," Reginald said.

"I want to know about this leak," Walter said, walking toward the door.

"Right now, I'm on a dead end with that one. The chief is on top of it. She's doing everything possible to squash it."

"And how does Officer Street figure in? You think she's a player in the Flight Arrangements?" Walter asked.

"Her record is impeccable. But that doesn't mean anything."

"What does The Boss think?" Walter asked.

"He wouldn't say. He was so rattled about the leak, he's taking it personally."

"Who's breaking the news story?" Walter asked.

Reginald rolled his eyes for the second time. "Your favorite girl, Channel 7 news reporter, Ashley Todd."

"You're kidding?"

"Nope. She at least had the decency to call to see if you wanted to make a comment. I told her to hold off for a bit. But it's breaking tonight. You need to learn to keep your women in check," Reginald said.

"That's why she's *not* my woman. She can't be kept in check," Walter said.

"Well, Ms. Ashley Todd is working her way up the network with this story, and we are going to be at the bottom of the food chain. And we're in a boatload of—"

"Don't say it. Remember you're working on the language—you don't want that baby to come out sounding like his father, do you?"

"Nope. And you owe *me* about a hundred dollars for the string of curses you let out tonight."

"Wait on it," Walter said as the two walked out the door.

Reginald's cell rang. "Yep."

"I killed the news story for now," Agent Delgado said. Reginald wondered how Agent Delgado had managed that, but he wasn't about to let on that he was impressed in any way. Jay Delgado was as cocky as they came. "And by the way, Officer Street is pregnant. That may be some information we can use to our advantage at a later date. I'll get back to you later." And he was gone.

"Well, Walt, I know we don't need a scandal, but we're skating on one now if you ask me," Reginald said.

THE TWO MEN rode in silence to the hospital. Orlando, the driver, sensed their mood and didn't bother with any small talk. Orlando had turned off his usual all-news station because it was broadcasting news about David and Officer Street being shot. The reporter had practically eulogized David, which set Walter on edge. All major news channels were running stories about the violence in Detroit, which had lessened tremendously since Walter Kincaid had taken office. Now, news outlets around the country were calling the senseless shooting of Pastor David Cole, one of the city's most prominent proponents of non-violence and saving the youth, a major setback for the city. And it was.

Walter's heart was heavy as he looked out of the window en route to the hospital. He surely hoped it was the will of God for David to survive, despite the gloomy news reports. David was a spiritual giant. They'd received news that prayer vigils were being held outside the hospital and at David's church. The city's police chief, Ms. Michael Darling, and Syvonne Wyatt, the mayor's press secretary, were already waiting at the hospital. Chief Darling had been waiting for the mayor to arrive so that they could be seen together. And Syvonne had been holding the press off for hours. Their first stop would be to check on Officer Street. Then Walter would check on his friend. He wasn't sure what kind of statement he would make. But Reginald had gone into professional mode. He was busy typing something on his tablet for Walter. He would connect with Syvonne at the hospital so they could discuss strategy. That was the only way Reginald could keep his mind off the gravity of the situation at hand.

Chapter 25

In the Midst of Darkness

David was out of surgery when Leah and Joseph arrived. It had taken them almost five hours to drive to the hospital from their cabin up north. They listened as the hospital's chief neurosurgeon, Dr. Arielle Smith-Blackmon, explained David's injuries.

"Pastor Cole suffered three gunshot wounds . . ."

"Oh, Jesus!" Leah said, covering her mouth with her hands. Her knees buckled. Joseph caught his wife underneath her arms and lifted her with his strength before she hit the floor. He walked her over to a nearby sofa, and they both sat down. Joseph allowed Leah to lean on him.

Dr. Smith-Blackmon followed them and continued, careful to use laymen's terms. "He suffered a wound to his right leg and his left shoulder. Both of those injuries are non-life-threatening, and the bullets were removed. However, the most severe wound was to the left side of his head."

Disoriented, Leah nodded while the doctor spoke. "O—o-okay—oo-kay . . ." she mumbled. But her thoughts were crowded together like a New York sidewalk. She couldn't think of anything without seeing an image of her holding David in her arms as an infant when he'd entered this world almost forty years ago.

Dr. Smith-Blackmon was patient and compassionate in her delivery of the prognosis that had to be shared with the family. "A bullet entered just behind his left ear. Unfortunately, it crossed both hemispheres, and fragments are lodged in his skull," Dr. Smith-Blackmon said.

Leah was visibly shaking. "Oh, Lord . . . Oh, Lord. Oh, Lord God . . ."

Dr. Smith-Blackmon remained professional. She was certain Leah did not recognize her. She looked Leah in her eyes and sighed. "Mrs. Cole-Montgomery, we have done everything medically possible for Pastor Cole at this time. We've placed him in a medically induced coma due to the trauma he's sustained. Right now our main concern is the swelling of his brain . . . "

"Wha-wha . . . what are you saying?" Leah stuttered.

Dr. Smith-Blackmon paused before answering. She wanted to be honest, but she didn't want to take away the family's hope. She believed in a God who could do all things. "We estimate a one percent chance of survival. We will continue to monitor him through the night and provide the best medical care we can . . . ." Dr. Smith-Blackmon's voice trailed off.

Leah collapsed onto Joseph's lap and sobbed profusely. "God's got the last word, Lee. God's got the last word," Joseph said, stroking Leah's hair. Normally, Leah Cole-Montgomery was strong and fierce in her faith. But the doctor's words had toppled her.

Deacon Lewis walked over to the couple and stood over them. "The Lord says to pray. If we gon' cry, then we gon' have ta cry and pray at the same time," he said. David was like a son to him; no one felt the pain worse than he did. Not even Leah could understand what David had done for John Lewis. David had given John Lewis's life meaning and purpose after the death of his wife. David was the son and grandson that God had never given to John Lewis biologically. "There are two hundred people outside this hospital, prayin'. And I'm told that the church is packed right now. We gon' put David's angels to work right now, Ms. Leah. I'ma keep on prayin'," Deacon Lewis affirmed.

Dr. Smith-Blackmon nodded in agreement.

LESS THAN AN HOUR after Dr. Arielle Smith-Blackmon delivered the saddening news, one of the hospital chaplains entered the area. Because of David's notoriety, the family was escorted to a private room on the floor just below David's ICU room. It was a quiet, serene location that overlooked a court-yard and an elaborate fountain below. Looking down eight stories, Leah could think of nothing. Her mind was a jumbled mess.

When Gus arrived, Leah's worry extended to him. She was perplexed by his overgrown facial hair and unkempt appearance. His dingy-blonde hair was shoulder-length now, and he sported a ragged beard and mustache. Gus looked just like a ghost—just like his nickname. His white skin was pale, paler than Leah had ever seen it. Gus looked like a madman. "I'm working, Ma," Gus said into Leah's ear and squeezed her to him. He didn't remove his black tinted sunglasses, which made him look even eerier. Leah nodded and released her emotions.

"Why would someone do this to my baby? He's done nothing but good for this city—for these kids—for everyone. Why would they do this?!"

"I don't know. But I'm going to find out, Mama Leah. And

they *will reap* what they've sown. I promise you that. I put my life on it."

Leah laid her head on Gus's chest. She wasn't sure what type of justice Gus was referring to. And at the moment, she didn't care. It was hard to think holy thoughts when her only son was lying in a hospital bed, dying. The neurosurgeon had all but said that David may not make it through the night. Feeling Gus's strong arms around her, the warmth of the love they shared for David cocooned them. When Gus pulled apart, Leah saw the trickle of tears slip from under Gus's severe, dark-tinted sunglasses. Then Walter Kincaid entered, and Leah raced to him and spouted one word.

"What?!"

"Mama Leah, they think it's gang-related—but we haven't confirmed anything yet. I've got everybody working on this thing."

"You better find every last person who had something to do with this!" Leah's demand broke into a cry.

Joseph walked up behind her. "Come on, Lee," he said, guiding his wife into a corner of the room. He made her sit down. Joseph was afraid that Leah would cause her blood pressure to spike and have to be hospitalized herself.

Walter Kincaid acknowledged Gus with a nod. Then the two embraced. Truthfully, Walter wondered what Gus was into these days. He looked horrible. Walter knew that Gus was into some type of law enforcement. He suspected Gus worked for the FBI or CIA. Neither David nor Gus had ever confirmed either way.

"What's your next move?" Gus asked quietly.

"When we find out what's going on, I'll be better able to say," Walter said, sounding like a practiced politician. Before the words had time to settle in the universe, Gus shook his head.

"Don't give me that, Walt. I already know everything—*everything*. Let's go out to my car and talk."

"Alright," Walter said. He nodded to his security detail. "Going out to the parking lot."

"No. No security. Just you and me."

Walter sighed. "Okay, but Reg is in."

Gus acquiesced. "Fine."

* * *

In Gus's rented SUV, he placed a small device on the dashboard that resembled a cell phone battery. Walter looked curiously before asking, "Is that some kind of recording device? If it is, I have nothing to say."

"It prevents others from picking up on this conversation," Gus said. Walter peered out the windows of the SUV. Reginald did the same thing from his position in the back seat.

"Ghost, what are you into, man? Who would be listening to you?"

"Walt, the question is: who would be listening to *us*? Not all the players in Flight Arrangements are *clean*."

There was no point in playing dumb, so Walter gave in. "We know that. We have people on the inside who are keeping track of some of our dirtbags. When the time is right, the arrests will be made," Walter explained.

"Man, this thing is way bigger than dirty cops! Even some of the higher-ups in the bureau are dirty. You better watch your back closely. And don't get too comfortable with the federal team, which is supposed to be here assisting you. They reek of impropriety," Gus said.

"How did DC get caught up in this, Ghost?" Reginald asked from the backseat. He scooted up closer and rested his elbows on the backs of Walter and Gus's seats.

"Officer Dominique Street," Gus said flatly. "Brent King, your main dirtbag and link to the drug cartel—he's a disgruntled lover. The hit was on Street. DC was collateral damage."

"Are you saying King ordered the hit on her—someone he's been uh . . . *cozied up* with on the regular?" Reginald asked.

"That's *exactly* what I'm saying," Gus returned. "And he's sloppy. He's got the drug cartel up in arms. I'll be surprised if he makes it through the night himself. He's brought too much attention to them. The hit was done by some fairly new members of the gang who call themselves The Sect. They do some drug running for King."

"We thought he had a bunch of renegade guys," Reginald said.

"No. It's all organized. The Sect is run like a business—better than any Fortune 500 company I've ever seen. Their management flow chart is incredible. The gang members you see on the street are low, low-level players. The Sect is worldwide. And they are heavily into sex trafficking." Gus refrained from telling them that the strong arm of The Sect—the brains behind the entire organization had been dabbling in cybercrimes that had turned into cyber-terrorism over the last three years. Gus's unit at the CIA had been tracking them for a while now. He was more familiar with The Sect than he wanted to be. "And just so you know, about an hour ago, The Sect's rival gang, Them Boys, retaliated by shooting up a known hangout of The Sect—supposedly on David's behalf. So you need to figure out how you're going to handle the PR on that. You've got a heads up," Gus said.

The members of Them Boys considered David off-limits because of a meeting he'd had with them about refraining from harassing any youth who didn't want to be recruited. David had never entered into any type of agreement with any gang because he felt that God's people had no business entering into covenants with unholy people. But he had asked them to respect his church and the youth who were members of DOC. Them Boys used David's shooting as an excuse to start a turf-war takeover with The Sect.

"DC wouldn't have wanted that kind of retaliation. He had more integrity than I've ever seen. He would have let God handle it," Walter said stoically. He looked out the window at the lights of the hospital. Being mayor was not a joy tonight.

"Don't speak of my brother in the past tense, Walt. He's still here with us."

"I'm sorry. I didn't mean to."

Just then, a tap on the window startled Walter and Reginald.

Gus drew his weapon and let his window down slowly with his gun pointed at the window tapper. The huge man on the outside had his weapon pointed at Gus as well. Gus stared down the .38 Special.

"Ghost, is that any way to greet a friend?"

"Pardon me, I'd rather be safe than sorry," Gus said. He lowered his weapon. So did Bones. Bones leaned into the car.

"Walt, Reg, DC is gonna be alright," Bones encouraged.

"Bones, you just made me pee on myself, I swear," Reginald said with relief, finally letting go of the breath he'd been holding for the last few moments.

Walter rubbed his temples. "What in the world is going on?"

Bones ignored them and spoke directly to Gus. "Timothy Archer. Lionel Kennedy. Thomas Banks. And Juan Dozier. It was Dozier's night. I'm out," Bones said and walked away from the vehicle back into the blackness of the night.

"Peace," Gus said before raising the window. Gus stared at Walt. "You need to get on it right away before I forget that one year ago I gave my life to Christ, and do something to those young men that I will regret for the rest of my life."

"What?" Walter asked, befuddled.

"The names, Walt. Those are the guys who shot DC. The trigger boy is Dozier, right, Ghost? Bones said it was *his* night. That means it was his night to prove himself," Reginald offered.

"Thou hast said," Gus replied, sounding like a page out of the King James Bible. He looked down at his cell phone. "The chaplain is ready. Mama Leah wants me to come in and pray with the family."

Walter was speechless as the three exited the car. He stopped abruptly as they neared the private hospital entrance. His security team followed loosely. "Ghost, what about Dominique Street? How connected is she to the drug cartel and the sex trafficking?"

"Walt, you run the city and your police department the way you see fit. But I'll tell you one thing: Dominique Street is *mine* to deal with. Her sins will not go unpunished. Pregnant or not. And that's all I have to say about that," Gus said. He walked briskly ahead of Walter and Reginald.

It was apparent to Walter that Gus had people in high places, in heaven and on earth. Whatever Gus did for the government, he had access to everything that had been going on with Flight Arrangements. He knew details that Walter Kincaid did not.

Chapter 26

Goodbye, Don't Go

Leah, Joseph, Deacon Lewis, Gus, and the hospital chaplain made a semi-circle around David's hospital bed while the chaplain prayed over David. Deacon Lewis was the only one of the four who'd had enough strength to continue praying after the chaplain had prayed and left the family alone to say their final goodbyes. Leah's body buckled for the second time. "I can't do this . . ." she said weakly, barely able to stand. Joseph raised her bent body and pulled her to his side. He escorted her out of the room. Deacon Lewis followed.

Gus was the last one left in the cold, medicinal-smelling hospital room with David. The smell made him sick to his stomach. He wanted to regurgitate the food that lingered in his stomach. Gus had been with the CIA for over fifteen years of his life, and he'd seen many things. But nothing was as horrible as seeing his soul-brother suspended between this life and the afterlife. Gus pulled the chair from the corner of the room, placed it right next to David's bed, and sat. David's normally honey-colored skin was ashen and devoid of vitality. It no longer held life's warm glow. Chapped, cracking lips made

David look as if his soul had already departed. Gus took in all the intimidating equipment. There was a sea of machines, wires, and tubes connected to David. Gus studied the grotesqueness of David's swollen head, which was supported by a cervical collar. He let his manly tears fall.

Gus lifted David's limp hand and cupped it in both of his. "DC . . . you can't go . . . you *promised*. I've never known you to go back on your word, bro." Gus said, choked up on his own words. He viewed David through stinging eyes that he found difficult to keep open. Gus squeezed his eyes shut. "You said we were gonna teach our sons to fish and scare our daughters' boyfriends away . . . you promised . . ." Gus opened his reddened eyes. He inhaled and exhaled, taking deep breaths to keep himself from coming undone. "You're the reason I got saved last year, DC. And . . . I need you around to keep me . . . in line, bro. This is all new to me—especially the women. You know God drives a hard bargain when it comes to His rules about me not getting any lovin' unless I'm married, bro. Because of that, it's been a minute since I . . . you know . . ." Gus said. His attempted humor was strangled by the flame in his throat. "It's not time yet, DC," Gus continued.

"I know it's better on the other side, but it's not time, bro. It can't be time . . . it's not supposed to end like this. We were supposed to go buy our orthopedic shoes together and feed the pigeons and stuff. It's not time, man. Come on back here, DC. We need you. I love you, bro. You are the only family I have, man. Please don't do this to me . . ." Gus couldn't take it anymore. His chest was caving in under a three-thousand-pound boulder. "I gotta go, bro. I'll be back. And you better be right here, man. I mean it. I love you . . ."

Gus returned the chair to the corner of the room. He bent down and kissed his brother's forehead. "Oh, I almost forgot . . . Cherelle wants me to tell you that she loves you, you lucky dog.

You better get back here and take care of her, bro." Gus took his dark glasses from his pocket and slid them back on. "Be back soon," he said finally and headed right to Dominique's room. Yes. She was going to pay.

Gus slipped into Dominique's hospital room easily after he'd asked Walter to briefly remove the security detail they'd assigned to her for precautionary measures. Gus did what he came to do and walked out casually. He went outside to the area where Deacon Lewis and the rest of the church had gathered in prayer on David's behalf. David's young assistant pastor, Clint Hobbs, was leading the prayer vigil outside. A galaxy of candles illuminated the darkness.

Cherelle stood right next to Deacon Lewis, and he squeezed her hand as she sobbed. He was the closest to David she could be at this dark time because no one had been allowed into David's room except for his mother, Joseph, Gus, and Deacon Lewis. Not even Walter had been given the privilege. She'd heard from Deacon Lewis that the chaplain had prayed with the family, and she felt as if someone were choking her to death.

Gus eased next to Deacon Lewis and Cherelle. He spoke into Deacon Lewis's ear first. "They're all going to pay," he said. Then he hugged Cherelle and told her what to do next. Gus walked to his rental and exited the hospital parking lot. Cherelle eased away from the crowd and walked toward the block Gus had told her. She pulled her thin shawl around her and eyed her surroundings to see if anyone was following, just like Gus had instructed. She kept her head up and listened for any unusual sounds. She jumped when the sound of a barking dog caught her off guard. She sucked in a gulp of air. Just then, an SUV without headlights pulled up. "Cherelle, get in," Gus said out of the lowered window. Cherelle released her breath and hurried inside. "Put on your seatbelt," Gus directed.

"Where are we going?"

"You'll see when we get there."

Gus's cell phone rang. "Yeah, I'm on my way," he said.

Ten minutes later, Gus drove up to the back entrance of The Ice Cream Shoppe. He'd killed his lights a half block down. He turned off the engine. "Cherelle, stay behind me. If anything goes wrong, get out of here. Live your life like this part never happened—as if you don't know anything about this place, okay? Like you've never been here before." Gus handed Cherelle the car keys. "You get to safety and don't worry about me. That's what you've got to do, okay?"

Cherelle nodded. "Yes . . ."

"Okay, let's go." Gus got out of the car and walked around to Cherelle's door. He opened it for her, keeping his eyes on everything in the dark morning. He closed the car door behind Cherelle and hurried to the Ice Cream Shoppe's backdoor keypad and punched in the code, unlocking the door. He locked it back as soon as they entered. They were in pitch blackness. "Cherelle, put your hands on my back and stay behind me," Gus said. Cherelle complied. They walked down a long hallway before they reached a door. Gus opened it and hit the light switch. "Stay here," he whispered. Gus descended the stairs. In a few seconds, he returned. "It's safe. Go on down."

Cherelle sat on one of the sofas and released all the emotion she'd been holding onto for the last several hours. She sobbed loudly. "I love him, Gus! I love him! I should have told him . . . last night . . . I love him. Oh, God . . . David . . . please!"

Gus sat down next to Cherelle and held her in his arms. In a way, he felt like he was betraying David for touching Cherelle the way he was. But the harder Cherelle cried, the more compelled he was to squeeze her closer to his body. "Cherelle, I need to talk to you . . ." Gus said in a whisper. Cherelle looked up at Gus through teary eyes. "I need you to listen to me. What happened to DC . . . it's because of that—" Gus started before taking a moment to contain himself. "It's because of Dominique. She is mixed up in some heavy stuff with the wrong people. And she dragged DC right into it. She'd been warned. She knew something like this could happen, and she didn't care. But I'm going to make sure that they all pay, Cherelle. I mean it." Gus reached into his jacket pocket and pulled out a small package. "Keep this," he said. "Put it in a safe place. If something happens to me and DC, I want you to give this to Mama Leah. And don't *ever* believe the lies that might be told about DC. I've known him almost all of my life. He's a good man. He's my brother. His only sin was getting involved with Dominique."

Confused, Cherelle asked, "Wh—Why are you giving this to me? David doesn't even know how I really feel about him. I should have told him. I don't know if he feels something for me, but . . . I just . . ." Cherelle explained before breaking down again.

"He knows, Cherelle. DC just got himself into something that blindsided him, that's all. He loves you. I know it for certain. And no matter what happens, if he makes it and I don't, make sure DC knows to keep Dominique away from this family with all her lies."

Cherelle's tears continued to flow steadily. "Why are you telling me all this, Gus?"

"Because when I first started my career, my boss once told me, 'When you don't know who you can trust, trust the one you can trust. Trust the obvious.' Cherelle, you are the obvious."

It was too much to take in, and all Cherelle could think about was losing David.

Chapter 27

Sweet Hour of Prayer

A day had gone by, and Leah's blood pressure caused her to be admitted to the hospital just as Joseph feared. She'd been near stroke level. Joseph prayed that somehow a miracle would happen for David. He feared losing his son and his wife. He couldn't stand a tragedy like that. He hid those things in his heart as he left Leah's room and headed to the ICU. When he opened the door to David's room, Deacon Lewis was at David's bedside.

Joseph stood over David. "Good Morning, son. It's Joe," he said, patting David's hand. "Good Morning, Deacon."

"Morning," Deacon Lewis answered without looking up at Joseph. He kept his eyes fixed on David. "I think the swelling is going down, Mr. Joe," Deacon Lewis said. "Young Gus just left. He was here all night. I told him to go on back to David's and shower, and get some rest. But I know he'll be right back. And Pastor Clint got the church prayin' round-the-clock, Mr. Joe. They're operating in shifts. Someone's been outside this hospital prayin' every hour."

"That's good. We're so grateful for the support."

Deacon Lewis rose from his chair and went into the restroom. He came out toting a face towel in his hand. He gently brushed the moistened towel against David's lips, carefully working around the tube in his mouth. He skillfully avoided bumping the cervical collar. He took a Chapstick tube out of his pocket and rolled it across David's lips. "Uh-huh. Looks good, son," he said to David before placing the tube back into his pocket. Joseph smiled. Deacon Lewis walked back into the restroom and returned the towel. He came out and reclaimed his seat. Finally, he looked at Joseph, who had taken a seat on the sofa bed against the window, where he was fighting sleep. "If you want to be alone with him, I can take a walk, Mr. Joe," Deacon Lewis said.

"No. You're fine, Deacon. I just want to sit here."

"How's Ms. Leah?" Deacon Lewis asked.

"They've got her pressure down, but her doctor wants to keep her here today."

"Uh-huh. She'll be fine," Deacon Lewis said. "And David's work here is not finished. No, sir. He's got more work to do. God is in control. Yes, He is," Deacon Lewis continued confidently. "One percent don't mean nothin' to my God, Mr. Joe. He don't need *no* percent to do what He does. See, David's still hanging on. He's strong in the spirit," Deacon Lewis said. He began humming "Sweet Hour of Prayer." "Yes, sir. That's your favorite hymn, ain't it, son?" he said to David. "I love to hear you play it on the piano. It would be real nice to hear you play it for me again," Deacon Lewis said. He continued to hum as Joseph drifted off into a deep sleep.

Both Joseph and Deacon Lewis were asleep when a woman entered David's hospital room. She stood over him quietly. She held David's hand. Then she bent down and spoke into his ear. She placed a soft kiss on his hand. She left before her tears came. She stepped out into the hall and right into Gus.

"Whoa . . ." Gus said.

The woman looked up. "I'm so sor—"

"Ari?"

The woman smiled and threw her arms around Gus's neck. "Ghost . . . it's so good to see you."

Gus hugged her tightly before releasing her to get a good look at her. She still had the most beautiful hazel eyes and café au lait skin. Her thick, wavy hair was pulled back into a bushy ponytail. "Wow, you have not changed—not one bit. You're still as beautiful as ever. And what are you, now?" Gus asked, studying her badge. "A doctor . . . *Chief of Neurosurgery*. Wow! You were always so smart."

"Thank you."

In an instant, the reality of Arielle leaving David's room alarmed Gus. He couldn't miss her watery eyes. His smile faded. "Is he okay?" Gus asked, stepping around her.

She placed a hand on his shoulder. "He's fine. He's still fighting. I'm in awe of God once again. I know that some of my team members didn't expect him to make it through surgery, but here he is a day later, hanging on strong."

Gus let a long breath. "Okay . . . good. He's a fighter. Did you—?"

"Yeah. I performed the brain surgery."

Forgetting himself, Gus lifted Arielle's hands and planted kisses all over them. "Bless you . . . bless you . . ."

"Come with me to my office," Arielle said, noticing the hospital personnel who were now observing the two of them.

* * *

"Have a seat," Arielle motioned.

"This is nice. I didn't know doctors had cushy offices at the hospital." Gus was impressed with Arielle Smith-Blackmon's glass and chrome desk and bookcases.

Arielle twisted her lips. "The chief of neurosurgery does."

"Oh, I see. She's beautiful and cocky."

"Why do you think DC and I got along so well?"

Gus smiled. The memory was fresh. "Yeah, DC was crazy about you back in high school. What were we in eleventh grade?"

"Yes. *Sixteen*. I was crazy about him, too—but you know DC was a mess. I couldn't take all his girls," she said.

Amused, Gus asked, "Is that why you broke up with him?"

Arielle's smile took over her gorgeous face. "Yes!"

"You know DC nursed that wound for the longest."

"Not as bad as Asa Miles nursed his! And I thought Asa would be safer than DC, but he was worse!" Arielle said with a hearty laugh.

"Oh, man! I almost forgot that DC clobbered that dude. Isn't he directing movies now?"

"Yeah, DC gave Asa the business. And yes, Asa is directing movies now."

"Wow. So, you are Dr. Arielle *Smith-Blackmon*?"

"Yes. I've been married to Kyle Blackmon for ten years. No kids."

"Is he a doctor too?"

"No, he protects and serves this city as a police officer."

"That's great. I love a lawman."

"What do you do now, Gus?"

"Oh . . . I work in private security—internet stuff," Gus said. He'd practiced the line so many times that the story seemed normal. It was to a certain extent.

"Do you live here?" Arielle asked.

"No, my home is in Tennessee. But I work a lot, so I'm hardly ever there. My job requires me to travel extensively."

"It seems like whenever I see people from high school, it's always under these kinds of circumstances . . ." Arielle admitted.

"Yeah. Life is like that sometimes," Gus said absently. "So tell me, Ari. When DC recovers, what kind of life will he have? I mean, how badly was his brain affected by the shooting?"

Arielle knew that it was okay to share information with Gus. There were four people listed on David's records as family members with whom information and updates on David's medical progress could be freely shared. Gustavo Merrick was one of the names. Because David was a high-profile patient, the staff had to be more keenly aware of his legal rights and requests, so that they wouldn't inadvertently leak information to the press or any other unauthorized persons.

Arielle sighed. She noticed how confident Ghost seemed about David's recovery. She didn't want to give him the impression that David would survive. She didn't know if he would. She'd been led to pray for David and exercise her faith, but she didn't have an answer to Gus's question. "Ghost, I wish I could say for sure . . . but we won't know until he wakes up. Normally, in cases like these, the patient doesn't even survive the surgery. But you know DC isn't a normal kind of guy," Arielle smiled. "The bullet crossed both hemispheres of his brain. I can't say for certain what kind of quality of life he'll have after this. Sometimes people with TBI—traumatic brain injury—are never able to go back to the jobs they had before the injury or live on their own again—even with substantial amounts of therapy and rehabilitation.

"And then I've seen cases where patients have partially regained their former quality of life after an injury. They may have lost sight in one eye, or may not be able to use their left or right side, or their speech may be limited. But they have a decent quality of life. They marry, have children, and live as normally as they can. The human brain is a wonder. We don't know. That's up to God. We'll have to pray and see what happens, Ghost."

"I see . . ."

"One thing is for certain: God is in the middle of this. We're going to give DC expert care here. Some of the best doctors in the country are at this hospital. And DC has some of these non-believing atheists re-considering their belief that there is no God because they experienced God in that operating room. And they are experiencing Him now. They see the way DC is hanging on. He's already a miracle."

Chapter 28

Here

Leah had watched doctors come in and out of David's room around the clock for a total of six days. Three days ago, David's medical team successfully reduced his medications enough to slowly bring him out of the medically induced coma. But still, there had been no response from David when his name was called or when he was touched. Leah held David's hand and said, "Punch, I love you, sweetheart. You have always been the best part of me. Where are you? Talk to me . . ."

* * *

IN A PICTURESQUE COUNTRYSIDE, *David lay on top of a blue picnic blanket, surrounded by plush green grass. With his arms cradling his head and his feet crossed at the ankles, he stared up into the blue sky. He heard voices and turned his head in the direction of the sounds. He saw his grandfather, Kent, and his grandmother, Rose, walking hand in hand toward him. They were both smiling.*

David sat up. "Grandpa Kent, Grandma Rose, what are you guys doing here?" He scooted over to give the couple room on his blanket. They joined him and sat next to each other with their hands clasped together.

"We came to see about you," his grandmother said. Her dark brown skin was vibrant and youthful. There was a beautiful color contrast between Grandma Rose and Grandpa Kent. While David's grandfather had fair skin like his mother, Leah, his grandmother was a deep chocolate color, like Cherelle. In fact, David could smell Cherelle. Her scent was more prominent than the spring flowers and the fragrance of the emerald-green grass that surrounded him.

He was staring into his grandmother's eyes when he heard babies crying. He looked down to find his grandmother and grandfather each holding a baby. The couple smiled at him before smiling down into the babies' faces. David could not see them. "Whose babies?" he asked before a heavy rain pelted him suddenly. His grandmother and grandfather were gone, but David saw Dominique in the distance, standing under a gigantic willow tree. Her fingers were spread across her bulging belly. Lightning struck the tree, and Dominique fell to her knees.

David got up and sprinted toward her. "Nik, move!" He pulled Dominique into his arms and walked her out into the open. The rain stopped, and the two were in a wooded area. It was fall now, and the leaves created a funnel around them. David put his hand on Dominique's stomach. He closed his eyes and kissed her. When he reopened his eyes, his lips were pressed against the roughness of tree bark. Confused, he backed away. Then there was nothing.

* * *

As soon as Dr. Arielle Smith-Blackmon walked into David's hospital room, Leah ambushed her. "Dr. Smith-Blackmon, why isn't he responding? It's been three days since you all supposedly brought him out of the coma." Leah lowered her voice. "Is my baby brain dead? You tell me the truth right now!"

"No ma'am, he isn't. Sometimes, it just takes time. Every case is different. Let's step out," Arielle said.

"Ms. Leah, let her do her job," Deacon Lewis called out as Leah and Arielle stepped into the hallway.

Deacon Lewis got up and sat in the chair next to David, where Leah had been sitting. He pulled the chair as close to David's bed as he could. "Son, you know how Ms. Leah gets. She gets all worked up. That's 'cause she loves you so much. I told her you gon' be just fine. I think that doctor can handle her, though. I went by to visit Sister Ruthie Mae yesterday. Her grandkids were there, and they are a rowdy bunch, sho nuff! Shoot yeah. I played every game and sang every song there is," Deacon Lewis chuckled. "Ms. Ruthie is still bedridden, but them youngins keepin' her spirits up. Heck, one of 'em showed me how to play chess on my cell phone. It's keepin' me in practice for when you get better. I let you win that last game. You remember, don't you? I was just being nice to you, but next time, not so, son. I promise to give you the whoopin' I shoulda gave you the last time we play—ed."

The sound of a baby laughing hysterically caused Deacon Lewis to look around. It persisted. "What in the world . . .?" He got up and walked over to his suit coat, from where the sound was coming. He checked the pockets and then fished out the cell phone. "Well, I'll be. Them little villains musta changed my ringtone. Now, I don't know how to set it back the way you had it, son." He pressed the decline call button so as not to disturb David. Then he fumbled with the phone in his hand. "Now, how did they do that? See what I mean, son?

They changed my phone right under my no—Ms. Leah! Ms. Leah!"

Leah rushed in, her eyes huge with fright. Her hand over her heart to keep it from beating right out of her chest. Arielle was right on her heels. "What's wrong?" Leah asked.

"He opened his eyes."

Astonished, Arielle walked over to David. "David, I'm Doctor Arielle Smith-Blackmon. Can you hear me?"

David didn't move.

"He opened his eyes for certain. I was lookin' right at him." Deacon Lewis said.

Arielle repeated herself. "David, this is Dr. Smith-Blackmon. Can you hear me?" This time, she touched David's hands. Leah stood with her breath held. The laughing came again, and Deacon Lewis struggled to turn his phone off.

Leah couldn't believe it. "Jesus! Punch! His eyes are open!" she said, but David seemed to be staring into the abyss.

Arielle nodded. "There you are . . . . Hello, David," she said, even though David's eyes were blank. His eyes closed again. "Can you hear me? Blink your eyes or move your fingers if you can." There was no movement. "Can you wiggle your toes?" Arielle pulled back the cover on David's feet. She waited. Nothing.

"Punch . . . please . . . talk to me . . . do something," Leah pleaded.

Deacon Lewis's phone rang again. The silly, hysterical laughing baby ringtone filled the room, and David's eyes flew open and closed again. "Sister Ernestine, I'm at the hospital. I'll have to call you back," Deacon Lewis explained, rushing Ms. Ernestine off the phone.

Dr. Smith-Blackmon smiled knowingly. "Did your phone ring the first time David opened his eyes?" she asked Deacon Lewis.

"Yes, ma'am. It sure did."

"So you like the sound of children laughing, huh?" Dr. Smith-Blackmon said, touching David's hand softly. She turned to Leah, "I think he's responding to the ringtone. He's definitely coming around."

Overcome with joy, Leah said, "I've got to call Joe."

* * *

LEAH SAT at David's bedside, praying along with Deacon Lewis and Joseph. Just four hours ago, David had shown signs of responding to external stimuli. Leah was filled with new hope now that David had given her a sign that he was *here.* She'd heard all the medical mumbo-jumbo about the human brain and how complex it was from Dr. Arielle Smith-Blackmon, but all she wanted was her son back—however God gave him back. Leah wanted to tell David that she loved him, and she wanted to hear him say it back. If he couldn't do that, she just wanted to feel his touch again. The world knew David as an extraordinary evangelist and teacher. The Turn-around Preacher. To Leah, he was still David Kent Cole, the little boy who questioned everything around him, and who had a habit of patting her head and smelling her hair. She wanted him back. The world wanted back its preacher-hero. Leah wanted her son.

Leah shifted in the chair she'd placed next to David's bed, realizing she'd fallen asleep. She lifted her head from David's left leg; it had become her pillow. She turned to see both Deacon Lewis and Joseph asleep again in the reclining bed chairs on the other side of the room. Still holding David's hand, she rested her head against his leg again. Leah rubbed her cheek against David's hand, and her tears trickled, moistening David's cold skin. It seemed that she'd been crying for a week straight—ever since that night those thugs did this to her baby.

Leah's curly bob looked like a frizzy mop on top of the white sheets and blankets covering David. She mumbled a prayer that only God understood and drifted off to sleep again. She was startled awake by something crawling on her face. Jerking, she yanked her head up and swatted her face. She dusted off her shirt, feeling silly that maybe she'd dreamed it instead. She took David's hand and stroked it tenderly. "Come back, Punch . . . I miss you . . . come back, honey . . ." Leah pleaded, gazing at David's handsome face. Seconds later, she felt something, a slight movement. Gasping, she loosened the grip on his hand without letting go of it completely so that she could be positive. "Punch, I'm right here. Come back, honey. Everyone is here waiting for you. This is your mother, do you hear me?" she asked. She watched David's hands intently, looking for any subtle movements.

"Punch, can you hear me? I know you're there . . ." Leah studied David's face; she watched the rise and fall of his chest and noticed that his breathing had changed; it was more rapid. "Punch, this is your mother. I need you to show me that you hear me. I know you can hear me, honey." David's forefinger moved slightly. Leah grabbed his hand and held it to her cheek, bathing it in her tears. "Oh, dear God, please . . . yes . . . Lord," she prayed in a hushed tone. "You are a merciful God, Lord. You hear our prayers, Oh, God. Bring him back, Lord. Let me have my baby again, Oh Lord. Thank you, Jesus," Leah continued to pray. Several minutes ticked by without David moving. Leah knew in her heart that he was on his way back. She felt it in her spirit, so she continued to pray. She prayed over the quiet snores of her husband and Deacon Lewis and the hum of the machines in the room. Her prayers went up to God, and she kept sending more.

David could feel his mother. He could smell her, but he couldn't open his mouth to speak. He couldn't move. He was weighed down by a heavy force he couldn't see. It had him locked in a space of nothingness. He fought against the invisible force that kept him from reaching out to his mother. Disoriented and weak, he continued to fight against his opponent, tiring himself out to get to Leah. In his dream, the room was one big watercolor blur, and in the midst of it was her.

* * *

Dr. Arielle Smith-Blackmon held her second press conference regarding the status of the city's beloved pastor. This time, instead of the stoic mood she'd had a week ago, her face was lit with the hope only God could inspire. Arielle and her entire team of surgeons sported black, Detroit-bling style T-shirts under their lab coats that read: *I Believe.* The rhinestone-studded shirts glittered and sparkled under the bright lights of the many camera crews. A husband and wife team, who were members of David's church, had used their T-shirt company to print the 'I Believe' T-shirts for the members of DOC who'd been praying for David's survival. At every prayer vigil, members were sporting the message that no matter what prognosis the doctors gave, they believed in a God who could do all things. The media did not miss it.

Reporter Jaden Stallworth addressed Arielle. "Dr. Smith-Blackmon, can you tell us about the fashionable attire everyone seems to be wearing?"

Arielle smiled. "Ah, yes. We believe that some things are beyond us as medical professionals. And what's happened with Pastor Cole is one of those things. He beat every odd to be with us today. So yes, along with the members of Disciples of Christ Ministries, we *believe.*"

Another question came from Katherine Irving of Channel 9. "Dr. Smith-Blackmon, can you tell us what to expect in the coming days? Will Pastor Cole be able to return to his work in the city? How well is he?"

"Okay. I'm going to answer all three of your questions, Katherine, and then we need to get back to work around here," Arielle said with a wink. The crowd chuckled. "In the coming days, we can expect a great deal of therapy to get Pastor Cole back to being as functional as possible with his injury, employing physical therapy, occupational therapy, neuropsychiatric therapy, speech pathology, and any other form of treatment that will give him what he needs to function. Right now, we can't say exactly what his quality of life will be. When you're dealing with the brain, it is a day-by-day process after this type of trauma.

"Right now, Pastor Cole is out of a coma. As I said earlier, he is responding to us non-verbally via eye contact and hand movements. We will start a therapeutic regimen right away after further tests have been administered. My staff and I are grateful to have been tools in this miracle. We thank you all. Good night. "

Chapter 29

Without You

Shortly after one a.m. on a Tuesday morning in October, Joseph and a member of the private facility, Great Day Rehabilitation Center, helped David out of a wheelchair and into Joseph's car. Leah sat in the backseat with Deacon Lewis, watching out for anyone who might have been spying on their clandestine operation. There had been a media leak indicating David would be released that afternoon. So with careful planning, the family arranged with the CEO of the facility for David to be released before business hours to avoid the slew of reporters and media outlets that would surely swarm the facility by daybreak.

David had spent the last six weeks of his life at Great Day Rehabilitation Center, learning basic life skills all over again—including how to walk again. It had taken him four weeks to master walking, although he still needed assistance. His fine motor skills had been severely impacted by his cranial gunshot wound. He suffered from retrograde amnesia. He couldn't remember any events leading up to the night he was shot. Even when shown a picture of Dominique, David was unable to identify her, and he didn't remember that he'd been with her on the night of the shooting.

This week, however, David had been able to recall scant details about that night. He'd spoken to his neuropsychologist, Dr. Monica Flemings, about a party he attended, but he couldn't remember whose party it was or what type of party it was. There seemed to be one hurdle after another because just when he seemed to be regaining his long-term memory, he realized he'd lost the ability to retain recent memories like the name of a person he'd just met or what day of the week it was. The long road ahead would be filled with daily occupational and physical therapy on an outpatient basis. Despite these limitations, the media had dubbed David *Mr. Miracle,* and by all accounts, he was.

* * *

CHERELLE'S HEART was all but destroyed. She hadn't seen David since Corey's birthday party, the night of the shooting. Two whole months had passed since then. She talked to Deacon Lewis several times a week, but Leah had made it clear that David was to have no visitors. Leah had medical power of attorney, and she strictly adhered to the guidelines David had given her before this incident. He was vehemently against anyone viewing him in a weakened state. The only people he allowed to have access to him in a time of medical crisis were his parents, Deacon Lewis, and Gus. Leah carried out David's wishes dutifully, not deviating for any reason.

Cherelle suffered. Each day without seeing David made her feel like she was fighting for oxygen. She'd spent the last year of her life working with David. They'd spoken to one another at least three times a week. And now, she couldn't get anywhere near him. She was in love with him, and she couldn't take another day of being absent from his life.

The day before David's release from Great Day, Deacon Lewis had listened as Cherelle poured out her heart and her tears. "I . . . I've got to see him. *Please.* Ms. Leah doesn't know me that well, but she knows you. I can't go on like this . . . please. Would you try to convince her to let me see him—just once—for a couple of minutes?" she begged.

"Ms. Cherelle, please don't cry, now . . ." Deacon Lewis said. "I'm gon' talk to David and Ms. Leah myself."

"Okay. . . thank you. Please see if you can do something."

Deacon Lewis reassured her. "I'm gon' do all I can. Everything gon' be alright. Okay?"

"Yes, sir."

STILL UNABLE TO HOLD HIS fork and other utensils properly, David struggled to scoop food from his plate and put it into his mouth. He was a child learning to feed himself. David, a man who held an MBA from Harvard University and a master's degree in divinity from one of the best theological seminaries in the country, had been reduced to a child in terms of self-care. Deacon Lewis reached over and helped steady David's hands as he gripped the fork in an awkward fist. David nodded his thanks.

Sometimes, the exercises that the occupational therapist engaged him in were so overwhelming that he wanted to cry a grown man's cry. Flash cards. Puzzles. Things he should have known, he could not process anymore. He walked with assistance now, but even that was toilsome on his body. His speech was fragmented and slurred as if he'd suffered a stroke, but every media outlet in the nation was calling him Mr. Miracle. Leah had done her best to protect David from the press on his release from the hospital, but a few of them were able to get some photographs. He was home with intensive outpatient services four days a week. This left Leah and Joseph with no choice but to move in with him temporarily.

As they sat in David's sitting room off his master suite, Deacon Lewis helped David wipe the gravy from the beard that was making an appearance on David's face, causing him to look a bit scruffy. Joseph had moved a small table into the area to help David practice table etiquette. "Tomorrow, we gon' have to get you shaved up again, wolfman," Deacon Lewis issued. David grunted.

Deacon Lewis removed his cell phone from his pocket and scrolled through his photos. He found a photo of David and Cherelle that had been taken at Corey's fortieth birthday celebration. He showed it to David. "Ms. Cherelle is concerned about you. She cried sho' nuff when I talked to her. She needs to see that you alright for herself. She's got a broken heart, son. Ms. Leah has been respecting your wishes, but I think you need to make an exception for Ms. Cherelle. She loves you."

Looking at the picture of him and the woman in the photo gave David a warm, familiar sensation. He stared at the photo and tried to remember her. In the photo, his eyes held admiration for the woman with the natural hairstyle. Finally, he said, "K-kit," with emphasis falling on the letter t. Something in David's brain told him that Kit was not the woman's real name, but that was the only name he could latch onto in his mind. He couldn't remember the woman's name. But he couldn't deny the feeling. "Yes. Kit can come."

Against the speech pathologist's recommendation, David used as few words as possible because his speech had been afflicted by the brain trauma he'd sustained. He hated the strained sound of his voice now. He struggled with articulation and fluency. It was embarrassing to a man like him.

"Good, then. I'll let her know that she can come by tomorrow after you're done with your sessions at the rehab center," Deacon Lewis returned.

David closed his eyes and nodded again. When he opened them, his eyes seemed distant.

"What's the matter, son?"

"Kit," David said absently.

Cherelle hadn't waited for Deacon Lewis. She took matters into her own hands by calling Leah herself, and Leah was so taken aback by Cherelle's candidness that she promised Cherelle she would check with David to see if a visit from her would be okay. Leah was still processing Cherelle's confession, *"I'm in love with David and I cannot go another day without seeing him or touching him, or hearing his voice without falling apart . . . please let me see him."*

Leah had heard David mention Cherelle on several occasions concerning working on the youth project and even meeting with the president about the city's youth task force. But to Leah's knowledge, the only woman David had been involved with was Dominique. After the Christmas Eve gathering, David kept his relationship with Dominique private, so Leah didn't know if they had become serious or not. She only hoped they hadn't. Now, Leah wondered what had been going on between David and *Cherelle Dupree.*

Before Deacon Lewis could broach the subject with her, Leah questioned him. "Deacon Lewis, can you tell me what sort of relationship Punch has with Cherelle Dupree? She called me today and said something that made me believe they were a bit more than friends. But the last woman I know Punch was courting was Dominique Street."

"Well, now, Ms. Leah, all I can tell you is that Ms. Cherelle loves David very much. They have a very special friendship, and I believe he loves her too. Sometimes us men can be slow to act on the obvious, Ms. Leah. It was something different with Ms. Dominique."

"But Cherelle said that she was '*in love*' with Punch. That's more than friendship."

"Yes, ma'am, it is," was the only response Deacon Lewis gave. Leah knew there was something Deacon Lewis *wasn't* saying. "David said it would be okay if Ms. Cherelle came by to visit tomorrow. It would be good for them to see one another," Deacon Lewis offered.

"Does he remember her?"

"Yes, I believe so. I showed him a picture of her. If I recall, he called her by some other name, but the look on his face told me that he remembers her."

"That's weird. He doesn't remember Dominique or much of what happened before the shooting. How is it that he remembers Cherelle?"

"Matters of the heart, Ms. Leah," Deacon Lewis said.

"If he said okay, it's fine. Whatever it takes to help him get better. But no other visitors," Leah commanded.

"Yes, ma'am."

* * *

CHERELLE CREPT up the stairs toward David's room. Some years ago, he'd had the wall to one of his spare bedrooms in his Tudor-style home knocked down to create a gigantic master suite with a sitting room. Deacon Lewis had helped ready him today. David sat in his sitting room wearing a pair of Harvard sweatpants and a matching T-shirt. His right eye was covered by a patch.

Leah trailed behind Cherelle. She wanted to witness

David's reaction to the poised, soft-spoken beauty. She hoped it would answer some of her questions. Cherelle's heart fluttered as she climbed each stair. Relieved and anxious all at once, her heart transitioned from flutters to thumps, not knowing what to expect from David. She knew from experience as a therapist that brain trauma was grueling. There was probably very little he remembered as he battled to be the man he was before the shooting. Cherelle hoped she would be allowed to visit with him alone.

She entered through the door that led straight to the sitting room. Deacon Lewis sat on the sofa next to David's double-person La-Z-Boy chair. He stood when Cherelle entered the room.

"Good evening, Ms. Cherelle," Deacon Lewis said, giving her a warm hug.

"Hi, Deacon Lewis. Thank you,"

"David . . ." Cherelle spoke in a hushed tone. She bent down and kissed his forehead. David looked up at her and stretched out his hand. Cherelle took his hand in hers and covered it with sweet, tender kisses. She couldn't stop the steady flow of relieved tears. She kneeled on the floor and laid her head against David's leg. Holding on to his hand, Cherelle threaded her fingers through his and cried happy tears.

David's strained voice penetrated the silence. "Kit . . . sit . . . here."

Cherelle stood and scooted next to David in his favorite chair. She leaned her head on his shoulder delicately and re-familiarized herself with the scent of him. David's clean, soapy smell was comforting. He reached out and placed his hands in Cherelle's natural twist-out. And the glorious scent of her body and hair oils wafted up his nostrils. He pulled her gently to his chest while he clumsily worked his fingers through her hair, rubbing her scalp. It was a sign of affection. Cherelle lay against him, saying nothing. She relished the only sound that mattered —the sound of his heart beating. She knew she could never love anyone else this way—the way she loved David Kent Cole.

Cherelle's presence brought David peace he'd never experienced with a woman before. So instead of trying to focus on remembering events that involved the two of them, David studied Cherelle's tear-glossed eyes as she gazed up at him. "David, I love you. I love you . . . I love you so . . . much," Cherelle confessed, speaking the words she regretted not telling him the night of her brother's birthday party. David met her gaze, and Cherelle understood all that he couldn't say.

Holding Cherelle brought memories of Dominique to the forefront of David's mind. They were memories he had not been able to access until this very moment. They were like puzzle pieces he had to constantly shift around to make sense of. The frustration of being unable to put the entire puzzle together was overwhelming. David's mind held the secrets of his heart. The secrets only God knew. His heart ached. In an instant, pain stirred in the pit of his stomach. It was a feeling so sorrowful that he released a tear. *Dominique.* He needed to see her. Then David inhaled Cherelle's scent and pushed all thoughts of Dominique aside. He was fulfilled. Leah and Deacon Lewis gave the two some privacy.

Two HOURS LATER, Leah walked in to check on David and found him and Cherelle sleeping contentedly next to one another in David's double-person La-Z-Boy, Cherelle with her head pressed to David's chest, David with his hands still gripped in Cherelle's hair.

"Excuse me, you two . . ." Leah said, clearing her throat. Cherelle stirred at the sound of Leah's voice. Her movement caused David to awaken. Cherelle looked up at David, feeling as if she'd been in a wonderful dream. It meant everything just to be with him again. David peered down at her and smiled a crooked smile. Cherelle righted herself and sat up slowly without putting any pressure on his body so as not to injure him in any way. "I know he needs to get some rest," Cherelle said, looking at Leah. She turned to David. "If it's okay, I'll check on you tomorrow or later on in the week." She stood and squeezed his hand one last time. Then she placed a kiss on his forehead.

"Yes . . . t—tomor . . . row," David responded.

Cherelle nodded. "Okay . . . see you later." She didn't want to leave David. She wished she could stay there with him and sleep on his chest all night. She knew he needed to rest, but she needed to be close to him. She had been denied for so long. Aching for so long. With watered eyes, Cherelle spoke humbly to Leah. "Thank you so much, Ms. Leah. My heart feels so much better. Now, maybe tonight I can get some sleep." Cherelle cracked a half smile.

"You get some rest, sweetheart. We'll see you tomorrow, depending on how his physical therapy goes. I will call you if something changes," Leah said.

"Okay. Thank you again."

Moved by the endearment Cherelle displayed toward David and the way he'd reciprocated, Leah hugged Cherelle and kissed her cheek. Her mother's intuition told her they shared a special bond.

Chapter 30

The Betrayer

Guilty as a criminal, Dominique stood before David, waiting for him to speak. She fidgeted with the belt on her trench coat. She knew she shouldn't be anywhere near him. Gus had warned her, and she believed he would follow through with every threat he'd made. He'd told her to consider his threats as *promises,* and she did. But what was she supposed to say when David sent for her? If she had refused David, surely he would have been suspicious. This was the first time she had laid eyes on him since that dreadful night. She hadn't called, sent a note, or anything. No contact at all. The reasons would remain between her and Gus Merrick as long as she lived.

David scooted to the edge of his chair, taking Dominique in. She looked curvier than he remembered. Even the radiant bronze glow of her skin was lovelier than he remembered. David reached out his hand, pulled Dominique closer to him, and rested his head against her belly through her coat. Dominique stiffened. A tear dropped onto David's head. He pushed her back gently and gazed up at her with pleading eyes. His face contorted into a horrifying grimace, and his breathing hastened.

"My ba-by?" he questioned.

"No," Dominique muttered, backing away.

A stinging vibration rattled in David's head. *Jesus! She couldn't have killed my baby . . . .*

"Why?" David asked. His voice sounded like a child's whine. His eyes looked as if he wanted to say more, but his mind couldn't formulate the words—couldn't locate them. He took in air and exhaled with quick, short breaths. The throbbing in his head intensified. Standing, he pressed both his palms to the sides of his head.

"Go," David managed. A siren rang loudly in his brain, making him dizzy and preventing him from maintaining his focus.

"Dave, don't . . . please . . ."

David's eyes could no longer keep back his tears. "Go, Nik!" he shouted.

Dominique watched the watery streaks slide down David's face. "Dave, you don't understand . . . I had to—"

"Go!" his slurred voice inched in volume. He stood and brushed past her, walking into his adjoining bedroom with mechanical steps, assisted by the cane that used to belong to his grandfather. He had to lie down. His head pulsed. He knocked over all of the items on his dresser. "Get out!" David yelled. His bedside lamp smashed against the wall.

Leah charged up the stairs. "Punch!" she screamed at David, just before he pushed his bookshelf over. The act caused him to lose his balance and fall backward onto his bed.

Dominique was frozen by his rage. David yelled once again, this time with all his might. "You!" he said, tossing one of the books at Dominique. "Out!"

"Please leave! Please . . ." Leah said to Dominique.

Dominique walked quickly past Leah and down the stairs.

"*David Kent Cole!* What is wrong with you?!" Leah screamed, picking up items off the floor. He'd frightened her. Her heart pumped as fast as David's. She was trying to make sense of it all. *A fit of rage.* The neuropsychologist had discussed the possibility of David having outbursts of rage and even displaying a lack of sexual self-control. She had said these problems were often associated with brain injury. On an intellectual level, Leah understood all of it, but right now, she was just plain scared.

"Leave. Me. Alone. Leah!"

"Punch!"

Joseph trotted up seconds after Leah. He was the voice of reason. "Let him be, Lee. Come on downstairs with me," Joseph said. He walked in calmly and pulled Leah out of David's room.

Downstairs in the den, Leah burst into tears. "I don't know who he is, and that's my child! I raised him! Who is that up there? Why did he do that? He asked for her to be here, so why would he do that, Joe? I can't take this!"

"Lee, you heard the psychologist say that there may be days like this. Something upset him. We just have to deal with it, honey. He'll be fine."

"He's been acting a fool all week, Joe! I don't know what on earth has gotten into him. I can't take all this throwing things and being violent. It's like he's not the same person anymore."

"Lee, it'll be okay. Just calm down."

A headache like the ones he experienced frequently trounced David, hammering him so hard that it weakened him. He buried his head in his pillow and cried out to God in his heart because he couldn't stand to hear the feeble sound of his voice. *"Why, Father? Surely I have paid for my sins against You!"*

The Lord had taken everything from him. David could hardly remember anything now. Not scriptures. Not music. Not even people's names or faces. Not even simple facts. He became dizzy and unbalanced whenever he walked. How could he ever lead his church again? How could he be the man that he'd once been? And now God had taken his child, too. Why had Dominique done such a wicked thing against him? David cried for his unborn child until he couldn't feel anymore.

* * *

At Great Day Rehabilitation Center, David sat at a table across from Laura Tyler, his occupational therapist. Today, she was reviewing life skills with him. She handed him a mock utility bill with a questionnaire sheet. He had been feeling agitated all week, and he didn't want to deal with Laura today. Her high-pitched voice grated on his nerves. Ordinarily, David could stomach her for an hour a few times a week. But today, he wanted to be done with his session. He'd had his physical therapy session earlier, and it had been challenging. He'd reached his physical and mental limits.

Laura stretched David far beyond his willingness. It was as if Laura Tyler and Mindy Morris, his speech pathologist, double-teamed him. He would only have a half-hour break after his session with Laura before he saw Mindy. David wanted to go home. And as soon as Laura began asking him questions, he knew his brain wasn't going to cooperate.

"David, can you tell me how much you owe on this bill?" Laura asked.

David concentrated on the bill. Something told him to

focus on the words: *Amount Due*, but he was distracted by all the other numbers on the bill.

"I don't feel like it," David slurred.

Laura could tell David was frustrated, but she pushed anyway. She ignored his statement. "David . . . I need you to relax, look at the bill, and tell me the amount you owe for services." They'd worked on this last week, but David's ability to recall simple facts was inconsistent.

David met Laura's eyes with a glare of disapproval. He studied the bill again. *So many numbers.* Finally, he said, "Two hundred seventy-four."

"Okay, that's right, but you're forgetting something. Two hundred seventy-four *what?*"

David's nostrils flared. Again, he studied the bill.

"Two hundred seventy-four *what?*" Laura repeated.

David knew Laura wanted an answer, and he wanted to give her one, just so she could shut up if nothing else. But he couldn't think of the answer she wanted. He grunted. Laura allowed a few minutes to pass to allow him time to recall. She was one of the best in her field. When she figured enough time had lapsed and David couldn't access the memory, she said, "Two hundred seventy-four *dollars*, David."

Dollars. Why couldn't he remember that? "I'm done," David said resolutely.

"No. We still have at least thirty minutes left. We do this so you can get better, David."

David grabbed the bill and tore it up. He threw the pieces at Laura. "Done!"

Laura backed down. His eyes revealed that he'd had all he could take for the day. She'd discuss it with his neuropsychologist and his psychotherapist when they had their weekly multidisciplinary team meeting. Laura understood how frustrating it was for David to relearn simple information. He was an extremely intelligent man; he'd commanded stages all over the U.S. and abroad via various speaking engagements. She was empathetic to the embarrassment and humiliation David was experiencing. He hadn't yet recognized that he was a walking, living miracle, even if he felt like his brain was betraying him these days.

Chapter 31

On Me

Hell on wheels. That's the only way Leah could sum up David's behavior for the last few weeks. She thought it only right to warn Cherelle when she'd called and said she would stop by for a visit. Cherelle assured Leah that she could handle whatever outbursts David was having. She missed him. Besides that, she had him texting again. He'd texted: *Come over.* That was all the motivation Cherelle needed. Despite all that David was forced to deal with in his new normal, he missed her. Cherelle knew his recovery process would be slow, but it felt good to be able to see him and spend time with him regularly. Those months she'd spent without him were some of the worst days of her life.

After talking with Cherelle on the phone, Leah kidded with Joseph. "Well, if Cherelle Dupree loves Punch the way she claims she does, we'll see how well she can handle loving him this week. Between his sudden mood swings and aggression, I've been ready to strangle him myself, and I'm his mother."

"She's a psychologist, Lee. I'm sure she's dealt with people who are worse off than Punch," Joseph said.

"We'll see. She may not know what she's getting into . . . ."

* * *

THE SOUND of David's cell phone ringing ushered him out of a nap. He saw Cherelle's image on his screen. Still groggy, he answered. "Hi, Kit." He'd been looking forward to seeing her, and the anticipation excited him. He missed her presence sitting next to him in his favorite chair.

"Hey, you . . . I'll be by around six. Is there anything you want me to pick up?" Cherelle asked.

"Chocolate. Chips. "

"You mean chocolate chip cookies?"

"Yes."

"Anything else?"

In his mind, David envisioned what he wanted. He could even taste it. But he couldn't recall the word. Scrambling in his head to connect the word associated with the picture he saw so vividly, he settled on saying, "White. Ice."

"Ice cream?" Cherelle questioned.

David sighed. He hated this, seeing something in his mind and not being able to communicate it to another person. Although Cherelle and everyone else around him were patient with him, David felt trapped in a mind that was no longer efficient. "No. White ice, Kit."

Cherelle paused for a moment. *Think simply, Cherelle. Something white and cold that isn't ice cream.* Oh, how silly could she be? What goes with cookies? "Milk?" she asked, feeling confident that she had the right answer this time.

"Yes, *milk*," David said. He tried to commit the word to memory again. "Thank you."

"You're welcome."

* * *

CHERELLE ARRIVED with cookies and milk in tow at six o'clock, as promised. David lit up as soon as he saw her face. Cherelle wished she could take his picture without him being upset about it.

David looked to the left as if he were accessing a memory. "Lookin'. At. You. Kid," he said slowly.

Cherelle beamed proudly. David was getting better at remembering lines from the movies they watched when she visited. She had even made up a game, where she would start a line from a movie, and he would have to finish it. Normally, she'd have to show David the DVD cover of a movie before he recalled a line. Today, he'd done it without prompting.

"Bogart?" Cherelle asked. David nodded.

"I got you," Cherelle said, using one of David's favorite phrases. David's face transformed into a cheery "Have a nice day" sticker.

Cherelle reached into her bag and pulled out the Bogart Collector's edition. It had cost her a hundred bucks, but David was worth it. He nodded. "Good girl. Come here," he said.

Cherelle walked over to his La-Z-Boy and bent down. He patted and smelled her hair. Cherelle giggled. "You are incorrigible, *David Kent Cole*," she said before kissing him on his forehead.

Deacon Lewis entered. "Ms. Cherelle, it's nice to see you again. How are you?"

Cherelle looked back at David. Her heart was content. "I'm good," she said, hugging Deacon Lewis.

"Hey, son. You lookin' good today."

"Thank you."

Cherelle walked over to David's wall unit entertainment stand. She bent over and placed the DVD in the player, unaware that she had caught David's attention.

"Nice," David said quietly, sneaking a peek at Cherelle.

"You gettin' better every day, son," Deacon Lewis snickered.

Joseph had gone out for Chinese take-out. Cherelle took a break from movie-watching to prepare a plate for David and allow Leah and Joseph to rest. Assisting David with his recovery had become a full-time job for the couple. Cherelle set a tray of food on a table stand, and she placed it in front of David's La-Z-Boy. She'd placed a generous portion of rice, lo mein, and sweet and sour chicken on his plate. David was still clumsy with his fork, but he was mastering the technique of getting food into his mouth without making too much of a mess.

"More rice," David requested.

Cherelle noted his pronounced slur. "It's 'more rice' *please*," she corrected. Her cell phone vibrated in her front pocket. She pulled it out and proceeded to check her voicemail. She hadn't realized she'd missed a call from her mother over an hour ago. Cherelle put up one finger. "Give me a second," she said to David as she listened to her mother's message.

Feeling a surge of anger, David's tone was firmer and louder, "More rice!" he insisted. He wanted Cherelle to comply right away. *Why was she ignoring him?*

David's tone took Cherelle by surprise. She walked closer to him, and he glowered at her. She shifted into therapist mode. "David, that's not necessary. You can wait. I said, 'Give me a sec—'"

David felt the need to exert his authority. Get Cherelle's attention in a way she would surely understand. Before Cherelle could finish her sentence, David purposely tipped the plate over on the tray, causing sauce to splatter on Cherelle's shirt and jeans.

"Son!" Deacon Lewis shouted.

Cherelle shook her head. She couldn't believe what David had just done. "What in the—?" she said. She hadn't had a patient become aggressive with her in years. A part of her wanted to laugh from the shock of it. The other part of her was ready to handle the situation as *Dr.* Cherelle Dupree. David's eyes dared her. The two were in a standoff. Suddenly, Cherelle flipped the entire tray onto David's lap. His eyes widened with surprise, then confusion. Cherelle got right in his face. "No! That's unacceptable, David! Do you hear me?"

The idea of Cherelle, who was normally soft-spoken and ladylike, giving David a taste of his own medicine, painted a smirk on Deacon Lewis's face.

Joseph entered the room, noticing the mess and the confrontation. "Hey, what's going on in here?"

"Behavior management, Mr. Joe," Cherelle said, without taking her glaring eyes off David. "You have medicine to help you control your impulses, but the rest is up to you! You will *not* yell or throw things because you feel like it—so don't try that mess on me!" Cherelle said before she snapped her head around and directed her attention to Joseph. "Mr. Joe, Deacon Lewis, behavior is *learned*—even in a case like David's. I understand what the psychotherapist and neuropsychologist told you, but if you allow him to treat you a certain way—even with his injury—he will continue to do it. I'm his friend. I love him, but I'm not having it.

"So if he is going to allow the impulses to cause him to tantrum, he better take that mess to the rehabilitation center where they are getting paid thousands of dollars a week to put up with it because I won't!" Cherelle turned her attention back to David. "You are *David Kent Cole!* You have an IQ of 155.

You earned perfect scores on the ACT and SAT. You have an MBA from Harvard and a Master of Divinity. You sustained multiple gunshot wounds—including a bullet in your brain, and here you are, three months later—a miracle. You are a man of God and a fighter! Along with your therapy and with your meds, you can get better. You can help control what's happening inside of you." Cherelle turned back to Joseph. "I'm going home to get cleaned up, and I will see you gentlemen tomorrow."

Cherelle had spoken so calmly and matter-of-factly that Joseph felt like he was in a horror movie and Cherelle was the psycho who would strike at any minute.

"Uh . . . okay, Cherelle . . . we'll see you tomorrow, then," Joseph said cautiously.

Chapter 32

What You Don't Know

After wrapping up an assignment in London that focused on curtailing cyber-attacks against the U.S., Gus flew to Detroit with a twofold purpose. First, he wanted to spend the holidays with David, Leah, and Joseph—his only family. Secondly, and most importantly, he'd come to tell David the *truth*.

Gus waited until Leah and Joseph had gone Christmas shopping. He couldn't believe it was December already. Christmas was just a week away. He didn't feel good about doing what he had to do. He'd been waiting until David was better, but now that the arrests of the players in Flight Arrangements had been made, it was time. Officer Brent King was behind bars under heavy security, awaiting trial. All the young men involved with David's shooting had been arrested, including the trigger boy, Juan Dozier, who was prepared to testify against King for a reduced sentence.

King had disappeared the night of the shooting, but the FBI and the city's police department received their Christmas wish early. They'd found King before the drug cartel found him.

They needed King to bring down some heavy players in the cartel. Leah and Joseph had shared the news story with David two days ago, but there were other things David needed to know in case Dominique was called in to testify when the trial started.

His speech stilted, David asked, "What is it?" He knew there was something on Gus's mind because he'd been uncharacteristically withdrawn.

"Bro . . . I need to talk to you about something . . ."

"Talk."

"It's about Dominique, bro."

David shot Gus a malicious glare and spoke slowly so that he didn't jumble his words. "What . . . does she . . . have . . . to do . . . with you?"

"When everything went down with you, I had a few of my sources check on some things . . ."

Agitated, David shifted in his chair. "*My* business?" he asked.

"Yeah, bro. Your business. You're my brother, DC. I did what I felt was necessary . . ."

"Talk."

"I know Mama Leah and Papa Joe told you what was reported on the news—that Brent King ordered a hit on Dominique that night. But the truth is that Dominique had been under surveillance for almost a year because of her relationship with King. They'd been seeing each other off and on for a few years—even while you were seeing her—the *whole* time you were seeing her, DC. Dominique was King's main chick. She was never loyal, bro . . .

"Maybe initially, Dominique didn't know King was dirty. But she had to have known something was going on when IAD started breathing down his neck. Maybe she was afraid of him. I don't know. But one thing is for sure: King told Dominique that he would kill her if she were ever disloyal. And she played between the two of you, DC. King knew Dominique saw other men from time to time—they had that kind of arrangement. So King was never worried about you. But when Dominique didn't corroborate one of his alibis during an IAD interview, it showed her disloyalty to him. And about the pregnancy . . . Dominique wasn't sure if you or King was the father."

Angry that Gus knew such private details about his life, David pinned his glare on Gus. But Gus continued. "She came to you because she didn't want to be connected to King in any way. She's made a lot of friends in the police department, DC. Someone warned Dominique that King was going down. So she told you that you were the father. She knew you wouldn't deny her if she kept the baby. You wouldn't question if you were the father, even if the baby turned out to be King's. Dominique planned to let you believe that the child was yours so that King would be out of her life. The night she called you to put her plan in place, it almost cost you your life. Any way you look at it, DC, Dominique is bad news. She's moved to Chicago, and she needs to stay there. If she tries to contact you, just stay away from her. King has a lot of pull—even locked up. There's no telling what he still has planned for her."

"She's been here."

"When? Why?"

"I asked her to come."

"Why?"

"My baby . . . I wanted to know . . . about my baby."

Gus huffed. Hadn't he warned Dominique to stay away from David? "What did she say?"

"She killed my baby . . ." David said, convinced that the child had been his and not King's.

"I'm so sorry, bro . . . I'm really sorry."

David covered his face with his hands. He pushed back

from the table where the two of them were sitting. He stood. Being somewhat unbalanced, he swayed. He held onto the table for support. Gus stood as well and inched closer to him, watching his movements, prepared to catch him if he lost his balance. David turned toward his bed. Scaling his hand across the wall as if he were feeling his way in a dark room, he walked over to his bed and sat down. Gus followed.

"I'm sorry, bro . . ." Gus said again. He knew he'd hit David hard.

"It's over," David returned. He lay back against the head-board, and Gus pulled the blanket over David's feet.

"There's something else . . ."

David didn't want to hear anymore, and Gus felt the heat of his stare.

"Uh . . . about Bones and Squirt . . ." Gus started. "Bones isn't who you think he is, bro. He's an FBI agent. He's been working undercover, and he's certain that Dominique's main man killed Squirt. Brent King murdered Squirt, bro . . ."

David's eyes glazed over. He wasn't listening anymore. When his doorbell chimed, Gus looked curiously at David.

"Kit," David said.

Gus picked up the remote on David's nightstand and punched in a number. The TV screen showed Cherelle at David's front door. Gus pushed the intercom button by David's bed.

"Hi, Cherelle, come on up," Gus said. He'd installed David's entire spy-grade security system a few years prior. David's doors could be locked and unlocked with the push of a button. And Gus had hacker-proofed the system Gus-style. He was CIA-trained, but there were some things Gus knew and kept to himself.

Cherelle trotted up the stairs cheerfully after putting her coat away. Genuinely happy to see Gus, her smile was a bright beam. "Hi, Gus!" Cherelle placed the plastic cake tote she was holding on David's huge dresser. Then she hugged Gus warmly.

"Nice to see you again, Cherelle," Gus said. "You look beautiful as usual."

Cherelle kissed him on the cheek. "Thank you, Gus. You're a hunk," Cherelle teased.

"Hi, David. How are you feeling today?"

"I—I . . . want . . . to be . . . a—alone," David said flatly. He eschewed eye contact with Cherelle.

David's response caught Gus and Cherelle off guard. Crestfallen, Cherelle said, "Well. . . okay . . . I—I baked you an apple pie. I'll just leave it here . . . I can pick up the carrier some other time."

"Okay," David said. There was no light in his eyes. He wasn't excited to see Cherelle today. One of those dark clouds that had been a constant in his life since the shooting surrounded him again.

Gus saw the pain in Cherelle's misty eyes.

"Gus, I'll see you on another visit," Cherelle said, checking her emotions as best as she could.

"I'm going to be here a few weeks, Cherelle. I will definitely catch up with you before I leave. Let me walk you out."

"Bye, David," Cherelle said.

David didn't answer. He had drifted off to another space in his mind. Cherelle couldn't take the emotional distance. She hurried out of the room, and Gus trailed behind her.

"Cherelle, don't take it to heart. DC is having a bad day today," Gus said quietly as they walked down the stairs together.

"He's been having a lot of those lately."

"Today is exceptionally bad. I had a heart-to-heart talk with him about some things concerning Dominique," Gus whispered. "So it's nothing personal against you, Cherelle. It's a lot for him to process, and he's trying hard to get back to his old self. In his mind, he's not even half the man he used to be. He's forgotten a lot of basic things he used to take for granted—like playing chess. Physically, he's struggling with balance when he walks or stands. He doesn't talk much because of the way he sounds. He can hardly remember anything—not even Scripture. He's really afraid that he'll never be able to preach again— to be the man he was. DOC is his *life*, Cherelle. We look at him and see a man who has made exceptional progress—miraculous. But in his mind, he sees himself as feeble. This is extremely difficult for a man like him. Please try and understand that."

Reaching the foyer, Cherelle pulled her coat from the closet. Gus helped her put it on before grabbing his. "I understand, Gus."

Gus walked Cherelle out to her truck and cleaned off the snow that had fallen. Cherelle sat behind the wheel, thinking about David as she watched Gus. She let the heat penetrate her heart. Gus tapped on the car window, and Cherelle lowered it.

"Hey, cheer up," Gus said.

"I'm trying. I was looking forward to spending time with him today. I know he's dealing with a lot. I just want to be here for him. I *love* him. And today I wish I didn't . . . "

"You don't mean that, Cherelle. David needs you. And he appreciates you being here for him. He may not be able to express that to you right now, but he does." Gus bent inside the window and kissed Cherelle on her forehead. He stared at her for a few moments, then said, "I'll call you later. Drive safely."

"Okay. Thanks, Gus."

"Don't mention it."

David watched Gus and Cherelle from his TV monitor. As numb as he felt about everything Gus had shared with him, another feeling prevailed when he saw Gus kiss Cherelle. And he didn't like it. When Gus returned to David's room, David flicked off the TV monitor and adjusted himself in his bed.

"You could have been nicer, bro. You hurt Cherelle's feelings," Gus scolded.

"D—Don't . . . kiss . . . her again."

"What?" Gus asked. Gus had understood every word of David's slurred command, but he couldn't believe that David called himself checking him about Cherelle.

"Don't. *Touch.* Kit. Anymore. I'm tired. Get. Out," David said, before turning his back on Gus.

Gus smirked then said, "Okay. I'll be in *my* room if you need anything." In the hallway out of David's presence, Gus chuckled. "His brain ain't that damaged. Not at all," he said to himself.

Chapter 33

Silly Fool

The weather was calm, and spring was sneaking in. It was seventy-three degrees. Unlike the previous year, there had been no snow. This April had been touted as record-breaking for high temperatures. It gave David a new sense of hope. The bright sunshine prompted him to reflect on how far he'd come since that fateful night last August. After months of intensive therapy and prayer, David had progressed far beyond what anyone thought possible at the onset of his treatment. He wasn't one hundred percent back to normal, but gone was the stilted, slurred voice, and the crossed right eye. He was now able to recall some scriptures and cite some verses from memory again. At times, however, he still experienced a total loss of recall for a few moments.

His short-term memory had been severely impacted by his brain injury. Now, he needed to use text reminders, voice recordings, and notes to keep up with short-term information like grocery lists, appointment schedules, and transferring his clothes from the washer to the dryer. Before the injury, he'd been a walking computer, rarely using notes, even when he preached or delivered speeches at conferences. But despite the shooting and the physical and cognitive limitations he experienced because of it, David knew his miraculous recovery was a result of God's grace.

As he walked down the hall of the rehabilitation center, after having completed his therapy sessions for the day, David expected to see Deacon Lewis. Instead, he saw Cherelle. Her back was turned to him. She was engrossed in a lively conversation with one of the staff members. The first thing He noticed was Cherelle's natural hair in a pineapple style. It was partially wrapped in a colorful pink head wrap. She was wearing a jersey-fabric, hot pink, maxi dress. It was stylishly accented by a denim bolero that was studded with rhinestones. Although she was covered from head to toe, the dress catered to her curves. She wore rhinestone-studded blue jean sneakers, and an oversized bag hung on her shoulder. She exuded a bohemian kind of flair. Only Cherelle could pull off an outfit like this. David decided that she looked sexy.

With her hands on her hips, Cherelle laughed gregariously as she stood close to the handsome man she was talking to. He was dark-chocolate like her, about six feet two inches tall, and looked to be in good physical shape. He certainly wasn't pushing a walker like David was. He still had trouble with balance from time to time, and the walker helped when he had to walk moderate distances.

Based on the proximity of Cherelle's body to the man she was talking to, it was unmissable that they knew each other. Cherelle rarely ever allowed strangers to enter her personal boundary space. David had watched her in enough meetings and social situations to know that she always initiated a handshake when meeting someone for the first time. It appeared to be a polite gesture, but David knew that was the main way

Cherelle kept people from entering her personal space. Her extended hand kept others at arm's-length.

The man closed the space between himself and Cherelle and whispered in her right ear. He stepped back, and Cherelle toyed with the bracelets on her arm. She eyed the man seriously. With her head tilted, Cherelle looked up at the man and then back down again. She was nervous. If David could have rolled the walker any faster, he would have. He wanted to know what the man had said to throw Cherelle out of her square. The dark chocolate mystery man took out his cell phone. Cherelle took out hers. It looked like the pair were exchanging numbers. The mystery man replaced his phone in his lab coat pocket, then took Cherelle's hand and planted a kiss on it. By David's estimation, the mystery man held Cherelle's hand about ten seconds longer than what was considered socially acceptable. David straightened himself as he neared them. He didn't want to look like a feeble old man in front of the mystery guy. As if on cue, Cherelle turned around to face David while the mystery man did a poor job of discreetly studying Cherelle's backside.

"Hey, you! You're all done?" Cherelle asked David.

"Hello. Yes, I'm good for today. What happened to Old Man?"

"Uh . . . Sister Murphy had to go in for emergency surgery on her ankle. She slipped at the supermarket and broke it. Deacon Lewis went to the hospital to pray over her because Pastor Clint already had several visits scheduled for the day. You don't mind having me as an escort, do you?"

"No . . . no. It's fine. Thanks."

"Oh, Pastor Cole, this is Dr. Warwick . . ." Cherelle said, turning back to the voyeur.

David extended his hand and gave Dr. Warwick a firm

handshake. "Hello, nice to meet you, Dr. Warwick," David said, wondering why Cherelle addressed him as Pastor Cole.

"Same here. I've heard a lot of great things about you around the center. We are blessed to have you here with us. Such a testimony and encouragement to others."

David smiled and nodded. *Who is this clown supposed to be, the public relations representative?* "Glad to be a blessing," David said. *This dude is sickening.*

Wonder Guy looked at his watch. "Well, let me get back to my patients."

No duh. Please hurry off. With a plastered smile on his face, David said, "It was nice meeting you."

"Dr. Dupree, I'll see you later tonight, right?" Dr. Warwick said, backing away.

"Yes . . ." Cherelle nodded before turning to David. "Do you need any help?" she asked David.

"No."

"I'll let the valet know we're ready," Cherelle said.

"Sure."

Cherelle smiled on the inside. She knew exactly why David was answering in those one-word responses. *Jealousy.* She assisted David into the car, then folded his walker and placed it into the back of her truck. She turned on an R&B station and wanted to fall out laughing when Beyonce's "Single Ladies (Put a Ring on It)" song came on. She hummed to the tune, trying desperately to keep from laughing. She was hard-pressed to keep the smirk off her face. *Yeah. That's right. Don't get mad if you see that someone else is interested.*

David sat in perturbed silence.

Cherelle turned the music down. "Are you in any pain?" she asked to get her mind on something else.

"No. I'm good."

"How'd it go?"

"About the same as every other time, *Cherelle*," David said, annoyed.

"Ooo-kay," Cherelle said. She turned the volume up again. If David didn't want to talk to her, she certainly wasn't going to force it today. She'd had enough of David Kent Cole. It had occurred to her recently that she was the only one holding her heart hostage. Not David. She'd been constantly by his side, demonstrating her love for him, and yet he had kept her at a distance emotionally. Now that he was better, nothing had changed.

It was time for her to open herself up to the possibility of dating again. If all David wanted between the two of them was a good friendship, then so be it. Cherelle was going to explore other options, and she was going to start with Dr. Zavier Warwick. The Range Rover filled with the sound of Minnie Riperton's "Lovin' You," and Cherelle sang along. She tuned out David and every other thing that was on her mind.

When Cherelle hit the high notes, something happened inside of David. It was powerful and explosive, like the forming of a new cosmos. Something he hadn't thought about in a long while was knocking at his door. The thought was as sudden as ocean waves rushing onto the shore. Though he chose silence, David was mesmerized by the beauty of Cherelle's voice. Everything about her was appealing. He couldn't blame Dr. Warwick for seeing what he'd known all along. Cherelle was *it*. And she'd been putting up with him for months now. She'd seen him at his weakest moments. She'd experienced his unprovoked anger and foul dispositions. And still, she was here.

Their interactions had changed in the last few weeks, though. Cherelle didn't visit him as frequently, and when she did, she limited her time to an hour or so. In the past, she would stay as long as David could stand to have company. Something was different now.

"So . . . how do you know Dr. Warwick?" David asked.

Startled by his voice, Cherelle stammered. "Huh—what?"

"I said, 'How do you know Dr. Warwick?'. You didn't just meet him today, did you?"

"Oh, no. We worked together at Riverdale, a psychiatric facility. I worked under him. He's a psychiatrist and a really sweet guy."

The light changed to yellow, and Cherelle slowed. She came to a complete stop at the red light and then glanced at her cell phone. Her smile was mischievous.

"What was so funny?" David continued to question Cherelle.

"Huh?"

"You were laughing about something before I walked up," David said. He wanted to ask Cherelle what Dr. Warwick had said in her ear that made her so nervous, but he didn't.

Cherelle chuckled. "Oh . . . Zavier was telling me a story about one of the patients who used to think she was a rock star. He said one night they just let her put on a concert."

So she's on a first-name basis with the clown. "What did he whisper in your ear, Cherelle?"

Cherelle knew David was dead serious because he was using her government name. He hadn't called her *Kit* at all since she'd arrived at the rehabilitation center.

"Excuse me?" Cherelle asked.

"What did he say to you that he had to *whisper* in your ear?"

"Usually, when someone whispers, it's because it's *personal,* David."

"If you don't want to tell me, then just say that."

"One, it's not your business. Two, it doesn't matter. Three, I *don't* want to tell you. And four, I'm not." Cherelle focused her attention on the road. David had some nerve being all up in her business like they had a relationship. They didn't, and from the looks of it, they weren't going to. So whatever Zavier said didn't matter.

"Can we just be friends for a minute, Cherelle?"

"We *are* friends, David. And that's all we are. So I don't need you asking me fifty questions about something that's none of your business."

David wasn't used to Cherelle speaking to him this way. She'd always demonstrated reverence and admiration for him in the past. "Cherelle?"

"What?" Cherelle snipped, annoyed by the very fact that David wasn't calling her Kit—the sweet nickname he'd given her.

"Forget it."

"It's forgotten," Cherelle returned. She pushed the CD button. Now she *was* sending David a message. He knew it as soon as he heard Teddy Pendergrass singing about how the whole town was laughing at him.

* * *

When Cherelle arrived at David's home, she was glad Joseph was there. The garage door lifted, and Cherelle inched her truck inside. David waited until the garage door was completely down before he attempted to get out so that none of his nosy neighbors would see him. Joseph entered the garage and grabbed David's walker out of the trunk.

"Cherelle, do you want to come in and have something to eat? Lee made lasagna." Joseph offered.

"No thanks, Mr. Joe. I'm going out to dinner with a friend later. I'm saving my appetite."

"Okay. We'll see you tomorrow, then?"

"Sure."

Joseph knew that something was off between David and Cherelle. He knew what the problem was, but he didn't want to overstep his boundaries with David, so he'd held his tongue on the matter. David went straight to his room without a word to anyone for the rest of the evening. He even passed on his mother's lasagna, which was a favorite of his. After hours of staring at his ceiling, he still couldn't sleep. This was a first. Sleep had been the one thing he'd been able to do a lot of since his injury. Between the medications and the physical and mental exhaustion, sleep had become a pastime. But not tonight.

David carefully navigated the steps down to his main level and entered his music room. He hadn't played his piano since before the shooting. He refused to practice at the rehabilitation center. It was the one thing they hadn't talked him into doing. David feared that he wouldn't be able to play—something his Grandma Rose had taught him at the tender age of three. If his hands betrayed him, it would crush what was left of his spirit. Tonight, however, he was moved by something more powerful than fear. He had to play. He had to release the thoughts that were bubbling inside of him.

He sat on the bench and lifted the fallboard. He placed his hands on the keys tentatively without stroking them. He closed his eyes and pictured himself and Grandma Rose sitting next to each other, him looking up into her eyes as he listened to her instructions, and then watching her hands. A melody sat on David's heart and commanded his fingers. He played without thinking, without anticipating. He let the song orchestrate his movements. A tear fell, and more followed. His soul praised God. "How Great Thou Art" floated around him and through him as he spoke to God.

David's playing awakened Leah, and she lay in the dark listening before waking Joseph. David played with such clarity

351

and perfection that it caused Leah to weep. Just eight months ago, he was fighting to stay *alive*. Joseph waited a while before going downstairs. Finally, he went down and stood in the doorway of David's music room, sensing that maybe David was ready to talk now. When David noticed Joseph, he stopped playing.

"I didn't mean to interrupt you, son," Joseph said regretfully.

"It's okay. I just was thinking . . ."

"Well, it sure sounded good. You mind if I come in?"

David smiled. "No. Come on in." Joseph sat on the sofa across from him. "Joe, I feel the hand of God in everything that's happened to me. I understand that I needed to see Him more clearly—be closer to Christ. The shooting has deepened my relationship with Christ. But there are some things I *don't* understand—like where certain people fit in my life."

"*Certain people* wouldn't happen to be Cherelle Dupree, would *they?*"

David smiled and nodded. "Yeah. Exactly."

"Well, son, I guess my question would be: where do you want Cherelle to fit?"

"I'm not sure, but . . . I don't want to lose her. The way she looks at me, or at least the way she *used to* look at me. The way she's always here for me—no matter what. I don't want to lose that. But I want to be able to give her what she needs, too."

"I have one question before I comment on what you just said, son. Do you love Cherelle—I mean, like she loves you? Because it's *obvious* to me that she's in love with you."

"Well, today, something happened after my therapy session, Joe. Deacon Lewis was supposed to pick me up, but there was a situation, so Cherelle came instead. When I first laid eyes on her, it was like I was seeing her for the first time. I mean, I've always thought Cherelle was a good-looking woman.

But today, *all* of her hit me. I was looking at the physical her, but I could see and feel all of her—her spirit, her intellect— everything. And it was a good feeling, Joe. Cherelle has been giving me the blues for the last few weeks, but today, I felt like she was mine. And yes, I love Cherelle—more than friendship. I think I've always loved her. I just didn't know how to handle what I was feeling, especially after all that had happened between Dominique and me."

"Does Cherelle know how you feel about her?"

"I'm sure she knows I care for her a great deal, but I've never actually told her that I *love* her. I think I've told her everything but that. To be honest, I don't like the idea of feeling vulnerable again, Joe. I've been trying hard to deal with that. But deep down, I've wanted to let Cherelle know how much she means to me. I admit I have allowed my pride to get in the way. And lately, she's been treating me differently."

"I noticed."

"Man, it's like she doesn't look at me with that same sparkle in her eyes anymore."

"So what's your plan, son? Why don't you talk to her about it?"

"I tried calling. She didn't answer. I think she went on a date with Dr. Warwick from the rehabilitation center."

"Ouch."

"Yeah. Ouch is right. You should have seen the way he was checking her out. Eyes roaming all over her. If he thought he was being discreet, he wasn't," David said.

"Well, Cherelle's is a nice package, so to speak. And she's a God-fearing woman. She's smart. She's a little spicy. And she's very caring and *loyal*. That's a nice combination for a deserving man."

"Tell me about it," David said. "Man, Joe . . . this is crazy."

"What, son?"

"Cherelle is driving me *crazy!* For the first time since the shooting, I looked at her and I uh . . . felt uh . . . I felt *it*."

"You mean you felt like you loved her?"

"Yes, definitely. And I also felt everything that comes along with realizing you're in love with someone. What I'm trying to say is that I felt . . . *it*. You know what I'm saying? Since the accident, I haven't had any of those feelings. Today, I felt like myself."

Joe raised a curious brow and then quickly caught on. "Oh . . . you felt *manly*."

"Oh yeah. It was one big bang when I looked at Cherelle. I felt my spirit, my heart, and my body respond to her all at the same time. It was strange—in a good way."

"So you're worried about getting involved with Cherelle because . . . ?"

"It's like this, Joe, Cherelle is a good woman. I love everything about her. I always have. And she's not the kind of woman who a man can half-step with. Cherelle deserves the best. She's precious. I don't think I've ever met anyone like her. I'm healing slowly and getting back to normal, but I know I'm not at one hundred percent right now. She's been so supportive, even when she just sat here with me and said nothing. She's so loyal and giving that it makes me want to reciprocate in a way that lets her know what's really in my heart. But until I'm one hundred percent, I know I can't do that."

"I see. So what you're saying is that you love Cherelle, but you're afraid that you aren't able to give her all that she needs right now—until you're better?"

"Yes. I mean, right now, she's probably out with that dude from the hospital, and he probably picked her up in his car and opened the door for her and all that. Getting around way better than me. He could literally pick her up and sweep her off her feet. I, on the other hand, I'm still getting around slowly. And I don't feel like I could protect her the way I could have before they shot me. I don't ever want Cherelle to see me as *weak*."

"Son, I'm gonna be honest with you, and I hope you don't mind. I don't think Cherelle has ever seen you as weak. I don't think she ever will. She's watched you fight through something that most people don't survive. She knows who you are on the inside, son. I think that's the man that she's in love with. Now, Dominique, I don't think she ever understood you or saw you for who you are. You can't fully love what you don't know. That's all." Joseph hoped he hadn't overstepped his boundaries by mentioning Dominique. But he had a feeling some of David's apprehension about opening up to Cherelle had to do with the rejection he experienced with Dominique.

David contemplated. Joe was right. "I need to pray about this. I know in my heart what I want to do. But I want to be certain of His will beyond a shadow of a doubt this time around. I need to make sure I'm making the right decision."

"Praying is a necessity. But I think the Lord has already shown you what you need to see. It's like when the people in the Bible were waiting for their king to show up and release them from Roman oppression. Jesus was right in their faces, revealing His character in truth. But they had this idea in their heads about how it was all gonna go down, and couldn't see the blessing right before them. Jesus was right there. He was it. The ultimate blessing. Prayers answered. The people were just too blind to see that," Joseph said.

"I hear you," David said.

"Now, that dude at the rehabilitation center, what do you think he saw when he looked at Cherelle? If he spent any time talking to her, he would immediately know how beautiful she is on the inside, too. You think a man of his status wouldn't want that kind of woman for himself? I know I would.

"When I first saw your mother, she was leaning up against

the building outside the plant where we both worked, reading a small pocket Bible. And she was a knockout. I said to myself, 'That's the kind of woman I *want*. That's the kind of woman I *need*.' And you know what? There were plenty of other men at that plant who noticed Lee was different than the rest of the women there. And they wanted her, too. But you know something? I knew the moment I saw Lee that none of those men could love and protect her like I knew I could. And I told Lee on our first date. I said, 'Lee, if you give me a chance, I promise I will love you like no other man has ever loved you or ever will.'"

David smiled. He rose from the piano bench and walked up to Joseph. Joseph stood. "If I never told you, I want to say it now, Joe. I appreciate everything you've done for Ma and me. You were the best father I could have had. I don't think I would have been the same man without you. I know I gave you a hard time, but I always respected and appreciated who you were."

Joseph embraced David, and both men stubbornly fought tears that persistently trickled down both their faces. "Thank you, son. You're a good man. I'm proud of you," Joseph said. He patted David firmly on his back. He put some space between them. "Now, for some real good advice: Don't let Cherelle get away. Women like her are hard to come by. It seems to me that she's exactly what you need. And she sure ain't bad on the eyes, either son. Unh-uh. But you know that . . ."

David nodded and smiled. "Yes . . . I know."

Chapter 34

Love in the Afternoon

Cherelle had been ignoring David ever since she dropped him off at home the day before. There had been no sweet text message or goodnight call. She was sending David another kind of message instead, and David hoped to turn things around for the better. Talking to Joseph helped him develop a plan. At seven-thirty a.m., he put his plan into place by calling Cherelle. She answered quickly, like she'd been expecting a call.

"Good Morning, Kit."

Cherelle rolled her eyes. Today, David was back to calling her *Kit* again. She wished he'd make up his mind about what kind of friendship he wanted. "Good Morning," she greeted politely, like she was addressing a stranger.

"I hate to bother you, but I need your help taking care of some business today."

Cherelle hesitated. ". . . Um, I have plans this morning and afternoon. Do you need me to take you somewhere?"

"Uh . . . no. I will explain everything when I see you. We can go over it here."

"I can come by about seven this evening if that's not too late."

"No. Seven is fine," David said.

Someone else was calling Cherelle. "Okay. I gotta take this call. I'll see you later," Cherelle said, sounding chipper. She hung up before David could say goodbye. She'd been in a rush to get him off the phone. David wondered if Dr. Zavier Warwick was calling Cherelle this early, and if the man was a part of Cherelle's morning and afternoon plans. He sure hoped not. It was time to get Dr. Warwick and any other would-be suitors off the scene for good.

* * *

DAVID FELT a sense of satisfaction about being able to get out of bed without a struggle, bathe and dress without someone's assistance, and stand and brush his teeth without feeling like he was tilting or going to topple over. He had freshened himself up with a long, hot shower and donned new clothes. He'd thrown on a new pair of Levis and a crispy white Disciples of Christ T-shirt. He even splashed on some cologne, which caused Leah to wonder what he was up to. But she was thankful to the Lord that her baby was getting back to himself. Leah had seen David struggle to form words and do simple tasks, such as holding a pen in his hands. To see him take so much care to prepare for company was a joy. She was grateful for the miraculous progress he had made and was still making.

David still experienced dreadful, debilitating headaches daily, but he was determined not to make a habit of taking pain medication unless it was absolutely necessary. He didn't want to be dependent on anything but God's provision. He realized that in sparing his life, God may have left the headaches as a reminder that His grace was sufficient. They were the thorn in

David's side, and he would in no way whine about them. Today, he'd been spared the pain, and he was feeling good.

David sat in his sitting room watching *Casablanca* in black and white. It was a favorite of his and Cherelle's. He'd fallen asleep in his two-person La-Z-Boy. Cherelle entered without a sound, mindful of her movements. She reached gingerly across David to pick up the remote and silence the TV. She was adamant about not having electronics on while sleeping; she swore it kept the brain from fully resting. David looked so peaceful that Cherelle wanted to kiss him, and just yesterday, she'd wanted to strangle him until his eyes popped out of their sockets. He smelled wonderful. It was a clean, soapy, fresh scent intermixed with the masculine aromas of sandalwood and musk. Just as Cherelle pressed the off button on the remote, David seized her suddenly and pulled her onto his lap.

"Ahhh!" Cherelle shrieked, startled by David's sudden movement. "I thought you were sleeping."

"I was until I smelled you," David said. He settled Cherelle on his lap. "Kit, I just wanted to thank you in person."

"For what?" Cherelle asked. She felt odd sitting on David's lap. And the way he was looking at her was unnerving. His eyes peeled away her layers, exposing her thoughts. She felt a surge of embarrassment, like David could see through her. She moved to get up, but David gently tugged her back into place. He toyed with her shoulder-length twists. The sensation of him doing that caused Cherelle to look away. If she didn't, her eyes would surely tattle on her and expose to him all the feelings he stirred in her. David turned her face to him.

"Thank you for everything. For being who you are. For being what I've needed over the last year and a half—ever since I met you."

"You're welcome," Cherelle said nervously. Her hands

were wet with perspiration, and she felt jittery inside like she'd had too many cups of coffee.

David studied her before saying, "I need to talk to you."

"Like this?" Cherelle questioned. David held her securely. He had never done anything like this before. He'd always been appropriate—even the night they shared a kiss in her office. He had never allowed them to get out of line. Cherelle wasn't sure what was happening with him at the moment. She knew that brain trauma could cause a lack of self-control. She wondered if this was one of those mo—

"No, like this . . . " David said, side-swiping Cherelle's thoughts with a kiss that began tentatively as he settled his lips over hers. Then, with expertise, he explored them more thoroughly—tasting, suckling, and teasing. David pulled Cherelle farther down into his arms and cradled her. He immersed her in a succulent tribute. Cherelle's soft moans assured him that she heard every word he hadn't spoken audibly.

For just a moment, David unwillingly separated his lips from Cherelle's, spoiled by the luxury of her taste. Her candid eyes were glazed over with passion. Connecting this way was like having an out-of-body experience. Satisfied that he had all of Cherelle's attention, David repeated his delicious kissing ritual before pausing. He pressed his forehead to hers and said, "I love you, Cherelle. I'm *in love* with you. I'm sorry about yesterday. I was a donkey."

"Yes, you were, and I love you too," Cherelle whispered breathlessly. She slowly fought past the delirium David's kisses had caused. "That's not the business you needed help with, is it?"

"Yes . . ."

"Well . . . mission accomplished, sir."

"No. That was like pre-mission. An appetizer. The real mission will be accomplished when you become mine in every way," David said. Cherelle blushed. If her skin weren't so chocolate, she would have turned beet red from David's brashness. "Kit," he continued, "I need to know if you would be willing to go the distance with someone like me, knowing that I have this injury—bullet fragments still lodged in my brain. By the grace of my God, I can hold you, kiss you, love you, and *feel* like doing all the things a normal man would want to do to you. I want to show you how much my heart feels for you, Kit. I want you to know that it is filled with *you*. And I need to know that if by chance something happens to send me back to a time where I'm learning how to do things all over again, that you'd still be here . . . " David choked on his own words. He thought he knew the answer, but he needed to hear Cherelle say it to him.

"David, I *love* you. I loved you when your heart was someplace else. I loved you when you couldn't walk or talk. I loved you when you couldn't remember my name. I've been here all this time because I love you . . . and I would travel any road God placed before us. I promise . . . I promise . . ." Cherelle confessed through teary eyes.

David's eyes welled. He examined Cherelle's face, and he knew. He knew what God was communicating to him about Cherelle. He knew what he felt for her was from God. "Oh, Kit . . . you are the biggest blessing . . ." he admitted. His lips found hers again, and he shared the depths of his heart with a passion-filled kiss that told its own story. Feeling her tears against his face, David kissed Cherelle more deeply, translating his love in a tangible way.

Leah and Joseph walked in with dinner, and Leah was stunned by David and Cherelle's afternoon love scene. To her, it was a scene out of place. Leah remembered that after the shooting, David had barely been able to put words together or take steps without a walker. Now, he was holding and kissing Cherelle as if none of those things had happened. When had their relationship transitioned to this sort of affection? She and Joseph placed the trays on the huge dresser without a sound. Neither David nor Cherelle heard them, and Leah and Joseph exited unnoticed, just like they had entered.

* * *

LEAH STOOD at the kitchen sink, flushed. "Well, if there was a question about all of his man parts functioning normally, I guess that answers that."

Joseph smiled proudly. "I guess so."

"I knew Cherelle had a thing for David. I'm not blind. But I didn't know the two of them were romantically inclined."

"You mean to tell me you haven't noticed the way he looks at her?"

"I just thought he—I don't know, Joe. So much has happened. I just didn't see it that way . . . "

"Well, Cherelle has been here just as much as we have. She has literally been taking care of Punch, too. If he had any doubts about Cherelle because of what's-her-name, I hope God has answered all of his questions by now."

"Honey, I really like Cherelle—I do. I just didn't know they were . . ."

"Baby, they were just kissing. You're blowing things out of proportion."

"Maybe I am."

"Stop being a mother hen. David is a grown man. That's our only child, but he's *grown*. He may have gone through a traumatic experience, but he's still a man, Lee. I don't see anything wrong with them expressing their feelings for one another."

"I'm just worried. He's not one hundred percent back to normal. I don't want him to get emotionally overloaded."

"Well, he looks like he's on his way back to one hundred percent to me," Joe chuckled, but Leah didn't laugh. "Come on, baby, you're uptight for no reason."

"Joe, Dominique almost destroyed him. I'm worried."

"Cherelle is a totally different story, Lee. You *know* that. Don't you think Cherelle is the kind of woman Punch needs?"

"Yes, but . . ."

"Lee, let go. He's grown. He's getting better every day. God has brought him a long way. It's natural for a man to want to kiss and hold the woman he loves. Ain't no sin in that."

"I guess you're right."

"I *am* right," Joseph said. He placed a kiss on Leah's forehead. "And I think it would be hard for any man *not* to love a woman like Cherelle. She's been with Punch through the darkest times of his life, and she's never wavered or strayed. She's been right here. That's the kind of woman you are, Lee. And if you want to know the truth, Cherelle reminds me of my wife. So why are you worrying?"

"I don't know, honey . . ."

"Don't worry about Punch. He's good. He's puttin' the moves on Cherelle like any *normal* man would," Joseph laughed.

* * *

DAVID FELT Cherelle pulling out of his embrace. "D—David, I —I . . . can't . . . handle . . . anymore kissing," Cherelle panted.

David's smile was everything. "I'm sorry. Me either. Just the sensation of holding you and touching you reignited something in me I haven't experienced in a long while."

"Are you experimenting on me?"

"No, babe," David chuckled. "It's just that I wasn't sure I was back to normal. Now I'm sure. But I'm afraid I'm gonna have to put us on a kissing moratorium, Kit. I want to safeguard us to make certain that we stay within His will. I never want to compromise you in any way. I love and honor you that much."

"Okay," Cherelle agreed, understanding fully.

"Good. And just so there are no questions in your mind, Kit, I *undoubtedly* intend to marry you. There will be *no* game-playing on my end, Kit. I want to spend a little time dating and courting you like you deserve. I want to give us some time to grow in a different way, as I get better. I'm never going to give you less than a hundred percent of me. I want you to be my lady, Kit. I just need you to be patient with me as I continue to heal.

"There's something I need to tell you. It's about DOC. You know I haven't been back there since the shooting, and DOC is everything to me. I realize I'm prideful. I didn't want anyone to see me in the condition I was in—not even those who love me and have been praying for my healing. I've been praying and asking God to give me the mental capacity to teach and preach His Word like I once did. My memory is improving, Kit, but I don't remember as much as I once did. My voice is back, but my *mind* is not all back. You know, I never used notes when I preached? I never had to. But this thing—this injury has changed me.

"My priority is getting back to DOC. I feel like God is telling me it's time. But I don't *feel* ready. Honestly, I'm afraid that I'm going to stand before my congregation and not be able to do what I've been called to do. And why am I afraid? I don't know. I should trust Him more by now—after all this. I should trust Him. So I need your support and patience as I ready myself to do what God is calling me to do. Can we do this together?"

"Yes, of course," Cherelle affirmed. She settled her head against David's chest.

"I love you, Kit. You're all mine . . ."

* * *

AFTER THEY'D EATEN, Cherelle volunteered to take the trays downstairs and put the dishes in the dishwasher. David could navigate the stairs beautifully now with no dizziness and no stumbling, but Cherelle wanted him to rest. Leah seized the opportunity to question David while Joseph occupied Cherelle with conversation in the kitchen.

"So what's going on with you and Cherelle, Punch?" Leah asked, taking a seat next to David's La-Z-Boy.

"Ma, it's simple. I love Cherelle."

"You loved Dominique."

"It's not the same. I *chose* to love Dominique. I can't help but love Cherelle. I had a special fondness in my heart for her before this happened," David said, pointing to his skull. "Now, I know for certain she's exactly what I need. She's who I *want*. And I know for certain she's what God wants for me. That makes me love her even more. It wasn't that way with Dominique. I fought God to have her—even when He had plainly told me no. God has shown me what true love is in Cherelle."

"I just want you to take your time, Punch. You've been through so much . . ."

"That's how I know how precious time is, Ma. What I feel for Cherelle is a complete love. We've never shared more than a kiss, so there is nothing clouding my judgment between lust and love. I just know what I feel. And I'm totally at peace on the inside. It wasn't that way with Dominique."

"What about Cherelle? Does she understand that even

though you are better now, and it seems that you are getting back to normal, something could happen down the line—a setback? What if something happened and she had to take care of you for the rest of your life and hers? What then?"

"*Leah*," David chided his mother gently, "you've raised me to talk to God about these things, and I have. I don't need a woman in my life. I can live without Cherelle, but my life is so much richer with her in it. I don't ever want to live without her. I believe that Cherelle is God's will for me. And I don't want to lose her to someone else because I'm too blind to see a gift right in front of my eyes . . . "

Chapter 35

Return of the M.A.C.

Disciples of Christ Ministries was packed to capacity. The glory of it was that it was filled with young people under the age of thirty. Although DOC had its fair share of mid-lifers and thirty-somethings, its uniqueness stemmed from the fact that it had a huge membership of young people who were carrying out the mission of the church.

David's young assistant pastor had given the invocation. The congregation was on its feet, worshipping on this glorious Resurrection Sunday. God's mercy rang true even in the weather. A comfortable sunny, seventy degrees was the appropriate climate for remembrance of the Lord's resurrection. Sunlight streamed through the stained glass windows, casting dancing kaleidoscopes on the walls. Only a dead man couldn't feel the Spirit of the Lord in the sanctuary.

Today, Pastor Clint refrained from focusing on the timeliness of the service schedule but instead allowed the Holy Spirit to have His way in the church. Clint listened for God's direction as he praised. Twenty praise-filled minutes passed before Clint addressed the congregation.

Twenty-five-year-old Stormie Greer sat two rows behind the deaconesses, admiring Clint. She had securely snagged him. The two were engaged and scheduled to be married in the fall. There were selfish sisters in the congregation who hoped Stormie didn't make it down the aisle with him, but everyone who knew Clint well knew that Stormie Greer was his heart and soul. Being a fairly young man, Clint was a babe in some of the older congregants' eyes. But his walk with God had made him mature beyond his years—more so than some of the members who claimed to have walked with God longer than he'd been alive.

Clint had received a special message during the week about tentative arrangements for Resurrection Sunday, but was told to prepare a sermon anyway. Clint sat in the pastor's chair on the dais as he had every Sunday since David's shooting incident. When he felt the unction, Clint stepped closer to the pulpit and prayed. It pleased him to see so many young people loving and worshipping God.

"Good Morning, DOC. It is a pleasure to be with you and serve you this grand Resurrection Sunday," Clint said. The young people shouted and clapped loudly. Some whistled. "That's right, go ahead and celebrate Jesus! It's a shame to shout more at a sports game or concert than you do for the One who gives you breath! Hallelujah!" Again, there was a roar in the church. "If you are wondering who is bringing the message today, I'm gonna tell you right now. It's the Lord!" He turned to the empty chair on the dais and pointed. "He's sitting right here, and if you can't see Him, it's alright, you've already felt Him. And you still feel Him. Hallelujah! And if you can't feel Him, I'm gonna send one of the nurses over to you right now to check your pulse and make sure you ain't dead!" There was shouting and clapping and praise going forth. After several more minutes of praise, Clint gave further instructions.

"Ms. Meagan Monroe is going to give a few announcements, and right after that, we're going to worship. And the Lord will bring forth the message." Some of the deacons looked curiously at Clint. As soon as the choir had sung three praise medleys and led the congregation in worship, Clint stepped to the pulpit and led the congregation in prayer. "All heads bowed, all eyes closed . . . Lord, on this glorious spring day, we honor You for Your magnificent blessing of Jesus. We honor You for giving us hope when we had none. We honor You for forgiving the multitude of sins we've committed against You. We thank You for loving us despite our shortcomings. And now, let all that You would speak to your people come forth. Amen."

As soon as the "Amen" had drifted off Pastor Clint's lips, there was thunderous applause, foot stomping, shouts, and tears. The congregation rose to its feet in unison. There was so much shouting and stomping, it felt as if the building were swaying. Clint turned to his right and saw David walking slowly toward the pulpit. Clint sprinted the short distance and grabbed David in a brotherly hug. There was not a person sitting. From the oldest congregant, who was one hundred and three years old, to the youngest who could stand alone, all were up out of their seats.

As David neared the pulpit, it seemed to Clint that the shouting and clapping grew louder, if that were even possible. Clint had never heard anything like this. Not at any concert or sports arena—nothing of this magnitude. And Clint knew that the congregation wasn't praising David. They knew not to praise men—David had taught them that. The members of DOC were praising God *for* David.

Through a broken voice, strained with holy tears, David spoke. "Well, hallelujah, DOC." He swallowed hard and tried to gain his composure, but he knew the smile he held was contorting because of his tears and sobbing. The young people stomped up a storm, which caused David to fall to his knees on the dais and praise the Lord. He lay prostrate and sobbed openly. Clint kneeled beside David and whispered, "Are you okay?" David could only nod. For every part of him was praising Christ. Pastor Clint stepped to the pulpit and said, "Come on and praise, church. Choir, come on, let's praise the Lord for what He has done and is doing! Praise Him!"

And they sang. Leah buried her head in Joseph's chest and heaved. God had snatched David from the hands of death and planted him firmly in the land of the living without any long-lasting disabilities. When David finally rose and stood on his feet, there was no mistaking that God had touched him. Normally prideful, David let his tears fall openly, and he was not ashamed. He looked around at all the members who were witnesses of his miracle. He hated that the media had dubbed him Mr. Miracle. But he was God's miracle. He was a tool God had used to reveal Himself more deeply to David and those around him.

David's quiet tenor voice quieted the crowd. "The scripture for today is Hosea 14:1-9. Read with me . . ." After the reading of the scripture, David said, "I know this is Resurrection Sunday, and every other preacher across the country is sharing scriptures on Jesus' resurrection. God wants me to tell you that *you* need to be resurrected! He was resurrected so that you could have that privilege. And He is the only One who can resurrect your life at any time and in any place. Sometimes, even those of us who have accepted Christ as our savior and have walked with Him get sidetracked and get off the narrow road God places us on. And that's when God calls out to us to repent and return to Him. Return to what's right. Return to what's good. Return to your peace. So our lesson title today is *Return of the M.A.C.* That's right, M-A-C," David spelled out."Man *or* Wo-man," David chuckled, "After. Christ."

David glanced over in the direction he knew Deacon Lewis had seated Cherelle. She stood out to him with her chocolate skin bathed in a heavenly white eyelet maxi dress. He nodded, and she nodded back. He would have a moment in the future to acknowledge all that she was to him, but today was God's moment. So David focused all of his attention on Christ and gave the message that was on his heart. Afraid that his brain might freeze up on him, he'd prepared extensive notes. He'd neared the end of his sermon before he realized he hadn't needed them at all. He knew it was evidence of God's mercy at work in his life.

After David preached, thirty people answered the altar call; twenty of them were under the age of twenty-one. David informed Pastor Clint that he would leave right before prayer and benediction. He didn't have enough strength for the receiving line today. The two men hugged and blessed one another. Deacon Lewis had been watching David carefully. The two had created signals. David winked at Deacon Lewis, and Deacon Lewis nodded. Pastor Clint readied the congregation for prayer and benediction. He gave David ample time to exit the sanctuary before the closing prayer.

Deacon Lewis chauffeured David and Cherelle to David's home, where Cherelle had left her car. David unlocked his front door and allowed Cherelle to enter first.

"I'm going upstairs for a while. I need to pray. Make yourself comfortable and relax," David said.

"Okay, honey," Cherelle returned.

She sat in the music room where she and David had often

worked on the youth project. She made herself comfortable on the sofa and rested. She knew David needed time alone. She saw how mightily God had moved in the church. A person needed time alone with God after an experience like that. More than an hour passed, and Cherelle had drifted off to sleep.

David stood over her for minutes without speaking before he rubbed her hands gently to awaken her without startling her. Cherelle awoke feeling refreshed. She looked up at David curiously. His blank expression made her wonder if he was attempting to hide the fact that he was feeling pain. Maybe standing up and preaching for an hour had taken more toll on him physically than he had expected it to.

"Are you okay?" Cherelle asked. She squeezed David's hands with tenderness. David took her hands in his and kissed them.

"Yes, Kit, I'm fine. I was just thinking about how much I truly love you," David said, sitting next to Cherelle. "A few weeks ago, I asked you to be my lady because I wanted an opportunity to date you. I knew in my heart then, and I know right now that you are the woman I want to spend the rest of my life with, Kit. I've never told anyone this, but when we first met—I think it was the first time we had a meeting about the youth task force. I touched your hand because I had asked to see your purity ring. And when I did, something happened that scared me to death—so much so that I flat-out *rejected* it.

"I don't consider myself a love-at-first-sight kind of man. I usually try to walk into things. But when I touched you, Kit, I felt like my whole future was somehow wrapped around you. At the time, I had just started seeing Dominique, and I was pretty sure you had something going on with Corey. So those thoughts about you and me together disgusted me. I'm not the kind of man who lusts after or covets someone else's woman, nor am I the kind of man who will pursue more than one woman at a time. I didn't understand what was happening to me. And every time I was around you or touched you, I felt it. Like we were somehow connected—like you were *mine*. It didn't make any sense to me then, Kit. But it does now. You *are* mine. You were mine from the *beginning*, babe. I just didn't understand what God was showing me.

I get it now. I love you and I want you to be my wife." David dropped to one knee and spoke earnestly, "Cherelle Eleanor Dupree, will you marry me and become *Mrs.* David Kent Cole?"

"Yes," Cherelle said just above a whisper.

"Are you sure?" David kidded.

"Yes"

"Positive?"

Cherelle nodded through her tears. "Yes," she affirmed.

David revealed the red velvet box that had been hidden behind his back. He took the circular solitaire stone from the box and slid it on Cherelle's finger on top of her purity ring. It fit perfectly. David kissed Cherelle's hand, which now held the symbol of his love for her. He stood, pulling her to her feet. He squeezed her to his chest, molding his lips over hers. He'd promised that they would have a kissing moratorium, but it seemed appropriate to seal his proposal with a kiss. However, as soon as their lips met, David was reminded of the reason they needed a moratorium in the first place. Cherelle had an effect on him like no other woman ever had.

Chapter 36

Ahh . . . To Be . . .

L eah had to tell several family members and friends
that she wasn't having her usual Resurrection Sunday
dinner. David had asked if they could keep it intimate
this year. He didn't want to be asked a lot of questions about his
injury. He only wanted to enjoy his family and close friends.
To David's astonishment, when he and Cherelle arrived at
Leah's, the classic white Maserati that belonged to Gus was
parked in the driveway.

David and Cherelle were ten minutes late. Leah was a
stickler for being on time for dinner, but she wouldn't start
without them. When David opened the door with his key, Leah
let out a huff. "It's about time. We've been over here starving,
thanks to you two. What were y'all doing that made y'all late?"
Leah teased. Everyone laughed. "On second thought, don't
answer that, *Pastor* Cole."

Cherelle and David raced to the table hand in hand.
"Sorry, we're late. We had to discuss a couple of things. I just
want to introduce everybody to Cherelle—" David started.

"Punch, shut up. We know Cherelle. We're ready to eat!" Leah said, squeezing David's jaw.

"No, Ma. Y'all know Cherelle *Dupree*. I want to introduce you to the soon-to-be Cherelle *Cole*."

"What?" Leah asked. Were they pulling her leg?

Cherelle held out her hand and the brilliant round stone danced in the light of Leah's chandelier.

"Ooh . . . look a dere!" Deacon Lewis shouted.

"Uh . . . are you sure you can handle your bills after that, bro? You need a loan?" Gus winked.

With tears flowing, Leah hugged Cherelle tightly and kept repeating, "Congratulations. Thank you . . ."

"Congratulations, son. You've done very well. And Cherelle, I love you. But I'm *hungry!*" Joseph joked.

As soon as Joseph had blessed the food, David kissed Cherelle and said, "Babe, you know I love you, so go ahead and fix my plate, woman!"

"Cherelle, you better get your slaps ready. 'Cause Punch is gonna need a bunch of 'em!"

"I see . . ."

"I'm just kidding, babe. What would you like on your plate?" David said, placing a wet, sloppy kiss on Cherelle's cheek.

Cherelle squirmed. "A little of everything," she said, laughing.

"I got you. Love you," David said seriously.

"Love you."

Acknowledgments

First, I would like to thank "Pastor David Kent Cole" (wink) for sharing his story with me; it truly blessed my soul—three books worth! LOL. Next, to my sands Aminah Steger (Number One), who constantly stays on my tail like no one else, to make sure I'm writing the next book, thank you, sands. You keep me on my toes. and I LOVE you for it—threatening, harassing and all!

To Nicole Williams and Cheryl Angelelli at the DMC Rehabilitation Institute of Michigan, thank you for your hospitality and expert knowledge. Nicole, I greatly appreciate you for taking time out of your busy schedule to answer all my many questions related to TBI treatment, and for being gracious enough to re-explain and clarify! Ms. Angelelli thanks for the opportunity to talk with Nicole. You guys do an awesome job at a wonderful facility!

I'd like to extend a gigantic thanks to the law enforcement personnel (you know who you are) who lent their expertise. Your input was invaluable. In the end, I took creative liberty to tell the story the way it played out in my brain, and I will take the heat for anything that doesn't align with the way things"usually go down." It's called writer's privilege guys! LOL.

To my FABULOUS beta readers: Elaine Hudson, Veronica Hollis, and Brunisha Brooks, thank you all so much for your honesty, questions, and keen insight! You read the manuscript before anyone else and helped me to polish the story! I LOVE you all so much.

To my readers, thank you once again for giving me your time and allowing me to share a piece of my heart and mind. I hope you enjoyed the journey as much as I did! Stay tuned for the second book in the series: *A Man's Love*.

Love you and God bless!

About the Author

Sherrhonda Denice is an author, speaker, licensed therapist, and educator. She is a graduate of Michigan State University and holds a master's degree in social work from Wayne State University and a master's degree in teaching from Oakland University. Sherrhonda writes realistic Christian fiction that takes her readers to places where faith and love intertwine to create juicy storylines, and non-fiction to help her readers conquer life's challenges and grow in their walk with Christ. She loves to read, write, and do absolutely nothing but look out the window with a steamy cup of French vanilla cappuccino in hand. Visit Sherrhonda on the web at **www.sherrhondadenice.com**

facebook.com/sherrhondadeniceauthorpage
instagram.com/sherrhondadenice

www.ingramcontent.com/pod-product-compliance
Lightning Source LLC
Chambersburg PA
CBHW021130260626
47169CB00005B/1543